"Be prepared to get enthralled by incredible, vivid imagery of scenic beauty, detailed and lively descriptions of characters… relish the writing and not get entangled in the mystery alone."

—Reedsy Discovery

"It was a page-turner, and the suspense kept me on the edge of my seat. The descriptions of New Mexico were so vivid that I could visualize them. The characters were intriguing and dynamic. I could relate to them, and they could be anyone I know. My favorite character was Peyton. I could relate to her struggle with her demons."

—Readers' Favorite

"I enjoyed the developing romance between Peyton and Blake. Relationships, self-discovery, and struggles were woven into the plot. The story was vivid and beautifully written, and it is a lovely story about family and love."

—Readers' Favorite

"Reine's painterly prose evokes her characters' creative endeavors as well as the gorgeous New Mexican landscape."

—Kirkus Reviews

"Peyton's struggle with her own inner demons is one that can resonate universally, regardless of class or position on the social ladder. And the vivid images Reine paints of the Southwestern landscape and its environs create a three-dimensional backdrop for a skillfully told tale."

—IndieReader

"Be prepared to get enthralled by incredible, vivid imagery of scenic beauty, detailed and lively descriptions of characters… relish the writing and not get entangled in the mystery alone."

-Reedsy Discovery

"A fine case of supporting characters adds to the budding romance between Peyton and Blake, and Reine's rich descriptions of New Mexico's architecture and natural landscape bring the setting to vivid life."
—*Publishers Weekly BookLife*

"An art-minded romance novel about love, legacy, and self-discovery."
—*Kirkus Reviews*

"Reine's dialogue and descriptions are robust, creative, and sophisticated."
—*IndieReader*

She Died Then Showed Me

THE PIONEER RANCH SAGA

Book One

SAMAR REINE

Published by

Carmel-by-the-Sea Publishers

Gilbert, Arizona

Cover Design by Tim Barber, dissectdesigns.com

Interior Design by Danielle H. Acee, authorsassistant.com

Library of Congress Cataloguing-in Publication

Reine, S.

She Died Then Showed Me / Samar Reine

p. cm.

Library of Congress Control Number: 2023909287

Paperback ISBN: 979-8-9884110-3-1

First Edition

She
Died Then
Showed Me

Dedications

Without my mother, Samira, I wouldn't be half the woman I am. Thank you, Mama, for being both the horizon and the shore.

My dreams come true because of my husband's support, patience, and love. Thank you, Zach, for piling stars in the palms of my hands. If a Yellow Brick Road ever existed…

Fred's affection, insight, and generosity transform barren lands into thriving ecosystems. I am humbled by your unwavering support and encouragement, even when my work was unpolished. Your generosity is unrivaled.

one

Abiquiú, New Mexico

"There's no money. I won't put you through the wretched reading of a heartbreaking will," Mr. Jennings said after the funeral. He had been the family lawyer since before Peyton was born.

She peered back at him, covered in mourning black. "Sorry? I thought this was only a formality. Every generation leaves the ranch to the next better than when they inherited it."

"Not this time."

Peyton loathed the way he fixed his hooded eyes on her, staring over narrow reading glasses. "What do you mean?"

He eased himself onto the sofa in her father's study and gestured for her to sit down, but she remained standing. "There isn't enough cash to maintain this massive estate, and there's no selling the land without the Big House, the stables, horses, the cars and whatnot, and furthermore…" Mr. Jennings huffed, hesitant, reminding Peyton of a horse prodded up a steep hill. "Your mother, rest her soul, asked me to take care of you, and I endeavored my best to honor her wishes, but attorney/client privilege prevented me from warning you earlier. Your father, may he rest in peace… err…"

9

Jarring memories of the last time Peyton saw her mother, Harlow, alive walloped her. On the day Harlow died, she had struck her twelve-year-old daughter hard enough to cut her lip. "Mom personally asked you to take care of me?"

"More than once."

Peyton rubbed her hands up and down her arms, a habit pirated from her mother. She recalled opposite moments when Harlow danced with her, twirling her from room to room until they both collapsed from dizziness and laughter.

Mr. Jennings went quiet.

She covered the divide between them in three steps and placed a manicured hand on his forearm. "Whatever it is, it's not your fault. I'm not a little girl anymore. Not at thirty-three. I don't need protection, but I need the truth."

He tugged at his collar and patted her hand. "There comes a point a fellow can't get any wetter, and a time when he can't get any sadder. Today is already dreadful. Might as well allow for the downpour." He reached for the bourbon at his elbow and quaffed it. "The estate is highly leveraged." He removed an embroidered handkerchief from his breast pocket and wiped his brow. "Even with some financial miracle, keeping all this property will make you estate poor. It'll reduce your life to a more modest lifestyle, and I've never known the Chases to settle for what's modest. That's not all…"

"Just lay it all on me, Mr. Jennings." Peyton poured him another drink with trembling hands. "Go on, please." She sat on her hands to keep from wiggling, and bit her cheek, bracing for the punch to come.

He cracked a sheepish smile and swilled his second drink. "The cars and furnishings are free and clear if you have room for them, but no more expensive horses, and something will have to be done about the cattle." He shook a thick finger. "I've been to a few of your father's lavish parties. I don't know what your style is, but it can't be like Sorensen's." He tried to keep judgment out of his inflection, but failed. "I know you're a reputable art restorer and earn your own income. I don't discount that."

Shock hijacked her tongue. For a moment, she froze, her heart thudding in her head. "Why didn't Dad tell me anything?"

"Wish I had an answer for you, Peyton, but I don't."

She thought of the paintings lining the walls of the upstairs gallery, what remained of her mother's work. She'd been famous for her audacious interpretation of everything indigenous. Like Georgia O'Keeffe, Harlow Peyton Chase captured New Mexico's gorgeous landscapes. She had also settled in Abiquiú—with hundreds of paintings to her name. To Peyton's knowledge, her mother had made a private fortune selling her works. Her obituary in *The Los Angeles Times* read, "Had she not lived only half a lifetime, she would've dazzled for the ages."

Peyton collected herself. "I can't imagine this life without the ranch. But there's more?"

Mr. Jennings removed his glasses and rubbed his eyes. "That's the worst of it, I'm afraid, Peyton. You don't have any paintings."

She shot to her feet. "Explain!" Her father's voice echoed from the past, reminding her of the Chase standards of decorum. "Please," she added, her tone lower, and sat down.

"Your father sold them privately. In fear of discovery or reprisal, he had them all copied and restored to their original spots in the gallery. Never disclosing he was no longer in possession of his—"

"—inheritance? *My* inheritance, you mean." She thumped a fist on her chest and hardened her features. "Not his—*mine*. He had no right. Mom left them to me." Her lips quivered. She was eager to cry at the betrayal, but had none to give. She shook her head, staring out the window at an expanse of mountains hued purple and gold, and at dunes of clouds seen only in the Land of Enchantment, some called New Mexico. "It's not even about the money. How can I live without her paintings? You're sure they're all gone? It's all I had left of her."

Mr. Jennings swallowed, sweating. "Well, legally, your mom never stipulated to whom she bequeathed those paintings. Why Sorensen never apprised you of that before is beyond me."

"What?" Peyton's chest heaved, and she balled her fists. "But I was always told they're mine."

"Your father may have considered them yours, but they were his to sell as far as the law goes."

She darted to the massive French doors leading to the terrace, every muscle in her body aching to run and keep on running until she collapsed in a mound of dirt.

"About the copies upstairs… err… they're superb. They might fetch a few thousand each."

It was like offering a sugar pill to a heart patient.

Peyton paced, clicking on the pink Numidian marble floors. She stared at the violet veins coursing through the rare ancient marble, as if they were runes capable of foretelling her future. "You can't buy Numidian marble any longer." She stared at Mr. Jennings. "Half of what built this estate is scarce, priceless. Why did Dad need all that money? Why sell and borrow us to ruin?"

He clasped the bourbon bottle, refilled and guzzled. "After the mines dried up, the expenditures didn't abate. Your father took to selling assets to maintain the same lifestyle. You knew him best of all. He was a *bon vivant* with expensive taste." He took another minute before saying, "Your father left this estate in good shape structurally, I must say. You won't need major renovations or expensive new equipment any time soon. He kept it all up. That would've also been expensive. It's an enviable house, but you don't need me to tell you."

"If I am personally debt free, it's because my father taught me how to budget. This makes absolutely no sense to me."

"Sometimes people advise others of what they wish they could do, but fail in themselves. Sorensen maintained the assets. Your problem is cash flow and lack of asset income."

"I have profound love for my father, but according to you, the bank owns my house." Peyton slumped on the deep leather sofa, frozen when her world felt on fire. She ruminated over clues she must have missed to be blind-sided to this degree. "I'll not be the one Chase to lose it all." She curtained her face with both hands, as if to shield from the carnage. "How long do I have to decide?"

With a creased forehead, the lawyer asked, "To decide on what to do with the estate?"

"Well, yes."

"You must list the estate. Certainly, don't default on any payments. You have months, not years."

"No! My family has lived on this land since before this country existed. This house was built when New Mexico had only two main roads. For God's sake, the heart of the house is still the original adobe built in 1671. How much does the estate owe?"

"The mortgage your father took out stands at a principle greater than five."

"Five what? You can't be telling me Pioneer Ranch owes over five million?"

"About that, yes. Sorry. It's all in the will."

Peyton stretched to her model height, straightened her tailored jacket, and smoothed down her pencil skirt. "My mother gave me her last name for a Christian name, so I'd never forget I come from hardworking, brave settlers. The first pioneers."

Mr. Jennings drank the last of his bourbon and placed the crystal tumbler on the nearest coaster. "Come and see me anytime. I'm in my Santa Fe office on Thursdays & Fridays, and in Albuquerque the other three." He pointed to the thick file on the massive vintage desk where her father composed much and read more. "I also had my paralegal email you the will, with annotations. I'm sure you'll have questions."

Fossilized in loss, Peyton had never felt more alone in the world. Her father was dead, her history was not as she'd known it, and her future was jeopardized. *Truth always comes at a price.* She worried it would cost her what she guarded, not owned—the Chase heritage.

"What skills do I have for this disaster?" Peyton looked at Mr. Jennings with a compressed chest. "Final thoughts?"

He tapped her on the arm. "You can't work for yourself, as you do, and not be enterprising. You'll know what to do."

Peyton extended her hands, her way of dismissing Mr. Jennings with the grace of her upbringing. "I'll drive you home." He protested, but Peyton raised a finger like a mistress reprimanding a schoolboy. "Ah-ah, I'll have your car transported as well, but perhaps not till tomorrow. I know how hard it was for you to deliver such dreadful news to me today. You're a kind man, Mr. Jennings. Thank you."

"It's a stupid question, but are you all right?"

Rooted in the middle of the desert, in the sunny space of what used to be her father's study—his inner sanctum—Peyton said, "I can't get any wetter."

"There are those who get wet—"

"—and there are those who walk in the rain. *The Book of the Samurai.* One of my favorites as well. Dad made sure of it." Peyton gestured to the thousands of volumes lining the walls. Her father had expected her to be a warrior. Was she that fighter now? She pressed her temples, wondering to what degree she had let her father down. She must have. How else could he have concealed crucial facts from her? Memories of her father sitting in his oversized leather chair rose like smoke out of an oil lamp. "Last I saw Dad alive was three weeks ago. He stood in the spring rain waving to me. I had no idea it would be the last time I'd see him."

A knock on the door was followed by a familiar voice asking for permission to enter.

"I'll give you some privacy." Mr. Jennings gathered his belongings. "I want to say hello to some folks out there."

At the sight of the man she considered the love of her life, Peyton's mouth went dry. Ashton's presence was as unexpected as the news Mr. Jennings had just delivered.

Dressed in a tailored black suit, he took decisive steps toward her. "I'm so sorry about your father, Peyton."

He was close enough for her to smell his Creed Aventus cologne—notes of musk, patchouli, and bergamot. A scent associated with the best days of her life—and the worst. "Ashton Grant." She realized he was about to hug her and took a step back. She was too fragile to handle the touch of someone once fused to her soul. Last she saw him he was supine and naked, sleeping in sunshine—an image seared on her mind by the trails of lava he left behind. "I'm astonished to see you."

two

"Did you believe I'd never show up?" Ashton asked. "I was at the cemetery earlier, but stayed back. I didn't want to rob you of your grief."

Peyton reflected on the paintings she whipped up after their breakup. Artworks she had created in the shadows, never telling a soul. She had longed for him to come after her, but he didn't. Until now. "When a year goes by and a man still acts as if he lost his lady's address, she changes the locks."

He shifted closer until she could see every fleck in his cinnamon eyes. "And did you change your locks?"

"I listened to Gloria Gaynor enough times." No one was ever as handsome—or as capable of wounding her. "Why are you here after all this time?"

"Because you need me. If anyone knew what your father meant to you, I do."

"Ah, you deem me vulnerable enough now?"

He flashed hurt eyes, and they didn't hold the same impatience. "Maybe I'm the vulnerable one now."

His effect was swift, but she didn't want to feel for Ashton, when their history had bitten off all it could. "Who says I don't have someone in my life? You're still presumptuous."

"And you're still a terrible liar. I'm here and you didn't even have to ask." He looked about the room, not having been at her house in Abiquiú before. It was always in California, where they had lived, loved, and then burned it all down in the brushfires of obstinance and immaturity. "For a historic house, it's bright and happy. Very well maintained."

"That enormous arrangement that arrived this morning with no card is from you, isn't it?" She had failed at hiding how much he discomposed her, even after all this time. "You came all the way from California. Thank you for that."

"I was in Canada when I learned your father had passed. You'd been on my mind, as always. Contrary to what you probably thought. I took the news as a sign and booked a flight." When she said nothing, just stared at him, he added, "I'm in Santa Fe, at The Five Graces. I'll stay for as long as you need me. And you do."

She wanted him to hold her and never let go, but that wasn't how things unfolded before. She didn't trust they would now. "I'm drowning in devastating news. Don't wait around."

"Devastating news? Tell me."

She hugged herself and shook her head. "You're still married, right?"

He inserted his hands in his pockets, and gave her his classic half-angel, half-shark grin. "We don't live together. You know that."

"Wrong answer." Peyton pointed toward the door, where beyond it some visitors remained. "I don't want to be rude, but there are guests I've yet to see."

Before he could reply, Royce, her mother's oldest friend and Peyton's godmother, found them. Taller than most men, Royce was always in heels. "You're a heap of misery, darling." Then, looking Ashton up and down, she said, "Pardon me, I interrupted."

Ashton extended his hand to shake Royce's. "Forgive me. I might have monopolized Peyton for too long. I'm Ashton Grant. You must be the incomparable Mrs. Kent I've heard so much about."

"As in the Texan Grants?" Royce had nailed Ashton as the heir apparent to an oil and gas dynasty. She shook his hand, though her intent stare wasn't on him. "How do you know Peyton?"

The more charm Ashton poured, the taller he stood. Peyton's familiarity with his ways was sadder than she could've expected.

"Oh, come now. Peyton must've told you about me."

With a raised eyebrow, Royce let Peyton know she assessed her demeanor in full. But the skilled socialite was adept at camouflage. "I must know your version, young man."

"Ah… it's that bad, is it?"

His dark, thick hair was recently cut. Peyton noticed the shaved skin at the base of his neck. Fine lines on the corners of his eyes had sprouted since she had last seen him. When he smiled, Ashton disarmed without trying, and now he displayed his confidence of which he had an endless supply, Peyton resented how much of her feelings he uncoiled in a few minutes. "I'm sorry, Royce. It's like I came in here with Mr. Jennings and took a year to come out. Let's just return to the others."

"Oh, no. Stay put." Royce gave Peyton propitious eyes. "I'll hold the fort and linger after everyone leaves. No rush."

Ashton said, "I may have thick skin, but I'm not thoughtless. You want me to leave and I will, but let's have dinner tomorrow."

If Peyton ever felt quicksand beneath her feet and resolve, it was then. "No. You don't need me to explain why."

He nodded, as if he was accepting the situation, and then stepped into her space, gazing at her like a predator. "This time, you didn't budge. You see? You not only need me, but you also want me, like I still want you."

Peyton arrowed out of the room as if goosed by electricity.

"Okay, I'm leaving, and you can run, but…"

She heard him, but hastened to the formal salons, where three of her allies lingered behind for a private goodbye.

The remaining loyalists huddled together like a human tepee, as if in a conspiratorial circle. They turned to face her all at once, framed by the tall windows.

Mr. Jennings stood next to Mark, who snuck a furtive glance at Peyton.

"Uncle Mark, you've known about my situation for a while, haven't you?" she asked New Mexico's former State Attorney, her father's top litigator, and his closest friend.

Tall, with grooves in his cheeks, his shoulders rounding forward now he was past sixty, Mark looked at her with sad eyes. "Your father told me in confidence… So, I brought you a fun brownies basket." He winked, grinning like a rascal.

"Sorensen told you what?" Royce asked.

"Oh, boy." Mark frowned, appealing to Peyton with an outstretched hand, his Chopard chronological watch gleaming in the light.

It reminded Peyton time was against her, though her father had always believed time was for her. She was among friends who would learn the truth, and most already did. "I may be forced to sell the ranch, but I was always groomed to shepherd it."

Mr. Jennings said, "Estates come and go, but people rebuild."

"Without Pioneer Ranch, it's like the Chases never existed!" Peyton flung her arms to the ceiling. "This is not an estate. This is a legacy, or it's supposed to be."

"Honey, you're not alone. You have us." Mark studied her, splicing a smile. "Where did the years go? You're your mother's mirror image, but more polished and not as infuriating."

Peyton laughed to avoid sobbing, but managed neither so well. "I'm the last Chase standing."

Like a hero from a romance novel, arriving not a moment too soon, Scarborough swept into the room, with his ten-gallon hat tucked to his chest—not a Stetson. Scarborough would never desecrate the ruggedness of a working cowboy. His cropped hair was almost as brown as it was in his youth, but his beard was the color of slate. He wore his trusted bandana wound about his neck. Today it was black like his shirt and his scruffy leather boots. For someone who worked with his hands, Scarborough was spruce and tidy. "I figured you still need me for something, ma'am."

"You must start calling me Peyton sometime, Scarborough."

"I will, ma'am." He stood tall, with a bronzed face framing brilliant blue eyes.

"You should've left by now," she said.

Mr. Jennings felt his pocket for his keys, though he'd had one too many, which prompted Mark to say, "If someone can follow me in Manny's car, I'll drive him home."

Santa Fe is an hour's drive away, but Peyton felt responsible for her lawyer's safety. "I'll do that."

"No, ma'am. Can't let you do that. Not today." Scarborough turned to the lawyer. "I'll ask Koda to follow me in your car, sir."

Peyton could always count on Scarborough to manage everything. He waited for her lawyer to mumble his approval, then raised his hat into the air and waved to all. "Folks, be bidding you goodnight now." Assured Mr. Jennings followed, he stepped into the crisp air, at his back a barrage of accolades, for everyone present knew how much the family had always depended on Scarborough.

Mark checked the time, looked down the corridor, and reached for his keys. "I won't say something stupid like 'I'll be thinking of you.' I'm here, just ask." He gave a decisive look. "Your father was a good man. Except at winning poker games. Sorensen Chase was the worst winner I ever met."

Royce pressed her fingertips together, her wine-red polish reflecting the room. "But the best loser, and that's more important."

Peyton felt wicked for thinking her father was good at losing. He had lost his inheritance and hers. But his love was strong and true. He always left her without any doubt of his devotion. She hated the meanness of her thoughts, but found them hard to rebuff.

"We'll be bugging the hell out of you," Mark said. "We'll pop in regularly and drink down your dad's cellar like we always did." He rubbed a hand between her shoulders. "Doors will open for you. And Royce and I are a stone's throw away."

Peyton saw Mark out. They stood in the foyer crowned by massive wooden beams engulfed by golden light, splashing down from the chandelier. The walls ribbed the foyer with stunning pale granite, insulating the room from all outside noises. Alone with him, she said, "I believe Dad confided most in you. He might have asked you to withhold information from me, but he's no longer with us and I need to know. What happened to all the money? Dad may have been a hedonist, but he wasn't irresponsible, and he loved me. He wouldn't have left me such a mess without a solution, at least."

Mark's characteristic smile faded, and he gave an empathetic nod. "I asked him the same question. He said the revenues had dwindled, yet the expenses hadn't. But he thought he could fix it without involving you."

"'Fix it' how?"

"He ran two ideas by me. A geological engineer found the ranch rich with perlite. He assessed it could be mined at the far end of the estate."

"Perlite? That'll scar the land something horrible."

"This was Sorensen's thought, too. He didn't want to return to those days, so he considered a hunting business. The state has been encouraging hunting to reduce the numbers of animals starving to death in winter. He thought maybe the ranch could capitalize on it."

"That's it? No other ideas?"

"Not that I know of."

Peyton waited until he got in his truck, and drove off, and waved to him, like the early settler women did on the range, standing on porches, watching riders gallop away. She let gratitude for the serenity of the ranch pulsate around her, then closed the massive carved doors. She needed two hands to close the panels, weighing over a hundred pounds each, though they swung into place obediently. Their heft created the mirage of having to steady them. Why wasn't she like those wooden titans lining up in this new frame of her life? Peyton turned to a big gong kept by the doors. Her mother had bought it in Japan on a trip the family took when Peyton was little. She picked up the polished wooden hammer and banged on the suspended brass gong. The unmistakable, classic sound resounded in her bones. She closed her eyes, listening to the complex blend of high and low notes, with warm overtones, and recognized what it was she drummed for.

The battle had begun, against circumstances and consequences not of her creation. Against a new life devoid of her father's counsel and wisdom, one bereft of explanations when her father's currency was words. "What does a Chase do?" her father would ask whenever she'd come to him with puzzling problems. This time, Peyton didn't know.

She removed her shoes, sighing with the pleasure of emancipated feet, and returned to Royce, carrying her shoes by their collars. "Let's go to the terrace. I need fresh air."

Peyton sat on the edge of a chaise, gazing at Abiquiú's cornucopia of colors, for which no artist had more shades. She knew from the way she'd agonize over her work—however kept hidden—critical of hues, texture, depth, proportion, and light. Facing north, toward the Tusas Mountains with Abiquiú Lake in the foreground, Peyton sighed at their stunning character. Above the mountains, a parfait of sky and whipped clouds stared back at her. The layers of contrast and complexity matched her present life.

Royce stretched her legs on her chaise lounge facing the long view. "I asked Layli for coffee and sandwiches. She actually smiled at me this time." She kicked off her shoes and rubbed her feet. "I swear my feet are getting bigger and I already wear the same size as Bigfoot." For someone of substantial height and stoutness, Royce was styled and coordinated. She made up in bravura what she lacked in beauty.

Peyton chuckled, and shook her long chestnut hair, messing it up. "How I love this perch on top of the world. To think I grew up here."

"Lucky, and you deserve it."

"It's more than luck. It shaped me, though I'm not majestic or stunning like Abiquiú."

"If not majestic, then rather magical."

"Oh, not true. For too long, I told myself, 'I'm fine, doing my best.' Neither is true."

The sound of clinking dishes and sloshing coffee caught their attention, now a steady helper, with a toothy smile, arrived with a tray. "Sorry to disturb, Ms. Chase."

"Lots of carbs are just perfect, Tansy. Thank you. Leave it. I'll pour. Do you need a ride? It's late."

"Layli is giving me a ride. Thank you. Goodnight, and sorry again, Ms. Chase."

Peyton gave Tansy a subdued smile and bid her goodnight. She filled two cups and bit into a biscotto. It was the first food she'd had all day. The coffee was intense, roasted in New Mexico, masculine like the desert, nutty like the pistachio and pecan orchards growing all over her home state.

Restored by food and caffeine, they sat blanketed by the last vestiges of pink light.

"How bad is it?" Royce asked.

"I must sell up, according to Mr. Jennings, but I won't. Generation after generation was born and died here. This is where my mother did her best work, where my father became his best self. It's where many people I love live, and… and…"

"Just say it, honey."

"Pioneer Ranch is part of my identity. Maybe it shouldn't be, but it is. I feel like my work is not done yet. Actually, I feel as if I'm only just beginning."

"What work?"

Peyton bit her lower lip. "There's so much I don't understand, and I've been cowardly about it. I thought I had all the time in the world to figure it out, but I've suddenly run out. This is where my mother, in her prime, one day dropped dead and left my dad emotionally crippled, and though it never sat right with me, I didn't ask enough questions, partly because Dad discouraged my curiosity, and told no one what happened that day."

Royce put down the plate of strawberry macaroons she was munching. "What do you mean?"

Peyton teared up, and her temperature rose. It was like hot needles were forcing their way out of her pores. "Do you remember how I rode to your house the day Mom died? I arrived with a bruised jaw and a cut lip."

"Yes, of course. You said you had fallen."

"Well, I didn't fall." Peyton gathered napkins, patted her eyes, and blew her nose. "I had found Mom in such a state. She was packing shoes in a suit-case—just shoes—crying and talking to herself. She scared me, but I was also worried about her. When I told her I was going to get Dad, she picked up one of her shoes and struck me with the heel. I was so shocked, instead of running to Dad, I rode to you, but when I got there, I couldn't tell you the truth."

Royce stopped breathing and covered her mouth with overlapping hands. "Then when you returned home, Harlow was dead and your father was in pieces."

"Yes, so I never told him either. My God, how hard he took her death."

Royce rose and sat next to Peyton, looking at her with empathetic eyes. "You didn't blame yourself all this time, did you?"

The way Peyton burst into sobs said it all. For a while, she cried waterfalls. "I might have pushed her over the edge when I said I was going to get Dad."

"No, no, no… impossible. You must give up whatever guilt you're carrying. You were twelve years old. A child. How could you have blamed yourself like this?"

Peyton shrugged and quaffed a glass of water.

"I'm so sorry, honey, but you should've told me sooner." Royce cradled her sideways and rocked her. "About the ranch… How much are you short?"

"Got five million in your piggy bank for me? Chump change, isn't it?"

"Lordy! I can come up with three hundred thousand without Edward's approval, but what will that do for you? And he won't agree to more. I know my son."

"I don't expect you to come up with anything. That's my job." Peyton bent her head until her wavy hair swooped down over her arms. "I'm not sure I can forgive him."

Royce shot her a cross look. "Of course you can forgive your father. It's only money."

"It's not the house or the money." She sobbed. "Dad sold Mom's paintings. All. Of. Them."

Royce covered her forehead with a hand adorned with weighty jewels, her expression no longer defending Sorensen. "No!"

Peyton shook her head and vacated her chaise. She walked to the edge of the volcanic red rocks covering the porch, where the dry wash sloped. The entire house was built of it, carted from Cerro Pedernal mountains. "I should have children by now, a family of my own, but I don't. What I had are the paintings and Dad, and now they're gone."

"I don't know what to say."

"I argued with Dad to take Mom's *The Last Start* with me to Mendocino, and thank goodness, or he might've sold that, too."

"Isn't that the unfinished one?"

"Yeah, you're right. He wouldn't have been able to sell it. Still, how could he?" Peyton sobbed again, hanging her head and clasping her arms. "I know he liked that floosy Flora, but I hated how he brought her into the bed where Mom slept." In the hall of mirrors conjured up in her mind, she pictured *The Last Start* depicting a dead Hopi woman shrouded in her white deerskin wedding dress, her body arranged in a sitting position in the corner of a room, in the custom of Pueblo people. The dead woman's apparition stands in the doorway, about to step off to begin her journey—her walk—into the afterlife. It was Harlow Peyton's final work—a seal for her daughter to break.

Royce inched closer to Peyton as if approaching a butterfly she feared scaring away. "You told me it was your favorite."

"Yes. I took the fact it was unfinished as a symbol of Mom's unfinished life," Peyton said. "*The Last Start* tells me what happened to Mom. Dad insisted it was a heart attack, but there was no open casket, a quick funeral. I know it was suicide."

Royce looked as if she found a squashed bug in her cake. "Don't say that! No, Peyton, it wasn't. Wouldn't she have left a suicide note?"

"*The Last Start* is her suicide note. I stared at it long enough over the years to know." Saying it out loud for the first time made her realize if her mother had communicated a message in one of her paintings, then she would've in others as well. Under the gravity of such an awareness, she balled her hand and clenched her jaw, recalling the most painful memory she had of her mother. Peyton's greatest aspiration was to grow up to be a painter—just like Harlow. She remembered how she once tried to copy one of her mother's paintings at nine years old. She would bring each new attempt for her mother to critique. After several attempts, Harlow tossed her daughter's painting into the trash and said: "Stop trying. It's a waste of time."

"Where did you go just now?" Royce asked. "What're you thinking?"

Peyton refused to share that kind of pain with anyone. After that day, she had stopped painting alongside her mother, yet Harlow never seemed to notice. "I fear for more than the estate. It's the people depending on Pioneer Ranch for their livelihoods that worry me most. It supports Layli's whole family, dozens of employees, and Old Ambrosia. Scarborough is in his fifties and has only ever worked here. I can't just drop them. It would be criminal."

"Who's Ambrosia? Is she LSD?"

"You mean LDS, of the Church of Latter-day Saints, right? LSD is a psychedelic drug."

"Same thing, darling," Royce said, flicking her wrist.

"Ambrosia is the cook who lived here when Grandma ruled with an iron fist. You must remember her. She came out of retirement for a stint when I was twelve. I have only faint memories of her."

"Vaguely." Royce tapped nails on her coffee cup. "What of this cook now?"

"Dad put Ambrosia on an annuity as she aged. Now she's my responsibility."

"I thought I knew everything. I can kill Sorensen!" She gasped and stretched out an apologetic hand. "Sorry, that was thoughtless."

"Don't worry, I share your sentiment, yet I miss Dad to the bone. All those evenings we talked with a book buried in his lap, the walks we took when he'd shared obscure historical facts, and hard evocative questions he'd send me away with." She cried and laughed all at once. "He used to say, 'If it's easy, don't bother with it, and if it tastes good, spit it out.'"

"Sorensen was always Confucius meets Oprah." Royce cracked herself up.

She hooked eyes to the sun, now but a red dot in a smoky sky, and yearned to dip her brush in it and smear it over her face like war paint. "I want to be in that movie, *What Dreams May Come,* and swim in paint."

"Sometimes, you're like your mother—impetuous." Royce raised her voice in excitement. "Like that time, she was supposedly driving us back from Taos. I fell asleep in the car, only to wake up in Colorado because Harlow felt like swimming in Pagosa Springs. No change of clothes, didn't let anyone know, nothing."

"Was it selfishness?"

"Maybe. Mostly it was fun," Royce replied. "How I miss your mother. Never found a friend like her since… except for you, darling girl."

Peyton handed her a fresh napkin, now she joined her in a tear fest. "I miss her too, though she could be downright cruel."

"You never said that before."

Ever since she learned of her father's passing, a dam broke, flooding her desiccated psychological terrains. Welcomed or not, the flash floods were here to stay. "Maybe because I'm starting at the beginning."

"Sometimes, honey, there's no better place. What's your plan?"

Peyton surveyed the land splayed before her. "Oh, I'm here to stay."

"Wouldn't this mean you'll have to resign at The Art Center?"

"And give up the Pacific to reclaim the desert with the hand of a ward, like I was raised to do. I expected as much, but when I'm fifty or sixty, not now. I thought Dad had another twenty, thirty years left."

"You're an art restorer. How can you give that up?"

"I don't see why I must give it up. I can restore art from anywhere given the right tools and products, and I already fly many places, restoring art on all sorts of premises. And some are shipped to me."

"And you're Harlow's daughter. That's gotta count for something."

"It counts for a lot," Peyton replied, jabbed by the nature of this reality. "Being Harlow's daughter increases my desirability in the world of art restoration. My career is safe, just not my estate."

"Will you have to sell your house in Mendocino?"

"God, I hope not. It can fetch about eight hundred thousand. If that sum ends up making a difference, then I'll have to. As things stand, selling the house won't shrink the liability enough. Besides, Mendocino is also home, with decent friends and a big art community. I hope to never have to sell my house there, but life seems to have other plans for us."

"Darling, is there a light at the end of the tunnel?"

"Yes, but it's mostly tunnel."

Royce raised her eyebrows as if about to be cat-naughty. "Does that light have anything to do with Ashton Grant? I'm surprised you didn't tell me about him."

Peyton hung her head and spoke in a small voice. "I didn't tell anybody about him—not at home, anyway."

Royce faced her more squarely. "He's the kind of man whose name you shout from rooftops, so I'm confused."

Peyton sighed and made a lip trill. "It took forever to get over him."

"Lordy, do you still love him?"

"He's married."

"He doesn't wear a wedding ring," Royce said. "I looked."

"He never wears one, but he's married… was married when we got involved, and I was an idiot. It was wrong of me. I didn't give you his name, but I let you know I had broken up with someone prominent. I paid for it, and don't want to discuss it anymore."

"He loves you. I'm sure of it."

Peyton shot to her feet, shaking her head.

"Why can't I say that?"

"If today wasn't my father's funeral, Ashton would be dating yet another woman, like he did soon after our breakup. I can't return to that place of not knowing what the future held for us. It was precarious and miserable when he wouldn't agree to a divorce."

"That place might not exist any longer. Call him."

Memories of Ashton's breath on her neck, his teasing play, and the way he would devote his attention to her when present lit her being. But she had replaced his impact with paint and brush, hadn't she? "I won't."

three

Before the birds could practice their notes, the perfume of her childhood—horses, manure, and hay—welcomed Peyton to the stables. She wore old jeans, rubber boots, and a worn white T-shirt. Baroness was her favorite horse. Not too big, not too fast, not too eager—her Goldilocks mare.

"Hey girl." From a bucket of sliced apples she had brought, Peyton fed Baroness a few chunks. She teared up at the horse's snort, but they were happy tears. She fed the white horse more and swished her messy blond mane. It felt good to bury her face in her Friesian. "You're as beautiful as ever."

There were other horses to greet and feed treats. One by one, she visited them all—Bishop, Blaze, Breeze, Bentley, Bennett, and Brandy.

A great-horned owl hooted from a cottonwood tree, coyotes howled, and larks and finches competed, singing dawn awake. Hummingbirds fought over feeders hanging outside the stable doors, bees buzzed over the fields of wildflowers, and the smell of burning wood rose above all other scents. Peyton brushed away at hides and manes, humming to each horse, and deciphering her father's will. Unable to sleep, she had braved reading his will, only to find out a mysterious person—listed as Recipient One—was entitled to a huge portion of a trust, of which Peyton was the ultimate beneficiary. The annotations explained it was confidential, but that didn't abate her curiosity. *Who's Recipient One?* Had her father sired a love child? But that wouldn't have been like him. She shook the thought out of her head, a pang of guilt slinking through her. On her last visit, a month prior, her father had asked her to stay longer, but he had taken up with Flora, someone beneath him. Why didn't she honor his request? Maybe he wanted to explain things. For eight years, ever since she moved away, she had been visiting every season like clockwork, yet none of it halted her guilt. Why didn't she do as he asked? She should've. Planted on clean hay with a brush in her hand, she heard Scarborough thump closer, accompanied by the panting of dogs.

"You're here, ma'am?" he said, somewhat disapproving.

She had heard the dogs, yelping earlier. "I smelled the burning fire and knew you were here. Only you light a fire every day. I may live in California, but I know this place and its people by heart."

"Sure know that, ma'am. A Chase is no tumbleweed… always a sycamore."

"Then, you're a Chase, too." She petted the Foxhound first, then the German brindled Shorthaired Pointer, though she looked about her for the Labrador. "Where's Cooper?"

"Looking for you." Scarborough coughed, more for attention than necessity. "The horses would've been attended to."

"I beat your handlers this morning, Scarborough, couldn't sleep. The horses don't need me, but I need them."

"Good morning," he finally added, dropping his shoulders a smidgen.

Layli arrived with two mugs of coffee. "Get away!" she ordered the dogs. "It's your ranch, last I looked. If you want to play at the stables, then you should be able to."

When the dogs didn't listen, Scarborough commanded them to stay put. They were too smart not to obey.

Layli's eyes, the color of cacao beans, stabbed at Scarborough. "You keep sending Koda over here and over there. I hardly see my little brother these days." She wore a red plaid shirt cinched at the waist by a substantial leather belt, studded silver and turquoise, she was almost never without. She, too, wore jeans, but hers were pressed. Patchouli and honeysuckle fanned the place—Layli's distinctive scent. She handed Peyton one mug. With reluctance, she handed the other to Scarborough. "Out of the generosity of my people," she said. "Lucky for you, cowboy, it's a virtue my ancestral mothers taught me." Her broad face gleamed, her long ebony hair swinging in the breeze of the high desert. For a forty-two-year-old, she was as energetic as a college freshman. Solid. Present and wide-eyed. She was Layli.

"Thank you, but you didn't have to come all the way down here." Peyton sipped her coffee. "Why does your coffee always taste better than when I make it?"

Layli stuck out her tongue. "You're not immortal like me. Gotta be Puebloan for that."

"Says the bossiest woman I ever met." Scarborough rolled his eyes. "This is good coffee because I bought the beans from Whispering Bean Coffee Roasters. Waited in line for twenty minutes."

"About how long you take to rope a bull these days, eh Scarborough?" Layli flung her hair away from her shoulders as if she just won a decisive victory. "Breakfast is ready," she told Peyton. "Yours, too, buckaroo boss, at your favorite spot, but I wasn't the one who put it there."

Peyton knew the routine. Koda would've done it, a nineteen-year-old who wanted nothing less than to fill his own ten-gallon hat.

Scarborough said, "Good boy that Koda, unlike his big sister, who's always mad at somebody."

Layli rolled her eyes. "Your food, missy, will only stay warm for a little while."

"I'll walk with Scarborough for a bit. If breakfast is cold, then it'll be my fault."

"I'll catch up with you at the house, then."

Peyton knew how Pioneer Ranch's heart hammered, had it in her blood, but she hadn't been its sentinel before. Together, walking at the pace of hot mugs in hand and feisty dogs ringing about them, Scarborough and Peyton ambled to the carriage house, today serving as storeroom and six-car garage.

Peyton took her time speaking, walking in silence for a while, but led with her real purpose. "Scarborough, Dad was planning a hunt, right?"

"Well, yes, ma'am, he was. Why we bought some of the high-end fishing and hunting kit in spring. Mr. Chase and Mr. Mark Wells discussed it at length. It was Mr. Wells who recommended some weapons and gear we stocked up on."

"Do you approve of the idea?"

"It's got bite."

"And Dad had no other ideas?"

"Not to my knowledge, ma'am."

Before Peyton could ask more questions, her phone rang. "Layli?"

"Not to alarm you, but there's an SUV speeding up the driveway I can spot from the upstairs. Might be that floosy Flora. She drives a big black truck like that. Just giving you the heads-up."

"Thank you. I don't want to deal with that woman." Peyton hung up and turned to Scarborough. "Might be Flora."

"You just say the word, and I'll haul her out of here before she could snap her heels." Kicking up dust, moving too fast, the SUV came to an abrupt stop. "What a rude woman," Scarborough said, though when the driver came out of the truck, it was no Flora.

At the sight of her maternal half-sister, Peyton excused herself and walked closer. "Lexi? Why didn't you tell me you were coming?"

"And you would've welcomed me?" She hooked her purse to her shoulder, removed her sunglasses, revealing pale blue eyes, and ran fingers through her short red hair. "Sorry about your dad. He was always nice."

"Thank you. He was much loved." Peyton noted Lexi's ruffled feathers and invited her to the house, if only to safeguard their privacy.

"Not yet. There's something I must say right away." Everything in Lexi's body language said her guns were cocked.

"Well, let's tuck in here, at least," Peyton said of one of the best kept buildings on the ranch.

Block walls made the place. Apart from the main house and casita, the ranch was built of dry stone with no mortar. Hard work and history glued those stones together, not much different from the Chase family.

Peyton leaned on one hip, bracing for what promised to be unpleasant. "What spurred a visit from California after all this time and this early in the morning when you didn't come for the funeral yesterday?"

Out of her oversized handbag, Lexi trawled a manilla envelope and handed it to Peyton.

"What's this?" Peyton took it, and ripped it open.

"You've been served! I just had to see the look on your face for myself."

Peyton never understood her sister's venomous attitude. Whatever discord fueled their past never justified the scorched fields of their present. "You're suing me?"

"Mom left to me half of her private collection. I have a letter from her saying that much before she died. I want what's mine!"

Peyton looked at the same vicious face her mother would make when nothing but ruthlessness filled her. "How long have you known about that letter? Why are you bringing this up now? Why didn't you address it with Dad when he was still alive?"

"Because he wasn't the one who owed me. You do."

And because a judgement against her was easier. "Is a lawsuit necessary?"

Lexi stretched her neck in triumph and inhaled as if until this moment, deep breaths eluded her. "I'm getting a court order for an appraisal of all the paintings you have in your private gallery. Looks like they're worth more than ever."

"Is this about money, or wanting Mom's paintings?" Peyton stepped to the side, holding the subpoena in a sunlit spot, scanning it as her blood pressure thundered in her eardrums.

Lexi lopped an accusatory finger. "What I want is for you to hurt and stop being the privileged girl who knows nothing of pain and suffering!"

"It's not my fault Mom stayed to raise me, but left you with your father! What's that got to do with me?"

"It has everything to do with you. Harlow used to take me for days and days until you were born. I curse how needy you were. If you hadn't been, she wouldn't have stopped having time for me."

"Projecting much? Needy as an infant and a toddler? Do you hear yourself, Lexi?"

"And to think my daughter thinks you're some great aunt. That'll change when she finds out you don't want to give her mother her rightful inheritance."

"I see. This is about making Margot hate me? Are you now using your daughter as a pawn?"

Lexi stomped her foot on the flagstone floor. "This is how you always flip the tables on me. You're the villain, not me."

Peyton ran a tongue over her teeth, her chest heaving, assessing the summons again. "I don't know if that letter from Mom has merit. If you only just asked me to take some of the paintings, then maybe we could've worked something out. But suing me like this and telling me to my face that you want to see me hurt changes everything."

At the sound of shouting, Layli entered the stone building with a bow and arrow, assuming she'd find Flora. When she saw Lexi, she lowered her arrow, but kept her bow taught. "Peyton, are you all right in here?"

"No, I'm not. Lexi was just leaving."

"You're kicking me out? Ha! You and Stands-with-a-Bow over here can go fuck yourselves." She began to leave, then stopped and scowled at Layli. "Peyton will throw you to the wolves, honey. You don't know my sister like I do." She hadn't counted on Scarborough standing like a statue of Paul Bunyan, blocking her car. "Move, asshole!"

"Ma'am, you clearly swallowed a horned toad backwards. Stealing coins off a dead man's eyes is more than robbing the grave. You might end up burying yourself in it."

Lexi scoffed. "That's what I hate about you cowboys. Every one of you thinks he's fucking Doc Holliday." She found her keys, but fumbled and dropped them in the dirt.

Scarborough picked them up, handed them back and said, "You know, ma'am, Doc Holliday won every battle. If he drew his gun, the other guy was already dead, and when he sat at the poker table, it wasn't to bluff. You're up against many Doc Hollidays here. Was this your plan?"

"Fuck you very much."

Peyton charged at them. "Stop it, Lexi! You want to talk to me in that disgusting tone, that's one thing, but talk to my people this way again, and I will hurt you."

"That's the Peyton I was talking about! All nice on the outside, but a snake on the inside."

"Just a little reminder," Peyton said, needing to settle an old score. "When you came to Mom's funeral, I took you to her jewelry box and told you to pick whatever you wanted because Dad suggested you should have some of her nice things. We didn't take turns choosing. I just let you have your pick. You took more than half. Some of it I would've preferred to keep. But that wasn't enough for you, was it? You went back and stole the rest. Didn't even leave me the box! The only reason I have Mom's emerald ring is because she kept that one in a drawer in her nightstand. I was twelve, and you were an adult, Margot's age. Why did you do that? Why?"

Lexi didn't deny it or defend herself. She climbed into a vehicle much too big for her and raced away.

"Are you two all right?" Peyton asked.

"Are *you*, ma'am?"

"Yes, just frazzled. But call me Peyton, like everyone else."

"Everyone else wasn't raised by my folks, ma'am. I was."

Peyton eyed the subpoena as if she could charm it into dust. "Thank you both for sticking up for me." She winked, repeating his old words of wisdom to her. "No one truly ever owns anything."

"But your sister thinks otherwise. From what I've heard, she's all fangs and claws. I'd take her threats seriously."

"They're not just threats. She's already set a legal battle in motion." Peyton thought she should strike the Japanese gong again. To diffuse her nerves, as adrenalin bubbled in her veins, she looked at Layli and snickered. "Lexi called you Stands-with-a-Bow. She's got wit, if not grace."

Layli slung her bow over her shoulder. "Might have been the best nickname I ever got, not the insult she meant it to be."

Peyton fished her phone from her pocket. "I need Uncle Mark's expertise. I'll see you guys later."

He picked up on the second ring. "I'm sorry if this is too early, but I have a big problem."

"It can't be early when I'm turning into your driveway. I forgot to bring you something yesterday."

Peyton looked down the drive and saw a dust cloud.

Mark parked his Hummer between two sandstone buildings with terra-cotta roofs, and slipped out of his vehicle, carrying an acorn fed *Jamón Ibérico* and other goodies from the Sage House. "Why do I feel whoever was flying down the driveway when I drove up left a sour taste in your mouth?"

Peyton accepted the basket and put it on a wooden bench, thanked him, plunked a kiss on his sateen cheek, and handed him the subpoena. "Can Lexi win against me for paintings I don't have?"

The diamond studs in Mark's earlobes belied his former life as the state's top prosecutor. His smile was genuine and his friendship with her father had been as steady as the Colorado River. "I'll need to learn more details," he said, looking over the summons, "but leave this with me. I'll follow up with the other side before assessing the legitimacy of the claim, all right?"

She gestured toward the house. "There's breakfast if you're hungry."

"I won't stay." He angled his face away from the sun. "I'll not sit on this lawsuit. We'll do some discovery and apprise you, okay?"

"Can't thank you enough, but could it have merit?"

He drew down the corners of his mouth and tilted his head. "Sorry, but yes, it might. Family court is a different breed. Too much gray, but we'll get through the muddle. I expect a quick turnaround."

Peyton drew on her knowledge of her mother's history. "She should already have paintings of her own. Wouldn't that matter?"

"If that's the case, then yes, but don't worry about crossing that bridge just yet. We're not there."

"She's looking into the current value of Mom's paintings, forgetting I'm in the business. Half would be over a million dollars. Could I end up owing her a sum that large, for real?"

Mark's loud exhale said enough. "I don't mean to scare you, but the chances are greater than fifty-fifty if Lexi can prove that letter came from Harlow. On the other hand, since it wasn't notarized, a judge might ask for witnesses. And like you said, she might have some paintings of her own already. It depends on the judge to a certain extent."

"I have one painting in my possession, *The Last Start*, but it's unfinished. Would it count?"

"I doubt it. People don't buy partial works. To be safe, I'll argue that one out of the deal, since it's impossible to evaluate it."

She bit her cheeks and plunged a nail into a cuticle to keep from crying. "One day at a time. Thank you." As she waved goodbye, she heard the golden Labrador coming from behind. "Cooper, you've never learned you're not human, have you?" The dog lunged and licked her face. She bent a knee, caressing him. "Gray hairs already like an old man? Aren't you only three?" She kissed the top of his head and stood up.

Koda materialized from a hidden corner, frightening Peyton into a hop that made him giggle. He wore his hair long, like his forefathers, today pulled back and tied with deer string and a foxtail.

Scarborough, coming a step behind him, said, "'Ma'am. Right, ma'am,' you say to Ms. Chase." He gestured for Layli's brother to repeat after him, but Peyton interrupted.

"But Koda has always called me Peyton. It's silly to suddenly start calling me ma'am."

"No, it's not," Scarborough replied, as tranquil as oil. "Koda aspires to be a proper cowboy and is no longer a boy. He has some learning to do, and it starts with respect, at least while he's on the job."

"I aspire to lead." Koda cuffed his hips and raised his chin for added drama.

"Then first learn to follow." Scarborough punched him in the arm. "Are you riding up to the ridge today to check on the cattle crossing?"

Koda nodded. "No later than ten."

"Take Bennett and a shotgun. He handles coyotes and mud best. It rained cats and dogs up there yesterday."

"Will do, buckaroo boss."

"And take the satellite phone this time. Last time your cellphone failed you. Scared me half to death, not replying for over an hour. I don't want to send the dogs after you again."

Koda's laughter was infectious. "But they need the exercise."

In the desert, the rains decided what flourished and what flagged. What decided for Peyton, and what didn't? She no longer knew. "Scarborough, I'll be making use of the old pickup soon."

"Stealing that dog again, I reckon?"

"Isn't that what I always do?" She released a guilty laugh and picked up the gift basket. "Stay safe, Koda," she said, and started up the path, Cooper close behind her, his nose pointing at the ham.

Muscled with stone and exposed beams, generous on wall-to-wall glass, the

Big House was quintessentially New Mexico. *Architectural Digest* featured it, and at about the same time, it adorned a limited edition of Abiquiú postcards. Harlow's paintings, some of them odes to Pioneer Ranch, made it famous yet kept it quaint.

Peyton strode through the kitchen garden, lamenting its poor state. How many times, as a teen, had she filled baskets with produce the kitchen hatched into culinary delights? How she missed the taste of tomatoes off the vine. The dog whimpered, reminding her that his belly growled. "Cooper, you stay right there. I'll get you a treat."

Cooper, who was fluent in human, wagged his tail. In the mudroom, Peyton removed her boots, wiped them down, and placed them on a rubber mat. She opened the top cupboard where miscellaneous items were kept, including dog and horse biscuits. "Come closer, Cooper, but stay outside or Layli will make dinner out of you."

"That's right!" Layli shouted from the kitchen.

She fed him six biscuits, more than Scarborough would approve, and petted him again. "Off you go now. You're on watchman duty." Cooper barked and appealed to her with his eyes. Fluent in dog, Peyton replied, "No, you can't come in and rub oily, mucky fur all over my clean house. Off now. I'll bring you eggs and ham later."

Peyton shed her dirty jeans and shirt, balled them up, and tossed them into the hamper. The room was spacious, with huge windows, heavy steel doors, and an oversized soapstone basin. She scrubbed her arms and hands with lemon verbena. There was such a joy in it, a simple, mindful pleasure.

Everything about Abiquiú was different. The cottage door that led to the kitchen was as old as pieces of eight—its top half habitually left open. With a practiced flick of her hand, she lifted the latch-lock on the bottom half, entered, and closed it behind her. Wearing only her spandex shorts and tank top, she stepped on the lustrous Azul Macaubas quartzite floor, and said, "I love walking on water. This floor is an ocean." The room was filled with bereavement baskets, sharpening her grief. "That accounting degree comes in handy, eh?" she told Layli. "We'll have to sit down and talk about household expenses and such. Aren't you excited?"

"Good to know you can still be sarcastic after what happened with Lexi."

Peyton smoothed her eyebrows and pressed her temples. "I can't believe how much she hates me."

"She's envious. Wants to uninstall you from your life and take it over, but it doesn't work like that. Everything the Power does, it does in a circle." Layli put on the kettle and sorted through the tea cannisters. "If I hadn't been there to witness how she behaved and what she said, I'd have a hard time believing it. She flew in just to rankle you and watch your expression. I thought I had nerve. Harlow had an edge, too. Luckily, you escaped it. Lexi didn't."

Lexi's accusations still whipping her, Peyton couldn't fend off the memories that invaded her. Her mother loathed neediness, punished it. When Peyton asked her mother to attend her painting competition, Harlow told her, "No one supported my art growing up, and look at me now. I'm a phenomenon because no one helped me. You don't need me there."

"That's some face you're making," Layli said. "What're you thinking?"

"Did you know the paintings upstairs are only copies?"

"They are?" The kettle whistled. Layli took it from the stove and looked at Peyton wide-eyed. "Your father was good at chasing me out of here whenever he wanted me blind or deaf, mainly with matters related to your mother."

"He did the same to me when Mom was alive. He sent me to singing and music lessons, riding lessons, art classes, too many places. Old habits die hard, I guess."

"In the past few days, you've brought up your mother more than you have in years. How are you?"

"Dad conditioned me not to ask questions about Mom, but now he's gone, I feel the need to delve, especially since he kept all the money troubles from me."

When Peyton was the height of sagebrush, Layli's father kicked her out, and she sat at the kitchen table with Harlow, discussing her options. She was no longer welcome in her family home, because she brought the White Man's world with her. Harlow convinced Sorensen to give Layli the lower cabin on the ranch and sent her to the University of Arizona in Tucson to earn her bachelor's degree in accounting.

"Educating a woman is saving an entire generation," Layli said. "I'm only in charge of the household budget. Your father didn't involve me in anything that led to this mess. My guess is he didn't want me telling you anything, and I would've."

Peyton nodded. "Through a trust, Dad's will includes two other people. Ambrosia Yazzie, and another, not named, labeled 'Recipient One.' Who could that be?"

Layli leaned on one hip and stirred sugar into the tea mugs. "You may confide in me, but your dad never did."

Peyton eyed the cold oatmeal and omelet but didn't touch the food. "I need to go through drawers and shelves. There's so much to understand. It's like I know it all, but I know nothing." An image rose to the surface of her mind like a watermark, a painting her mother had made of her father writing at his desk. She knew he wrote essays, but in Harlow's painting, he had a tower of letters. He always wrote on Italian linen paper using a stylus. Such care meant he would have saved what he wrote. "Did Dad keep a journal? I know he typed up stuff and sometimes kept handwritten drafts in a box in the study closet." Her father had never been emotive, and avoided discussing their history during the years Harlow was alive. "Dad had to have put those feelings somewhere. Did he write letters?"

Layli brought the steaming cups of tea to the table and took a seat. "Peppermint, skullcap, catnip, and licorice root—my mix. You'll sleep deeper and better with it, and frankly, you look like crap."

"He did, didn't he?"

"Hmm… clever girl." Layli hesitated for a moment, then said, "I never snoop, you know that."

"But of course. No need to qualify anything for me. I trust you like my parents always trusted you."

"You're right. There are letters."

"How do you know?"

"A couple of years ago, I supervised a carpenter who was fixing the drawers in your father's desk. We had to unlock it, and I noticed a bundle of envelopes. He wrote letters he sent to no one. He kept them locked in his desk, at least then. They must be meaningful."

Peyton sipped her tea, with unblinking eyes, soothed by the aroma. "I'm so mad at myself. Why didn't I probe sooner?"

"You know why. It would've bothered your father if you disrespected his privacy. Rummage through his study, and you'll find everything. After he passed, I locked it all down—his bureau, the glass-door bookcase, the walk-in closet full of boxes. I'll get you the keys. I haven't gone through any of it. You'll be the first. But brace yourself, Flower Child, you might not like what you find."

"You haven't called me Flower Child in ages."

With searing eyes, Layli said, "Uprooted plants don't bloom, you know. You came back for visits, but left a big part of yourself back in California."

Memories of Ashton ribboned through Peyton's mind. The damage he caused her, or she caused herself, also strained her connection with her family.

"Maybe you can bloom again now."

Peyton stood up and gathered the plates. "Thank you for breakfast. I'm sorry. I have no appetite. Don't bother in the future, Layli. When I'm hungry, I'll figure it out for myself. But I'll give this to Cooper."

"So, no more setting up in the breakfast or dining room?"

"The pomp was for Dad. Those days are over. When I have guests, it'll be different, but I prefer to eat right here with you guys, like we did when Dad was out." She teared up again at the thought of her father and tucked her head down, hoping the letters would shed light.

44

four

Armed with the keys to the kingdom, Peyton whizzed to his study, a mini gallery of historic Americana artifacts and mechanical wonders, from automatons to intricate multi-tiered music boxes to clockwork jewelry. His sandalwood cologne still lingered there. Masculine. Classic. Peyton knew she'd preserve the room and wished he'd done that for her mother's studio and paintings. She pictured his intelligent blue eyes, his hair neither short enough to look modern, nor long enough to look hip. It had thinned on top, yet he had kept it longer in the back, like a sheep's rump.

She used a combination of numbers, letters, and a fingerprint to open the safe where she'd packed away his will and fineries. With a pang of sorrow, she realized she was the only Chase left. She flicked on the desk lamp and tested the keys, inserting them one by one into the lock. One of them unlocked all the desk drawers. She slipped her hand into each drawer with care, searching for letters her father might have written. The drawers were sparse, their contents organized, ordinary. No letters. Nothing of consequence.

Where could those letters be?

The small dial on the clock jumped three numbers, but she continued her search, opening boxes, riffling through leather valises and wooden chests. Stacks of beautiful satchels, valuable in themselves, contained missives, souvenirs, postcards from as far back as the 1970s. Finally, she found a few letters that had yellowed from the leakage of time. With a racing heart, she scanned the pages for dates and noticed they were in chronological order. But the stack was short. Would her mother have painted him writing letters at his desk if it weren't a frequent habit? It struck her as odd that all of them dated from before Harlow's death.

Peyton sat cross-legged on the sofa and began to read them in order. Most were an intellectual, internal dialogue, like a diary. But one was enlightening. In it, her father wrote about his vasectomy. She'd never known he'd undergone that procedure. The letter was dated before she turned two years old.

Why did her father have a vasectomy? Where were the letters he'd written after Harlow's death? What was in them if well hidden?

The longer she sat pondering, the better she heard the ticking of the clock. Once a month, Sorensen wound his American mahogany banjo clock. He'd find the winding key, kept in the pendulum case, and place it in the winding hole. He habitually sang and hummed "Over the Hills and Far Away," then turned the key clockwise until it met a gentle resistance. It was his favorite clock, with a perched eagle finial, a steel engraved dial under glass, and a hinged door with a reverse painting of Monticello, in homage to Thomas Jefferson. He'd show it to fellow clock enthusiasts, elaborating on its maker, Willard of New Haven, Connecticut, and its original paper label dating to the early 19th century. It made a soothing ticking sound, reminiscent of rain drops. Peyton understood why her father loved old clocks.

The hours measure the day, but only time measures the man. And now that time was measuring her, she feared it would find her wanting.

Peyton scanned the books on her father's floor-to-ceiling shelves. He had such a trove of words. She wished he'd used them to show her the way… or absolve her. She was sure she needed absolving. Of what? But she knew. Could she admit her sin aloud, even once? She thought of Father Gabriel. She could confess to him. Her father was no longer around to lid the hole she'd carried in her chest for more than two decades. Perhaps if she confessed, the hole would refill. At random, she chose a leather-bound book and thumbed through it. She was looking for something specific. Tucked in its pages would be a laminated bookmarker with a quote by Mark Twain. She loved her father's idiosyncrasy. It read, "Thunder is good, thunder is impressive; but it is lightning that does the work."

Royce phoned. "Come down to Santa Fe and have dinner with me at the Coyote Café."

"I was thinking I'd shower and nap. Haven't been sleeping well at all."

"Nap tomorrow."

"I haven't been that hungry."

"Lordy, I want to talk to you about something important."

Peyton knew this was one of those moments when Royce could be relentless. "I'll make a simple but nice meal. How's that?"

"Screw simple. You're not getting your way, young lady. I want you to put on a dress and some goddamn lipstick and come down. Heels, too. In my book, they fix everything." When Peyton took her time replying, Royce said, "I may have a solution for your problems. Say yes to your favorite godmother."

"Five, okay with you?"

"Perfect."

In a red and white polka dot dress worthy of Audrey Hepburn, and red patent leather pumps not meant for walking, Peyton strode to the Coyote Café on Water Street. She'd had to park her car near Saint Francis Cathedral, forced to walk farther than planned, but the physical discomfort was welcome, like biting down on an achy tooth, something to pinch the flesh instead of the spirit.

A host with full red lips and a top the size of playing cards showed Peyton to her table. A red Dale Chihuly chandelier hung in the center of the restaurant, and the walls were decorated with images of animals in a vibrant patchwork design.

"I didn't want to leave the house, but now I'm here, I think I needed it. Thank you." She bent over and plunked a kiss on Royce's cheek, then slipped into a semi-circular brown and powder blue booth.

"Oh, honey, you look amazing. If Harlow could see you now."

"That's sweet, but only a godmother holds the magic wand."

Royce looked as if she hid her wand in her hair. It had been teased into a voluminous mass and parted down the middle. "I ordered you a cosmopolitan."

"That's the ticket. How're you?"

"I'll be better after some squash blossoms and elk tenderloin. You?"

Peyton scanned the menu: beef cheek empanada, stuffed quail, duck leg confit, mesquite grilled lobster tails. "Hard to choose."

"How do you get your lips so perfectly red and glossy?"

"Don't let anyone tell you differently. Sephora has all the secrets, not Victoria." She scooted in her seat and whispered, "Did you know Dad had a vasectomy soon after I was born?"

"I wasn't privy to your dad's balls. Is that a big deal?"

"Could be. Dad was methodical." Peyton decided on her meal, then put the menu face-down. "You said you have a solution for the ranch?"

Royce flitted the false eyelashes she was never without. "I've been worried about you, so I powwowed. Turns out Sorensen had a plan that would one day spare you the burden you have now."

"Do you mean the hunt Dad was contemplating?"

"How do you know that?"

Peyton spread the serviette on her lap. "Uncle Mark told me."

"Well, that took the wind out of my sails."

Peyton giggled. "Why? Did you think I'd love the idea? I don't. It's not me or my style. I'm not vegan… I realize it's hypocritical to judge hunting. Just doesn't feel right."

Royce stretched forward and slapped her on the arm. "What's feelings got to do with it? Mark can get you any license, can also take care of any legal ends, and I'll organize your launch for you, to boot."

A tuxedoed server brought their drinks and asked if they were ready to order.

Royce replied, "Not just yet. Thank you. Give us a few, please." Then, refocusing on Peyton, she added, "It'll be a posh hunt, and I'll get you the right guests. We decided—"

"—who's we?"

"Your triumvirate, that's who. Mark, God, and I. We decided you'll have to make the ranch work harder to save it." Royce felt her sprayed hair, making sure every strand was where she glued it. "You need paying guests for a proper stay that includes a hunt. I know who's who all over. I got you."

A man flailed his fork about. His way of getting a server's attention. "I hate when people confuse being rich with being rude," Peyton said.

Royce took a big gulp of her cocktail. "Hey, don't change the subject."

"What do you want me to do? Goad a bunch of strangers into giving me their money by selling them an expensive hunt? Because it would have to be exorbitant to make a difference to the ranch."

The queen of Abiquiú grinned and fluttered her ringed fingers. "No, no, my dear. This won't do."

Peyton sipped her drink, maintaining eye contact.

"My birthday party is coming up in three weeks, as you know. I'll gather just the right people at my house. Then, you'll pitch to them. We'll do it the old-fashioned way—buy, not sell."

Peyton clicked her apple red nails on her cocktail glass. "I suddenly feel like an idiot. What do you mean?"

"Wealthy people sell nothing. They buy. You'll have to *buy* their confidence, Peyton." She buttered a warm sourdough bun. "Just be your-self, darling."

"And that will do it?"

"God, no! Fireworks, Louis VIII cognac, and flamenco dancers will do it, but you'll still have to be yourself. They must see the descendant of money, *le vrai de vrai*."

"Won't you be disappointed if I change my mind?"

Royce flung fingers into the air, casting her spell. "Pish-posh, I'm already spending all that on my party. A hunting pitch or not, makes no difference."

Peyton considered the idea. She found it unappealing, but had no alternative way out. "What if it fails miserably?"

"This is cattle and big game country. It's a way of life for us. Rich men hunt with or without your help. Only you'll give them something extra. Why not?"

"Something extra?"

"You're the one putting on the hunt, not me. You figure it out."

Peyton laughed and clapped her hands. "Classic Royce."

"You have horses, a humongous house, staff adept at the outdoors, and an estate to rescue. You can't just ride your horses and treat them like pets, Peyton. Put them to work as your father was planning to do."

The server returned for their orders.

Royce checked the time. "Can we wait just two more minutes, please?"

"I'm ready to order, aren't you?" asked Peyton. "Or are we waiting for someone?"

Royce flashed a partly naughty, partly sheepish smile, and looked past Peyton. "Well, he's here now."

"Hello, Peyton," Ashton said, standing beside her.

Peyton took her time looking up, but she recognized him. No one had shinier shoes or a silkier voice. Here he was again, to tempt and torment her. Reluctantly, she met his eyes. "Hi."

"Don't give Royce saucer eyes," he said. "I asked her to invite me, not the other way around."

"Sit down," Royce said, looking at Peyton. "Ashton sent me a divine box of Sprinkles Cupcakes. I just had to invite him."

Peyton tucked her hair behind her ears, considering her next move. "Sugar and spice, and everything nice is how it starts, but how does it end?" It was like time hadn't passed. Ashton had infused her self-confidence and showered her with love and generosity of soul.

"I like your neck of the woods," Ashton said. "Thought I'd spend some time in it and catch up."

Royce pounced. "You like our little kingdom, do you? Fabulous. I'm having a soirée soon, up in Abiquiú. May I send you an invitation?"

Peyton knew Royce was being kind, but it felt cruel.

Another drink arrived for Royce, but she gave it to Ashton. "By soirée, I mean you won't be allowed to leave until you've taken a dip in the lake at dawn. Preferably naked." She chuckled. "You must come."

He swirled the swizzle stick in his drink, smirking. "When?"

"In three weeks." As if he needed more enticements, she added, "I have a helipad. Others will fly in, as well, and I have plenty of rooms for overnight guests."

"Ah, that kind of party."

"Is there another kind, young man?"

"Will Peyton be there?" he asked, forcing her to bury her face in her cocktail, steeling her nerves.

"Well, yes. Wouldn't be much of a party without her," Royce answered.

Peyton shot her a chastising glare. "Ashton is busy, far away."

His relentless eyes paused on her. "I miss Peyton very much."

"Super. I'm the largest house on the lake. Can't miss it. Just show up in three weeks. Come the day before. Stay the day after. Just come."

He shifted his chair close enough to touch Peyton's face if she'd let him. "I'll do my best to come if you'll allow me to cover dinner tonight. I insist."

"Lordy lord, is there no end to your generosity?"

Peyton pressed her lips together, tension clamping down on her body. "You don't have to do any of that, Ashton."

"Yes, I do." He inhaled with the air of someone only getting started. "You smudged your lipstick, beautiful." He tried to wipe the smear, but Peyton turned away as he clenched his jaw.

Royce said, "Maybe you should take Peyton riding while you're here… unless you don't ride."

"Do I ride, Peyton?" he asked, but when he couldn't force an answer, he said, "We met when she came to one of my polo matches. Probably the best day of my life."

Royce raised her glass for a toast. "Now that's what I call a real match."

Peyton wondered if she'd end up having to kick her under the table. Then Royce excused herself and left them alone, making her wish she had.

Ashton walked his fingers in the narrow space between them. "You want me. I can see it plain as day. Why are you acting as if you don't?"

Peyton lowered her voice. "You forget I know you. I know your tactics, too. You're Prince Charming, but what I want is Prince Honest."

"I didn't lie."

The anger stringing her voice surprised her. "I wouldn't have waited around for years if for one minute I'd doubted we'd get married and start a family."

He grabbed her hand and tugged her toward him. "I wanted a full life with you, but so much is entangled in that damned marriage of mine. I couldn't get free."

She asked about the most painful memory with him. "Then why was having a child with me so horrifying?"

"It wasn't." He leaned closer until she could feel his breath on her cheek. "I have ambitions and enormous responsibilities. I hardly saw my father because of his own ambitions and responsibilities. He and I talk business and that's it. Half the time, he forgets we're related, and when he remembers, it's to push me to be like him—a relentless workaholic. But I told you all that, Peyton."

"Then don't be like him. It's a choice, isn't it?"

He placed his hand on her knee, rocketing her temperature. "I choose you."

She shook her knee free. "I'm not going down that road with you again. You gave me false hope then, and you're doing it again now."

"Stop saying I'm lying. I'm not."

"There's blatant lying, then there's promising me what you can't deliver. Don't build castles in the air for me again." She grabbed her purse and tried to hightail it out of the restaurant, but Royce intercepted her.

"Where're you going? He's beyond perfect and you're leaving?"

Peyton led them to a private corner, sandwiched between a pony wall and a tall red and blue vase.

"Royce!" She waited until she lost the glint of exuberance in her eyes. "You shouldn't have invited him. You acted as my ambassador, but it's not what I want. I know you thought you were helping me, but you're not."

"Honey, look at what he's doing for you."

"What is he doing for me? He showed up at my father's funeral with a big flower arrangement and sent you some cupcakes. I'm worth considerably more than that."

"But they're from Sprinkles." Royce saw Peyton didn't find her funny, and said, "I'm sorry I stepped in it."

Peyton scanned their surroundings, verifying they were still alone. "When Ashton didn't get divorced, didn't want children, my embarrassment morphed to shame, because… because…" She bit her cheek and her tears drizzled.

"You can say it, darling."

"Because I had lost respect for myself."

Royce pulled her into an embrace. "He clearly was important once. Maybe he still is."

"I learned a lot from that relationship, but I'm better off without it." She fiddled inside her purse for tissues. "I allowed myself to invest wholeheartedly in a man to whom I was only an option. Of course, he denies that characterization, but it's true." She patted her eyes dry, careful with her makeup. "I had to fix what made me settle for part of a man, when I clearly give all of me to him. I had options, but I chose wrong."

Royce tucked Peyton's hair behind her ears. "It wasn't a mistake if you could grow and learn this much from it. But did you ever figure out what made you settle for so little?"

"The reward was small, but the man was big. I learned the hard way that any life with a man has to be as big as he is, if not bigger."

"This is heavy stuff, calls for an old-fashioned whiskey."

Thoughts circled in Peyton's mind like vultures over dead prey. She chastised herself for having been so cowardly, avoiding the necessary questions, treating them as corpses when they were very much alive. "Tell me again. How did you see Mom? What was she like in your eyes? Was she fun, intense, what?"

"Unpredictable, to say the least, also stunning, fun, unforgettable."

"And how do you see me?"

Royce said what Peyton feared most—she feared the entire world saw her that way. "You're Harlow's daughter."

She tucked her head down, huddling deeper into the corner, and cried.

"I just said something dumb, didn't I? I meant, you're unforgettable, too."

Peyton closed her eyes, her mother's paintings wheeling in her head like a Rolodex, and she scanned them one after the other, until one stood out—the painting that had pivoted the trajectory of her life. The sin she needed to atone for. She vowed to visit Father Gabriel the next day, as the painting she could only share in confession crystalized in her mind. "Look, don't feel bad. I'm not mad at you, just at the situation, but I should go. It's taking everything I've got not to get lured in again. Ashton can't believe there's room for him in my life."

"But why?"

Peyton pivoted, preparing to dash out. "Because there *is* room for him. I'm human, want to be held at night, and I yearn to be adored and cajoled, but he can't know that. I'll see you soon."

With insistent steps, Peyton traversed the restaurant, feeling Ashton's eyes on her, not breathing until she disappeared from his view. She took the stairs, almost running. Halfway down, she paused, breathing deeply, shocked at how shaken she was. It wasn't the love she once felt. But it was more than she wanted to feel for a man who was magnetic but married.

five

Bucolic, aromatic, and vast, Abiquiú displayed its colors in stone rather than foliage. Roads curved through rocks the texture of honeycombs. Ensnared in its beauty, Peyton and Cooper trundled to Saint Thomas's in the truck to see the kindest friar she knew. At Abiquiú creek, she turned onto a dirt road, mindful not to kick up dust, and parked by the humble white wooden cross staked near the iron gate. Some reservation churches were pre-fabricated buildings, more fit for storage than prayer, but not Saint Thomas's.

Quaint and inviting like the Pueblo of Abiquiú, the adobe church welcomed all with lavender bushes growing strong and resolve growing stronger.

"Come on out, Cooper." Peyton opened his door. She was dressed in shabby jeans and a plain shirt, blending into the surroundings. Her father had taught her the importance of mirroring the conditions of others when on their turf. She'd never forgotten that.

An old lady was sitting on cracked front steps. Her thin braids were tied with Hopi medallions, and they dangled as she hunched over a pile of hatch red chiles, stringing them with calloused, arthritic fingers. Beside her, bunches of chamomile were piled into a tall pyramid.

"Good morning," Peyton said. "You've been busy, I see."

The old lady muttered, nodding. Cooper whimpered, sniffing the herbs.

"If those beautiful chili ristras are for sale, I'd love to buy some, ma'am."

The old lady struggled to her feet. Peyton made to give her a hand, but was leery of causing offence. "I can help."

The woman ducked inside her house, returned with a hunk of acorn bread, and handed it to Peyton on a napkin. "Made it this morning."

"It smells delicious. *Askwali*." In respect for tradition, she bit off a nice chunk. "Buttery. Thank you."

"How many ristras would you like?"

"Five if you have them."

The old lady nodded and quoted Peyton a price of twenty dollars per garland.

"Heavens, no, these ristras are each at least four feet long. It would be criminal to pay you less than forty each. I'll be right back." Peyton leaned into her truck and retrieved the cash from the wallet she kept in the glove compartment. She surreptitiously gave half her acorn bread to Cooper, then returned with the money. "Two hundred, as promised. Thank you for the ristras. I'll pick them up before I leave. I have some business with Father Gabriel."

The old lady beamed through missing teeth and tiny eyes. "*Askwali*."

From the flat bed of her truck, Peyton heaved a basket filled with peach roses, white Asiatic lilies, and green echeveria succulents, and another filled with dried meats and cheeses.

"For me?" The old lady asked. "I didn't get anything this beautiful when I was in my twenties."

"Ladies don't age past twenty-nine."

"Ah, I love you said that."

"May I place them on your kitchen table? They're heavy."

The old woman nodded hard, clapping.

"I'll be back for the garlands in a while."

Peyton grabbed another basket of flowers and walked to the church.

She opened the low iron gate with her free hand, stepped into the small courtyard, and was relieved to find the front doors open. Father Gabriel was rearranging prayer books in the pews.

"Need help?"

He turned and grinned in recognition. "Blessed be. It's Peyton Chase! Come in, come in."

Not finding a suitable surface, she placed the flowers at her feet, and dipped her fingers in the holy water that shimmered in a small marble bowl by the door. The church beckoned her to take a knee and cross herself. The stone floor was bracing and cool. She closed her eyes, inhaling traces of incense. Then she walked toward the altar, and the breeze followed her inside, as refreshing as her long friendship with Father Gabriel. As always, he was in a gray robe, tied loosely with a hemp rope, his tonsure freshly shaven, his fingers twined with rosary beads—a true Franciscan.

"No expense was spared on this one," he said of the bereavement basket. "Just look at those huge blooms."

"Your church deserves them," she said.

"There's a wedding coming up. Perfect timing." As if sharing a secret, he whispered, "I'll give you holy oil before you leave."

"I can use it. Thank you very much." She commented on the pigeons and jackrabbits in the front yard. "Saint Francis must be proud, Father. I also noticed a donkey in the back."

"She keeps coyotes away from my chickens better than any dog." The friar took her hands in his. "Sorry, Peyton. Your father was excellent to us."

She acknowledged his statement with a bob of her head. "I'm sorry I spoke so little to you after the funeral service. It was crazy."

"No explanation needed. You have nothing to apologize for."

An image of her father in his coffin intruded, and she struggled to keep from crying. "I would've asked you to the vigil, but…"

"Child, you carry more guilt than God All Mighty permits. Your father had his own priest, so you called upon him. It was proper and just."

Her eyes misted, but she resisted the urge to cry.

"Maybe if you confessed, you'd feel better."

Peyton had come, in part, to confess, but she feared saying out loud what she wished had never happened.

He twirled his rosary beads about his fingers. "Your mother was Mormon, rest her soul. Correct?"

"Mormon six days a week, Catholic on Sundays." She pointed to her truck and turned to walk outside, politely urging him to shadow her. "I brought you some things."

The friar trickled behind her. The truck was brimming with baskets.

"It's a lot of food. More than we can eat at the ranch before it spoils. I wanted to share it with the families here."

"Smoked meats, dried fruits, and is that Godiva chocolate?"

"I didn't bring you anything impractical, like pâté or pickled gooseberries. It's stuff with decent shelf life, only the fresh fruits and spreadable cheeses are perishable."

He made the sign of the cross over her, then with bent head and clasped palms, he prayed aloud, and Peyton joined him. "Blessed are we, O Lord, because we have known You. Blessed are we because You are our great hope." When he finished the prayer, he chuckled. "You don't know how needed that food is. My parishioners suffer, but they don't complain. These are better donations than we usually get."

"My father would say a real cowboy would never let his horse drink water, he wouldn't drink himself."

"Sorensen, rest his soul, was just." He grew ever more enthusiastic and rubbed his flat belly. "Ooh, San Francisco Bay coffee—keeping this one for myself. There's such kindness in this. You *are* your mother's daughter. It's such a Harlow thing to do. Your father was generous, too. Followed through on anything your mother promised."

"What do you mean, 'what she promised?'"

The friar twiddled his rosary beads, still inspecting the goodies.

"Harlow, rest her soul, would show up unexpectedly, full of life and joy. She'd give me checks. Eventually, I learned to verify with your father for funds, and he always honored them."

Resisting a frown, Peyton asked, "Mom would give you checks she wasn't sure you could cash, and then rely on Dad to secure the funds?"

"Quite right," he replied, tallying the donation before him.

She felt a resurgence of compassion for her father and wondered if she'd misjudged some things, if she'd been harsh, unchristian even. "I apologize in advance for asking, Father, but were those sizeable sums?"

"The largest was just before her passing. Your father was obliging. You'd think he'd tithed himself. His donation bought fuel and food for many families."

How often had her mother gotten her father in financial jams, forcing expenses on him he couldn't sustain? Is that what had happened to the money? But Harlow had passed twenty years ago.

The friar glued his eyes on Peyton. "Why didn't you send someone? Why did you bring all this yourself?"

Before she could reply, a scrawny boy called out and dashed to the friar, his hair styled in a blue mohawk. Another boy, shorter, chubby, with cheeks the color of pomegranates, followed with much effort.

With his hands on his bulbous knees, the taller of the two said, "Grandma sent us to help you." He had an aquiline nose and penetrating eyes.

"Well, good morning there, Mikey," Father Gabriel said. "And you, Ricky. Thank you both."

"I'm Awanata the Swift," Ricky whistled through his missing two front teeth, and raised his arms like a wrestler. "I don't want to be called Ricky today."

Father Gabriel laughed. "Did you give yourself that name?"

"Grandma gave it to me." He pointed to his brother. "He's Honovi, and I'm Awanata. I'm seven years old and he's nine."

"I know."

Ricky pointed to Peyton. "She doesn't."

"That's true, and I'm Peyton. I'm thirty-three."

Father Gabriel wobbled his head, amused. "Alright, boys, let's lug all this stuff into my office."

When the brothers had grabbed a basket each and were out of earshot, the friar murmured to Peyton, "Honovi means strong deer."

"And Awanata?"

"Turtle."

She burst out laughing. "Grandma mustn't have explained the names very well."

It took multiple trips to unload the truck. Peyton noticed that the older boy studied her. "Do you want to ask me something, Mikey?"

With focused, mature eyes, he said, "You're stuck because she is."

"What did you say, kiddo? Who?"

He hunched his shoulders until they almost touched his earlobes. "That's all they said."

"They?"

"Reward time." Father Gabriel let the boys have first dibs on the snacks. They left with armfuls, satisfied with their wages. Cooper helped by jogging back and forth beside them, that earned him cashews and peanuts.

For more information, Peyton said, "Mikey is precocious, it seems."

"He's more than that. Quite special, that one, but I want to talk about you." Father Gabriel's smile faded, and he fiddled with his rosary beads. "You smile, even laugh, but your spirit is heavy."

The church was empty. "You asked me why I came here myself. Please, get your purple stole."

Peyton sat in a pew with her elbows on her knees, preparing for her first confession in a long time. She was about to divulge a secret she'd kept snug in her heart for twenty-four years.

Father Gabriel harnessed his neck in a long purple stole that gave him the authority to mediate with God. He sat beside her.

Peyton swallowed. "Since Dad died, I've been invaded with difficult memories of my mother. It was as if he were the shield, but it's down now." Encouraged by Father Gabriel's closed eyes, she continued. "By the time I was about nine, I'd stopped painting alongside my mother, though when I was a toddler she gave me food coloring to paint with."

"Ah, so she encouraged your artistic side."

"Then she started working on a portrait of me. She'd do that from time to time. Over the years, she painted several of Dad and me, but she said that this one was for me to keep. But I overheard her selling it over the phone. The client came to preview it before it was finished and paid for it upfront…"

"Go on, my child, go on."

Peyton's tears burst through. "I was furious because she was giving away what she'd promised was mine. But more so because she'd depicted me with paint on my face and hands."

"Why was that painful for you?"

Peyton couldn't tell him that her mother had declared she lacked talent, as she saw it. "Because it felt humiliating, as if she'd painted me with egg on my face, and showed it to people."

Father Gabriel gave her his profile and bent his head. "What about that is sinful?"

"I was so angry with her, I hid the painting the day the buyer came for it. I wanted her to get in trouble, and I wanted to keep that man from showing my portrait to others."

"Still no sin there, Peyton."

"The problem is the man demanded his money back, so that involved Dad. I spied on my parents after the client left, but they didn't know I was there. One thing led to another. Dad accused Mom of having been irresponsible, made it her fault. At one point, Mom slapped him. It might not have been the first time she did that, but what shocked me even more was that Dad hit her back, and it seemed to me he'd never done that before. I felt so bad and got so scared, I hid the painting in one of the unused buildings on the ranch, so my parents would never find out. I hadn't planned on stealing it, but I did."

"And?"

"My parents were never the same after that, and it was all my fault, Father." Peyton sobbed and buried her face in her sleeve.

"You were a child. You're carrying false guilt." He made the cross over her again. "What happened to that painting?"

"Years later, when I could face it, I dug it up, but it had been damaged from improper storage. That was the first painting I ever restored—a portrait of myself I found hideous."

"That was a travesty, Peyton, but it wasn't your fault in quite the way you describe. What you did might have been the straw that broke the camel's back, but that camel would have had no chance by then. By the grace of the Lord, who sanctifies repentant sinners, you are absolved of all your sins. In the name of the Father and of the Son, and of the Holy Spirit. Amen."

Peyton fidgeted and placed her hands on the pew. "How many Hail Marys, Father?"

"What you really need is to hail Peyton."

It was an icy truth that burned, but one effective at reducing the inflammation in her soul.

"It always helps to pray to the Mother of God. I do so daily." He squeezed her trembling hand. "Do you know what you really said to me today? Your father's death reminded you of what restoration really is. Forgive your mother, forgive your father, and forgive yourself, for God loves and forgives you."

She nodded, wiping away tears. "Thank you. I feel somewhat relieved, but I must go now, Father."

"I'll walk you to your truck."

In true Puebloan character, the chili ristras had been boxed, together with a loaf of acorn bread, and placed on the hood of Peyton's truck. She searched for the old lady, wanting to thank her one last time, but found Mikey instead. He was watching her with the same intensity as before. She waved to him, sensing a significance she couldn't comprehend. Mikey waved back, then slunk away. Peyton let Cooper jump onto the front seat, and the dog comforted her with head nudges. "May I ask you for a favor, Father?"

"Of course."

"If I send a car for you, would you come bless Pioneer Ranch?"

"It needs an exorcism, does it?" He laughed, but it was odd, like a sputtering muffler.

"It has its share of ghosts."

He sputtered again and gave her his number. "Just call me."

"You helped me a great deal, Father. Thank you."

He looked at her sympathetically. "What do you need most?"

"I don't know what to do. I need divine intervention."

He gestured toward the altar. "Just talk to Him. Remember, my child, He'll give you what you need, not what you want."

She knew Father Gabriel meant to comfort her, but what if God decided she didn't need the ranch?

six

Peyton slowed down when she turned onto the estate. The three-mile-long, scenic, private drive was lined with aspen trees on both sides. Wildflowers poked in pockets, adding a kaleidoscope of color. Swallowtails and eagles dominated the sky; pronghorns, mule deer, and coyotes the land. On special days, golden eagles appeared as did oryx antelope, brought from South Africa, now an integral part of the landscape.

Peyton muted the radio and listened to nature's music instead. Huge iron letters, flanked on both sides by terraced walls with pierced belfries, loomed in a big arch, spelling Pioneer Ranch.

She parked in a space the size of a small piazza, between the main house and the casita, the oldest building on the ranch. Cooper jumped from the truck. She gathered the box of chilis and headed to the kitchen. Again, the state of the garden bothered her. She stared at partially collapsed beds, at weeds, and spindly bushes that reached the windows. More mental notes.

Tansy, a young woman with a toothy smile, met her in the mudroom and relieved her of the box. "Are these what I think they are, Ms. Chase?" With sausage fingers, she unwrapped each garland of shiny, fleshy red hatch chiles the size of dinosaur talons. "They smell intense. Nice to use the hooks on the porch again. Five, right?"

"One for each hook," Peyton said, washing her hands.

"Can I take next week off? My family has a pie stand at the rodeo this year, and they need my help."

"Yes, of course."

Layli came in with a vase of orange and yellow gladiolas. "Can't wait for the rodeo to begin."

Tansy flashed her beaver smile. "Don't forget to stop by for some pie."

Layli opened the fridge and pulled out three thick sandwiches.

Through the cellophane, Peyton could see pastrami on rye glued together with Russian dressing.

"We'll walk and eat. I have one for Scarborough, too." She handed Peyton a sandwich and a stack of napkins. "Let's go, we're burnin' daylight."

Scarborough tidied the trunk while he waited for them.

"Do you ever stop?" Peyton asked.

He was wearing a sky-blue plaid shirt, a bright yellow bandana twined around his neck, his attitude smooth as molasses. "An honest day's work, that's all."

"Left the keys in it."

He tipped his hat. "I reckoned, ma'am. I'll move her later." He took a sandwich from Layli. "Is it safe to eat?"

"I poisoned it myself."

Peyton swabbed at the corners of her mouth. "What's in the converted stables now?"

"Old furniture in good condition, boxes of extra housewares, surplus horse gear, and all the fishing and hunting gear, but those are locked up."

Peyton thought of what the guestrooms would need if she were to move ahead with the hunt. "Chairs, desks?"

Scarborough nodded. "Some… most disassembled, but we're dabsters here. We can put them back together in a flash. I'll email you an inventory."

"The hunting gear should be substantial."

"I'd say so. Only good stuff. Shimano and Daiwa for rods, and Bergera for rifles. Real good kit. Cabela's never had a better customer."

Peyton pointed to a rotunda. A well-curated hunting exhibition could become part of the ranch's purpose. "Layli, the casita is as ready as always, right?" She thought she could offer the casita as a premium accommodation.

"Let's take a look."

They strolled to the casita, the original house on the property. Gravel crunched underfoot, but it was no cover for the Wood Thrush serenading the ranch. Five crescent steps led to a round casita built of limestone and sandstone with giant beams painted a reddish brown.

The door creaked, opening onto a rustic space with a high ceiling, a loft, and a small, dim and cool bedroom made comfortable with layers of linens, blankets, and throws, and an en suite bathroom. A baker's hutch painted a pale country green and a butcher's block counter lent the kitchenette character. Stone walls and floors in natural tones contrasted with colorful Mexican tiles of cobalt blue and yellow. Textiles collected lazily over many years, Navajo blankets and Kachina dolls added a touch of hominess.

"Cheerful as ever," Peyton said, recalling how she'd played house in it as a child, pretending she was the mother of two. Now she feared she'd never become a real mother.

She stood at the bedroom door, assessing with the eyes of a custodian. "I think a wealthy patron will pay a bundle to sleep in a bed made by early settlers." She fiddled with the handle and its skeleton key. "How can anyone resist a historic building furnished with locally hand-crafted linens?"

Layli ran tan fingers through her straight dark hair. "What're you thinking, then?"

Peyton sat on the leather sofa facing the hearth. "Look at the view behind me, at this fireplace older than the Liberty Bell. This old ranch needs old money. A by-invitation-only hunt requires the right man and the right seduction."

Horror curtained Layli's face. "A commercial hunt like your father had in mind? I'm not opposed to hunting, but not for sport. Doesn't seem like you."

"It's not me, but I don't have a better idea for now. It's worth exploring, at least. Besides, this is not about me. I was up last night, looking through spreadsheets and income statements, studying liabilities and assets." She wrinkled her forehead. "This place is hemorrhaging from hefty expenses, especially the mortgage. We need a lucrative endeavor that wouldn't insult it."

Scarborough scratched the back of his head. "In Europe, manor after manor hosts tourists to keep afloat, and many with hunting as the primary draw. Why not us?"

"How do you know this?" Layli raised her eyebrows. "Through your readings?"

He sniffled and squinted. "I watch *Britain's Great Manors* on the BBC."

Peyton said, "I don't love the idea, and I'm not sure I'll go with it, but I have to test every avenue until something opens up for us." She crossed her legs and fanned her arms on the back of the sofa. "This house spent ungodly sums over the decades entertaining in style. It's time it earned its keep." She could see Layli give Scarborough a sharp, critical stare. "Scarborough didn't even bring it up. Don't blame him. I asked Uncle Mark. Besides, it's a seasonal business, December through April. The house won't be engaged all year. Only one week each month for four months a year. If... and it's a big if... the hunt can bring us a substantial income in only four weeks, I want to look into it."

"At least we have that going for us," Layli said. "Four weeks are manageable, but with all the preparations, they'll feel longer."

"We'll have to focus on big game, bears, big cats—"

"—no predators, can't stand that. Only prey, and even that's uncomfortable."

"As you wish, ma'am. There's elk, Persian ibex, Barbary sheep, oryxes, grouse, pheasant, other fowl."

"Uncle Mark can get me any licenses I need. He's a hunter himself. Dad's friends offered their services. Time to take them up on it."

"Many are well to do," Scarborough said. "And they know others who are. That's how we'll find hunters itching to scar the hide and tell the story."

Peyton pasted her elbows to her knees and leaned forward. "Scarborough, what'll we need?"

"We'll need to line up some key people like a taxidermist who'll prioritize us, a licensed arms dealer who'll come to us in case some guests want to buy their own weapons. We mustn't forget a single detail."

Peyton loathed the image Scarborough painted. "I'm probably going to nix this idea, but it doesn't hurt to explore it. Layli, you're our accountant. Can you run some numbers for me and let me know if this can work, regardless of how little enthusiasm we have for it?"

"Sure."

"The kill has to be guaranteed for such a price," said Scarborough. "You'll need someone who'll scout the forests and educate the guests. Someone who can teach them our ways up here. I reckon they'll also need a moving feast."

"Who'll that be, old man, you?" Layli asked.

Scarborough stabbed a finger at her, his irritation bringing out his Southwestern accent. "You watch it now. Lettin' the cat out of the bag is easier than puttin' it back." He fished his cellphone from his side pocket and scrolled through his contacts. "You'll need Adler, but he won't do it."

"Who?" asked Peyton.

"He's not some nut, is he?" Layli asked. "We don't need crazy."

"We all got pieces of crazy in us, but some got bigger pieces than others."

Layli pursed her lips, tapped her foot, and mumbled something in Tewa, her native tongue.

"Will someone explain to me who we're talking about?"

"Blake Adler, ma'am. The best at scouting, at leaving no trace behind, and he knows these woods better than anybody. He's unrivaled, but I doubt he'll do it."

"Is he to be trusted?" asked Peyton.

Scarborough squinted. "He's one of them folks. He doesn't go in if he doesn't know the way out."

"Why wouldn't he want to do it?" Layli asked.

"Because he's Adler."

"I'll pay well if we can get the money we'll be asking for," Peyton said.

Scarborough stretched to his full height and scooped a pocketknife from his jeans. "See this here? Damascus steel and dinosaur bone."

"So?" Layli sneered.

"Valuable knife!" His voice pitched higher. "Adler gave it to me just because. The man doesn't do things for money. He makes good dough from his security business. Another reason he'll refuse, I reckon."

"Are we in so much trouble that we need this?" Layli asked.

Peyton stood up and looked from Layli to Scarborough. "This never leaves the room under any circumstance."

Both nodded, focused.

"I can't be sure, but my estimate is we have less than six months to fix it or list it, and I can't stomach the idea of losing Pioneer Ranch. It would be a betrayal." She had betrayed her parents when she stole the painting. She didn't think her soul could handle betraying them in death, too.

Layli flopped her arms. "Just six months?"

"If that, but I'll fix it. If we plan wisely now, we'll be in time for the upcoming hunting season."

Scarborough wiped his face. "I have a house of my own. Where would Layli go? She and Koda live here. Not to mention the seasonal wranglers who crash here for weeks on end each year."

Peyton swallowed, scattering her eyes all over. "Whatever solution I come up with for this estate will include all of us. I promise." Silence canopied the room as she gathered her nerves. "Scarborough, are you familiar with the hunting treks closer to the Colorado border?"

"Know them some, but Adler knows them best. He's from Chama."

"Do we have enough Jeeps to ferry guests up there?"

"We'll need to pack up a feast for them each time. We only got two such vehicles, but they're on their last legs. Not lavish."

Peyton exhaled hard. "We have enough trailers and working trucks, but not luxurious SUVs. To keep the expenses down, we'll need to borrow some. Uncle Mark has an arsenal of them. He'll lend us a couple. The horses and mules are all in decent shape, right? We'll need them."

"Two yearlings arrived today, ma'am. I'll show you. Part of what Mr. Chase was planning when he decided on this hunt. Let's head to the corral."

They ambled along a winding paved path and crossed the wooden pedestrian bridge that arched over a stream, splitting the property from stem to stern. Peyton pointed to a roadrunner rushing in front of them. "It's an omen. The roadrunner is the symbol of steadfastness and endurance. Is there a better sign?"

Scarborough wrapped a fatherly arm around her shoulders, which he hadn't done in ages. "I only know the way of the cowboy, ma'am. If you climb in the saddle, be ready for the ride."

She realized they both saw through her bravado and knew she was afraid. "I was Rodeo Queen once."

"That's no beauty pageant, ma'am. You have to be darn skilled with horse, dog, and cattle to win that crown." He doffed his hat. "And you were a greenhorn, then. Imagine what you can do now." He took a pair of leather gloves from his back pocket and hung them on his belt. "Now, about the new horses… Mr. Chase bought the foals recently. They got delivered this morning."

"Tell me the veterinarian issued their certificates."

"Oh yeah. They're healthy, just underfed. Koda is with them now."

In the afternoon, the corral was shaded, butting against a tall rock.

Koda, shirtless, wearing chaps and a wide-brimmed hat, stood in the middle with an Appaloosa and a Paint Horse. A long thick braid bisected his shoulders, and he whistled and chanted in Tewa, calming the newcomers.

Peyton opened the gate and entered the corral. The horses seemed on tenterhooks but consolable. She knew how to avoid spooking them, and let them smell her, get the measure of her. The Paint Horse was curious, ducking his head and neighing. Peyton gave him a loving pat, but her eyes were on the Appaloosa. "Such a beautiful, speckled specimen." She continued to stroke the Paint Horse, feeling its white belly and brown legs. "You're right. They need TLC."

"Why your father bought them. He was kind that way," Koda said, whipping his braid around his neck like a pet snake. "Are we renaming the horses?"

"Want to be the one to do it?"

He touched the Paint Horse. "The Calico should be called Whiskey Jack. The Appaloosa, white with black polka dots, should be named Cookies N' Cream."

Peyton burst out laughing. "We're not naming a horse this gorgeous after food."

"What should we call him then?"

"I don't know yet. We'll wait on the Appaloosa, but, Koda, you can name the Paint Horse, so long as it's faithful to the alliteration."

Layli snickered and counted on her fingers. "Baroness, Brandy, Bishop, Breeze, Blaze, and all the others."

"How's Brocco for the Paint Horse, and Bonanza for the Appaloosa?"

The Paint Horse bobbed his head, as if he approved, making them laugh.

"Brocco it is, then. Thank you. But the Appaloosa hasn't divulged his name yet."

"What if he refuses to tell?" Koda asked.

"Then you're not asking the right questions. These babies need setting loose in the grassy fields. They can rest and eat for a while."

Scarborough tapped Koda's shoulder. "Do it right away, cowboy. They look thirsty, too."

Koda led the horses from the corral toward grassy paddocks, then turned to Layli. "The sandwich you sent with Tansy was puny. Send, like, two more."

"Told ya," Scarborough said, chuckling, and hooked a boot on a horizontal post.

"I should make some phone calls before the day disappears," Peyton said. "Got Blake's number for me, Scarborough?"

"Everyone calls him Adler. You go see him, ma'am, if you want him."

In a paddock, jackrabbits were nibbling dandelions. "Go where?"

"He won't be rocking away the day at home. I'll have to ask around. Maybe I can ferret him out for you."

"What is he, Scarborough, a professional hunter?"

"A military man for years, a cowboy by breed. Quiet, precise, methodical, has a reputation."

"Reputation?" Layli shot. "That's all we need."

"If you'll let me finish, I mean a *great* reputation." They followed him out of the corral and he closed the gate.

"You should speak sense to her, you, not spur her on," Layli told him. "Military man, group hunting licenses, taxidermists. Seems complicated!"

Peyton nudged her old friend. "We're Pioneer Ranch. For pioneers, everything is complicated." She shaded her eyes with her hand, scanning the horizon. "This land needs guardians more than ever, but nothing comes without sacrifice."

Scarborough patted his belly. "I'll go up to Chama, try to find Adler and grab a real lunch at the saloon up there while I'm at it, since Layli only gave me a snack."

Layli turned on her heels, muttering under her breath.

He watched her punish the ground with each step as she hammered up the path to the house. "Layli always comes through. It's her history coming to haunt her."

"What history?"

"I helped her move into her cabin way back then. She didn't come out for a week. Shellshocked people do that."

Peyton thought of the ghosts she'd mentioned to Father Gabriel. Some of them weren't hers. "I'm not brave, you know."

Scarborough stared at her. "You raced a horse bareback, with nothing, not a saddle or a bit. Remember? And why? Because some nitwits at the rodeo dared you. You're brave, alright. You just haven't had to be this brave in a while."

After another day of strain, grief, and little appetite, Peyton skipped dinner and ate one of Mark's magic brownies instead. She sat in her bed admiring the liberal sky through massive windows, contemplating the colors she'd mix to achieve the same glow. Her thoughts bounced from brush to pen, and she grew convinced her father would've written more letters. But where were they, if not in his room or study? He mustn't have wanted them found. She questioned her right to read them, and if the hunt was a mistake, but resolved to roll the dice on both. And she still needed to find Blake Adler and refine the projected profit margin for a hunt she knew nothing about.

seven

Roosters crowing awakened Peyton. It was her ring tone for Scarborough. The sun had already breached her room, and tractors hummed at a distance. The ranch at work meant she'd slept past breakfast.

"Did I wake you, ma'am?"

She sat up in bed, surprised she'd slept as well as she had, until she remembered Mark's brownie. "I needed waking. Good morning, Scarborough."

"I found Adler, ma'am. Word is he's fishing at Abiquiú lake. I'm still up here in Chama. Waited for him, but I'm told he's been camping down there."

"Thank you for finding him."

"Problem is, he was supposed to leave today. Might've done already."

Peyton flung the sheets off and jumped out of bed. She put him on speaker and threw on jeans and a plaid shirt. "He's in my neck of the woods. I'll go the fast way. Maybe I'll catch him."

"No, ma'am, there's no urgency. Wait for me. We'll track him down, eventually."

"Of course, there's urgency. Royce's party is in less than three weeks. How will I recognize him? What does he look like?"

"Look like?" Scarborough paused too long, as if he was asked about the last time he had sex. "He's a fella, you know."

"Scarborough, is he tall, short, old, young? What?"

"Yes."

"He can't be all the above. Help me here. Am I looking for someone handsome, not handsome?"

"What do you mean, handsome?" Peyton could picture Scarborough's face and just how hunched his shoulders must be when he replied, "A man… A good guy, ma'am."

"I'll try to find him," she said. "Worth a shot."

Peyton dialed Koda while brushing her teeth. "Thank God you picked up. Saddle up Baroness and a horse for yourself. I'm on my way."

In the mudroom, she pulled up her Dubbary boots in practiced fashion, slipping them over her slim jeans. The lake had its share of visitors, so she wasn't sure she'd find Adler, but she felt better trying. She bolted to the stables, secured her hat, and spotted Cody, a Foxhound, white with brass and brown dapples. "Come, boy, follow me."

Koda was fast at his task, saddling Baroness for Peyton and Brandy for himself. Chipper like a quokka, he greeted her with high energy. "Where're we going, Peyton?"

"Down to Abiquiú Lake. We'll take the shortcut. Do you know a man named Adler, by any chance?" She tightened the strap of her hat under her chin, gave Baroness a loving pat, and climbed on.

"Nope." Koda mounted Brandy with envious finesse. "What kind of name is Adler?"

"We're about to find out. We're looking for an ex-military man who's fishing down there."

The Foxhound, Cody, followed as they headed down the canyon toward the lake. They rode with purpose, but not too fast. The horses and dog had to cross washes, hoof in between sagebrush, duck under junipers, and mind thorny chollas and pointy yucca. The air smelled of mesquite and hot sand, with the occasional whiff of Agastache or hummingbird mint, as the locals called it. Sometimes Cody trailed them and sometimes he ran ahead of them, all the while honoring his job as lifeguard.

"Might he be at the campground?"

Peyton rubbed Baroness's neck as she undulated this way and that. "I don't think his kind would hunker down among the campers to grill hot dogs and make s'mores. I think we should try the higher ground most hate to hike with the best views of Pedernal Peak." She chuckled. "Glad he's not *on* Pedernal Peak. It would be a trek and a half."

"Amazing mesa top, though. Broke my mountain bike up there."

"Oh, you don't have one anymore?"

"No, but don't tell Layli I told you that."

Peyton tugged on the reins, and the white mare slowed down. "Why can't you tell me?"

Koda's sweet demeanor misted away. He pressed his hat over his brow, but Peyton gathered his true feelings. "Layli says I mustn't complain, considering everything that's happening."

"You're a man now, Koda. A young one, granted, but a man. You can talk to me about anything."

"Can I leave Pioneer Ranch, then?"

Peyton was glad she was wearing her sunglasses, which hid some of her surprise. "Of course. This is home, not prison."

"But Layli will be alone. Don't know. It's challenging."

"Are you asking for my help?"

His broad smile returned, exposing his gums. "Maybe."

Peyton clamped Baroness with her legs, ready to ride fast. "Then you have it, but not until the hunting season is over if we take that route. It's foreign to me. I can use all the help I can get."

"I wouldn't dream of abandoning you now, but at some point..."

"As far as Layli goes, she's the strongest person I know, and for a while, she ventured far herself. She'll understand. I'll help you go wherever you choose. For now, let's dash."

Cody raced on ahead. They rode with momentum until they came across a few hikers and bathers laden with coolers and wet towels. They urged their horses higher, to the tops of flat rocks overlooking the lake below. When they passed the steep rise, Cody reappeared with a Weimaraner, dripping wet. The gray hunting dog barked, but quickly turned friendly when Cody rubbed against him.

"Who's your buddy?" Peyton asked Cody, who turned tail and ran closer to the edge with his friend. She took it as a sign and followed them until they reached a squat, dark-skinned man with a black band around his biceps, scraping the detritus of fish and rice.

With efficient, swift moves, he rinsed plates and mugs in a bucket of water and set them on a rock to dry. "Can I help you?" He wore a camo muscle shirt and upland pants, and his gun was where they could see it.

A number of fishing rods leaned against a tree trunk, together with spears and a kayak. Beside them, creels teamed with fish.

A hint of androgyny about him caught Peyton's attention. It made it difficult to look away. All ease and smiles, she deleted that thought. "Seems like our dogs are friends."

The man ran his fingers through his crewcut. He shifted from foot to foot, then turned sideways. "Not my dog."

"I'm Peyton Chase." She dismounted, pretending not to notice his discomfort, or that he didn't give his name in return. "This is Koda Hoarnhorse, the pride and joy of Pioneer Ranch, where we live."

The man gave no reply.

She removed her sunglasses and tucked them in her saddle. "We're looking for Adler. Do you know him?"

A flicker in the stranger's eyes confirmed she had found her target. It took effort to disguise her disappointment. She hadn't expected someone debonair, charming or friendly, but she expected someone more striking, and for whatever reason, she pictured Adler as taller.

"Why are you looking for him?"

She extended her hand, initiating a handshake, but he seemed reluctant to take it. "You wouldn't disappoint a lady, now would you?" The man shook her hand, squeezing hard enough to hurt. Peyton needed a better introduction. "Scarborough sent me."

"Don't know any Scarborough," he said, spreading his short legs and barricading his chest with muscled arms.

"But I do," rose a voice from behind her.

Peyton twisted around. At her back stood a dark-haired man with a beard, tall with strong features worthy of a gold coin. She flagged the way he scrutinized her, but pretended not to notice. "Oh good," she said, sighing with relief. "I'm Peyton Chase. I live at—"

"—I know who you are and where you live." His briskness irritated her, but she grew hopeful when he dried his hands on his camo shorts and extended a flat palm. "Blake Adler. Nice to meet you."

Peyton took his hand, hoping he wouldn't crush hers, and he didn't. "I'm delighted to have found you."

"Why, I owe you money or something?"

There was a curtness about him she found disadvantageous. "This is the highest jumping point at the lake. This time of year, forty feet at least. Is this what you've been doing up here?"

"The Corps of Army Engineers doesn't allow jumping."

"But people do it all the time." She smiled, puzzled at her inability to solicit much warmth from him.

The other man snickered. "Adler is afraid of heights."

The tall sailor raised a hand to silence his friend and locked his intelligent, distrustful eyes on her. "We're not that kind of people."

Peyton was careful not to huff or roll her eyes. "What kind of people is that?"

He pointed to his already half-packed gear. "We were about to leave."

Her lack of effect on him disconcerted her. She was used to having a sway over men. "I understand you're something special with hunting, fishing, scouting."

If he was flattered, he didn't show it.

"I'm organizing a substantial big game hunt. I need a proper scout and lead."

He raised his angular eyebrows and lifted his chin, accentuating the length of his neck and the strength of his jaw. "Why come to me?"

She tucked her hands in the back pockets of her jeans, formulating the best response, as his companion tossed water on the campfire. "I would appreciate it if you agreed to escort my group to where you know they can successfully hunt."

"I'm not a servant!" he shot, making her flinch.

"I beg your pardon. What language did I use to make you think I view you as a servant?" Goaded by instinct, she stepped on a rock, adding to her height.

"Your group will most likely be like you. No, thank you." He turned his back and threw items in his duffle bag.

His companion took several steps away, standing closer to the edge of the cliff with an apathetic air, though he'd trained his hearing on them.

Peyton hid none of her indignation. "What do you mean, like me? Have I offended you in some way?"

He didn't look at her. "Your kind doesn't offend. You're too refined for that."

"Say my kind one more time and I'll deck you one, buddy!"

His companion chuckled, but bit back his snickering when Adler slanted eyes at him. "See how entitled you are?" He turned to face her, taking big steps closer. Koda shuffled his horse, but it didn't faze him. "You're already treating me like I owe you something." With an even voice, he said, "I don't answer to you."

"Wow! What was her name?" Peyton held her ground and read the look in his eyes. "And I thought you were tough. Did one woman make you scared of all of us?"

He sneered. "Arrogant much?"

She needed another angle. "I'm not arrogant. Your reputation said you could be trusted, so I'm here. Asking."

They glared at each other, neither backing down, though he seemed a hair more malleable. The dogs were fighting over a frog, which broke the tension.

"Cody, Nuke, stop it! Sit!" he said.

The dogs froze and obeyed.

"I see you tell my dog what to do."

"I see you want to tell *me* what to do."

She took a deep breath and stared at him, surprised by his heated reaction.

"This conversation is not bringing the best out of me," he said. "You asked. We're done here."

Fed up, unable to remain quiet any longer, Koda said, "Quit being mean to Peyton! To Ms. Chase, I mean."

"Ah, you have him trained."

Koda dismounted, thumping to the ground. "She's a very nice person, unlike you."

Adler incised his jaws. "Sorry, I got worked up. I respect Scarborough… It's why you're still here. But this conversation is over."

The other man laughed like an audience watching a sitcom. "Who're you again? No one riles Adler like this."

Peyton softened, seizing the opportunity. "The compensation is great, and the guests are well-to-do. This is a great opportunity, worth your consideration."

Adler shook his head. "I'm not looking for opportunities, notably not with spoiled, gutless, rich people."

"Gutless? That's it!" Peyton whipped off her hat and spun it, but Koda caught it. She yanked at her boots, lanced Adler with hurt, livid eyes, and then ran to the edge, diving headfirst into the lake.

When she came out for air, the shorter man, hanging over the edge, brought his fingers to the corners of his mouth and fired off a whistle, then cackled and clapped.

Koda leaned over and formed a cone with his hands, shouting, "Are you okay?"

Peyton hollered back, making sure Adler heard her. "Of course, I am. Unlike some people, I'm not afraid of heights." She swam to the shore, shaking off the sting of cold water.

By the time she reached the bank, Koda and the sailor were already there.

She waded out of the water, her clothes weighing her down, and squeezed her long hair. Her shirt clung to her form and goosebumps assaulted her skin, but she was vindicated.

Koda balanced on a rock and gave her a hand, asking if she was cold. "I wish I had a hoodie for you, Peyton."

"No, don't get wet."

"Some bravado!" He helped steady her as she stepped on rocks. "That was a Layli thing to do!"

"That was a Harlow thing to do." Her mother coursed through her veins as she shivered in the breeze, invigorated.

"I like you quite a bit," said Adler's companion. "Who knew Wonder Woman lived in Abiquiú? I'm Joe, and you're right, no one knows these forests and rivers like Adler. I'd help you, but I'm from the Bronx. Know nothing about this area."

"Hello, Joe." Peyton wiped her face and wrung her hair again. "I need him," she appealed in an elegant voice.

Joe looked her up and down. "I think he needs you, too."

Adler was holding the horses' reins. He cocked his head and gestured for Joe to climb back up.

"Just find someone else," Joe said. "Don't worry about the horses. We'll tie them to a tree. You can come for them once we've left. We're pretty much packed."

"I don't understand. Have I hurt his feelings?" asked Peyton. "I didn't come here for that."

Joe slapped her on the arm, hard enough to sting. "He's a big boy, but you better learn not to go for the jugular so fast."

Peyton's eyes narrowed. "He insulted me."

"Nah…" Joe waved his hand. "He tested you, but you were loaded. Hell!" He started up the hill. "Women!"

"What do we do now?" Koda asked.

"We go back to the drawing board, I guess." She knew without a skilled scout, the hunt would be a bust, but she had no other answer for saving Pioneer Ranch. And failure wasn't an option.

eight

Peyton returned Baroness to the stables. Her clothes had dried enough, but she was covered in dirt and dross. She missed the outdoor shower she'd installed at her Mendocino house. "I'm a mess," she said.

"Yes, you are, and you have straw in your hair." Koda laughed. "I can hose you down."

"Don't you dare!" She faked slapping him, but he shuffled out of her reach. "You were brave down there, Koda," she said, unsaddling her filly. "Those guys are built and armed, but you showed no sign of retreat. You had my back, kiddo."

He gathered his hair and started braiding it with a gratified smile on his face. "Why was Adler mad at us?"

Peyton shook her head. "I mishandled the situation. Should've waited for Scarborough, like he told me to."

"You were fine. He's just weird."

"I don't think he's weird, but that massive chip on his shoulder could crush an elephant."

Koda covered his mouth with his hand. "He's so commanding. Oh my God, when he yelled at the dogs to sit, I almost sat down myself."

She liberated Baroness of her gear, and Koda did the same for Brandy.

"I'll take them to the fields to graze and rest, but I'll see you for dinner. What do you feel like?"

He grinned. "Meat anything."

"You got it. Plan on seven. I'll tell Layli. We'll eat together on the patio under the stars."

"Can I have a beer, then?"

"Not with your family history." She saw his face fall. "I have plenty of fun brownies left."

He faked smoking a joint. "Like the real fun kind?"

"Totally! They're mild. We won't tell Layli."

Dosed on nature and squabbles with military men, Peyton formulated a dinner menu as she headed back to the house. She settled on two savory dishes and a pie for dessert. She'd have to make a trip to Bode's General Store. A swanky black Maserati was parked outside. She figured who the driver must be and dialed in reverse, about to scamper away.

"Oh no, you don't," Ashton yelled, stepping onto the loggia.

She froze, her back to him. Not only did she not expect him, but she also looked like a cat dunked in a swamp.

"I drove an hour and I've been waiting another. Please, Peyton." He descended the double staircase wearing tailored black pants and a black and white Sebastian Cruz button-down shirt. "I almost had to extort your maid to let me in."

She turned to face him, defeated before she could start. "Who, Tansy?"

"Fuzz on the upper lip and ashen cracked feet, then that's the one. Why do you have riffraff working for you? Your servants represent you. Choose better."

"Servants? What's this, the Gilded Age?" She gave him a frustrated stare. "Ashton, what're you doing here?"

"I brought you these." He held out a wrapped, rectangular box, but Peyton didn't reach for it. "Aren't you the least bit curious?"

"Why didn't you call first?"

"I did, but you have me blocked."

Peyton had also burned most of his letters and deleted photographs and files from her computer and phone. She moved up the gravel path flanked by lavender and orange globemallow. "I don't mean to be rude, but—"

"—then don't be." He looked her up and down. "What happened to you? Did you fall in a beaver dam?" He saw her face and said, "Sorry, don't be peeved. I didn't come here to get under your skin. Or maybe I did." He placed the box in her hands. "Have dinner with me."

She could smell his Creed Aventus cologne. She'd awakened to that scent for over three years. "I made other plans. Can't."

"Break them," he said, inching closer.

"What do you want from me, Ashton?"

He stressed his words. "You just cut me off, Peyton. I want an explanation for what you did to me."

"What I did to you? You've got nerve!" She shoved the box back in his hands. "What you did to *me!*"

"Then explain it to me over dinner."

"It's been years. Please, not now."

He made to tuck her tousled hair behind her ear, but she wouldn't let him. "Things are different now. Hear me out."

"Your timing is off."

"Then come out with me tomorrow," he said with a face she'd always found adorable.

"You understand my meaning perfectly, but you're choosing to ignore it."

"Change your mind, come on."

She remained neutral in a way she knew he detested.

"You. Owe. Me."

"No, I don't."

She headed into the house, but he gripped her wrist and spun her to him. "Stop acting like a petulant child, and take this gift from me, for God's sake."

"Will you go if I do?" She closed her eyes, waiting for his answer, but he gave her something else.

With gentle lips, he kissed her, reminding her why she once felt she couldn't breathe without him. He'd made her feel she could do anything. She kissed him back, and there was longing in the kiss. It took all her willpower to pull away from him. Ashton was spellbinding, riveting, but he was also pain and suffering. She placed a hand on his chest and pushed away.

"Why?"

"Because of all the reasons I left in the first place. Now, will you please leave while we're still friends?"

"Yes, but you must promise to call me, and we're not done here. Not by a long shot."

"Yes, we are, Ashton."

"I think you're lying to yourself. I can see you're tempted, and there's no reason not to be." His patience was fused with determination. He forced her to take the box, ran a hand through his dark hair, installed himself in his car, and lowered his window. "The time to act, Peyton, is always now. Unblock me, for God's sake."

Every moment she spent with him melted her resistance like hot water on ice, and she needed to stay strong to avoid yet another emotional rollercoaster.

A long, hot shower was one of her favorite remedies. Motionless under the steaming waterfall, Peyton recalled seeing her mother dance fully clothed in the shower. Sorensen had coaxed her out of the shower, but she fought him. Who would do such a thing? Peyton's life was so uncertain now, she needed normalcy, a feeling of family about her. She pushed the memory away, dressed in a casual summer frock, and headed to the market.

The golden hour descended, dusting Abiquiú with a gilded veneer. Pioneer Ranch twinkled with torches and light posts. Layli set the table for four under the grapevine, and decorated it with candles and fresh flowers, while Peyton finished garnishing the serving platters and brought them out. She'd used the smoked duck she'd found in a bereavement basket to concoct a dish of amaranth and blueberry porridge served over crispy sweet potatoes and blueberry maple syrup. From Bode's, she'd bought boar tenderloin and braised it in juniper and sage until it was spoon-tender, then shredded it. She served it in its aromatic gravy over white corn porridge and wild dandelion leaves.

Scarborough brought a pack of Sunbru beer and his pipe to smoke with a glass of whiskey after dinner. Layli brought white chocolate and peanut butter cookies. Koda brought his appetite.

The large, stately patio was furnished with a full-size dining table and chairs, and a comfortable sofa, with additional seating around the firepit, and an upholstered swing.

As they sat under the fairy lights, Peyton raised a glass of peach wine. "To absent and present loved ones."

"*Da'ohdlá!*" Koda shouted with a raised glass of sparkling lemonade.

"*Da'ohdlá!*" they all cheered and chinked glasses.

"Say something, Scarborough," Koda said.

"To evenings we won't remember, with the people we can't forget."

"This is amazing, Peyton," said Layli, savoring the smoked duck. "I knew you cooked with some skill, but this is gourmet. Did you take lessons or something?"

"I make a few dishes well enough." Peyton thought of the two years after she left Ashton, when she dated no one and tried to fill herself with more than food. Had she succeeded? She'd filled herself with her artwork she'd treated like a secret society—or thought she had. "Between Julia Child and a Santa Clara Pueblo cookbook, I learned some tricks."

Koda filled his plate to the brim and shoveled forkful after forkful into his mouth.

"Seriously, Koda, I could swear I fed you before in your life," Layli said.

"This is like something Grandma would make only way better," he said through filled cheeks. "It's like the food of my childhood, but nothing like it."

Scarborough took a second helping of smoked duck. "This is weird fancy chew, but delicious."

Peyton had prepared three envelopes to distribute to her guests. "There's much work yet to come. You deserve something extra. Consider these signing bonuses. No need to open them now."

"Flower Child, you mustn't!"

"I'm making the biggest investment of my life. You're the embodiment of it. I'll be asking a lot from you, so accept this now."

Layli asked, "What if you don't go through with the hunt?"

"Then you'll have gotten something extra. If I am forced to sell, I won't be distributing much. But I have to do something. I'm not losing this ranch."

Koda flailed his envelope. "Enough to buy a new mountain bike?"

"There's more than that in your envelope, Koda."

Scarborough's smile was even wider than usual, and he tipped his hat. "I gladly accept this, ma'am. I have my eye on a steel roof. Would be nice to install it before the snow comes. There was no need. We're all in this together, but it's mighty appreciated."

Koda peeked inside his envelope. "It's the biggest check of my life."

"You're not twenty yet, kiddo. It should be," Peyton said. "For dessert, we have key lime pie, but I didn't find key limes. Had to substitute a mixture of limes and lemons."

"It'll do," said Scarborough. "Ma'am, when you said stay for some grub, I didn't expect something fancy like this. Here goes it. Say it with me now…" He raised his beer. "May your belly never grumble…"

They joined in, "May your heart never ache, may your horse never stumble, may your cinch never break!"

Nature had drawn her sable dress and stars twinkled above when Peyton stood to clear the table. Her phone rang. Father Gabriel's name appeared on the screen. She worried that he was calling so late.

"Sorry to call you, but I'm stuck."

"Glad to help. What can I do for you?"

"I'm embarrassed to say, but the old Pacer I drive just died on the main road, about a mile north of you. Oh dear, can I trouble you for a lift?"

"It's no trouble at all."

"I'm broken down on the side of the road, where there's hardly any shoulder. Look for a hunk of junk."

"You're nearly here. I'll come get you."

She could hear him wince. "Worse yet, I promised I'd substitute at tomorrow's Mass at the Sanctuary down in Chimayo."

"No worries, I've got you covered. Sit tight."

"Thousands will be there. Many pilgrims will have walked miles. Sweet Lord, I'm supposed to lead them in morning prayers, but I have no car to speak of."

"I'll make sure you can get there and back. Will call a tow truck. In the meantime, you should just join us here. I'd appreciate a blessing from you, and your timing is terrific. We're having drinks and dessert. You must stay."

He stuttered, "I have no toothbrush, no pajamas."

"I have all that, Father Gabriel, plus key lime pie."

"If God wills it."

"I suspect he does. I'll be there faster than you can say a Hail Mary."

"Tomorrow we'll pray for your mother at the Hall of the Lost."

Her heart drummed behind her eyes, spiking her blood pressure. "The lost, as in missing people?"

"Yes, a good-sized portrait of her is in the hall. Didn't your family put it there?"

She clutched the edge of the table. "My mother is dead, Father. Why would we put a picture of her in the Hall of the Lost?"

"Sorry, maybe I'm mistaken. I must be confused."

Her heart drummed faster as she hung up. "Layli, is there a picture of Mom at the sanctuary in Chimayo?"

She gave a puzzled face. "Chimayo? I don't think so."

"All right. Thank you. Tell you what, just leave everything. I'll deal with it after I pick up Father Gabriel."

Scarborough stood up with a grunt. "Since the father is distributing blessings, I'll fetch him. My truck could use it."

"No, I got it," Peyton said. "You're my guest tonight, and it's only a few miles."

"Right, so I'm doing it."

"In your yellow '44 Fargo truck?" asked Koda. "This I gotta see. I'm coming with you."

"I'll put on coffee," Layli said. "Decaf for you, Scarborough, I know, and a large whiskey. Now don't go riding a bull."

Scarborough sighed. "Getting old for nurses to be worth a bullhorn in the rump. Don't worry."

Peyton said, "I'll put a plate together for Father Gabriel, and a round of pie for all of us."

"Tomorrow is Sunday, ma'am. Who'll take the friar? Chimayo is a ways down."

"I'm taking him, of course. Haven't been to the sanctuary in forever." Peyton could've lent the friar a car, but she burned to learn more about the picture he'd mentioned.

nine

The sun peered over the mountains, slicing through the peach horizon like a golden razor. Peyton was sipping her morning coffee, preparing for an outing with the clergyman. On her bed, covered in blue and white linens, lay the book she'd taken from her father's study and the box Ashton gave her. She hoped it wasn't an expensive gift she'd be forced to return. She unwrapped it to find all twenty-five shades of Stila Stay All Day Lipstick. Ashton had made her laugh until he made her cry. She felt played in a way she enjoyed, which increased her resentment. The last time she'd succumbed to him had ended in agony. She'd have to try it if the description was accurate: not a smudge or a smear all day. He'd enclosed a note, handwritten on the same watermarked linen paper her father used.

Come slowly – Eden!
Lips unused to Thee –
Bashful – sip thy Jessamines –
As the fainting Bee –

Emily Dickinson's poem softened her. It was a reminder of a summer vacation they once took, driving from Manhattan to Québec City, stopping at historic places. They had a memorable and intense night at an inn in Amherst, Massachusetts, where they toured the poet Emily Dickinson's house. Ashton knew which buttons to push. And when.

Alas, she'd have to send a thank you note.

Her father had made his last exit, but his departure brought back Ashton. What if he was part of her destiny? Did she believe in a predetermined destiny, or did she make her own? She wanted her father alive, discussing these matters with her with probing eyes and endless questions. She recalled how he'd walk through the house in slacks and button-down shirts, often with a finger tucked in the pages of a book. It was as if he had accessorized his hands with them. The saddest part was the truth. Had he still been alive, her closed-off self wouldn't have brought up Ashton. She should've told him of such a man; should've introduced him to her type. It was all part of what made her feel stuck. Is this what that Puebloan boy meant? Little Mikey had said, "You're stuck because she is." Regret hailed down on her, and she sobbed. She took too much for granted. Never again. Her thoughts weren't done burglarizing her peace just yet. Lexi's lawsuit confiscated her present, but she'd have to compartmentalize better to survive the avalanche of trouble.

Adorned in pink from top to bottom, she looked for Father Gabriel, and found him on his third newspaper, full and merry. "I've got the keys. If you're ready, I am."

"Child, blessed be, you're like an angel." He came to his feet and grabbed the wooden crucifix around his neck.

Peyton beamed, thinking she looked especially good. "Okay, perhaps an angel with only one wing."

He grabbed his Bible and rosary beads, the only things he'd brought with him, and strolled beside her. "A single-winged angel? What's the use of that?"

"It carries half a person—their good half." Her dark side trailed her like a six o'clock shadow, but she was a painter, even if no one knew it. And she owned a box full of titanium white—if she had the nerve to use it.

Sorensen's car was immaculate. It shimmered a deep blue, a mirror of well-engineered steel. Peyton put the car in reverse and pulled out of the garage. "This is only the second time I'm driving Dad's car. He'd tell me to use it, but I always felt it was best to let him have it to himself. The irony is now that I have it to myself, I feel sharing it is better."

Father Gabriel raised his index finger. "Ah, I espy a philosopher."

She turned onto Route 84, a scenic road that culminated at the most popular Catholic pilgrimage in the United States. "Father, you're a man of God."

"Is it the frock?"

She tittered, but she was serious. "Sometimes I confuse the consequences of my decisions with destiny. Do you believe human decisions and actions follow God's plan? Humans have free will, yes?"

"Well, circumstances are part of God's universal network of fate."

"All right, but human actions are voluntary. Doesn't that mean we can pivot our destinies to meet our deeds?"

"It would be possible… if God wills it. What brought on this discussion?"

She wouldn't tell the priest that she had lived with a married man. "Let me ask you something else. Do you then believe God puts certain people in our path, though they might not be for our highest good?"

Father Gabriel squinted, running his rosary over his fingers. "Some people are meant to melt us down, and others are meant to re-forge us."

"But why?" she asked, enjoying the smooth road and lagoons of sky.

"Because to enter His kingdom, one's soul must withstand the journey. Only those who have been put to fire and ice prove their merit. If they come out of it worthy, they can enter the Pearly Gates."

Peyton wished she could be worthy but wasn't sure she was.

Father Gabriel said, "You're your father more than you know."

It was also what she thought. In temperament and personality, at least. "How so?"

"Harlow was like a ship's sails. She took one places with stunning power. But, Sorensen, rest his soul, was the ship without which there's no purpose to sails or sailing."

"Ah, I espy a poet."

The friar sputtered, his way of laughing.

She wished she had mined her mother's paintings earlier, but realized things happen in their own time. "Sometimes I feel stupid, Father. I ignored the clues, but they were there."

"I don't think stupidity is your problem."

"What is?"

"Too many leaves, too few blossoms."

Peyton took her foot off the gas pedal. "What do you mean?"

"You cloak yourself. You hide. And perhaps that's because you've blamed yourself for too much. You feared that if you were seen for who you are deep down, those around you would withdraw their admiration. But is that true? Are you as culpable as you feel?"

She hid her talent, and with it, much of her pain. "My sister thinks so. We didn't grow up together. We know each other a little, but she claims she has me figured out better than anyone else. To her, I'm evil."

"Then she's no authority over you. Her claims have no merit." He mumbled a prayer, as if asking forgiveness for what he was about to say. "You're of the desert. You know very well what I mean. The best survivors balance toil with equanimity, balance fight with flight."

Peyton took a deep, strung-out breath, and stepped on it.

"Just remember to stay in the light now you're under the desert sun, Peyton."

The ride to El Santuario de Chimayo felt like half the distance. She knew they were close when pilgrims carrying crosses appeared. As she drove by, Father Gabriel blessed them.

"Welcome to the Lourdes of America."

"What happens to all those crosses, Father? I've never seen them before."

"The invalid and wounded plant them upon arrival. The diocese removes them later, together with the crutches."

"Crutches?"

"Some leave healed, no longer in need of them."

Peyton wasn't sure she believed in miracles. She'd never experienced them herself and believed God wanted people to solve their own problems. "Because of the holy dirt?"

"But of course! It's holy dirt in the small pit that never empties." He raised his hands. "*Nuestro Señor de Esquipulas* is also miraculous, and he is present at this sanctuary."

Peyton found a parking space near the fence by the seven stone arches. "It's going to be busy."

"Yet you found a suitable space for your special car. Someone must have just vacated it. God is good."

"Can you show me that picture of Mom? I promise to entertain myself after that."

Her thoughts drifted like tumbleweed as they strode through the garden, past the Sculpture of Our Lady of Lavang and the Native Last Supper chapel to the Hall of the Lost, where thousands of pictures hung from floor to ceiling.

Some were of the dead, others of the sick or the lost. She saw faces in old photographs and new ones. Infants peered back at her. Centenarians, too.

"It's this one right here." Father Gabriel showed her what looked like Harlow at the time she'd passed.

Peyton tingled all over, her brain convulsing with questions. Could her father have done it? No, it wasn't his style. He was private and loathed public displays. Who would've hung it there, then? And why on the wall dedicated to the lost, not the dead? "Thank you, Father. I won't keep you any longer."

"I'll come get you fifteen minutes before Mass. Meet me at the Three Cultures Monument of the Spaniard, Cowboy, and Chief."

"I'll be there."

Peyton pulled her phone out of her purse and snapped a closeup of what she believed was her mother's photo. The image was old, blurry, but she was sure she was looking at her mother's face. Agitation nicked her as she texted the photo to Layli and Royce.

Royce called immediately. "Where did you find this?"

"Is it Mom? I found it at the sanctuary in Chimayo."

"It could be her, but I can't believe it."

Before long, Layli texted. She was unsure, but thought the resemblance was uncanny. Peyton steadied her breath. Was she seeing what she wanted to see, or did her family have more secrets than she knew?

She headed to the Three-Statue Monument, absorbed in her thoughts.

Near her, a dog whimpered. Peyton looked in its direction—Weimaraner, this time dry. The dog recognized her as surely as she recognized him.

"Hello, Nuke." She gave him her hand to sniff before petting his head. He yelped and softened his blue eyes. "Where did you come from?"

"Where did *you* come from?" asked Adler.

Seeing him, Peyton thought that maybe miracles really did happen. "Ah, good morning, sailor. I didn't think I'd see you this soon."

"Especially not at a holy pilgrimage sight." He chastised Nuke, who tucked his tail between his legs and sat panting and looking up at Peyton with lovely eyes.

"Nuke is beautiful."

Adler gazed at her as if she'd described herself. "He doesn't disobey me, but he did when he smelled you. That's my story, anyway."

"Here you are, Peyton," Father Gabriel said. "Oh, happy me! If it isn't, Adler. How wonderful to see you here."

Peyton and Adler spoke at the same time, "You know Father Gabriel?"

The friar looked from one to the other. "My children, you're loaves and fishes. Adler brings us fish and meat, and you, Peyton, bring us bread and other delights."

She re-evaluated Adler anew and saw that he was doing the same to her.

"Why are you here, my son?"

"Atonement, Father. If anyone knows my sins, you do." He looked at Peyton with eyes like scales. "And Peyton? Why is she here?"

"The same," she blurted, surprised at how easy it was to speak such a profound truth.

The friar shook his head, smirking. "Out there, God is in our hearts, but here, everyone is in the heart of God." He tapped his watch and grinned as if he'd interrupted something, then walked up the ramp in long strides, leaving them alone.

Adler said, "I'm sorry about yesterday. I behaved like a jerk."

"I'm sorry, too. Didn't mean to ambush you."

"Are you here for Mass?"

"Father Gabriel's car died. I offered to drive him."

"That car is a hundred years old. Nobody drives Pacers anymore." He laughed in a way that lit up his face. "I should take Nuke back to the truck, but I'll see you inside the church."

Peyton leaned forward, capturing the moment. "Sorry, this might be pushy, but have you considered my offer?"

He moved closer. "You can die from shame for failing, or you can be proud of trying."

"Like you did yesterday at the lake, chasing me away?"

He petted his dog. "Hard to believe, but not what I wish I'd done."

With a clean shave, he'd look much younger.

"I tried calling to apologize, but my calls went straight to your voice-mail and it was always full." He lifted his chin, elongating his neck as the sun illuminated him. "I haven't considered your offer again, but I will... and you have nothing to apologize for. Quite the opposite." He cocked his head toward the statue. "It's my favorite."

She ran her fingers through her long, wavy hair, relishing his company. "Three different people, sharing the same purpose. I love it because it's about coexistence, tolerance, and equality."

His eyes said there was more to her than he'd thought. "Are you going to the rodeo this year, by any chance?"

Her hopes leapt. "Yes, on Saturday, midday. We're all going."

"Perhaps I'll run into you there."

The bells tolled, forcing Peyton to start for the stucco chapel in the style of Medieval Spain. "Fair enough. See you up there."

Peyton ferreted her way into the packed chapel and signaled to Father Gabriel, who beckoned her to the front, but she chose to stand in the back. She could feel Adler's eyes on her. He was a hunter. If she hadn't known it before, she knew it now.

ten

Huddled over her laptop on her father's substantial desk, Peyton read Mark's reply to her inquiry about Lexi's lawsuit. He wrote that he'd like to go over her deposition with her and that it was impossible to predict the outcome until he read the deposition her sister would give.

She was preparing the pitch she'd make at Royce's party. She loathed the idea of a hunt. It had no scout. And Layli's preliminary projections showed a moderate, unsustainable profit. But she had no other solution.

Her phone rang, rescuing her from her anxious thoughts. She glanced at her father's mahogany banjo clock and saw that it read the wrong time.

"Geraint, am I happy to hear from you!" She pressed her ear on the clock's guts. It wasn't ticking.

"Marvelous. Have you had enough time off?" A Welsh accent flavored his words.

"It doesn't feel like I've been off, but if you're asking me if I can return to work, the answer is yes. I want all the income I can get. What do you have for me?"

"Thank heavens. Can you fly to L.A. right away?"

"How big is the damage this time?"

"An early Renaissance painting, nine by twelve, water damage, looks like urine… yuck. And something else is causing it to flake in places. Several days of work, and I'm pressed for time."

"Ah, you sold it sight unseen, but the buyers will come knocking soon?"

He chuckled. "You always could guess my motives. Clever lass!"

"Is it one of those pieces destined to hide in some airport vault?"

"Tax evasion is all we're about. Now, stop being so smart."

"It's a terrible practice, hoarding art in vaults instead of allowing it to be enjoyed."

Geraint rapidly clicked a pen he held too close to the phone. "I need a conservationist, not a curator, deary."

"I'd love to help you, but my kit is at home in Mendocino. Can you wait till I go get it?"

"I'll fetch it. Jane can let me in. Don't say no."

"You'll have to fly."

"I must," he replied. "This deal is hot, so the painting has to be restored ASAP."

"Wow! You must be offloading it to a billionaire."

"But of course. It's a Jan Van Eyck."

"Book my ticket and I'll be there."

"I already did." His adorable smugness seeped through the phone. "Tomorrow, Albuquerque to L.A., at six forty-five."

"Will be there. I'll also need a car."

"Already reserved one. I'll email details as soon as we get off the phone, and I hope you've been sad enough, because there will be no blubbering here."

"Of course not. No one blubbers in L.A. It ruins the Botox."

"Glad you understand." He made kissy noises into the phone. "Happy you're coming. I wouldn't trust a work this delicate to anyone else."

She hung up and focused on the clock. She found the winding clock key, corrected the dials, and inserted it in the clock's face, then wound the dial until she felt a gentle resistance. But the clock didn't start. Even the clock was sad at her father's passing. Her thoughts floated to her family in California, so she called her niece, Margot.

"Auntie Peyton! I'm so glad you called. Can I visit you in New Mexico for a while?"

"Well, I called to tell you I'm coming to you. Let's go out for a lovely dinner tomorrow night. I'm in town for work, but we can still spend time together. Would you like that?"

"Tomorrow is good. Where?"

"Sugarfish like last time? I can't confirm the time until much later in the day."

Margot sounded nasal, as if she'd been crying. "I'm down with that. I'll expect to hear from you on the late side, then."

Los Angeles wasn't Abiquiú. No serpentine roads, oryx, or hypnotic land-scapes. Just congestion, concrete, and people looking at themselves on re-flective surfaces.

Slim, tall, and white-haired, Geraint greeted her outside his gallery as she prepared to park, removing the orange cones he'd used to secure a spot for her. She'd live at his gallery for the next few days, and he'd do anything he could to speed the tedious, protracted process.

He gave her a California hug—shoulder taps with hips kept far apart. "You're stunning, and here's silly me thinking you'd look sad and shriveled up."

"I'm sad and more, but I'm also a professional." She followed him into the gallery and scanned the works he'd accumulated since her last visit.

"I gained two pounds. Tell me you don't see them on me."

"I don't see two pounds on you, more like four?"

"Mean lass."

Each wall of the sprawling gallery was painted a different color. Geraint loved contrasts, a smorgasbord of styles and moods. They walked through the main rooms, down a corridor with lesser works to the multi-purpose backroom, half of which Geraint used to store inventory. A glass divider separated the space from his office.

"Before you ask, your house is fine, your garden is fine, Jane is fine, everything is fine, especially the painting above your fireplace." He clamped a hand over his mouth. "It's to die for. If you want to do something with it—"

"—never ask me that again. Got coffee, like a bucket of it?"

"Fine. Starbucks is to the left and right of us, but, seriously Peyton, if you have finished works and you're saving them for a nest egg, someday you may want it to hatch."

"Oh my God!"

"Okay… Well, maybe I can borrow *The Last Start* for a bit, just as a draw to my gallery?"

"Don't make me threaten you with broken bones! *The Last Start* will never see a catalog or the internet. It's held and loved in private, and always will be."

"Oh my, some work! Scrupulous. Detailed, and one of the largest I've seen of your mother's. Harmony of colors, stirring, yet peaceful, almost a contradiction… like Harlow was, I suppose. I knew her way back then. From mild to wild in a flash. That was Harlow."

Peyton was relieved his take on her mother confirmed her memories. "Tell me you didn't photograph it, because I swear if you took pictures, I'll kill you, Geraint."

He brought his hands to his cheeks. "Would I ever?"

"Give me your phone this instant." She held out her palm, glowering at him.

"Okay, you can't have my phone, but you can watch me erase them." He shook his head in disappointment. "That isn't your only treasure, now is it?"

Peyton's heart sank at what he might say next. "You didn't go into my studio, did you?"

"Of course I did." He reached out and pressed the tip of her nose. "Whose paintings are piled so neatly against the long walls?"

Peyton stood frozen like a possum, pretending to be dead.

"You're a closet painter, you naughty, naughty girl. You've been painting up a storm, and you never told me! How could you?"

Peyton amazed herself by bursting into violent tears.

"What did I say? Why are you crying?"

She sat on the nearest stool, shaking. "No one was ever supposed to know."

"Know what?"

Peyton said what she feared most. "That I'm no Harlow. That my work isn't good enough." Geraint fetched the box of tissues from his desk. When she finished mopping her face, he touched her forearm. "Ask me how I knew the paintings were yours. Please, ask me."

She took a deep breath.

"They're vulnerable and tender. Some are cagey with a serious play of light and darkness. Overall, they lure and invoke hope. The way you use ancient techniques with modern colors and make the focal points, expressions, and postures of your subjects gave me butterflies."

She straightened her back. "But they're not like Mom's."

He pulled up another stool and leaned forward. "Ready for the brutal truth? When you tried to copy Harlow's painstaking detailed work, sharpened into a mirror, it came across as—"

"—cold."

"No, not cold. Rigid, perhaps, because you weren't being authentic. But the paintings of cowboys on cattle drives crossing rivers and rescuing lost calves, or people around campfires in reverent conversations, have a superior and enlivening feeling. My favorites include the portraits of your father engrossed in reading by the kiva fireplace—must be your house in New Mexico. And those portraits of a gorgeous man who shall not be named."

Peyton thought of the three portraits of Ashton she'd painted from photographs and memory. She'd never told him they existed. "Mom was a hyperrealist painter. I'm not."

"Yes, but you don't need to paint like that. Some people don't even like it. You use *sfumato*, like Vermeer, Raphael, and Leonardo, but updated, with a modern geometry. It's a difficult technique. Laymen don't understand that, but we do, and we educate rich clients who don't get it." He used a finger to smooth his flawlessly microbladed eyebrows. "I can't believe you never asked for my astute opinion. I'm hurt. The way you do fire, twilight, and the powerful trust between man and nature is stupendous. In those paintings, you tell *your* story, not Harlow's, and that makes all the difference."

"You're serious?"

"Your lack of confidence has betrayed you. I'm a professional, and that's my seasoned opinion." He crossed his arms over his narrow chest and tapped his pointy leather shoe.

Peyton tittered, but she was sad. Her mother's voice telling her to quit trying echoed in her head. "Mom thought I didn't have it."

"Lassy, your mother was a gifted cherry bomb, but when she wasn't creating masterpieces, she said too much. She also called tall people short and attractive people ugly."

"I never thought Mom machine-gunned unfounded observations."

"She once called me fat. I have a twenty-eight-inch waist! She did it to horrify me." He turned his hands into upturned claws. "Why don't children ever know their parents? She loved stinging people as much as she loved doting on them. So, stop lugging around an empty jar and listen to me. I wouldn't want to exhibit all your paintings, but at least thirty or forty."

Peyton slipped off her stool. "What?"

"Why do you think I'm bringing it up? I'll want to hold some originals and print *giclées* to sell, so they'll produce more money in the long run. You must sign them all. I can't believe you hadn't."

"And risk the world saying the apple fell far from the tree? Critics are ruthless!"

"Fuck the critics! I resent that characterization of yourself, and you should resent it, too."

She knew he was right. Her head understood it, but her heart was far from believing him.

"You didn't fall far from the tree." Geraint stretched tall and made circles with his hands like a magician conjuring a rabbit. "You're no apple, deary. You are your own tree."

She began sobbing again. "I can't."

He went to the mini-fridge, took out two bottles of water, and handed her one. "You can't what, Peyton?"

She thought of the painting she'd stolen as a child. "I'll end up with egg on my face, and everyone will see it."

He rocked back on his heels with his hands in his pockets. "Okay. You're in mourning, fragile from grief, hence you've lost your mind. I forgive you… for now. You need time to reflect on this, but I'm earnest. I want to exhibit your work, and I know some seriously deep pockets."

Peyton wanted to say it was no guarantee they'd appreciate her work, but she'd exposed herself too much already. "Geraint, please, don't mention this conversation to anyone."

"That's your problem, right there." He placed his hand on her shoulder. "Truth hurts, but secrets damage."

She knew he was right.

"Hey, I wish I hadn't said no blubbering when I called. I might have cursed you."

She laughed through fat tears. "I'll go wash up. When I come out, I'll be fit for work."

"Let's get you that coffee." He called his assistant and asked her to go over to Starbuck's.

"No, I'll go, it's okay."

He blocked her way. "Not letting you out of my sight for a second, deary. Must start the restoration right away. Everything I brought from your house is by the easel. Do you want mocha? Cappuccino?"

"A gigantic doppio dark roast, lots of cream and sugar." Peyton organized her brushes, sponges, knives, needles, and bottles of chemicals, then slipped on her smock and rubber gloves.

She had asked for divine intervention, but she already had it. It was about time she stopped asking and started acting. "Let's see what we've got." She lifted the protective linen cover, peered through her magnifying loop, and shone a beam on a canvas painted more than five and a half centuries ago. Before beginning a new conservation project, she always recited these words written by Leonardo da Vinci: "While I thought that I was learning how to live, I have been learning how to die."

"Amen," said Geraint. "It never gets old."

Peyton was already at Sugarfish, sipping a cosmopolitan when Margot arrived. At nineteen, she looked twenty-one, and wore the shadow of someone who used to be athletic. Her straight red hair swaddled her slender arms like a wrap.

Peyton gave her niece a proper New Mexico hug, embracing her with warmth and tenderness. "It's official. You're as tall as I am."

Margot swirled three-hundred-and-sixty degrees like a dancer, showcasing her body. "I'm straight fire like you now, Auntie."

"You're prettier, honey." Peyton shook her finger at Margot's outfit. "Twirl some more. Not everyone has seen your butt cheeks yet."

Margot inspected her bottom, attracting even more attention. "Why? What's wrong with my shorts?"

"Oh nothing, except you're not wearing any."

She stuck her tongue out and sat across from her aunt. "Everyone wears these now. They're so Gucci."

"Not everyone. They're like underwear. I'll only say it once and then

I'll shut up. You don't need to walk around half naked for people to notice how sexy you are."

"Hot is the word. Sexy is what old people say."

"I'm not old."

"Nope, you're dope." Margot tucked her hair behind her ears. "If you got it, flaunt it."

"If you flaunt it, you don't got it. But I understand." Peyton didn't like the recent changes in her niece and thought she might have more to say.

Margot reached across the table, took Peyton's cocktail, and stole a sip. "I prefer espresso martinis." She lifted off her seat and leaned in for closer inspection of her aunt's face. "That's lit! How do you do that with your eyes?"

"It's just makeup, and I can hold a brush, you know. I can show you, if you'd like."

"You should make videos and post them on YouTube." Margot downed the rest of the cocktail and flopped down again.

Peyton had begun the evening with a lecture. She didn't want to perpetuate it by criticizing her niece's drinking. "Are you feeling better today? You were distraught last night."

Margot looked down and played with her phone. "Don't know. Mom throws shade on everything I do." The server came and took their order, a sushi and sashimi platter for two. "My aunt will have another cosmo, please," she told the server.

Peyton wondered who the drink was really for. "What're you up to? Ready for the fall semester?"

"No, not feeling it. Sort of salty on it."

Peyton thrust her neck. "Since when is college optional?"

"I'm seeing someone. We're planning an expedition with our squad, you know."

"An expedition? Who're you, Lewis and Clark? Where to?"

She laughed lethargically. "Tasmania, Lord Howe Island, New Zealand. We're going to blog and stuff." When the food arrived, Margot ate with little appetite.

Peyton popped salmon sashimi, swimming in soy sauce and wasabi. "You have money for such a trip?"

"Doing it with my fam. Like I said, we're going to blog and Instagram. People make lots of money from that."

Peyton hid the extent of her skepticism. "Such people seek sponsors and put a lot of work into it. What looks like fun is a contrived exaggerated advertisement. Don't believe all these social media platforms. They're a ruse."

Margot swallowed two pieces of sashimi, then vaped an e-cigarette.

"Is that legal in a restaurant, Margot?"

"I don't care." She stretched her hand, showing off her red and white polka dotted nails. "Should I get an infinity tattoo on my finger?"

"Rings are better." Peyton chose a plump tuna, eel, and avocado hand roll and held it at her niece's face. "Eat more, honey, and tell me about your boyfriend."

Margot accepted the hand roll, then stood up. She was more legs than torso.

"He's okay. I'll send you a link to our Instagram."

"Are you leaving?"

"Sorta gotta. Is that okay?"

Peyton hid her concern behind a benevolent smile and stood for a goodbye hug. "You call me if you need me, all right? Because, honey, I'm your real fam."

"Cool." She leaned into her aunt's embrace, lingering a while. "Do you have to go back to Abiquiú right away?"

"I have obligations there, but it's also the place I need to be. You can come visit. I'll send you a ticket soon. And I can see you again tomorrow."

"Good." Margot looked on the verge of tears. "I don't know where I'm supposed to be. Tasmania, I guess."

"Talk more tomorrow," Peyton said, and watched her niece listlessly walk away.

Lexi called while Peyton was driving to the hotel. She'd had a long and emotional day, so she didn't pick up at first, but Lexi bomb-dialed until she did.

"What?"

"If you think I'm going to let you take my daughter away from me, you've got something else coming!"

"Is that it?"

"How dare you fill her head with ideas about going to Tasmania and wherever else?"

"That has nothing to do with me."

"You're so fucking controlling. Just because you're barren doesn't mean you can have my child. Go to hell!"

"Barren?" Peyton sneered. "Not all of us are morons who have kids at twenty-one, and you should be glad Margot has an aunt who loves and values her. It takes a village, Lexi." She wanted to add that Margot felt her mother neglected her, but she wouldn't betray her niece's confidence.

"You know, Mom once said you were one big speed bump in her way. I think she described you precisely. Stay the fuck away from *my* daughter."

Peyton remembered the night her mother yelled at her so venomously, her father ruptured into the room and carried her out without saying a word to his wife, who cursed him for intervening. He told her not to be afraid, that he'd always make sure she was safe. Soon after, he signed her up for singing lessons.

eleven

Being back in New Mexico after spurious Los Angeles was a relief. Peyton was happy to slide through the desert on roads that hug the mountains, cuddle the mesas, and race beside white rivers. The two-hour drive from Albuquerque felt like a quick spin. She melted in thought, admiring turquoise skies rich with lustrous clouds. She couldn't stop thinking of what Geraint said. What if the critics called her a failure, a pseudo-Harlow? She didn't think she could bear it. She'd called Royce from L.A. to arrange for a visit sooner rather than later.

Royce's mansion, rising from the land like a wedding cake, appeared in the distance miles before Peyton reached it. She parked in a driveway the size of a football field and admired the quarry stone and galvanized steel façade. The interior was decorated with colorful Talavera ceramics, spectacular crystal chandeliers, and pink quarry stone.

Dressed as if she were going to a ball, Royce met her in the magnificent foyer with a frescoed ceiling and hardwood floors. "Do you have it?"

"Don't I always? Only one this time, though." Peyton held out the gold box containing a Sophia cake from Artelice Pâtisserie.

"Lordy, how I love this stuff. If only they shipped." Royce took the box and kissed Peyton. "Come, we're in the tearoom."

"Royce, why are you in Cinderella's dress?"

"Oh, do you like it?" She pivoted this way and that. The dress was meant for a smaller waist, but it was chic. "I'm trying on dresses for my birthday party but can't decide. I look like an ice cream sundae in this dress, don't I? Too poufy?"

"I'd choose something more streamlined."

"What're you wearing?"

"Something I wore only once, and haven't since, but it's red-carpet worthy."

The tearoom was the most impressive space in the house. A skylight and Moroccan stained-glass windows elevated the room to the level of art. "I hope you didn't buy me a present. Don't want any. Too old for them now."

Peyton imitated Royce's hand gestures and the way she liked to stretch her already long neck. "Pish-posh, a lady is never too old for pampering."

Royce gave a belly laugh and plunked down on a chair, her dress billowing about her. With utmost care, she removed the mousse cake from its box and placed it on a table set with Victorian teacups and little pink plates. Then cut two slices of cake and handed one to Peyton.

"Now tell me why you sounded strange on the phone."

"I sounded strange?"

"Like you had a monkey on your shoulder."

Peyton took a bite. "I have to admit, this cake is worth carrying on the plane. If I hadn't had my kit with me, I would've bought more. I will next time." She wiped her lips and gestured for the teapot. "May I pour?"

"I'll pour... you talk."

"Why did Mom marry such an independent intellectual?"

"Did you ever ask your father for his take?"

"Tried, but he discouraged questions about Mom. He never told me he had a vasectomy. My parents were married for fourteen years before Mom died. At first I thought he did it because Mom didn't want more kids, but it turns out, it was Dad who didn't."

Royce drew the corners of her mouth down. "Not so strange. I only have my Edward." She finished her mousse cake layered with crème brûlée and cut another. "When he was born, we thought for sure we'd have another child, but I didn't get pregnant again, and at a certain point, he was too old for siblings, and I was having an affair."

Peyton put down her cup. "You had an affair?"

"God, no… I had *many*. Did you seriously believe I wouldn't?"

"I'm taken aback, but not in a judgmental way. Didn't expect you to say that."

"Affairs mean you'd better use pills and condoms. After all, we want romance, not illegitimate children, and nothing kills romance like a baby." Royce finished her second piece of cake. Peyton was silent, deep in thought, her eyes on the stained-glass windows. "What're you thinking?"

"Did Mom have affairs, too?"

"Only when she was flying high. Not that often. I sought it. Harlow didn't. For her, it just happened."

Peyton sat still, wide-eyed.

"What's the matter with you, Peyton? You look like an electrocuted mouse."

"Would you say she burned energy like a missile?"

Royce chortled. "On almost no sleep. How I envied her get-up-and-go attitude."

"She was an insomniac, too?"

"Sometimes." Royce cocked her head. "Harlow had her flat days, her boring days, her hardworking days, her sedate days. She also had her highs, like the rest of us. She was an artist. It came with the territory."

"But is it like the rest of us, Royce?" Peyton went to the French doors and stood there hugging herself, looking out at Abiquiú Lake and the curl of mountains on the horizon. "Let's consider the evidence. She spent money like a gambler, sometimes crashed, totally zapped, at other times fired on all cylinders. Did outrageous things like hijack you to Colorado, and though at times she punished me for the smallest thing, at others she'd play with me and think everything I said was funny. She burned her candle at both ends and was apparently prone to insomnia."

Royce's wide skirt dragged across the Moroccan tile floor as she joined Peyton. "Harlow was special, unforgettable in every way."

"Mom was bipolar!" Peyton's eyes were saturated with tears and her nose burned. "It must've been harrowing for Dad."

"Maybe, but you don't know she was bipolar."

"Oh, I know. I see the writing on the wall, ceiling, floor. She may have suffered from other disorders, like depression and anxiety. Dad protected me by sending me off to music and dance lessons, art classes, to distract me and keep me safe. I've been so blind. I gave him too little credit and blamed him for over-scheduling me." She moved to get a better view of the lake. Children in school uniforms were tossing rocks into the water.

Royce said, "Most of the time, she was fine."

"You didn't live with her. I think Dad had a vasectomy because she scared him. He didn't think he should have more children with someone so unstable."

"You're jumping to conclusions. Come back to the table and finish your cake."

Peyton had no appetite. "She could be jubilant. Do you remember when she brought a snowman into the house? I used to think she was a *bonne vivante,* like Dad. Now I know those were her manic days. And there's more. Lexi called me needy and said Mom viewed me as an obstacle. Were those Mom's words?"

"What do you mean?"

"Harlow punished neediness. She chose Dad because he was extremely self-sufficient. She loved me best when I wanted her to be my friend, when we played or had fun, but she hated me when I wanted her to be my mother."

Royce's eyes were filled with compassion. "I'm sorry, honey. I know she was hard on you, but what you're describing is much worse than I understood.

Sorensen was difficult in his own way. He could've left Harlow, but she tolerated his brooding and silence. He never let her into his private being, which was partly what drove her to partying. Well, that and mushrooms."

Peyton laughed, then cried into her napkin. "Mushrooms? You guys had so much more fun than I do."

"Honey, we didn't turn to other lovers simply for sex. Sometimes, we just needed someone vulnerable who'd allow us to be vulnerable with them. Remember that when you choose a life partner. Sorensen was an intellectual, generous, supportive and kind, yes, but he was also a vault, emotionally unreachable. I think you know that."

Sorensen, the intellectual, had laid himself bare for Peyton, but Sorensen, the emotional man, was as inaccessible as a snow leopard. "It's taken me forever to understand Dad's attraction to all those floosies. I'm downright embarrassed."

Royce nodded, as though she'd figured it out a long time ago. "Those girls are easy to please, predictable as birds on a wire."

"That's what they were. Chicks. Easy plucking. I hate that word for women, but it fits them. He gravitated to the bottom of the barrel. It was safer and simpler that way."

"Harlow was a blast, but she was exhausting."

"Did Dad have affairs as well?"

"I don't know." Royce poured more tea for the two of them. "He seemed glad she was off with her friends, away from his sanctuary of books. Maybe he thought he'd never keep her here without letting her be away when she needed it. Know what I mean?"

"I guess. Live and let live. That was Dad." She took a deep breath, and stretched, suffocating a yawn.

Royce put an arm on Peyton's shoulder. "Honey, why are you so angry at realizing she was bipolar?"

"Because now I have to forgive her, don't I?"

"And why is it so terrible to forgive her?"

"Where would I be without my anger?" Tears tracked down Peyton's cheeks. "I blamed her for so long. I forgot it was my job to put my adult feelings on my own adult shoulders."

Royce sliced a straight hand at her, hiding none of her pride. "That's a Sorensen thing to say! You're also your father's daughter."

Was Peyton's identity too wrapped up in her parents'?

Peyton Chase needs to chase Peyton, she thought. And no one else.

She hadn't told Royce about Geraint's offer to exhibit her paintings. If Royce tried to persuade her, she wouldn't be able to deal with it, and if Royce was skeptical, she didn't think she could deal with that, either. "Is it possible Mom was the reason Dad spent so much money?"

"Lordy, I wish I had all the answers for you, but I don't. Some secrets died with your father. Accept that, Peyton."

She laced her fingers on the top of her head. "Come to the rodeo on Saturday."

"I can't go anywhere. I still have a ton to plan for my party. Besides, horses hate me. Did you see the mess those workers made of the dancefloor they're building outside? I should gut that contractor with a spoon."

Peyton bent over and touched her toes. "I haven't slept much lately, and my back is killing me from sitting in the same position for hours. A day out in the air with bucking riders will loosen me up."

"You need a bucking rider, alright. Called Ashton yet?"

"You know better," Payton said, shaking her finger. "I should shove off."

Royce walked her to her car, checking her appearance in every mirror they passed. "Don't think harshly of your mother."

"I don't. It's not like I didn't love her. I just stuffed so much way down, it got compressed and hard to separate into layers. Can't say I'm not terrified and confused, but my hall pass has expired. I've gotta go back to the lessons I missed." She touched Royce's arm. "I have more compassion for both of them, but I haven't healed."

"And compassion for yourself, I hope."

"I'm trying."

"Do you feel defeated?"

"I feel awake and overwhelmed by what I see." She kissed Royce's cheek. "But sometimes, ignorance is bliss."

"Oh no, it never is. As you unfortunately found out, you can't stay ignorant for long."

"Because ignorance only postpones the pain?"

Royce cast her fingers into the air. The fairy godmother in Cinderella's dress. "It postpones the healing, darling, and that's a shame."

Peyton checked on the stew she'd started earlier. The aroma of garlic, roasted poblanos, and cumin infused the kitchen. She'd made a pot of coffee and was waiting to share a cup with Layli.

"Smells delish," Layli said as she came into the kitchen and looked Peyton up and down. "Dressed for the harvest, I see."

"Today is all about the garden, but tomorrow is the rodeo. Yeehaw!"

"What's your plan?"

"First, I have to fix the raised beds, weed, and pull bushes. I want them ready for the fall vegetables. My design also includes herbs, tall grasses, flowers, and climbers."

"Is it like your garden in Mendocino?"

"More flowers than anything up there, and a much smaller courtyard. I have stunning echiums and massive succulents. You should visit and see it for yourself."

Layli added cinnamon to her cup. "This garden is enough work for a brigade. Are you sure you don't want help?"

"I enjoy playing in the dirt. I'll have it looking splendid by fall." Peyton poured herself a mug from the French press. "Uncle Mark called with the court date. I never thought I'd be labeled a defendant, and the plaintiff would be my only sibling."

"How's it looking?"

"On a fast track. Uncle Mark says the judge likes a quick turnaround."

"What'll you do if you end up owing Lexi a million dollars? I can't wrap my brain around owing someone that much."

Peyton grimaced. "Selling my house might not be enough. I might have to dip into my nest egg. And none of it is earmarked for the ranch. Let's talk about something more cheerful. I have to find Adler at the rodeo. He has to give me an answer. Otherwise, we'll have to line up somebody else." She topped off her mug to take to the garden and set the timer on the stove, then slipped on her yellow gardening boots and went outside, relishing the smell of moist earth.

Scarborough had piled a heap of red cedar planks beside the kitchen garden fence. He was squatting over a toolbox with a hammer in his hand.

"Are you doing my job for me?" Peyton asked.

He played with his slate beard. "You won't fix those raised beds by yourself. That's heavy soil pushing out on the corners. They give too much, we'll have to rebuild them."

Peyton went to the garden shed hidden behind lilac bushes and returned with a shovel. "I'll trowel out dirt, while you nail the frames together. Deal?"

"Is that your grandpa's shovel there, ma'am?"

"I believe so. Over a hundred years old."

"They don't mak'em like that anymore."

"Shovels or grandpas?"

"Both, I reckon."

Peyton pressed the shovel into the soil with her foot and heaved out mounds of earth. It made a satisfying sound. "This soil is poor," she said. "I'll have to amend it. Can I use some of the compost by the carriage house?"

"I'll bring you some. Add kitchen scraps and worm castings to it, and you'll make black gold."

For a while, they worked in silence, each dedicated to their task. The magnitude of the project inspired Peyton to fight harder for the ranch. "Do you remember old Ambrosia?"

"The old cook? I could've sworn she tried to scalp me once."

Peyton froze with her foot on the shovel. "I'm sure she didn't."

"Oh yes, she did. Said she confused my head with a hog's." He returned to his hammering. "When I was in my prime, her grandson came to get her. Said they lived in Monument Valley."

Ambrosia had been there the day her mother died, but Sorensen had dispatched her soon after. Her instinct told her the old cook knew more than she should've about what happened that day, and she resolved to find her.

Scarborough wiped his brow with his wrist. "Everyone up there gets mail at a P.O. Box on Red Rock Road. My guess is she lives on the res there, which doesn't come with house numbers." He chuckled and pushed his hat back, letting the sun illuminate his blue eyes. "You could stalk her mailbox until someone comes to get the mail."

"Or I could ask Mr. Jennings." Peyton gulped coffee from the mug she'd put on top of the fence. "Have you seen Adler at all?"

"Adler is like a mountain lion. If he doesn't want you to see him, you don't. He's selective, though he carts around his strange buddy."

"Do you mean Joe?"

"Yeah… Something ain't right with him. Seen him with no shirt on. He had strange scars on his chest."

"Like what?"

Scarborough pointed to his pectoral muscles. "One under each ribcage like."

Peyton recalled her first impression of Joe. Now she got it. He was trans. It dawned on her that Adler was a complex man with conservative values, but open-minded about individual freedoms, and that made her like him more. "Joe seemed like a decent guy the one time I met him down by the lake. Do you think otherwise?"

"In my book, if Adler likes you, you're all right."

"Why do you like him? Turns out Father Gabriel appreciates Adler, too."

Scarborough got to his feet, groaning as a knee cracked. "Because he's authentic, the genuine article, and God bless him, he's still young and virile, not like this old man here."

"Ha! No old man here, Scarborough. Just a very productive cowboy."

He stretched his lower back, scowling. "I take it Adler hasn't gotten back to you yet."

Peyton pulled rocks as she found them and piled them into a wheelbarrow. "He said he'd think on it. Only I need to get a move on. Can you think of someone else we could use?"

"Adler is a man of his word. He'll not dodge you or lie to you. He'll tell you straight up how it is. Maybe too much, so. Why the urgency?"

"I'll need him to help me sell this stupid hunt at Royce's party. There'll be questions only he can answer."

"And if that doesn't happen?"

Peyton stopped digging. "Then I might as well look at getting the estate valued for today's market. But I'm optimistic it won't come to that." She thought of Geraint's offer to exhibit her work and wasn't sure which was worse, losing the ranch or exposing herself to ridicule. "Glad you're coming to the rodeo tomorrow."

"I never miss it, ma'am." His relentless blue eyes zeroed in on her. "Just don't go racing horses bareback."

She'd been racing bareback since her father's death. "How're the colts? I went to check on them this morning. They were already out and far off."

Scarborough removed his gloves and hooked them to his belt. "Out to pasture, which reminds me I've gotta move the cattle in lot sixty-seven. I'll send Koda with the colts for you to see them."

By the time the sky blushed at the horizon, the wind had whipped up. Koda came running, pulling the colts behind him, his long hair flapping.

He wore a deer hide and claw necklace, and black chaps over his work jeans. "The Appaloosa is temperamental, but Scarborough said to bring them both."

"I like horses with attitude," Peyton said, straightening up.

"I like them with names."

"He hasn't told me his name yet." It had been days since the foals arrived at the ranch. They were more relaxed, with shinier coats. Peyton greeted Brocco first. "He's ready for a ride. What do you think?"

"I agree," Koda said, "but the other one is stubborn."

She circled the Appaloosa, running her hand over him as he jostled with irritation. "You're quite the beauty, aren't you?" She checked his freshly shod and oiled hoofs, examined his legs, and studied his eyes. "You can win prizes, but you haven't bonded with anyone, have you?" A life without horses she called her own would be alien, and without the ranch, she wouldn't be able to keep them. She still had a shot at convincing Adler, though every impulse in her body told her she hadn't found her solution yet. Maybe she had but was too cowardly to act on it. She pictured Lexi's spiteful face, reminding her that she might have to sacrifice at least one place she called home. "Layli said you're leaving for the rodeo early tomorrow."

"I'm a barrelman this year," Koda said, grinning. "Gotta show up early."

"You have to be gutsy for that."

He let fly an ululation that spooked the horses. "I was born for it."

"I'll cheer you on, but do me a favor. If you run into Adler, let me know."

"Assuming he doesn't yell at me."

twelve

The locals flocked to the rodeo in groups, eating brisket sandwiches dripping with barbeque sauce or toasting a win with boots filled with beer. Some were already in the bleachers, claiming the best seats, but most sauntered about, enjoying the food stalls, bars, and well-groomed prize animals. Younger children elbowed to get a good look at the winning heifers and chickens. Older kids participated in sheep and pony riding contests. Country pop blared from loudspeakers, and bets had already been placed on horse and bull riders, chuck-wagon, and barrel racers.

Layli ate strawberry shortcake topped with vanilla ice cream. She'd brought her bow and quiver for a round at the range. "Let's bet on something."

"Do you feel lucky, punk?" Scarborough asked in a terrible Clint Eastwood imitation.

"Do you? Maybe I should bet on you. Perhaps you'll win this year."

Scarborough had never won the sharp shooting competition, although he'd been trying for years. "I sign off on that."

"You're only saying that because you want me to lose my money," Layli replied.

Peyton was sitting on a post fence, surveying the crowds and savoring a strawberry ice cream cone. She'd walked around, looking for Adler, but hadn't found him. "Tell you what, Layli. I'll bet on you. Can you still make smiley faces with your arrows?"

"Who'll Stands-with-a-Bow compete against, anyway?" Scarborough asked.

Layli grinned. "Ha! No one around here is better than me."

"My grandpa is," said a little boy with ketchup on his nose. He'd weaseled his way between them, and craned his neck to make eye contact.

"Who're you?" Layli asked.

"William Charles Kelcy Loving the Third." He had auburn hair and chocolate eyes.

"Why do I feel like I should curtsy or something?"

Peyton jumped off the fence and took his chin in her hand. "That's a mighty name, Bill."

"William is the name, ma'am." He bowed and doffed his cowboy hat. "What's your name?"

Scarborough chuckled. "Well, little man, this here is Ms. Peyton Chase. And this here is Ms. Layli Hoarnhorse. I'm Scarborough."

William wiped his nose on his sleeve. "Why do you only have one name?"

Peyton took a wet wipe from her shoulder bag and cleaned William's face and hands. "Because he's special."

William didn't seem to appreciate that answer. He looked up at Layli with big, curious eyes. "I challenge you to a duel, in the name of William Charles Kelcy Loving the First."

"Okay, that's it!" Peyton picked him up and pecked kisses on his plump cheeks. She might have had a child about his age, if Ashton had agreed to it. "And you have a hundred, do you?"

"I do," he said, "but it's in Grandpa's pocket."

"Where's Grandpa, anyway?" Peyton asked, bemused.

William scanned the crowd. He spotted his grandfather at the bar, smoking a cigar and drinking a shot. "Over there."

Peyton squeezed him. "How about I get you an ice cream, and then we go see Grandpa? Otherwise, he might think you're lost."

"Cowboys don't get lost, Grandpa says. They explore. And you smell nice, like lots of flowers."

William led the way to the bar, this time with ice cream on his face. "Grandpa is the one who looks like Teddy Roosevelt." He pointed to a man with blue eyes, brimming with jovial energy, with a chevron mustache, and a sharp part in his thinning salt and pepper hair.

Layli raised her eyebrows. "I'd say."

"Grandpa, I made you a bet."

William almost stumbled, but his grandfather caught him. "Here you are, Tiger. Where'd you go?"

"This is Peyton Chase, and this is Layli Hoarnhorse, and this is Scarborough. He has only one name."

"Jake Scarborough, sir, but everyone just calls me Scarborough." He shook the man's hand, cowboy-style, lingering and maintaining eye contact longer than the norm. "We already know you're William Charles Kelcy Loving." He winked at the boy. "And that's William, not Bill."

In a genteel Texan drawl, Grandpa said, "Ma'am, and ma'am… everyone calls me Kelcy, except my ex-wife. She calls me a son-of-a-bitch."

Peyton took out another wet wipe, cleaning ice cream from William's face and hands. "You have a proper gentleman here, Kelcy. How old is William?"

"Five going on fifteen, but he luckily takes after his mother, not his grandpa." He tugged William close. "What're you doing dragging these friendly folks here?"

William grabbed Layli's quiver. "I bet you can beat her at archery."

Kelcy looked Layli up and down. "How good are you?"

"Enough to advise you not to accept the bet."

Kelcy put out his cigar, smirking. "How much did my grandson bet?"

"A hundred," Peyton replied. "But we don't expect you to accept. We just wanted to return this remarkable kid to his grandpa."

"I accept," said Kelcy, and gulped his last shot of whiskey.

Layli made a face that said, *what do I do?*

Peyton asked, "Do you have a bow?"

Kelcy made a puckish face, eyeing Layli's primitive bow. "Mine is in the car, unless you prefer a gun shooting match." He pulled his shirt up to show them his now not-so-concealed weapon. "I'll meet up with you at the range, Layli Hoarnhorse."

As they went off to the range, Scarborough patted her arm. "I got it, if you'll reimburse me, but you won't need it."

"You're betting on me?"

He took five twenty-dollar bills from his wallet. "A hundred on the most annoying woman I ever met."

"I'll reimburse you," Peyton said.

William came running, Kelcy trailing him with an expensive professional bow. He was wearing a black brace on his right wrist.

"Holy! I'm changing my bet," Scarborough said.

Layli elbowed him in the ribs. "I swear, you do that, I'll take away your breakfasts."

Peyton watched in awe.

"What's the bet?" Kelcy asked, facing his target.

"Smiley faces," Layli replied. "We'll each make one and see whose is more accurate."

Kelcy stroked his chevron mustache. "Too simple. We'll go best two out of three: smiley face, a cross, and a diamond."

"Okay, you first."

William bounced up and down. "Go, Grandpa, go!"

Kelcy aimed at the target and pressed his bow to the corner of his mouth. He made a cross with twelve arrows, five horizontal holes, and seven vertical ones, then assessed the result, massaging his chin. "Not the best cross I've ever made, but let's see if you won't do worse."

Peyton bit her lip, watching Kelcy do a better job than she'd hoped. William stood close, studying her.

"You're very pretty," the boy said. "And your hat is nice."

"And you're very cute." She took his hand and swung it. "Your hat is nice, too."

Though her bow was primitive, Layli made a perfect cross with the same number of arrows. The way she controlled her breath was impressive enough for Kelcy to comment on it. "Sure you want to continue?" she asked.

"You won the first round, but that's not the whole battle, is it? We're yet to see whether it'll be the queen or the *king* of diamonds at the end."

Peyton thought of her multiple battles and hoped she wouldn't end up being the queen with no clothes.

Layli smiled but didn't reply. She completed the diamond accurately, but he was just as precise.

"My smiley face is gonna make you frown. How many arrows?"

Layli puffed her chest. "Ten."

Kelcy called for the guys at the range to refresh their targets and wiggled his hand, loosening it. Once more, he focused, performing better with his last attempt, but it wasn't perfect.

Layli massaged her fingers before aiming at her target. She fired the first nine arrows, pleased they landed close enough to where she'd intended them. The nose was slightly askew, but not by much.

Only one arrow remained to complete the smile. Peyton found William frozen in disappointment.

"Gonna take that last one, or what?" Kelcy asked, toking on a fat cigar.

Peyton looked at Layli with a question in her eyes.

Layli saw William's dispirited face, and winked at her, agreeing to prioritize the boy's feelings, and plunked the arrow a little too far out, ruining the smiley part.

"What was that, Layli?" Scarborough threw his arms into the air. "You just cost me a hundred bucks!"

She shrugged, smiling, pleased with herself.

William asked Peyton if Layli had won. "No, William, your grandpa did. You're right. He's excellent."

The boy clapped. "He's a hero, and the best grandpa ever… has medals and everything." He twined his body around Kelcy's leg. "You did it, Grandpa!"

Kelcy looked at Layli with doubting eyes. "Tiger, why don't you help get Grandpa's arrows? Those men over there will give you some to carry back to me." When the boy dashed, happy to be of use, Kelcy said, "You ladies threw this competition. Why?"

"Because William needed to see his grandpa win more than we needed a hundred bucks," Peyton replied.

Layli prepared to go fetch her own arrows. "Never seen a boy this proud of his grandpa."

Kelcy toked on his cigar and pulled his earlobe. "Not sure how I feel about that. With a better wrist, I'd beat you fair and square."

"Thank you for a wonderful time." Peyton held out the money. "A bet is a bet."

"Keep it till we can do this again, minus William and my sore wrist. Next time, at least a grand. Deal?"

"Minus the whiskey too," Peyton said.

"The whiskey is half the preparation, little lady." He cocked his head and squinched his eyes. "You're strange folk."

"No stranger than a man who keeps a bow in his trunk," Scarborough said, "but we all come armed to the rodeo, don't we?"

"Well, if you're not packing, you're no Texan." He waved goodbye and sauntered off, looking as presidential as Roosevelt ever did.

"Where to now?" asked Layli.

"I'm off to the shooting range," Scarborough said.

Peyton said, "There'll be shootin' and there'll be tootin'. And by God, there'll be rootin', too."

Layli laughed as Scarborough headed to the opposite end of the rodeo. "I'll stay here and practice."

"After a dose of that adorable boy, I'll go watch bucking riders."

It was time for the rodeo riders, a dangerous event and the one Peyton loved the most. She bought curly fries and headed to the big arena where men with high testosterone levels mounted animals aching to stampede them to death. She passed the pens, fascinated by the bulky, aggressive animals waiting to mangle their riders. The stench of sweat and manure assaulted her, but she didn't mind. She knew she'd never find a place to sit at this late hour. Koda was standing where spectators weren't allowed to loiter, and he signaled her to join him.

"You're still in one piece, right?" she asked.

Flushed with adrenaline, he adjusted his belt buckle. "I could live here. Comfortable?"

"I have a good view, thanks to you."

He ate some of her fries. "Guess who I spotted earlier? Adler! He was nice this time, said hello, then asked if you were around. I messaged you, but you didn't reply."

Peyton checked her phone and saw the missed text. "Where's he now?"

They both scanned the crowd. "He was walking up to the bleachers opposite us. Don't know."

Peyton was determined to find him. Koda said the barrelmen had been called, and he had to go, but she ignored him. She soon spotted Adler's face peering back at her. Spectators around him leapt and swayed, jeering with painted faces and festive hats, but he sat perfectly still, decked in black. He stood up and waved, inviting her to sit beside him. She gestured and started toward him, squashing a few toes as she plowed through the crowd, then sat beside him, and pulled her hat down to hide her flushed cheeks.

He was clean-shaven, and she got a whiff of his citrus and sandalwood cologne. "I like it when you actually show up," he said.

She passed him the curly fries. "I pride myself on being a woman of my word," she said, but his remark puzzled her.

He splayed his legs, but not enough for his thigh to touch hers. "Well, you're here now."

She studied his straight nose and strong chin. "I'm sorry, Adler. Our first meeting was such a disaster."

"It wasn't our first meeting."

The spectators rose in an uproar as a rider fell, but Peyton was fixed on Adler. "What?"

"I have a confession, but not here. Let's get a beer." He led them out of the arena to a picnic table, and they sat opposite each other, away from the noise but close to the smell of fried dough emanating from the food stands.

"You have a confession to make?"

He smiled in that way he had, lighting up his face. "You didn't ambush me at the lake. That's not what set me off."

"What did?"

He clenched his jaws and looked down. "You didn't remember me. Even confused me with Joe."

Peyton remembered that he'd recognized her instantly, that he knew her name and where she lived.

"One year, you were Rodeo Queen. I'm sure you remember it."

She ran her manicured fingers over her chin. "The summer I turned twenty-one."

"You were a Chase, and I was just a local, bucking at the fair. I couldn't peel my eyes off you all day. It wasn't the first time I'd seen you, but you didn't see me. The thing is, I wrote my name and phone number on a scrap of paper but didn't know how to give it to you. You gave me an opening when you dropped your gloves. My courage pricked, and I followed you with them… Maybe you recall?"

"Why don't I remember this?"

"Maybe because when I handed them to you, as I prepared to give you the scrap of paper, you tried to tip me. To the richest girl around, I was nothing but a hired hand. After that, I couldn't say anything. I just froze and watched you run off."

Peyton brought her hand to her mouth. "I might have thought it was the polite thing to do. I was so young." She searched her memory, hoping waves of recognition would come crashing. "Wait… I remember someone tall and scrawny, with a hat too big for his head, trying to stop me on my way to making good on a bet. Yes! You gave my favorite gloves back. That was you?"

He flexed his biceps. "Not scrawny now."

"Sorry. I was full of myself then. My father's only child. If I didn't remember you, it's not because you weren't memorable, but because I was self-centered. I never would've wanted you to feel bad, though. It's hard to remember such a thing, right?"

"True, I overreacted, but I didn't feel bad back then. I felt crushed. Here's why. Do you remember Danielle?" He took off his hat and fluffed his dark hair.

He needed a haircut, but his ruggedness was beautiful. "How can I not? Danielle was cute, spunky, and smart."

"Good. Do you then remember that she invited you to a gathering by the lake because she wanted to introduce you to the guy who handed you the gloves you dropped?"

Peyton winced, aware of where he was headed. "Oh my God, don't tell me. You got all spruced up, then I pulled a no-show."

"Yup, and that was after you said you would come."

"I don't remember the details, but it wouldn't have been because I thought I was too good for the locals or for you. You thought that though, didn't you?"

"I did, and arrogance is a sin in my book. That said, you had the right to be full of yourself. I saw you race that horse bareback after you fled me. You were a vision—Geronimo-brave."

"Foolish, more like it. I was challenged and wouldn't back down."

"How could you? You had a cliff to dive off, even back then, eh?"

"If I had agreed to meet you at the party, I would've thought you were darn cute."

He put his beer bottle on the table and straightened his back. "Am I still cute?"

Peyton snickered. "That's an understatement, if I ever heard one."

He stared at her, rotating his bottle. "Y'see, there you were down at the lake—Peyton Chase—unable to recognize or remember me and trying to tip me. Again."

"I don't see you as the hired anything, Adler. You're…"

"I'm what?"

She managed a pretty grin. "A man whose hat fits perfectly."

"I see." He looked at her with the energy of a sniper. "Anything else?"

"In all fairness, I showed up at the lake after all… some twelve years later."

He laughed heartily. "You're a slow mover."

"Now tell me, is making me chase you a payback?"

"Would I try to get even?"

Peyton locked eyes with him. "Are we even now?"

"Did you take notes?"

Peyton looked past him to Koda, who was scampering in their direction, kicking up dust and waving his hat. He collapsed beside her on the bench. "What's the matter?"

"Oh hi, Adler. Sorry to interrupt." He was flushed. "There's a colt show competition next month in Los Alamos," he said, rushing his words. "I think the Appaloosa would be perfect. I can get five thousand dollars if we win. Can I use him?"

"Why not? We have trucks and trailers."

"Really?" Koda straightened his bolo tie. "Five big ones, Peyton!" He pulled on his gloves, ready to return to rescuing riders. "The Appaloosa is still waiting for a name, though."

Adler said, "A horse without a name can take you places, but he can't bring you back."

"I'll name him soon."

"Okay, see you later and a million thank yous." Koda turned on his heels and went back to work.

"Nice thing you just did, Ms. Chase."

"Ms. Chase?" She held his gaze. "Does this mean I have *you* trained?"

He shook his head, grinning. "Touché."

"Happy to help. Maybe my kind is nicer than you think."

"Just maybe," he said and brought a hand to his chest. "Last time I saw you, those many years ago, you were wearing red. There was something about the way you moved, spoke, laughed that I found mesmerizing."

Peyton wanted Adler to herself, but several guys descended on them, insisting he join them for a beer, so Petyon told him to go.

"Can we talk again before you leave?" he shouted over the clatter.

"I sure hope so."

She wasn't sure where she'd find him again, but trusted she would.

Layli spotted Peyton at the picnic table and sat opposite her. "Who's that towering hunk?"

Peyton grinned and took a swig of beer. "That, my dear, is *the* Adler."

"G-i-r-l! You kept that glaring detail out? You only said he told you to get lost." Layli fanned herself for added drama. "You said nothing about the heartthrob he is."

"You're right. I should've said a heartthrob told me to get lost. That would've made me feel much better."

Layli drummed the ground with her feet. "Is he gonna do it?"

"Don't know, but he didn't yell at me this time, so I'm hopeful."

"I called three taxidermists so far. No one has called me back. We're more on an egg timer than ever."

"Don't remind me." The loudspeakers broadcasted the news that the dance floor was officially open. Peyton said, "I haven't danced in forever."

"Especially not with the cowboys of New Mexico." Layli checked a message on her phone. "This guy I met at the range is inviting me for a drink. You're okay here by yourself?"

"Of course. Go."

Peyton noticed an attractive young couple walking hand-in-hand. Her thoughts threaded through the needle of a past still stitching itself together. Ashton flickered in her mind. She hated having let him kiss her like old times. He'd be more difficult to rebuff. The sky morphed to strawberry jam, lights twinkled, and George Strait blared on the loudspeakers. She got up and moved toward the music, singing along to "I Gotta Get to You," and joined the crowd surrounding the dance floor.

Adler came up from behind her and offered his hand. "May I?"

Not since meeting Ashton had she been this elated at another's presence. "Timing is everything, isn't it?" She accepted his hand, enjoying the way he towed her to the dance floor.

He pulled her to his body until her skin prickled. "I'll do it."

"Thank you, Adler. I was hoping you'd say that."

"I have conditions."

Peyton took off her white hat and fluffed her hair, inviting him closer. "I'm listening."

"Condition number one: I'm in charge of the hunt, not you."

She nodded.

"And safety is paramount. I don't care how important or rich someone is. If they ignore safety protocols, they're out, and they don't get their money back."

"Anything else?"

"I choose my guys, not you."

"Is that it?"

"No, the list is long."

His sturdiness made her feel sheltered. Copious descriptions crowded her mind, but they distilled to a single word: true. "Come to dinner tomorrow. We'll discuss everything in private."

"At the ranch?"

"About six, if that works for you."

He jerked her so close she could feel his pulse race. "You and me, and Scarborough?"

She giggled. "Just the two of us."

His lips almost touching her neck, he asked, "It's a date, then?"

Peyton wasn't sure what she was getting into, but it felt right. "I'll wear red."

"In that case, I have something to give you." He reached into his pocket and took out a scrap of paper with a phone number scribbled on it. "If you call this number, you'll find the voicemail is never full."

She looked down, hiding her eyes.

He placed a hand under her chin and lifted her face to his. "Peyton Chase races bareback and dives off high cliffs. She can handle a scrap of paper from a scrawny guy with a hat too big for his head."

She touched the brim of his hat. "People hang on to their hats so they can hang on to their hopes. You grew into yours."

"I've known you five minutes, and you already understand me. Not sure that's a good thing." The song ended, and the lights grew dimmer. Adler brought her hand to his lips and kissed it. "I'll be there, but do me a favor and wear this perfume again."

"I accept that tip."

He chuckled, doffed his hat, and left.

She watched as the night swallowed him. He was a stallion with a name. She reached for her phone to let Layli know she could stay as long as she liked. She'd find her own way home. Peyton found a text from Geraint, asking her to call him right away. She distanced herself from the noise and called.

"Don't kill me," Geraint said, as soon as he picked up. "You made me delete the photos I took of *The Last Start*, but not the ones of your paintings."

Anxiety snaked through her belly, and she pressed her earbud. "You photographed my work?"

"Not my fault, you didn't guess that."

"Geraint!"

"Well, good thing I did, because I believe I have a buyer for one of them."

"What?" Peyton gunned toward the parking lot.

"This woman walks into my gallery and asks for paintings with the spirit of the West. She launched into a description that made me show her your work. She said it was perfect, picked one, but you haven't named them, so I can't tell you which. It's the one of the Grand Tetons with a cowgirl cradling a lamb, carrying it toward a cabin."

"That one is called *Girl with Ewe and Double-pen Cabin*," she said, "at least in my head, it is. But what? I'm floored."

"Listen. She asked to see it, but she's not in a hurry. I price nothing in my gallery for under ten thousand, and she knows it. This means she accepts it's worth at least that much. So, I have to organize a show for you… like yesterday."

Peyton needed to sit down. "Geraint, I'm not ready. Oh my God! No, no… I haven't spoken a word of it to anyone, and… and…"

"Will you grow a spine?" She could hear him push back his desk chair and stand up. "You said you needed money. I found you some."

Anxiety and eagerness clashed within her. "I need much more than ten thousand."

"You're making my argument for me. It's time for a show in the City of Angels. Enough hiding in Bumblefuck, New Mexico."

She paced so fast she almost tripped on a rock. Royce was preparing her pitch about the hunt. She had just gotten Adler onboard for it. And that spine Geraint told her to get was still in storage. "There's this thing I need to see through in a few days. Need a little time, okay?"

"To do what, lassie?"

"To throw up a few times." She laughed, though she was a ball of nerves.

"Okay, but have respect for my professional nose. It's big for a reason, and it sniffs a colossal success."

"Or a colossal failure with all eyes on me, not on your big nose."

thirteen

After a robust evening of cowboys and stallions with names, Peyton woke with a bluster of energy. Today, she'd meet the sun on its terms. At the slice of dawn, she rode to the range with Cooper for company. The silence of daybreak was broken only by birdsong and the horse's snort. Winged by the enormity of land rolling away from the mountains of Rio Arriba County, she reached the top of the mesa. The mist on the Tusas mountains surrendered to the sun, revealing myriad shades of green dripping from Van Gogh's paintbrush. The sky turned shades of tender pink and peach. She dismounted and sat on a rock, inhaling the savory scent of sagebrush, cuddled Cooper, and took photos for a possible painting, hoping to capture not only the beauty of the moment, but how she felt in it. If she ever wrote her memoir, it would be as her mother had done, with brush and canvas. There was a fortune in such serenity, a hearth against the blizzards of the unknown. The sun climbed in the sky, bringing welcome warmth, spurring Peyton to return to the house.

"You're my favorite for many reasons," she told Cooper, who at seventy pounds, tried to sit in her lap. "You're not little anymore, but you talk to me without speaking, and you're always right." He stretched to all fours. "I guess it's time to give you biscuits and ham and give me some piping hot oatmeal."

As she'd hoped, the kitchen was empty. She found harmony in cooking alone. Sorting through the selection of coffees for a strong cowboy brew, she turned on the radio for the morning news. Though she'd moved to California after college, her seasonal visits to Abiquiú always included morning radio time with her father and interesting discussions about man's relationship to nature or of how older doesn't translate to easier. Now that life had become hard for her, she could draw on the strength of his wisdom.

The ranch had begun humming. Scarborough, who was the true sunrise of Pioneer Ranch, was already whipping the day into shape. There would be no rushing today. No mistakes in the name of efficiency, especially since Adler was coming for dinner. Her phone rang. When she saw it was the friar, she decided to answer it.

"Good morning, Father Gabriel."

"Good morning, my child. Am I disturbing you?"

"It's been a lovely morning, and you just added to it."

"I'm sorry to always be calling with requests, but I have a big one today." He took a deep breath. "Do you remember Mikey and Ricky? The boys who helped us unload all those baskets?"

How could she forget Mikey? He'd told her, *You're stuck because she is.*

"You mean Honovi and Awanata?"

"Their grandmother had to be taken to the hospital," the friar said. "I can't find anywhere appropriate with proper supervision. Checked with the few responsible people I know, but no one agreed. I thought maybe you wouldn't mind having them on the ranch. Sorry, I know, it's a big ask."

"For several days?"

"I'm afraid so."

Peyton bit her lip. She thought of Adler coming for dinner and the preparations for her pitch at Royce's party. "For something like this, Father, I'll have to check with Layli. At least for this evening, I can't look after them. Can I call you back?"

"Oh, bless you, Peyton. Yes, of course."

She texted Layli, inviting her to come over for coffee and oatmeal.

Layli was there in minutes. "Are you adding cinnamon to that oatmeal?"

"Loads of cream, too. I know how you like it."

"Good ride? I saw you coming back with that dog who thinks he's your boyfriend." She sat at the table with Peyton and spooned oatmeal.

"My son, maybe. Speaking of sons, Father Gabriel called."

"Okay, I like that man, but he always needs something."

"Well, yes. He is *the* charity."

"No, I think we are. What now? The roof collapsed?"

"An old woman is in the hospital, leaving behind two unsupervised grandchildren. Father Gabriel thought maybe we could care for them for a few days."

"We or me?"

Peyton scraped the bottom of her bowl. "Yes, *we*. I only need your help with them tonight. Where'll we put them? This evening I need the house to myself."

Layli reflected, draining her mug. "This coffee is delicious. Okay, where to put them? No, not here, Peyton. It's too much of a departure from the pueblo, too grand. They'll have Koda's room. It'll feel like a palace. He can sleep on the sofa. How long will they need to stay?"

"Several days. I think Koda should sleep here, though. He's a grownup, and there are plenty of rooms in the house."

"You're spoiling that kid. I know he told you about his mountain bike and then you went and gave him a fat check."

"He's not a kid, Layli, however much he's your little brother. He has ambitions, and he's quite capable."

"Oh God, what ambitions?"

"I just mean he's a man now. His needs have altered."

"Fine, I'll tell him to bring his things here. I'd rather keep my sofa for sitting. During the day, the boys can putter about. Help, maybe." She spliced a wicked grin. "Scarborough would love it if we gave him two boys to entertain, wouldn't he? How old are they?"

"They're nine and seven."

"I'll go pick them up," Layli said. "Help them pack. Will you call Father Gabriel, or should I?"

"I told him I'd call him back. What time to pick them up, eleven?"

"Yeah, great."

"Bring them to say hello first before taking them up to the cabin," Peyton said. I'll give them lunch and feel them out. Want them to know they're welcome, and I'll put a care package together for each of them. They must be petrified, poor things."

"You're going to make this a holiday for them, aren't you?"

For years, Peyton had wanted to spoil a child or two. She brought the tips of her index finger and thumb together. "Well, just a bit."

As the sun receded to the horizon, Peyton stood at an upstairs window on the lookout for Adler. She wore a fitted, bright red, one-shouldered dress. Her hair was loose. Her whole being unfurled, and she was spinning with a combination of excitement and ease.

At ten till six, she spotted a black BMW entering the gates. She took as much time walking to the front door as it would take Adler to reach it. For fun, she banged on the gong and swung the heavy doors wide open, attempting a big welcome. But there was no car in the driveway, and certainly no Adler. She stepped onto the loggia to be sure the driveway was empty. It was. A knock came from the kitchen.

"Hello…" Adler hollered. "Peyton?"

She hurried toward the voice and found him standing in the mudroom outside the half-open kitchen door, carrying a bouquet of yellow tulips and something wrapped in butcher's paper.

She unlatched the door and stepped aside. "Thank you for coming."

"When a goddess invites me to her house, the thanks is mine." He handed her the flowers and the package, removed his hat, and inhaled the aroma of food still simmering on the stove. "Smells delicious. What you got cookin'?"

She noticed he'd gotten a haircut and a mirror-close shave. "Tulips are such a gentle flower. Thank you."

"They don't last long, but while they do, they're unforgettable."

"And what's this?" she held out the package.

"Trout, ready to cook." He shrugged. "Father Gabriel called it right."

"Come in, please. I'll make something appetizing out of that tomorrow. Grill them, perhaps."

He threw a thumb over his shoulder. "You're digging up a garden outside, it seems."

"There's always been one there. I'm bringing it back to life." She closed the kitchen door. "Why did you come through the backdoor? I went to meet you at the front."

"Your father brought me in this way once before. Seemed natural."

Peyton put the trout in the fridge and the tulips in water. "I have hors d'oeuvres and drinks out on the terrace for us." She took the vase and led the way. "Tell me how you knew my dad."

"I wouldn't say I knew him." He sat opposite her. "Mark and I are hunting buddies. That's how I met Sorensen."

"Uncle Mark, Mark? Reprobate, tall and—"

"—and always smoking marijuana? Yes, Mark Wells." He ran his eyes everywhere. "Your father showed me several things when he had me over, but he didn't show me this. You have some views from this house."

"Thank you. I'm happy to share them with you." She gestured to the ice bucket. "Beer or wine?"

"If Chardonnay, wine. Otherwise, beer is fine."

She poured two glasses of wine and offered him a platter of stuffed mushrooms and rolled prosciutto, replete with arugula and ricotta cheese. "What did Dad show you?"

"Everything with gears. We'd been talking about our grandfathers. I told him how my pappy repaired clocks, and how he'd shown me a thing or two. Took it up as a hobby. He invited me here to look at some of his babies."

"Then you've seen the banjo?"

"Loved that one." He chose a stuffed mushroom, slipped it into his mouth, then took another. "Did you make these?"

"Yes, I made the entire meal. Well, the banjo clock stopped working recently. I wound it, but it didn't help."

"Can I take a look?"

"Of course, but I didn't say that to stick you with it."

He got up. "Don't be silly. Show me."

She led him to her father's study. "Why didn't you return for another visit?"

He laughed. "You sure ask a ton of questions."

She bit her lower lip. "Sorry, terrible habit of mine. You ask *me* something." Peyton watched him inspect the clock with a gentle touch.

Adler pressed where she didn't think a hinge existed and popped it open, then lifted it close to his face and tested the main wheel and gear train. "What do you do?"

"I'm an art restorer, some sculptural work, but mostly paintings."

"Really? Like museum quality stuff?"

"Not bragging, but I get called for valuable artwork."

"Oh, someone said you were an artist like your mother."

Peyton felt as if he'd asked her to show him her breasts. Could she tell him the truth only Geraint knew? She hadn't even told Royce or Layli. But something about him made her feel safe, the way her father had all her life. "Until recently, I would've said I can paint, mimic to a tee sometimes, which is why I can do my job. But I would've also said I am not gifted like Mom was."

He looked at her with his full attention. "And what would you say now?"

Peyton braided her wrists behind her back and looked down. "I'm a different kind of artist than my mother. Perhaps not as good, but perhaps not terrible, either."

The look he gave her was supportive, saturated with understanding. "I get the sense this is a difficult topic."

"Mom's work has hard edges, but it's hyper realistic, like photographs. It's actually my favorite form of visual art. I'll show you if you'd like. Some of Mom's work is upstairs." Peyton realized late the paintings upstairs were only copies. How could she have forgotten? She thought the copies of her mother's work were a mockery and hadn't looked at them. She hoped he'd refuse to see them, but to her horror, he accepted.

"I'd like to stow away the banjo in my car first. Is that okay?"

"Please, do whatever you like."

He looked at her from the corner of his eye and smirked.

"About the clock, I mean," she added, blushing.

"If you'll give me a blanket to wrap it with, I'll take it with me and open it up properly at my house. Looks like it needs a part or two."

Peyton cocked her head, studying him. "That's very generous."

She was trusting him with the future of her estate. Why not the clock? "Are you sure you want to take on this trouble? It's a sizable, heavy item."

"It'll be a while before I can devote my full attention to it. I have a few jobs coming up. But I'll get it done." He stared at her with a tenderness she hadn't expected. "Nothing about you is trouble to me, Peyton."

"I'm touched," she replied, averting his eyes.

They climbed the pink Numidian marble stairs to a landing decorated with paintings and rich fabrics.

"Which one is your room?"

She giggled like a juvenile. "I'm not showing you my room."

Energy pulsated between them, and he looked about to kiss her. "I just want to know the direction."

"It's a corner room. Faces northeast."

"Toward Chama," he said.

"Yes, your neck of the woods." They stood on the top landing, looking at each other in the gloaming, hush.

"The gallery is this way." Peyton opened the door, turned on the lights, and braced herself. To her surprise, the copies were deceiving, at least to the untrained eye. "Natural light showcases Harlow's work best, but…"

He strode from painting to painting, his hands twined behind his back. Peyton noticed that he dressed in monochromatic colors, as she preferred. He was wearing dark blue jeans, a blue shirt, and boots polished to a mirror. He was a sailor, a cowboy, an intense presence, and more.

"I don't know much about art, but I see passion in these paintings. Do you have a favorite?"

"Yes, *The Last Start*, but it's at my house in Mendocino."

"That's where you've been?" He homed in on the smallest canvas in the room, a young native woman with a baby carrier on her back, grinding corn outside her tepee in late autumn. "What's this called?"

"*Apache Mother & Child*."

"And the big one of the Lakota going through a valley? Are they moving camp?"

Peyton was amazed he showed so much interest. "That's *Journey*. It's about changing camps after the bison hunt."

He turned to a large, vertical portrait of a girl with hazel eyes and wavy chestnut hair. "And this one?"

"I think you know this one is me. Cut it out."

He paused before a portrait hanging low on the wall of a woman with large blue eyes, dainty features, high cheekbones, full lips, and red hair. "Is this a self-portrait of your mother? There's such a strong resemblance. It could be you, except Harlow's hair was red."

"Correct. What do you see?"

Adler leaned on one leg and tilted his head. "I want to say loneliness. There's roaming behind the eyes." He studied the other works. "Any of the ones here your favorite?"

"I have a confession to make. Sorry, I didn't mean to mislead you. These paintings are excellent copies of Mom's work, not the originals, but

I only learned that two weeks ago. I know it's hard to believe, but I had forgotten they weren't originals when I offered to show them to you."

Unphased, he said, "In all my life, I've never heard anyone speak faster than you just did."

"I didn't mean to be voluble. I feel bad. Don't want you to think I'm a liar. I'm embarrassed."

"You have nothing to be embarrassed about."

She clasped her fingers together, her eyes cast to her feet. "I'm downright ashamed."

He moved closer and pulled her into his embrace. It was loving, sheltering, the hug of a well-meaning friend. "You mustn't. There's no shame in trying to fix things."

She let him hold her until she could smile again. "Thank you for not judging me."

"No point in judging. Either we've been there, or we will be."

She gave him a quizzical look. "Wait a minute, you don't seem surprised."

"I wouldn't have said anything, but I saw one of these paintings at Mark's. He made it clear it was an original."

"Which one?"

"Your mother's self-portrait. I figured something must've happened when I saw it again hanging here, but I wasn't going to ask."

She beamed at the possibility of seeing the original of at least one painting again. "You're very decent."

He gave her his best smile and patted his athletic torso. "And very hungry, but first answer my question. Is there a favorite of yours here?"

"Yes, this one of my parents. At least I find it the most intriguing." She stood before a sizeable tableau of her father sitting at his desk in a shaft of bright light, surrounded by books and a notebook with scribbles on it, while her mother stretched on the sofa in shadows.

After inspecting it for a minute, Adler asked, "I don't know if I'm interpreting it right, but before I tell you what I see, maybe you can give me your take."

Peyton told him the raw truth. "Dad wrote letters. Mom journaled too, but her medium was her artwork. I didn't always understand that, but this painting is an example of it." She swallowed, not used to voicing such deep-seated reasoning about her family. "Dad is in the light, engrossed in intellectual pursuits, connecting to what lacked a pulse, blind to his wife's state."

Adler nodded and thrust his face closer to the tableau. "At first I thought your mom was napping, but she's not, is she?"

"That's what most people see. Me, too, before, but if you look closely, her eyes are open. I believe she was expressing sadness, a feeling of neglect and malaise. I fear Mom was asking for help in some of her paintings, but no one understood that."

"Why is it one of your favorites, then?"

She chuckled. "And I thought I asked a lot of questions."

"Sorry, I'm being overly curious."

"No, no, I want to tell you." She took a deep breath. "Because I need reminding that my parents were flawed humans. Emphasis on human. I don't know in what way Dad tried to help Mom, but somewhere along the line, he gave up hope or just couldn't deal with her trials. I don't know. He and I shared many deep discussions over the years, but not much about their marriage or Mom's mental state. If he hadn't been such a staunch Catholic, I think they would've gotten divorced."

Adler stared at her with ruminating, potent eyes. "Thank you, Peyton."

"For what?"

"For trusting me."

She turned and gestured toward the door, feeling as though she could cry. "You said you were famished. I made some New Mexican favorites. Go on ahead to the terrace. I'll bring out the food. I just have to plate it."

"Then I'll help you carry it out. And I understand your father. Once sealed in the Catholic Church, there'd be no divorce for me, either."

Peyton filed that note away but said nothing.

Installed at the table, Adler unfolded his serviette and placed it on his lap. Arabian jasmine scented the evening air. As the light disappeared, the edges of mountains grew sharper. Coyotes howled their night watch, and hummingbirds stole their last sips from the honeysuckle bushes that surrounded the terrace.

"You went to too much trouble."

"Not at all. Gourmet meals are on the menu once a week."

"And the rest of the time?"

"The rest of the time, I enjoy fitting into my jeans. That's why God made fruits and vegetables. But once a week, I gotta make something extra yummy. Posole?"

"Yes, please." He held out his wide-brimmed bowl, and she filled it.

She watched as he tasted the rich, brothy soup of pork, hominy, and red chili. He narrowed his eyes. She was unfamiliar with his expressions, not sure how to interpret them. "You're in deep thought," she remarked, serving herself some soup. "What is it?"

He paused for a moment, smiling. "You're not quite as I expected."

"What do you mean?"

"You're sweet."

Peyton stopped eating and raised her brows. "And you thought I'd be mean?"

"No, but haughty, someone who'd avoid being vulnerable or real."

"But that's who you are. Why not me?"

He finished his posole and helped himself to stew and to cornbread stuffed with chorizo and cheese. "I mean this tender and bare. Don't take it the wrong way, but I didn't grow up with a cook, a maid, and a master of the horse."

The last bit, she found titillating. "You read too many romances. I'll tell Scarborough you called him master of the horse, though. It's a big house and a bigger ranch. It needs all hands on deck, so we all chip in. Dad didn't keep regular chores, but he fixed all electrical and mechanical things, including appliances and equipment. We may wear gloves, but we get them dirty. Did you find Dad haughty?"

"I didn't find him grounded like you are."

"Hmm, you're buddies with Uncle Mark. Is he haughty?"

"He's a self-made man. You're old money, and I mean no disrespect."

"Some people I know with serious money are as you describe." She picked up a square of cornbread and bit into it, thinking of Ashton, who fit Adler's description. "Not all."

"Maybe. Anyway, I'm happy the build-up of how you could be wasn't wasted."

"Is there's a compliment in there for me?"

"I made you big in my mind, Peyton, way back then. In time, I told myself you'd be a rotten person, that it was no loss. Then you came to me and were impossible to ignore. Now I'm at your house and find that I… I…"

"You what?"

"I think I've had too much of everything. My filter is off." He made a swooping gesture over the table. "You made all this?"

"Yes. Why so surprised?"

"You're supposed to be afraid to break a nail or something, and yet you dig holes, dive like a champ, chauffeur a humble monk, and elevate cooking to gourmet cuisine."

She laughed. "I *am* afraid of breaking a nail, so I get gel manicures. See?" She held out her hand, flailing her neat fingernails.

He took her hand and brought it to his lips, then came from around the table, sat beside her, and pressed her palm flat against his cheek.

Peyton held his face in both her hands. He'd touched her in so many ways. "I can't believe you didn't chase me down with your phone number, Blake Adler." His skin was silky, and in the twilight, he looked closer to thirty than forty. "Maybe you wouldn't have liked me then."

"You bruised my ego enough. Can't do that to a cowboy." He kissed her, and it was strong. "Was it okay that I kissed you?"

"Only if you do it again."

He stood, pulled her to her feet, and kissed her longer this time, pressing his sturdy, warm body against hers. The sun was diffused behind the mountains now. Night fell like black gossamer, and a chill set in. Fairy lights suspended from tree to tree above them twinkled, and crickets chirped.

"How about some bourbon and coffee?" she asked.

He accepted. "Did you think I was a total ass down by the lake? After you left, I felt like you pushed a button I didn't even know I had… and I'm trained to remain cool under extreme duress."

"Maybe showing up unarmed was to your disadvantage."

He laughed. "Maybe. I can manage looking down a barrel just fine, but a pair of beautiful hazel eyes pulls my strings. I guess my training didn't cover how to behave around you." He caged her to his body. "You have goosebumps. Let's get you inside. You must be cold."

She didn't tell him she owed her goosebumps to him. Together, they piled dishes in the sink and on the counter.

"I'll make coffee, and I have *tres leches* cake with strawberries for dessert. It won't be long before I fill up the dishwasher. Rest anywhere you like."

"I'll sit with you." He swiped a flat palm over the polished ironwood grain table. "I love solid wood."

"I get the feeling you gravitate most to what's closest to its original nature." She thought she might have strayed away from hers by hiding her greatest talent and wondered what it would take to trace back to it.

"Haven't thought about it," he replied, "but sounds accurate."

She gave him coffee the way he liked it, with sugar and cream, then got busy picking up the kitchen. "Should we talk about the hunt now?"

He laughed, and it sounded earthy and hearty. "We haven't yet? I hadn't noticed. No matter. We talked about the important stuff."

"Royce Kent, my godmother, is having a big party on Saturday. She'll be gathering potential clients for us in a private room. We'll have to explain why they should pay us an arm and a leg to hunt big game with us."

"Us?"

"Of course, *us*. I'll answer questions about accommodations, transportation, peripheral entertainment, but only you can answer questions about the marrow of it—the hunt."

"What kind of party?" His tone said he wouldn't enjoy it.

"A sophisticated one. The important thing is that they leave feeling confident they'll have a time worth bragging about."

"We'll do a PowerPoint presentation?"

She shut off the faucet and swiveled in his direction. "No, Adler, nothing should remind them of being at some board meeting. I'll deliver. Your job is to inspire confidence in what they'll do with you."

"I won't entertain them," he said, with an edge.

She dried her hands and moved closer to him. "I don't expect you to. I need you to show them why hunting with you will be different. The outcome is the entertainment."

"That's easy. I guarantee that."

"Great, say that, and I need an excellent taxidermist who'll return my calls. Can you give me a reference?"

"I know a guy with a big operation. I'll negotiate with him for you. And I'm assuming you want him to deliver in a timely fashion?"

"Precisely. I have an idea to run by you, but we'll discuss that tomorrow after I clear it with Royce." By the time she finished up at the sink and glanced his way, she found him asleep with his elbow on the table, his cheek buttressed by a fist. Symmetry and confidence shaped his face and a lifetime of movement shaped his body. Having him at her table felt as natural as morning dew. She wanted to kiss him again, even as he slept, but she enjoyed letting him rest, and poured herself a cup of coffee, instead. At the sound of a spoon stirring in a cup, he woke up.

"I wasn't asleep," he said, with a guilty smile. "I could hear everything."

She brought her cup to the table and sat opposite him. "I was up at the crack of dawn, too."

"I can't believe how relaxed I feel here," he said, stretching his arms. "Peyton, I've never had an evening like this, and not because I dozed off." He pointed to her cup. "My favorite part of sleeping under the stars is brewing coffee over an open fire."

"One of my paintings is of cowboys brewing coffee under the stars in the desert."

"Really? I'd love to see it."

"When I'm brave enough." She grinned and bit her lip. "This has been a night to remember. Thank *you*, though. Would you like a slice of cake?"

"I'll call you tomorrow and plan more for Saturday." He came to his feet and took her hand. "Save me a piece of that cake, will you?"

She stood up and threaded her fingers through his. "I can give you some to take with you."

"But I want an excuse to come back."

She paused, the way a woman does before she tells a man something he must never forget. "Blake Adler, you never need a reason to come see me."

He took her hands in his and kissed her tenderly. "I have many reasons." He walked to the kitchen door, pulling her behind him. "It's been surreal."

"Surrealism is supposed to destroy the shackles of our limitations."

"Said the artist."

His comment sent currents through her. She didn't know what look she gave him, but it made him gaze at her intensely. "Vulnerability may be the most beautiful attribute of all," he said.

"That's the first time anyone has referred to me—not to my mother— as the artist." She didn't cry, but tears were fighting to prick through, and she was sure he saw it. "Thank you."

"For what?"

"For seeing me."

He pulled her to him and kissed her again. It was the most meaningful kiss yet. "I was right to single you out during your college years. Because, Peyton, look at you now. Goodnight, and thank you for pure beauty."

"Thank you for pure honesty."

She returned to the kitchen to clear the coffee cups and wondered if Ashton would show up at Royce's party.

fourteen

If ice sculptures and flower arrangements the size of mules weren't enough to impress guests arriving at Royce's party, the towers of food and fountains of drinks would be. Pyramids of croquembouche, truffles, and petits fours abounded. A massive tent decorated with lights and fresh flowers hopped with life. Peyton had been to these parties before and knew what to expect, but every year Royce added a new twist. This year, the theme was *la corrida*, the bullfight. Servers dressed like matadors circulated with tapas, and waitresses dressed like flamenco dancers distributed drinks. Banderillos passed pastries drenched in liquor, and picadors offered cigars.

Peyton arrived early, worried about the framework for the pitch of her life. The party churned outside, where music played for tango dancers who entertained guests with two left feet.

In a plunge silver mermaid dress, backless with spaghetti straps, Peyton descended the stairs to the back gardens and handed an attendant the Bernardaud bone china tea set she'd brought as a gift.

"Lordy lord!" said Royce, coming to meet her in a gypsy inspired red and gold dress, and heels that gave her the height of a basketball player. "You stun, darling."

"I like this dress way more, Royce. You look ten years younger, quite the Esmerelda."

"Pish-posh, I look like two of Esmerelda's ugly sisters mashed together. But you, my dear, will break many hearts, especially Ashton's."

"I was hoping he wouldn't come." Ashton always thrilled her, but she knew the dangers of his magnetism. She didn't want him and Adler in the same space.

"You'll soon see for yourself. He's dashing, Peyton. Brought me a case of Bordeaux worth a crown jewel."

Peyton spied him meandering their way in a blue pinstriped Italian suit, a champagne glass in each hand. "He's a showoff," she whispered.

"Generous, not a showoff. And here he is." Royce straightened her spine and checked her bosom. "Ashton, darling, how're you enjoying the party?"

"Your party, your house, your guest list. All primo."

"Oh, happy to hear."

He cocked his head toward Peyton. "Your choice of friends is phenomenal."

"Duty beckons. You two have a good time. Peyton, darling, dinner is at nine, breakfast at four, and I made those special arrangements for you at eight."

"What're we talking about?" asked Ashton.

Peyton said, "It's business. You don't need to worry about it."

"Next time, you're doing my makeup," Royce said, "because those eyes of yours are breathtaking." Royce elbowed Ashton. "How can you stand it?"

"Who said I can?"

"I just love him, Peyton. Okay, take care of my goddaughter, you, or I'll drown you in your Bordeaux." She flung her jeweled fingers in the way only she could.

"I think she means it," Ashton said, watching her leave. "Isn't she too old for that dress?"

"Aren't you too old for that cynicism?"

"Oh, stop it. I didn't come here to fight with you." He gave her a glass of champagne and a perfect smile. "You're radiant, Peyton, as always."

The longer he cornered her, the weaker she felt. Ashton wasn't perfect, but he ticked all her boxes except her biggest one—a proper family. "Why did you come?"

"We have unfinished business."

She sipped champagne and took a chocolate-dipped strawberry from a circulating tray. "I think not."

He leaned in closer than she wanted him to and whispered, "I'm getting a divorce. You finally get what you want."

"Too late for that." Peyton made to move away, but he held her by the elbow and nuzzled her neck. "Ashton, behave or I swear…" It was then she saw Adler standing a few feet away, watching with a neutral face. She wished he showed more emotion, any emotion at all, and took a decisive step back, smiling at him. "You're early."

Dressed all in black, casual yet stylish, Adler didn't return her smile, but came closer. "I've been here awhile, alright."

Ashton extended a hand with a skeptical look on his face. "Ashton Grant, and you are?"

He took his time accepting the offered hand. "Adler."

"Rattler, you said?"

Peyton scowled at Ashton. "You'll have to excuse us. *We* have business to attend to."

"Wait, who're you?" Ashton asked with a faint scowl.

"We're together," Peyton said, but neither of the men budged.

"Together?" he asked, raising his chin, giving her the I-don't-think-so face she knew too well.

The men sized each other up—one refined and powerful, the other confident and resolute. Peyton wrapped her lips around the chocolate-dipped strawberry and bit into it, wondering what to say next.

"That must be the lipstick I bought you?" Ashton asked. "Velvety red. Look at that. Not a smear, not a smudge."

She resented his act of sabotage and made sure he saw it on her face. "Adler, can we just go and organize?"

He pulled back, waiting for her to lead the way, and tucked his hands in his pockets.

"Ashton, excuse us." After a few steps, when Adler was directly behind her, Peyton gathered her hair to one side and walked slower, exposing a delicate bare back and a silver train. She tucked under a sycamore and turned to face him. "I'm sorry about that back there. How are you?"

His mood was as dark as his clothes. "So, this is your world."

"It's a small and occasional part of my world."

He looked at her without the warmth and budding bond she'd felt at her house, as though he didn't know what to do with her. "Still on at eight?"

She smiled away the awkwardness. "Yes. Come, I'll introduce you to Royce. She's been a tremendous help."

He gestured for her to lead the way, his attitude too apathetic for her liking. Peyton beelined to Royce, but Adler stayed a step behind, unnerving her. Royce was socializing with Mark.

"Uncle Mark!" Peyton opened her arms and hugged him. "Where's your suit?"

He kissed her on both cheeks and turned to Adler. "You're the last man I expected to see here, but the first man I'd have invited if this were my party."

At last, cracking a smile, Adler shook Mark's hand. "Good to see you, too."

"Peyton is with you?" Mark asked, with a look of joyful surprise.

"I'm with her is more like it."

She wondered if he hadn't judged as harshly as she feared and moved closer to him.

Mark laughed. "It's always ladies' choice, isn't it?" He clasped Adler's shoulder. "Royce, why did you seat me at a table with old farts when this man is here?"

"You mean people like you?"

Adler gestured to his simple outfit. "I'm not staying, Mark."

"But you must," Royce said, shaking his hand. "Just look at Mark. He's practically in pajamas. I'm Royce Kent and you're most welcome at my home."

"Ma'am, I'm Blake Adler. Much obliged, but I'm here on business, not pleasure."

"I'm not sure there can be business without pleasure, but what do I know? Well, if you change your mind." Royce signaled for another old-fashioned. "We're having Japanese wagyu steaks, also oysters and Alaskan crab, fresh off the boat."

Adler made no sign any of Royce's enticements affected him, which Peyton knew Royce was privately judging.

"Have a drink, at least."

"Thank you, ma'am. I'm fine for now."

"Call me Royce, please. I'm tall and wide, but accessible."

"What business is that?" Mark asked.

Royce rolled her eyes. "I already told you. Peyton is pitching your hunting idea, remember?"

"Tonight?" Then focusing his attention on Adler, he said, "If I had known you'd ever agree to such a thing, I would've asked you myself, but I suppose coming from Peyton it meant more, eh?"

Adler smiled politely, but said nothing, which made Peyton cringe, though she hid it well.

Royce slapped Mark's elbow. "Do you ever listen? Just follow my lead."

"I love it when women order me around. Do it again…"

"Be at the library at eight and say yes to everything. Can you do that?" Royce asked Mark.

"You're still ordering me around." He plucked a joint from his case and lit it. "Anything for Peyton, who's luminous tonight." He gestured to Adler. "What's this man doing to you?"

"I'll see you soon, Uncle Mark. We'll go prepare now, Royce, if that's okay?"

"Do as you like, darling. I'll round them up and drive them at eight."

Mark said, "It's flattering when you treat your guests like cattle."

Royce punched his bony arm. "Only the icky rich ones."

Adler smirked. When a server offered him a canapé, he rejected it.

The library, with its redwood panels and green paisley rugs, was as Peyton had hoped. "Your taxidermist came through for us. This is impressive." She scrolled her hand over an ibex, assessing the others. The longer she touched and observed, the more wrong it felt. If she had been second guessing this venture, she now triple guessed it. Hunting was a way of life in the Southwest, but it wasn't her way. "Such beautiful animals. I don't mean to sound judgmental, but I couldn't shoot something this incredible."

"If we don't hunt some, more die of starvation in winter, and that's the real brutality. We hunt the few to spare the many."

Peyton knew the importance and benefits of hunting, but wished it wasn't necessary. She moved to a bighorn sheep and clasped its huge, curly horns. "Stunning."

He looked at her with camouflaged eyes. "As you can see, I brought Barbary sheep, pronghorn antelope, javelina, and oryx, but not bears or cougars. I chose not to."

"I'm pleased to hear you say that, because it's a sore point with me. You wouldn't want potential guests to think they'd be hunting predators on your watch. My sentiment as well."

His eyes showed admiration. "Right, not my style. For food, it's one thing."

In a small voice, she said, "I know your style. Just maybe."

He seemed touched, but his look didn't match what he said next. "This was a good idea. It's better to see these creatures up close and personal. They can't be appreciated in pictures or videos."

She liked the quiet, the aloneness, and hoped for a more intimate conversation. "I still have that slice of *tres leches* cake. It's dry by now, but I have it."

Voices drew close. Adler checked his watch. "It's time."

She noticed he wore an aviator watch, and realized she didn't know what he'd done in the military. "Jet fighter pilot?"

His face disclosed he loved her astuteness. "The watch is a gift from one. I'm too tall for a jet fighter pilot, though. Navy SEAL."

"Lieutenant?"

"Captain."

"I didn't realize you were an officer."

There was bite in his inflection. "There's a whole lot we don't know about each other, turns out."

Silence thickened. Peyton let it, tired of stoking the conversation, and used the time to read a text from Geraint, asking if she'd thought more about the art show. It only added to her apprehension about the hunt, though she was minutes away from pitching it.

"You studied art?"

"Yes. The program I attended was art history intensive. It helped me understand the correct feeling for every period. Did a semester in Florence to live at the Uffizi so-to-speak. I intended to return for a year, but that didn't happen."

"Why?"

Memories reeled as she recalled how she had nixed those plans when she met Ashton. He had filled her enough to turn a single room into the entire globe. "What did you study?"

"IT security." He locked eyes on her and exhaled. "I like to know the ins and outs. It's in my nature to learn what's worth protecting and what's not."

Peyton took it as a message. But the window for private conversation had closed as Royce entered the library with her herd.

"Here you are, my darling!" The queen of Abiquiú ushered in a string of guests. "This is Peyton Chase, daughter of Sorensen Chase and renowned painter Harlow Peyton."

Even now life put her on stilts, her mother's shadow grew longer. She didn't want to be Harlow's daughter—tonight, or any night.

"My darling girl," Royce said, "Allow me to introduce Jack Hemmings, James Lancaster, Henry Vacca, and Michael Suffield. Mark you know, and my special gift to you, Susan Penn, and—"

Before Royce could continue, a boy in a tiny tuxedo flew into the room, his legs spinning like tires. "Peyton, Peyton… I'm here!" William exclaimed.

"Oh my, don't you look handsome, sweetie. It's not a party without you." She gathered him into her arms. "Are you just about everywhere I am?" The longer she held him, the more she pined for a family of her own. Lexi's accusations about Margot revisited her. Maybe not becoming a mother had increased her attachment to her niece.

"Does this mean you already know Kelcy Loving?" Royce asked.

"Little lady," Kelcy said, smoking a cannon of a cigar. "Fancy seeing you here. You scrub up nice, unlike me. The more they soap me up, the uglier I get."

Peyton shook his hand warmly. "It's a small world." She kept William in her arms as she shook hands with the others.

Ashton strolled in, unnerving her, especially while she held a child in her arms. She refocused by rubbing the tip of William's nose, then put him down. "Ladies and gents, this is the talented Blake Adler, my partner." She drew a meaningful, deep look from him, but he said nothing. "Navy SEAL captain, entrepreneur, and avid hunter."

Murmurs and nods followed as the guests turned chipper, swaying among the taxidermy display. "What's this here?"

Peyton could feel Ashton boring into her. "It's what you can hunt guaranteed if you come to my house for a week's stay."

"What would something like that cost?" Kelcy asked.

"You big hick," Royce said. "You pay whatever Peyton charges you, and you pay it happily, you who belches dollars."

Kelcy grabbed his protruding belly and laughed like the Jolly Buddha.

Mark said, "The only reason I ever shot anything worthwhile is because of Adler. No one scouts like this man right here. On my own, forget it… grouse or pheasant maybe."

Peyton said, "The stay will be all-inclusive. Abiquiú doesn't hop with shops and gourmet restaurants, as you know. You'll get the works, including entertainment."

Ashton stood to the side, his arms crossed, his face wearing the disapproving look she knew too well.

Henry Vacca, a man with a long face and meaty shoulders, asked, "What happens after I shoot an oryx or a pronghorn?"

"We have a taxidermist lined up. The same guy who prepared these. Top of the line work, as you can see," Adler replied. "We won't wander aimlessly or leave you to freeze just waiting. I'll scout beforehand. By the time you show up, you'll get what you want."

"Adler identifies tracks, distance, and direction," Mark said.

Peyton paced between them. "If you want steaks, we'll also have a specialist who can package sous-vide and ship on ice."

"Working alone, Adler?" Mark asked.

"I'll have Joe, and depending on the size of the party, I may need one more sailor with a killer instinct. If I can convince him, that is."

"Who?" asked Kelcy.

"Willie BearClaw, lives in Utah."

"Don't tell me *the* Willie BearClaw who killed a mama bear without meaning to and raised her cub? He's a legend all the way down to Texas."

Adler replied, "That'll be the one, and that's not why his name is BearClaw. It really is his name."

"Imagine," Mark said.

Peyton interjected. "We'll transport you to the woods ourselves and provide everything you might desire, down to hot packs."

Susan Penn, a small woman with clipped copper hair, leather pants, and a snakeskin shirt, spoke with the raspy voice of a chain-smoker. "Would we cover lots of ground?"

"Into Colorado, if need be," Adler said. "I'll provide safety training, and weapons are available if you want to invite guests who don't own their own. If you can vouch for your guests, that'll be good enough for us."

Susan said, "I'll bring my truck and gear."

"We can accommodate most special requests," Peyton said. "The timetable is January through April, but all dates are predetermined. January is our biggest month. I brought pamphlets and we have a website accessible by password. This is a by invitation-only hunt." She grabbed a small stack of what looked like magazines rather than pamphlets and handed them out. The large glossy pages featured Abiquiú, the woods of Northern New Mexico and its animals, and Pioneer Ranch.

"Classy rooms," said James Lancaster. "If this is the view from your house, I'm inclined." He had dark circles around his eyes and pudgy cheeks, reminding Peyton of a racoon. "Towel warmer and freshly baked cookies before bed?"

Kelcy puffed his cigar and shook his head. "She'll tuck you in, too, Jamie, and sing you a lullaby."

Peyton snickered and held the centerfold open. "Pioneer Ranch dates back to when conquistadors were still populating the land with horses, since before *El Nuevo Mexicano* ever existed, never mind New Mexico."

"Is this a casita?" Kelcy asked.

"The oldest part of the property. Original and authentic."

"I want it. Doesn't need to have a towel warmer, but I'll take the cookies."

"First come, first served." Peyton gave the boy her hand. "If William isn't in school, he can come and learn to ride."

"I can ride," William said.

"A horse, boy, not a tricycle," his grandpa said. "What do you say, Tiger, want to visit Peyton at her house?"

William tugged at Peyton's dress. "Do you have ice cream at your house?"

Peyton got a great idea for Koda, who'd been angling for more money. "I have much more than that, William. I also have a riding instructor, and he's very nice."

"I want to see Peyton's house, Grandpa."

"What's the charge?" Kelcy asked.

Peyton quoted him twice Koda's usual rate. "Only thirty per hour. He's young, but he might as well be half horse. He's a proficient and safe rider, and he can teach adults as well."

Kelcy played with his chevron mustache. "Send me the dates, little lady, but on one condition." He made sure Peyton gave him her full attention. "I insist on a rematch with Layli Hoarnhorse. A serious one this time, with preprinted diagrams, a judge, and everything."

Susan Penn said, "Now, this is getting interesting. What match?"

"Archery," Peyton replied.

"I want in," she said. "I'd like to see a woman kick ass. Who's Layli Hoarnhorse?"

"Layli is stupendous," Mark replied. "I want in on the bet, too. We should make this ultra-interesting. Big money, like we did in Macau. Who's in?"

"Uncle Mark, what stakes are we talking about?"

He crossed his arms over his chest and puckered his lips as he cogitated. "From what I've seen, Layli is accurate, but uses a primitive bow, and isn't a hunter like Kelcy, who uses a sophisticated one. I'd say it's negative two hundred for Kelcy, so you'd have to spend two hundred dollars to win one hundred. And for Layli, it's a plus one hundred."

Peyton asked, "So to make a hundred, the bet must be for fifty bucks?"

"Precisely." He chuckled, waving his hand. "But no bet under twenty thousand. Otherwise, what's the fun in that?"

"Fifty thousand," said Kelcy, chewing his cigar. "To be fair, I'm betting on Layli, contributing at least that much to the pot."

"On Layli?" Peyton asked.

"Enough has to bet on her or it won't work. And I want to beat her fair and square."

"I want in," another said, "whether I come or not."

"I want ice cream," William said, making them laugh again. The five-year-old raised his arms, wanting to be picked up.

Peyton lifted him and ran fingers through his hair.

He placed his head on her shoulder and drooped. "You smell nice," he said, yawning. "Mama used to, too, before she went to heaven."

She brushed his bangs away from his eyes. "Maybe when you come over, I'll read to you." She couldn't help but glance at Ashton's frustrated face.

Royce drove the guests out, her eyes on Peyton. "Dinner is served in a few."

Ashton meandered her way, looking casual, but she knew better. "I run a multi-billion-dollar company, but you don't come to me for business advice?" The daggers he threw at Adler turned him into pure Navy SEAL.

"You know why I haven't."

Ashton stepped closer and leaned in. "We'll talk at dinner." He didn't acknowledge Adler, just tucked his hands in his pockets and started out.

Adler looked at her as if he had volumes to say. "I'll have all the taxidermy cleared out by tomorrow. Allen wants them back right away."

"I don't know how you convinced him to lend us these, but thank you. You were a great help. This wouldn't be possible without you. I'm more grateful than you know."

"It was nothing, Peyton."

She didn't like the atmosphere between them. It wasn't like before, and she didn't know how to fix it. "Adler…"

"What?"

She just looked at him with appealing eyes, her hand on the back of a Queen Ann chair.

He said, "I'd better turn in."

She stepped closer. "Where're you going? Talk to me. What's happening?"

"Do you have any friends who aren't loaded?"

"What's that got to do with anything?"

"Answer my question, please."

"I have Layli, Koda, Scarborough—"

"—no, they work for you. Got any friends?"

"They're family, and I work with—"

"—friends, friends, Peyton? Not colleagues or employees. Are any of your friends average folk?"

Peyton had many artist friends who struggled to make a go of their craft, but she wouldn't explain further. "That's unfair!"

"What's unfair is *this* situation."

"I don't understand."

"You have something with this guy, Ashton. I don't know what it is, and that's not all."

She hugged herself and rubbed her hands up and down her nude arms. "No. It was once something, but not now."

"I know what I saw, and it wasn't nothing. I'm not angry, just sad you're not ready for me." She tried to speak, but he held out a hand. "You said timing is everything. You're grieving, dealing with many changes right now, and I don't want you to toy with me."

She wrinkled her brow, and her nose burned. "I don't toy with you. Why are you saying that?"

"I know you're not doing it on purpose, but I want you to want me, not merely need me. Do you understand?"

"You're being hard on me, Blake."

He grew discomposed, but not displeased. "Look, right now I can't be sure if you want me for who I am, or whether you need me for your business or because you're undergoing so much. And you can't be sure whether I'm here because I'm a reliable, upstanding person, or because I have selfish motives."

"You're assuming a whole lot about me. I know what I want, and I think you do, too. We're not children here."

"How do you even know if I want you for you, or because you're out of my league?"

Peyton stepped back and hardened her face. "That's cruel!"

"I don't mean to be," he replied in a quieter tone.

"What do you mean?"

"Listen to me, please. After our deal is done, if you'll still look at me like you're looking at me now, I'll come to you. In the meantime, I'll do all I can to help you finish the hunting season successfully, but that's it."

"But. That's. It."

"Sometimes I say things the wrong way," he said. "Forgive me if I've hurt you. I just don't want any ambiguity between us."

"Oh, I'm pretty clear now. Thank you."

Royce's resonating voice reached them, thanking everyone for coming and letting them know dinner was served.

"You should go," he said. "A conversation with Ashton awaits you."

"For the record, I haven't misled you or misrepresented a thing. Not once." She lifted her dress and hustled out, wondering more than ever if the hunt was for her.

fifteen

Peyton stayed at the party just long enough to appease Royce and woke up the next morning with a headache. She took an ibuprofen and trudged to the coffeemaker, sure she was on the wrong path.

"Good morning, Peyton." Ricky was sitting at the kitchen table, his legs dangling.

"Good morning, guys."

"Tansy said to stay for breakfast, but she went somewhere," Ricky said.

"Ah…" Peyton wasn't sure whether having the boys there amid her trials had been such a good idea, then she remembered they were children without parents, and she was a well-to-do grown up. She'd have to help them. She had an income of her own and would never find herself with nowhere to go. Peyton gathered her hair into a messy bun with chopsticks. "How about a cowboy's breakfast?"

"Sausages, eggs, and cinnamon raisin toast?" asked Mikey.

"Pancakes with whipped cream?" asked Ricky.

"And buttermilk biscuits, boys, but first, the strongest cup of coffee I can make." She set up drip coffee and waited for it to brew, trying to ignore her headache. The boys looked bored as she made breakfast, listening to the howling of the wind. Out the window, a falcon gunned a pigeon, and clouds gathered on the horizon like rhinos ready to charge. "Looks real stormy," she said, piling scrambled eggs, sausages, beans and pancakes on two oblong plates.

"The oven beeped," said Ricky.

She took out the biscuits and buttered them while they were still piping hot. "Jam too?"

"Yes," Ricky whistled through his missing two front teeth. "That looks so good."

She brought the plates to the table. "Dig in, guys."

Layli came through the back door, humming.

"I made extra food in case you're hungry."

Layli put her hands on her hips when she saw the boys at the table. "What're you, hobbits? First you eat breakfast and then you ask for a second breakfast?"

Mikey laughed, lifting his head to the ceiling. "That was cereal, but *this* is breakfast."

"Uh-huh. Help Koda load up hay in the back of the truck when you're done eating. What do you say?"

"Looks like it'll be pouring soon, Layli. Better keep them inside for now."

"White woman, don't turn them into wussies afraid of rain."

Peyton gestured for Layli to move a healthy distance away from the kids, then said, "Two important things to share with you. I met a woman hunter last night." She snapped her fingers, goading her memory. "Susan Penn. She's psyched about you, especially when Kelcy asked for a rematch. She emailed asking about the bet."

"Teddy Roosevelt is coming here?"

"Oh yes, to put the record straight. He wants to beat you badly."

Layli flared her nostrils. "No mercy. I'll let it rip and see what he thinks then. Bring it on!" An impish glint sparkled in her dark eyes. "Wait, there's money involved?"

"Big money. We can clean up if you win."

Layli hopped from one foot to the other, as if warming up for a boxing match. "Like how much?"

"You're the underdog, so Mark gave you a plus one hundred for odds, meaning if we bet fifty thousand dollars, we'll double it."

Layli slackened her jaw and expanded her eyes as wide as she could "What, fifty big ones? I thought maybe like a thousand."

"No… Fifty thousand is the minimum bet."

"I gotta sit down for this." Layli pulled out a chair and sat with her knees apart, her fingers spread on them. "So Kelcy is expected to win?"

Peyton pulled down the corners of her mouth and bobbed her head. "They know his abilities, but not yours, and Mark took your bow into consideration. But Kelcy is betting on you to make the match happen."

Layli came to her feet. "My people fed entire tribes and held back redcoats and bluecoats with those weapons!" Stands-with-a-Bow made a fist. "I'll show them."

"Well, I'm glad you feel that way because I'm plunking two-thirds of my nest-egg on you."

"What?" Layli sat back down. "Wow… Why? To save the ranch?"

"I can't save the ranch with so little money, but I'm aiming to raise more to add to the sale of my house in Mendocino. Just don't know how else to pay Lexi." Peyton leaned against the marble counter. "I called Uncle Mark for an update. He suggested I at least get the house priced. So, I checked out recently sold houses in Mendocino. I'd have to risk money out of my savings to raise a full million, since I'll have to pay the realtor, too."

Layli loosened her jaw and softened her gaze. "Sell your house, for sure?"

Peyton played with her nails. "Uncle Mark said from the expert reports and Lexi's deposition, things look ominous. Let's just hope I won't have to sell the ranch, too, which brings me to my next point. Can we make enough money from this hunt to justify it? You were waiting for the rest of the entertainers. Did you hear from the falconer and fiddler yesterday?"

"Yes, finally, and they're way too expensive. To put on a posh hunt with entertainment and gourmet meals, the profit will be slim."

Relief washed over her. No hunting beautiful wild animals. No disrespecting the history and legacy of her estate by treating it like a hotel. Now she'd have to admit that letting Geraint exhibit her work was her only possible hope of saving the ranch. "I'm ditching the hunt idea," she said, unpacking her spine. "But I'm going to push the competition between you and Kelcy, so maybe we can win some money."

"I'm ecstatic that I don't have to turn this historic house into a B&B, but did you say *we*? I don't have fifty thousand dollars." She watched the boys reach for second helpings of sausages and pancakes.

Peyton winked. "If you can double the money I've saved over the past ten years in a single day, I can at least pay you a commission."

"If you can keep me in my cabin, in the lifestyle I've grown to love, you don't need to do anything else," Layli said, squeezing her arm.

Peyton grabbed her phone and scrolled through her call history.

"What're you doing?"

"Calling Adler to let him know I'm scrapping the hunt." She hustled to the hallway with a pounding heart. Why didn't he pick up? She left him a message informing him of her decision and asking him to call her back with questions, though she didn't think there'd be any.

The doorbell rang, and they heard Royce calling "yoohoo," as she always did when she let herself in through the front door.

Layli said, "The boys don't look done yet."

"I'll make sure they're all set with something entertaining. No worries."

Layli nodded, and vamoosed, leaving them to visit alone.

"We're in the kitchen," Peyton called.

Royce appeared in a tracksuit wearing her habitual false eyelashes and bright lipstick, and carrying a teacup piglet wrapped in a blanket. "I had to hurry before it rains."

The boys giggled at another woman avoiding the rain, their cheeks inflated with food.

"Who're you?" she asked them.

"Who're *you?*" Ricky asked.

"I'm Royce, and you?"

"The boys are my guests. This is Mikey who loves to run, and this is Ricky who doesn't."

"I'm with Ricky on that one."

Mikey said, "But you're wearing a tracksuit!"

"Real runners don't wear tracksuits. They were made for people who pretend to run but eat pasta and meatballs instead. Didn't you see *Goodfellas?* Of course not. What're you, like eight and ten?"

"Seven and nine," Peyton replied.

"Oh, perfect age for learning the piano."

"Why, you play?" Ricky asked, then immediately followed with a dismissive, "Nah…"

Royce gave him a bug-eyed look with prissy lips. "What're you saying there? I don't impress you much?"

"Is this really a pig?" Ricky came over to pet it. "It's so eency weency."

Royce held her pig as if it was a newborn. "Isn't she cute? She's a birthday gift. I named her Colossal."

Ricky tucked his chin until his neck disappeared. "Colossal? But she's tiny!"

"You name them based on your aspirations for them, kid."

"Why is your name Royce? Not like a Rolls Royce, is it?" Ricky asked.

She stabbed her jeweled fingers his way. "You underestimate me one more time, you little twerp, and I'll feed you to my pig."

Ricky laughed and attempted to retort, but Peyton wagged her finger. "You'll lose this argument, trust me. Royce, want some breakfast?"

"Maybe a little something for Colossal." She made a distorted face. "But not sausage, you know."

"I'll get coffee for us and pancakes for Colossal. Ever read the book *If You Give a Pig a Pancake?*"

Royce frowned. "No, and I don't care to. Sit with me. I have something to speak to you about."

"Peyton, we're done eating. Can we play pool?" Ricky asked.

Mikey shoved his brother. "Layli said not to ask about that. We should be ambassadors, not *ambarassers* of our people!"

"Mikey, ambarassers is not a word," Peyton said, "but use your words only, not your fists, and Ricky, I don't think you're tall enough to play pool, but you can play foosball in there, and cards."

Ricky stuck his tongue out at his brother. "See?"

"In a while, I'll bake chocolate chip cookies for a snack and make hot chocolate." Thunder boomed. Rain clashed over the landscape, slapping against the windows and doors. The boys slunk out of their chairs. As they scuttled away, Peyton yelled loudly enough for them to hear, "No racing or shouting, all right?"

"You sound like a mother of a whole brood. When did this happen? Have I been in a coma?"

Peyton cracked up and gave the pig pieces of pancakes to nibble. "Colossal will become gigantic, you know."

"Who cares? Just sit for now."

Peyton brought two cups of coffee and sat at the table. "Your party was phenomenal, and what you did for me was a miracle, but I can't go through with it."

"Why? Everyone was psyched about it."

"The math doesn't add up, and my heart isn't in it. It would be hard enough to make it work if I had a passion for it, but I feel the opposite."

"Hmm. I'll circle back to this. First, tell me, why did you leave before breakfast?"

Peyton didn't see the point of bringing up Adler. "I was just tired, that's all. But shouldn't you be sleeping?"

"Stayed up too late, then I got talking with Ashton. He's like a horse whisperer, so charming."

"He's charming, I give you that, but he's no horse whisperer. What did he tell you?"

"He told me what you're not letting him tell you. He's getting divorced, looking to buy a house in Santa Fe to be closer—panoramic views for the gods. Showed me pictures, and he wants kids now."

Peyton didn't buy any of it. "He lives in California, and I don't believe he'll ever get divorced. When big money marries bigger money, marriages last, and as far as kids go, he won't make a good father if he doesn't want them for himself, and he doesn't."

"You sure aren't making it easier. Have you seen those genes? Of course, you have… looks to die for, breeding, style, education, culture, I can go on and on. He's a catch."

"Is he the reason you're here?"

"Well, I did come with a purpose."

Peyton sipped sweet coffee, her eyes transfixed on Royce.

"I saw how you were looking at your hunter buddy. Came to get the dish on him."

"Honestly, nothing to tell."

"I'm an old lady in a tracksuit with a pig for a pet. Who're you kidding?"

Peyton got up and plopped a kiss on Royce's cheek. "I just love you and your suspicions to pieces, but there's no juicy story to tell."

"Like there wasn't one with Ashton, who'll slip through your fingers and into the grasp of someone less worthy."

"Okay, this is the I'm-worried-about-you talk. I'm fine."

Royce shifted her chair forward, as if about to litigate. "Hmm, but this guy is dry and stiff."

"Adler?"

"Who else?"

"No, he's not like that."

"And you say there's nothing going on. Puhleeze!"

Peyton went to the cupboard and took out a box of biscochito cookies. "Good with coffee. Have one."

Royce squinted. "Stuff your words, Royce? Is that what you're saying?"

"Why are you concerned? Let's say Adler is in my bed right now. Why do you care?"

Royce's jaw dropped. "No, he can't be! … Is he?"

"No, he's not, but what's the big deal? He's a fascinating man, in fact. Honorable."

Royce made circles with her hand, jiggling her bracelets. "Well, he's not Ashton, you know, not of your class."

"We believe in classes now?" Peyton ate a cookie, chewing fast.

"I didn't until my goddaughter got mixed up with someone who smiles little, refuses good hospitality, has no charm and no panache, and frankly, shows disdain for our lifestyle. Uh-uh, don't even think of defending this point. I could read it all over him last night."

"He's authentic, kind, and respectable."

"Oh no, I'm too late, aren't I? You already slept with him!"

Peyton cackled and bent a leg, resting her heel on the seat of her chair.

"If it's only sex, who can blame you? He sizzles, but don't get involved."

"Seriously, Royce? I don't do casual relationships."

"He could be after your money!"

"Money? He drives expensive cars, lives in a delightful cabin on hundreds of acres. Okay, I'll admit I looked up his address in Chama. He carries expensive gear and weapons. I don't think he needs anything from me."

"I think he needs *all* of you, in fact… and… seems like you're stalking him. Are you?"

Peyton knew Royce was kidding. She laced her fingers and stretched her arms over her head. "Well, I like him. I want to understand him better, but don't worry, he's not interested."

"What, not interested in you? How dare he?" Royce raised her voice, spooking her pig. "Now, I really hate him!"

"I don't want you to dislike him. Please, don't."

"My girl, you're preoccupied with the wrong man. Ashton is gallant, not judgmental. He's like that thunder outside."

Peyton's mind kited to the Mark Twain quote on the bookmark she'd found in her father's study. "Funny you should say that because 'thunder is good, thunder is impressive; but it is lightning that does the work.'"

"Is this a quote?"

"It's Dad's message to me from the grave."

Royce looked horrified. "What are you on? Did Mark give you something? Strange boys in your kitchen, a strange man in your bed, and now messages from the beyond?"

Peyton rolled in her seat, clutching her knee to her chest, laughing until tears trundled down her cheeks. "I swear, you're the funniest person alive, Royce."

"Honey, I just don't want to see you get hurt."

Peyton stopped laughing. "This life I lead isn't likely to hurt me in the ways you imagine. I may have missed the boat on having a family, but…" She reached over and squeezed Royce's arm. "I have a magnificent support system, and a career I enjoy, though I always find a pile of laundry when I return to it, and I'll find another one when I get back from Salt Lake City."

"Salt Lake City?" Royce ran a finger between the piglet's ears.

"Yeah, next week, a big job for a private collector. I'll be gone a while, especially since I'm going to Mendocino first for five days."

"Sightseeing? You should."

Peyton shrugged. "I want to see Ambrosia, the old cook I mentioned to you at Dad's funeral. I have some questions I'm hoping she can answer."

"And Ashton?"

"Right now, my focus is on saving the estate and not screwing it up. If I don't, I'll be the one who didn't live up to the family name. The only

Chase who let down the people depending on her."

"So, what'll you do now? What's the plan?"

Peyton braced for what she was about to say. She knew once Royce learned of it, she'd be relentless in pushing her to do it. "Okay, here it is, and don't kill me. Understand I've struggled in this area for years and continue to hemorrhage from it."

Royce's sassy face slacked. She placed the sleeping pig on her lap, freeing her hands. "I know this face. I'm listening."

"You remember, I'm sure, that I used to paint with Mom. I was a kid but showed promise. At least Dad thought I did."

Royce nodded and leaned forward, her hands in the air, as if preparing to catch a child falling from a window.

"I returned to painting five years ago. I didn't think the works were worth showcasing, but an art dealer friend of mine thinks some of them are."

Royce glued her palms together, wide eyed with excitement. "Harlow's paintings are mostly in the six digits. This might be the answer!"

"Hold your horses. Mom spent years building up to that level, which her premature death hastened. I'm a nobody."

"You're Harlow's daughter!"

Will everyone see me this way forever? Peyton teared up. "If that's all the critics say about my work, I'll have failed miserably."

"But why?"

"Because I'm *Peyton* Chase! Not Harlow. Not Sorensen. *Peyton*!" She realized she was yelling and apologized, horrified at her reaction.

Royce did something Peyton would never have expected. She clapped. Then clapped some more, nodding her head, and grinning wide. "I've been waiting for you to say that." She kept on clapping, brimming with pride, making Peyton cry again. "Bravo, Peyton. Bravo!"

Peyton dabbed at her face with a napkin. "Why didn't you confront me about it before?"

"If you want to feed a frightened kitten hiding in a hole, it's best to leave the food and take off. I didn't leave, but I knew you'd come out when you were starved enough."

"And now I'm starved enough?"

"Of course, honey. Sorensen is gone. Your paintings are gone. You clearly could never replace Ashton. Your estate, your very legacy, is in jeopardy. And when you picked up William, I saw how much you yearned to be a mother. So, I wasn't at all surprised to find children in your kitchen on the very next day."

In a flash, Peyton went from crying to giggling. "Thank you for always soothing me and making me laugh."

"Good. Remember that when I'm old and infirm."

Peyton hugged her. "Thank God for you. If Mom hadn't died, I wouldn't have benefited so much from your guidance and wisdom... or laughed so much."

"You're the daughter I never had. We're even. Now, when is the show going to be?"

"I know I should let Geraint give me a show. But it's the quagmire of my life."

Royce raised an eyebrow and batted her curly lashes. "Is the kitten going back into her hole?"

Peyton exhaled long and hard. "I'm no kitten, Royce. Not at thirty-three."

Peyton was in yoga pants and an athletic top, with chopsticks in her messy bun, mixing cookie batter when Adler called, asking if she'd see him for five minutes. She wasn't ready to face him again so soon.

"I'll need to finish what I'm doing and throw on some jeans. Can you give me thirty minutes?"

"I would," he said, "but I'm dripping wet, standing outside your door. I can go back to my truck and wait in it, I guess."

Peyton walked to the back door and saw him standing outside with his phone in his hand, sodden, unshaven, and tired looking. She hung up, crossed to the mudroom and grabbed a clean towel for him. "That was manipulative," she said, letting him in and handing him the towel. "I would never let you sit in your truck, wet and waiting."

"I know, my bad, but I needed to see you."

He followed her into the kitchen. She was embarrassed that he'd caught her a mess without makeup and was surprised at the way he looked at her. "I'm in the middle of baking cookies, but sit down. I'll pop on the kettle. It's raining sheets out there. You can use something hot."

"I'm sorry about last night. I have a way of saying it as I see it. It can be mean, though I don't intend it to be."

"I have Irish Breakfast, Oolong, and Darjeeling. Preference?"

"Anything not fruity, anything strong. Thank you."

"I like the idea of the competition, but unless enough people bet on Layli, it won't work."

"You have no reply, Peyton?"

She faced him, resolute but soft. "I hold no ill will. You spoke your truth, and that was that."

He hung his head as she handed him a mug of Darjeeling tea. "With lots of sugar."

"How did you know?"

"I remember how you take your coffee. You take your drinks like I take mine, Adler."

"Did you cancel the hunt because of what I said? I don't want to come between you and your solution. I promise to come through for you if you want to change your mind."

She appreciated his concern, and made sure her face showed it, though his words from the night before made her feel that a piece of the puzzle didn't quite fit. "I was never onboard with the idea. It's not who I am. I picture guests dirtying my carpets and smoking indoors, and I get repulsed."

"Was it because of Ashton's counsel?"

She was surprised he brought up Ashton, and wondered if he had regrets. "The math proves he's right, but this is about what feels like the correct solution. The archery competition will be for one day, held outdoors, with a potential boon. Good for the ranch even. Are you planning on betting?"

He looked at her as if her question was a double entendre.

The sound of pitter-pattering feet was followed by two boys who could eat more than grown men. "Cookies ready yet?"

"They'll be ready in a short while, Ricky. I promise I'll come get you."

Mikey stared at the new guest. "Are you like Indiana Jones? I see you on adventures and stuff."

"What do you mean, you *see* me?" Adler asked, but Mikey didn't reply.

Ricky chimed in. "Do you have a whip?"

The kids made him laugh. "I'm Adler. Not as exciting as Indiana Jones, but I'm messy enough to look the part."

"Are you staying for cookies?" Ricky asked. "Peyton said we'll have hot chocolate, too, maybe help in the garden after it dries up."

"That reminds me." Adler fished an envelope from the inside pocket of his raincoat. "Seeds for your garden. Father Gabriel asked me to give them to you when I told him about your project."

"How nice, but that also reminds *me*. Hey, Mikey, what did Father Gabriel say about Grandma yesterday? What's the update?"

"He just asked if we're okay staying here longer."

With his fingers and chin on the kitchen counter next to the cookie dough bowl, Ricky reminded Peyton of a puppy. "I could stay here forever."

Peyton fluffed his hair. "Adler, do you know what happened to Father Gabriel's car?"

"That was no car. More like a big roller skate. I gave him a truck. He's all set now."

"*Gave* him one?"

"My dad passed away a year back, left behind a truck with only fourteen thousand miles on it. It's just been sitting in the garage. Now it's on the road again."

"Oh, I'm sorry. Neither of us has our fathers, yet we're not that old." Peyton scooped dough in a clump and placed it on a cookie sheet.

"Or our mothers."

She gave him a look of recognition. "That was seriously generous of you."

"So, guys, how do you know Peyton?"

Mikey played with his faded blue mohawk. "Grandma died. Father Gabriel sent us here."

"Honey, your grandma is not dead. She's in the hospital."

He pulled at his earlobe. "She told me she was dead, that we should stay here, but she was an owl when she said it."

Peyton tilted her head. "Was this a dream?"

"I don't think so."

Adler gave her a look that said, *don't ask questions.* And she didn't.

"Can we call Grandma?" Ricky asked.

Adler dialed Father Gabriel. "Let's see." After a quick hello, he explained that the boys wanted to speak to their grandmother. The longer he listened, the paler he grew. He thanked the friar and hung up. "Father Gabriel is on his way here," he said. "Peyton, can I talk to you in the mudroom?"

"Boys, wash your hands and take a seat. Cookies will be ready soon." She followed him into the next room. "It's bad, isn't it?"

"That boy might be a seer. He's right. His grandmother has… you know… walked on."

Peyton brought a hand to her mouth and placed the other on her belly. She knew what it was like to lose a loved one in childhood. But the brothers were orphans. They'd had no family but their grandmother. "Father Gabriel is coming to explain it to them, I hope?"

"Precisely."

"Thank you."

"For what?"

"For being here." She rubbed her face as if she were clearing away cobwebs.

"I'd like to check with you later. Is that okay?"

"Adler, friends check on friends."

He looked at her tenderly. "At least you know I'm your friend."

"Yes, of course."

He seemed as if he were debating whether to say something else.

"Whatever it is, ask."

He played with his wet hat, spinning it. "Did you ever consider that God took your mother early so you could paint?"

She'd never thought of that. "What?"

"I'm not saying God took her on purpose, more like it was her time, but her talent wasn't wasted because it lives on in her daughter. Her talented, capable daughter."

His comment confirmed that the divine intervention she'd asked for had been granted a long time ago. She wasn't sure if she wanted to laugh with joy, cry, or kiss him. "That might be the most impactful thing anyone could say to me right now." She stared at him, emotions crushing her. Three words solidified in her mind: But. That's. It.

"What'll happen to the boys?"

"I don't even know what'll happen to me, never mind them. But I want to help them."

"Are you scared?"

There was intimacy in his voice. She feared getting tugged away, only to be marooned again. "I'm not frightened. I'm terrified."

He held her gaze, analyzing. She thought he might hug her. "I don't say this lightly. I'm here, Peyton."

"I take you at your word. Wish you'd take me at mine."

sixteen

When Layli arrived, Peyton and Father Gabriel were soothing the boys. Ricky's sobs interrupted the crackling fire. Mikey sat upright on a loveseat.

Layli's voice fluttered like moth wings. "They are not dead who live in the hearts they leave behind."

Ricky sobbed harder, and the friar handed him more tissues.

Mikey said, "I know Grandma started her walk."

"Is that why you're not crying, honey?" Peyton asked. "It's all right to cry, you know."

"Grandma used to tell me our best teacher is our heart. I saw her. She's young again, no more pain. She's free. Why would I cry about that?"

Peyton thought of the days and nights she'd spent weeping when her mother died, though some of her tears were from guilt and confusion. She was filled with admiration for this gaunt boy with a blue mohawk. "I wouldn't cry either if I knew what you know, but sometimes we miss a person we love." She brushed Ricky's hair back, soothing him. "Why don't you guys watch a movie in the family room? We'll come check on you in a while. Maybe we can have pizza for lunch?"

"I love pizza," said Ricky, tearful.

"It's settled then," Layli replied, weeping with him.

"Can I paint?"

"Well, Mikey, this is the perfect house for art." Peyton smiled at them with the fondness of the mother she wished she was. "I have pretty much everything. Come, I'll set you up in the family room with watercolors, charcoal, crayons, and art paper. Cool?" She saw how drained Ricky looked. "There's a cozy throw on the sofa in there. If I were you, I'd take a nap on this gloomy day, and I'll wake you up for pizza."

Peyton squatted beside Mikey, who sat on a stool by the window facing an easel. "Mikey, when I first met you, you said something interesting to me, but I'm not sure I understood it."

He picked up a piece of charcoal and drew a horizon.

"Why did you tell me I was stuck because she was? Who were you talking about?"

"Your name is Peyton," Mikey replied, then dipped a brush in water and lifted the lid of the watercolor box.

"Uh-huh."

"Paint… paintin'… Peyton."

Tingles prickled her skin. She sat back, her palms pressed to the hardwood floor as if she'd been pushed down. Her mother had named her, not her father. She had given her daughter her maiden name as a reminder of her lineage, but now Peyton saw deeper meaning, thanks to Mikey's insight.

"Names tell a lot about a person, don't they?" She felt like hugging him, but knew he wasn't open to it. "Thank you, Strong Deer, or should I say Honovi?"

Mikey sliced a faint smile and swished the wet brush over blue paint.

"Would you like to live here, honey?" She asked Ricky the same question.

"I see us here," Mikey replied.

"I love it here, but I miss Grandma so much," Ricky sobbed again, springing Peyton off the floor. She hugged him and kissed the top of his head. "I have to go speak to Father Gabriel and Layli, but I'll be back, okay?"

Peyton traversed the vast hallway, leading to the great room with its considerable kiva fireplace and thirty-foot ceiling. The walls were white-washed and Southwestern textiles and vibrant artwork brightened the room, but today it felt gloomy and sedate. She sat by the fireplace, seeking its warmth. "What will happen to them if they can't stay here?"

Father Gabriel counted his rosary beads, sadness drooping his cheeks. "They'll be put in foster care. The state will prefer someone Native as their caretaker. It will be hard for me to monitor them if they're placed far away, and I don't want them at an orphanage."

Layli asked, "Will it be all right, Peyton, if Koda were to stay with you pretty much permanently?"

"Since he's moved in, I've hardly felt it. He's up at dawn, returns basically at dusk, but when I see him, he's pure joy. He often eats dinner here, anyway. Koda is not an issue. I like knowing someone else breathes in this house."

Layli said, "I'm Puebloan, granted, but why would the state let the boys live here?"

"You're the best choice," said Father Gabriel. "They've been happy here. And look at where you live. You raised your brother, so we know you can parent, and if they stay here, they can continue to go to the same school and attend my church. I'll write you a stellar recommendation."

Peyton said, "No pressure at all, Layli, but there's no legal paperwork Uncle Mark can't push. I'll help with everything. I'm planning on requesting more commissions sent to me, no matter where we end up living. You have my backing, and my financial and practical support, regardless. I wish I could be named guardian, but the state won't allow it."

Layli nodded, focused. "So, we're agreeing on at least fifteen years of rearing?"

Peyton replied, "Of course. It'll take all of us."

"Let us pray on it." Father Gabriel got on his knees with them and led them in a long prayer. When he finished, he looked at Peyton. "Has God answered you yet?"

She laughed louder than she meant to. "I wish God talked to me promptly, Father."

"I think he did when you first accepted these boys. A part of us knew it was a one-way ticket," he replied, moving closer to the fire and shoving a pillow behind his lower back.

"Maybe I'm crazy, maybe I miss my brother being a kid, or maybe the boys are a blessing. They should stay."

Peyton nodded. "Feels right. We have the room and the resources. Father, what about the funeral?"

"A small life insurance policy covers what'll basically be a hole in the ground." He puffed his cheeks before adding, "There's the issue of her belongings. The house was rented. We'll have to clear it out."

Peyton made a list on her phone. "We have men, and we have trucks. We'll take the boys to their grandmother's place so they can get whatever they want. That's no biggie, and I'll speak to my lawyer about social services." Peyton concealed her ulterior motive for speaking to Mr. Jennings. It was about time she pressed him again on Recipient One.

Layli pulled her hair to one side and braided it. "I'll go tell them."

"No, wait, we'll tell them together, since they'll have two guardians." Peyton froze, sculpted in a lightbulb moment. "I'm someone's guardian?" She wanted a child of her own, a baby with Ashton. The boys were well beyond the age of being babied, and not Ashton's, but her instinct was to shelter the brothers and see them through.

After seeing the friar to the door and loading him up with sourdough bread, lamb stew and cherry pie, Peyton knew she could no longer avoid looking into the abyss.

Mikey came to see her holding a small canvas. The way he stood in the doorway, not entering until she invited him in, made her say, "You and Ricky are always welcome. Unless a door in this house is closed, in which case, please knock, you're always welcome to move about as you please. This is your home, too."

Mikey moved closer and handed her his painting. She took one look at it, then back at him, astounded at his artistry. "And you're only nine years old? Honey, this is mature work. You delineate well, there's an abstract touch, yet clarity and vibrancy. Hold the brush with less tension, though, and consider breaking up some of your blues with yellows, but this is fantastic. I'll show you a technique for reducing back-runs and how not to lose luminosity, if you want."

He nodded. "Can I also use oil paints?"

"We'll get some, and you have to show me everything you create, okay? Now, who's this, and why is she holding shards of glass?"

"It's you, and for you," he said, then left.

Peyton's enthusiasm was replaced by a different perspective. She was no longer critiquing his skillfulness, but entranced by the depiction. She stared at the painting, dissecting it, until Layli joined her and stood over her shoulder.

"Did Mikey do this?"

"I wonder why he depicted me squeezing shards but suffering no injury."

"He'd better make one for me, too," Layli said. "Come on, it's just a painting."

"Artists put pieces of their souls in their works, and sometimes they also incorporate pieces from the souls of others. Art is the other church."

"So, what does it mean?"

Peyton was sure what it meant. "Hmm... I need to put down those shards or use them."

"How?"

Peyton called Geraint and put him on speaker. She signaled for Layli to wait a minute. When he answered, she asked, "When do you want my paintings?" She giggled when he fired off a cheer.

"Drive-thru speed, deary."

Layli gave her an intense, quizzical look, but Peyton held up a finger.

"I'll have to clear three rooms for you, and I want to hype it—a lot! Autumn till Christmas is peak season, and I want cocktails under the stars because of all your outdoor themes, so let's shoot for the first Saturday in October."

She could hear him clicking on his keyboard. "That's less than three months away."

"This way, if we need to delay, we'll be running into November, my second-best month of the year."

"I was thinking I'd ship them to you next week while I'm in Mendocino, or is that too soon?"

"What?" Layli mouthed and punched her in the arm.

"Not at all," he replied. "I want to study them more so I can figure out how to present them and arrange a couple of friendly reviews. A blurb in *The Los Angeles Times* before the opening will do us a world of good. We need the rest of the summer. We'll video conference when you get to your house. Decide together."

"Thank you, Geraint. You don't know how much this means to me."

"It means a lot to me to get back some of the money I've been paying you for years. It's about time you paid me!"

Peyton laughed and hung up.

"I couldn't have heard right," Layli said. "You've been painting?"

"Yes. Geraint is willing to take a chance on me in October." Peyton clasped her fingers into a ball, scared of facing what she dreaded most.

Layli shook her head, as if flicking something out of her brain. "Start at the beginning. And why aren't you jumping up and down?"

"The abridged version is Geraint found out I've been painting and offered to exhibit my work. If I didn't have to save the ranch, I'd be too afraid to expose myself to ridicule."

"Ridicule?"

All Peyton could see was the painting she'd stolen, the portrait of her with what she saw as egg, not paint, on her face. "I feel like an imposter, and now the whole world will see it."

"What? Feeling like an imposter is not the same as *being* one." She waited until Peyton sat down and stacked one stockinged foot over the other. "I'm assuming you didn't tell me you've been painting because you didn't think yours are good enough. Is that it?"

Peyton's eyes filled with tears. "Right now, I'm the talented, successful art restorer. If my paintings don't sell, and the critics descend on me harshly, I'll lose the ranch. On top of it, people will look at me as the artist who restores other people's paintings because she can't produce anything decent of her own." She saw Layli's skeptical face, and added, "Even if that's not what they end up thinking, I'll interpret any strange looks that way." Her chest heaved and her temperature rose. "I'm forced to put everything important on the line: my ranch, my house, and my reputation. Only *The Last Start* is still safe. Thank God for that."

seventeen

Ricky stood in the cabin doorway, pronating his feet. His shirt fit him like a sausage casing. "I hate trying on clothes. Most itch."

Peyton was sitting in the car with the door open. "I promise it won't take long, and Santa Fe is beautiful. You need proper clothes for Grandma's funeral. Don't you want cool clothes for when you go back to school?"

With pouty lips, Ricky sunk into his spine, not budging.

"If you're cooperative, we'll get burgers and fries for dinner, and a new storybook."

"You'll read it to me?"

"I can try, if you try now."

A glint of assent flickered in his eyes, and he shuffled to the car, joining Mikey, who was in the back seat playing a video game on the tablet Peyton had given him. She drove down scenic Route 84 to a store she'd liked as a child.

"Have you ever been to Santa Fe?" she asked, eyeing them through the rearview mirror.

"Isn't Santa Fe in Arizona?" Mikey asked, his head in his game.

"No, it's about an hour south of here. Well, Santa Fe is gorgeous. Got restaurants, boutiques, amazing art galleries, cathedrals, beautiful architecture, and the best Georgia O'Keeffe museum."

"Who's Georgia O'Keeffe?"

"Are you kidding me, Ricky? She's the famous painter who lived at Ghost Ranch right here in Abiquiú. The Tourist Center is named after her."

He looked away and rested his head against the window.

"Would you like to visit her museum? If we shop quickly, we can go."

Mikey asked, "Is she the one who paints skulls and music and stuff?"

"It's exciting you should know that. She also painted animal carcasses, macro flowers, and landscapes."

"I'd like to see what music looks like," Ricky said.

"We'll try to go then, but I have to stop and see my lawyer first."

"What's a lawyer?"

"A man who gets you out of jail, dummy," Mikey replied.

"Are you going to jail, Peyton?"

She chortled, looking at him in the rearview mirror. "No one is going to jail, honey. He's a different kind of lawyer, and Mikey, don't call your brother names. You need to look after each other, always."

For the first time in days, Ricky smiled.

Everything the boys needed was in a single section of the store, so shopping was painless.

Mr. Jennings's office was in a traditional adobe building, with walls three-bricks thick, arched doors, and notched, exposed logs. He met them at the door wearing a three-piece suit and wingtips. "You look well, Ms. Chase," he said, shaking her hand. He smiled at the boys and asked if they'd like something to drink.

"Juice, please, for Mikey and Ricky, if you have it. They're my buddies."

She left the boys to hydrate in the reception area and joined Mr. Jennings in his office.

"I have two items on the agenda," Peyton said, nestled in a leather chair with a tufted backrest. "I'd like to know about Recipient One. Who's that?"

Mr. Jennings slipped on his reading glasses and pulled up a file on his screen. "I think you know that Ambrosia Yazzie is the other recipient. She gets an annuity, but the rest I can't disclose. However, when the recipients expire, all the benefits revert to you."

"Come on, Mr. Jennings, who's the other recipient?"

He gave her a stern look from above his glasses. "What's the next item on your agenda?"

"Well, if you can't tell me because of confidentiality laws, who can?"

"Ms. Chase—"

"—Uncle Mark, perhaps? Someone must tell me. Who?"

"If you were my daughter, I'd tell you to let it go. Let sleeping dogs lie. No good can come from this digging. Move on. Let the past be the past."

Peyton shook her foot. Not dealing with the past that was constantly in her present was why she jeopardized her future. She was done running away from zombies. "I want to keep those boys on the ranch, officially under Layli Hoarnhorse's guardianship. They've been recently orphaned and need fostering. I'll be just as responsible for them, though Layli should be listed as their primary guardian since she's Native and I'm not."

"You're sure you want this trouble? They're little. They'll need a house-ful of money."

Peyton clasped her hands over her knee without replying.

"Okay, we'll fill out everything for you and arrange for an inspection from Social Services as a formality. They'll be glad you already found a suit-able home for them. If Mark can make a couple of calls, the whole affair will be settled by Halloween."

She took a mint from the bowl on his desk. "There's nothing you can't do. I'm grateful."

"You might not be when you get my bill. In the meantime, I'll email you questions and go from there." He offered her more candy. She took chocolate truffles for the boys.

"Where are you off to next?" he asked.

"The O'Keeffe Museum, but that's mostly for me, then the best burger joint in town."

"Art and burgers? Can I come?" He sighed with envy and escorted her out. "Those are some lucky boys."

She thought of Mikey's transcendental insights and Ricky's sweetness. "It's a two-way street."

Peyton brought the kids back to Layli's cabin with new clothes, shoes, and school supplies. The funeral was a couple of days out, but Layli had prepared them, explaining about the rituals and chants.

"I'd say you're spoiling them," Layli said, as she helped carry packages into her cabin, "except they have nothing, so you're not."

"Their clothes are too small, their shoes are ripped. Everything I bought them, they need, but the O'Keeffe Museum was an indulgence."

"Weren't they bored?"

"Mikey has my genes. Ate it all up. Ricky just tagged along. He's too young still, adorable, but so sad."

Layli pulled items from the bags, grouping them into categories. "They listen, I must say. I couldn't do it otherwise. Scarborough hasn't complained. Calls Mikey 'locomotive.'"

"He told me they took to Koda."

"Koda as a role model. Who knew? They should be given work and responsibility. It's good for them to feel needed, I think."

"Not too much. They should study and play, mostly." Peyton bounced her car keys. "They've had their dinners. Ice cream, too."

"I know you want them to like you, but stop giving them all the junk they ask for. They should eat what we eat."

Peyton nodded. "You're right. They're no longer visitors, and I have many years to catch them up." She angled her body toward the front door. "It's been a good day, considering two boys tagged along."

"Then why do you look frazzled?"

"You read me too well, you!" She snickered, but soon her face fell. She'd searched everywhere for Sorensen's missing letters, but never found them. "Some of what Mr. Jennings disclosed, without actually disclosing anything, gnaws at me. I opened a can of worms, and I just know something horrible is awaiting me. I feel it in my gut." She exhaled, steadying her nerves. "Anyhow, it's almost bedtime. The boys shouldn't need much more than showers."

"I'll give them five minutes before they tell me they're starving. I don't know where Mikey puts it. He eats like Henry VIII but looks like Oliver Twist."

"I'm gonna skedaddle, take Lightning out for a quick ride. Gotta talk to a horse about a man."

Layli frowned, confused, but figured it out. "Oh, you finally named the Appaloosa. Whatever happened to the alliteration?"

"Lightning is his middle name. His first name is just between Lightning and me."

After a long shower, Peyton lit a candle in a glass jar on her nightstand and slipped under the sheets. In its amber light, she picked up the novel she'd been reading and was falling asleep when her phone rang.

"Hello, Adler…"

"Did I wake you?"

"I'm lying down, reading. It affects my voice."

"I'm in bed, too. Been a long day. I was wondering how the boys are doing."

Peyton sat up and leaned forward. "They're in mourning, but they're good natured and, hopefully, they'll adjust well."

"You sound worried," he said in a night voice she hadn't heard before.

She loved talking to him, cuddled up in bed. Still, three words reverberated in her mind. But. That's. It. "You called for a reason?" She could hear him stirring.

"I was thinking I'd take the boys out fishing this weekend, get their minds off the funeral."

"It's a great idea, but you might have to teach them everything. They haven't experienced much. Probably never went fishing."

"Quite a contrast to the way you grew up."

She pictured his strong features and wished she could trace them. "Polar opposite. By the time I was Ricky's age, I'd already been to Europe and Asia. But that's another extreme. Now that they have a home with us, I want to expose them to more."

"Wow! You're keeping them?"

"Layli gets the credit. They have nowhere else to go. How can we abandon them?"

"And you want children?"

His questions both pleased and confused her. Had something changed now that their business connection had been severed? "I've wanted them for years." She chuckled. "Didn't think they'd show up already in elementary school, but we take what we get. How about you?"

"Been waiting for the right lady." Quiet sat between them, then he said, "Come fishing with us."

"I can't. I have to go to Mendocino, then Salt Lake City for a job, but I'll take a raincheck."

"For how long?"

The hesitation in his voice caught her off guard. "Till the job is done. Some weeks."

"What other surprises do you have in store for me?"

She remembered how unhappy he'd been at Ashton's flirtations. "I thought surprises were precisely what you don't want."

"Surprises I can handle. Fate, though, has the upper hand."

Peyton wanted to ask if he'd changed his mind about her, but pride stopped her. "These days, I fear fate doesn't like me very much."

"Fate may have chosen you to lose. Give her hell, anyway. And if fate has chosen you to hang, try not to drown."

She looked up at the ceiling. "What if fate has chosen me to win?"

"I hope she has, Peyton."

Goosebumps erupted on her skin, but he'd drawn a line in the sand, and hadn't erased it. Maybe he never would. "Goodnight, Adler. Thank you for wanting to give our boys attention and kindness. They need it."

"Will you call me when you get back?"

She didn't like that he left the ball in her court. *Not what a hunter does.* "Don't let your voicemail get full."

"Not for you, it wouldn't be. Goodnight, sweet Pey. Is it okay if I call you that?"

She wasn't sure it was. Then again, life was telling her to be ready for anything. She filled her lungs and sank deeper under the sheets. "Sweet dreams, Captain… Are you afraid of heights for real?"

"Yes, but my training was brutal. I've been trained to sky dive, scuba dive, leap off cliffs, despite any fear. I do what I must."

"Did the Navy also teach you how to retreat?"

His chuckle told her he understood her stacked question. "Sometimes, we advance best by first retreating."

How many times had she failed to advance against her inner battles when she should have? "Life's training, I suppose."

eighteen

After a single knock, Koda opened his bedroom door. "Okay to come in?" Peyton asked.

The breeze blowing through the open terrace door carried the music of a new day. A rooster crowed, birds chattered, shovels scraped against stubborn earth, and the horses neighed.

"Came to tell you I'm leaving tomorrow, but also that I volunteered you as a riding instructor when I pitched the hunt."

"What?"

"I didn't tell you because I ended up canceling it, as you know. But a Texan I met at Royce's party called me this morning to ask if you'd give his grandson lessons."

"Me? I don't know how to do that."

"I told him you charge thirty dollars an hour—cash."

Koda's eyes almost leapt out of his face. "I'm the best riding instructor that ever was!"

She surveyed the bedroom Koda had chosen, the only one on the third floor, and the smallest in the house. "Why did you choose this room? There are way bigger ones on the second floor."

He finished making his bed and arranged the pillows. "I figured if I take the smallest, I'll keep it longest. It has a nice terrace with the same view I had from my room at the cabin. Not to mention the huge loft space. I have an entire floor to myself up here."

"Are those geraniums?"

"And herbs. I love the smell of basil in the morning. Is it okay that I put pots out there?"

"Perfectly all right, kiddo. Be comfortable, but I didn't take you for a romantic."

He laughed. "I don't know about that."

She noticed a paper map pinned to the wall, with Seattle, Savanah, and D.C. highlighted. "Going somewhere?"

"Everywhere, if I can." He checked his appearance one last time in the long wall mirror. "I've only been to Colorado and Arizona. I love it here, but I want to see more."

She read the titles of the books lining his desk. Most of them were about animals or science. "Is this why you want to leave the ranch?"

"That, and to go to school." He shifted, as if he couldn't find a comfortable pose. "Don't get me wrong. I love it here—"

"—goodness, you don't have to explain it to me. I moved in my mid-twenties, attended college in California, and it was important I did both. It gave me confidence in my decision to move back here. Besides, you can visit all the time, like I did. Sometimes, the only way to be satisfied with where we are is to first circumvent the globe."

He put his hands in his back pockets. "Do you think Layli will hate me if I leave?"

"You mustn't think that." She counted on three fingers. "Layli loves you and wants to see you happy. She's more preoccupied now with two boys to raise, and you have to allow adults to own their feelings." Peyton touched his elbow. "In this life, Koda, you have to decide what's right for you. I'm not saying not to consider others, but you can't be a sacrificial lamb. There's a difference between supporting others and laying down your life for them. Not what Layli would want."

He grabbed his hat. "Thank you, Peyton. I feel more grown up here."

She embraced him and patted his back. "I've watched you grow into a fine man." She took his hat from him and arranged it on his head. "I have an idea. Hopefully, Scarborough won't kill us for it."

"What?"

"Come with me to Mendocino. You can fly back on Monday, same day I'll have to leave. It'll be a quick trip, only five days, but you'll see some of California."

"There's an ocean there!"

"Oh yes, and we'll go swimming in it."

"I've never seen the ocean."

Peyton's heart crumbled. "Well, it's about time you saw the best of them. I'll tell Layli and Scarborough I need you to help me shutter up the house and pack up the artwork for shipment, but I don't, really. You'll get a mini vacation out of it."

"For real?" He hugged her hard enough to suffocate her. "The beach, oh my God!"

Peyton and Koda were at the airport in Albuquerque when Margot called, crying.

"Honey, we're about to board a plane. What's the matter?" Peyton huddled in a corner. The cacophony made it difficult to hear, so she pressed her earbuds deeper into her ears.

Margot sniveled and spoke in a nasal voice. "Can I come to you in New Mexico?"

"I'm on my way to Mendocino. Can you wait a few weeks until I return?"

"I'll come to Mendocino, then."

"I can call you when we land in California. Let's talk about it some more first. It's an arduous drive, and my stay will be brief." The rest was garbled. Peyton hoped Margot had heard her.

Koda asked, "Everything okay?"

"My niece, Margot, as California a girl as I've ever seen. She asked to join us."

"Have I met her?"

"She came to visit me here once. If I recall correctly, you were away." She saw the worry on his face. "I have four bedrooms. She won't be in your way or in mine, and I doubt she'll come. Mendocino is way up from Los Angeles. Margot doesn't realize how far, but when she puts the address in her GPS, she'll change her mind."

"Is she nice?"

Peyton pulled up pictures of Margot on her phone. "She tries to be. Looks like me, doesn't she?"

Koda's jaw loosened, and he swallowed. "Is this a recent picture?"

"Sort of. She's more mature now." The flight attendant called their group to step forward for boarding. "After we land in San Francisco, we'll take a small plane to Little River Airport. My neighbor will pick us up. I hope you don't mind small planes."

"I haven't been on any planes before, but I don't fear flying, if that's what you mean. I haven't been this excited since your dad took me to the Cirque du Soleil."

"Did he take you anywhere else?"

"He gave me tickets to concerts a few times, and once he took me out for a steak in Santa Fe. It was like I never tasted steak before."

Guilt blazed through Peyton. Why hadn't she reflected on the lives of others more carefully? "I'm sorry, Koda, I should've invited you, Layli, and Scarborough way before today. I sort of have, casually, but maybe I didn't show how much I meant it."

He nudged her. "I never thought anyone would take me anywhere. Never mind somewhere as beautiful as Mendocino. When Layli took me somewhere, it was to visit distant family or participate in powwows. It's all nice, but not like this. I've been looking at pictures and maps of Mendocino." He whistled and kissed the tips of his bunched fingers. "Can't wait."

The views from the small plane they took from San Francisco to Mendocino were spectacular enough to make Peyton regret their arrival. Surf crashed into vast farms in what looked like a quilt of colors framed blue on one side, with the occasional whales breaching and feeding.

"It's so green down there, all those fields of food. I knew the ocean was big, but it keeps going and going," Koda said.

"Why I live on the coast," Peyton replied as they disembarked on the tarmac. "It's more like a field than an airport, isn't it? Jane will pick us up just beyond the fence."

Ashton was leaning against a glossy red convertible, his arms crossed over his chest, one leg enfolding the other—a bewitching postcard of luxury. Peyton was more vulnerable than ever, yet there he was, ready to push all her buttons.

"You're not Jane," she said. "How did you know I'd be here?"

"You're not alone." He smiled at Koda, then wrinkled his brow and looked away. "There's barely room for luggage, let alone another passenger. Oh well, you'll have to squish in, won't you?"

"Why didn't Jane come get us?"

"I convinced her to let me pick you up, that's all." He pointed to his trim body. "Besides, would you'd rather a squat woman pick you up?" He opened the passenger door for her while Koda hopped in the back. "Good thing it's a quick ride."

"But take it easy, please," Peyton said.

Ashton lowered his sunglasses, giving her a familiar look. "Are you ever happy to see me anymore?"

The genuine feeling in his question made Peyton slump her shoulders. "I'm sorry. Thank you for picking us up."

He pulled onto the single-lane road hemmed in by conifers and stared at Koda in the rearview mirror. "I was thinking we'd go to Flow's for cioppino like we used to."

He needed closure, Peyton realized. "You want to talk? We'll talk." With his seductive flair, the wind blowing through his hair, and the white linen shirt he wore, he reminded her of the Ashton of long ago. She had missed him, and now she was in his car, she missed him more. A reminder of what might have endured. Until she opened up the subject of marriage and children, they'd been ecstatic together. Maybe she could be happy with him now. She had Mikey and Ricky, who, in time, would feel like her own. Maybe she could live without biological children. Perhaps God put them in her path so she could rejoin Ashton. "How did you know I'd be in Mendocino today? You didn't say."

He flashed a smile worthy of a toothpaste commercial. "I have my spies."

"You mean, you have Royce?"

"No, my love, *you* do."

She thought Koda must be listening, but pretending to check out the scenery with earbuds in his ears. "Don't call me that."

"Okay, my darling."

Peyton's house was at the edge of a dramatic bluff. Foamy waves crashed on rocks below. How many times had Ashton driven to that house?

"Don't park under the mock orange tree," she said, as she had many times before.

"But it's my favorite spot," he replied, and parked there anyway.

It wasn't a big deal, but it showed her that he still resisted compromise.

Koda jumped out of the car, dashed to the edge of the cliff, and spread his arms like a soaring condor. "Ah, I can't get enough of the sea!"

Peyton studied her yellow and white Victorian house. The court hearing was scheduled after she got back to New Mexico, and Mark had prepared her for an adverse outcome. This might be the last stretch she'd spend there. During the eight years she'd lived in the house, she'd grown her reputation, made most of her friendships, and spent unforgettable times with Ashton.

"Ladies first," he said, carrying her conservation kit.

She hadn't brought any other luggage. The house had all she needed. Peyton took Koda's backpack from the car, then opened the garden gate leading through the courtyard and inhaled the fragrance of summer.

Ashton roamed eyes over her garden. He hadn't visited in four years. "You've done more planting."

"Rosemary by the garden gate for good health and freesias by the porch for good fortune." She unlocked the front door and disarmed the alarm, kicked off her shoes, and stepped into the bright living room. She'd restored the house that had been neglected for years when she bought it. "I've been gone less than a month, but it feels like a year. I'll open the windows to air out the house… Left in a hurry once I got the news about Dad, but there should be drinks in the fridge."

"Yeah, I know. You still have good taste."

She was surprised to see a lavish bouquet of tropical flowers on her kitchen island and turned to Ashton. "Thank you. They're stunning, but this is gigantic, and I leave on Monday." Then, it hit her. Ashton had entered her house unsupervised. She glanced toward her studio and found the door closed.

He looked at her with knowing eyes. "You're worth it, but why are you ogling the door to your studio? Could it be because you painted my portrait, not once. Not twice. But three times?"

"Are you ever going to respect my boundaries?"

"You mentioned you wanted to return to painting, but I didn't think you would. Maybe you needed to miss me to go back to it."

That was true enough. "We were still together when I started. You came up here less during that time. I also painted less. It was easy to hide them among ones I restored."

"They're much better than I would've expected. When you told me you painted as a child, I didn't understand. Your work is superb." He sat in a plush chair and hooked his hands behind his head, mimicking the position she'd used in one of her portraits. "You should've told me you're super talented."

Ashton had always validated her, and she needed support more than ever. "What is it you want from me?"

"You missed me so much you wanted to hang my face in at least three rooms."

"If you didn't notice, Ashton, your face hangs nowhere."

"That's because it hangs in your heart. You want to know what I want? Okay… I want you to admit you miss me. To make another go of it. I was the happiest with you and it's the same for you. Don't deny it." He sprung out of the chair about to grab her, but she stepped back. "Stop acting like you hate I'm here."

Peyton enjoyed his playful nature. It was one of the reasons she'd been attracted to him. "Can we not muddy things, please? Did you file for divorce? Of course not."

Koda burst in, and Ashton shot him a frustrated look.

Peyton was happy about the interruption. She needed time to process Ashton's presence. "Come on, Koda, I'll show you to your room." She climbed the hardwood stairs and watched Koda scan her bedroom from the hallway.

"Such a beautiful house, Peyton," he said, as she opened the sliding doors that gave way to a small balcony with an ornate balustrade.

"Thank you. It's from the days of the lumbermen who built this town."

"Did you plant the flower boxes on your railings?"

"I did. The annuals died in my absence, but the perennials are resilient and drought tolerant." Her thoughts drifted to her father's last visit. He'd bought the succulents she could see from her bedroom.

She led him to the room opposite hers. "This one is yours. Check out the view. The inlet shimmers turquoise in the mornings and gold in the evenings. Gets overrun by harbor seals and dinghies in the afternoons." She stood back, wanting him to enter it first.

"I've never seen seals in person." Koda put his backpack on a chair facing the window that overlooked the steel-blue sea and ran a hand over the marble fireplace mantel. He felt the grain of the armoire. "What's it made of?"

"It's aspen wood. I have it in my room and downstairs almost everywhere. It's sensational, isn't it? Ashton introduced me to it."

He took quick steps to the chair by the window and lifted his backpack. "You should save this room for your niece, too nice. I'll take the one facing the back."

"Put that down, and don't let me tell you twice, mister."

He cracked up, but hung on to his bag.

"Margot invited herself, if she even makes it. All the bedrooms are lovely, but this one has an ensuite like mine. Relax and unpack. I'll see you downstairs whenever you're ready."

"Hey Peyton, am I intruding?"

She sliced a reassuring smile. "Ashton is, though you're both welcome." Every day, Mendocino had all four seasons. Peyton washed up and threw on a thin fuchsia sweater before heading downstairs. She found Ashton sitting on the sofa with legs stretched on a stool, scrolling through his phone and drinking beer from a glass.

He turned to her when she reached the bottom landing. "I see you still keep glasses in your freezer."

"I used to do that just for you, then it became a habit."

"Called Flow's, got us a table."

"For three?"

Ashton took his legs down one at a time, rolling his eyes. "Y-e-s, for three."

Koda had gone to the edge of her property again. Any farther out and he'd fall onto jagged rocks. "Don't scare the bejesus out of me. Step back a smidgen, or a whole yard!" she called.

Ashton stood on her porch, holding a jacket for her. "It'll be a chilly night."

She debated whether to reprimand him for going into her closet without permission. "Koda needs one, too." She headed upstairs, to her closet, and found a wind breaker that would fit him. Ashton followed her. She resented the pull she still felt. They'd spent so many intimate moments in that room.

"I live in more modern houses, and my bedroom is twice as large as yours, but when I'm here with you, everything is the right size and feel."

She clutched the windbreaker, resisting the urge to cry. She was too weak to be alone with him for another second. "Let's go to dinner. Koda is waiting."

He brushed his hand over her bedspread. "You want me here. I feel it."

"My heart wants many things. But my head vetoes them all."

He stepped aside with a grin that said it was only a matter of time. "Okay, beautiful. Let's go to dinner."

Peyton's house was a fifteen-minute walk from the main strip, but since Ashton was taking them to the beach afterward, they elected to drive and rolled down Main Street through the lethargic heart of Mendocino with its architecture reminiscent of Cape Cod, with steep-pitched gabled roofs, large central chimneys, dormer windows, and cedar shingles. But its friendly locals and lush gardens, rich with succulents, were quintessentially Northern California. Koda seemed alight, his eyes on the raised water cisterns as they climbed the stairs to Flow's and sat on the upper deck overlooking the Pacific.

"The sunset is red this time of year, but hazy and tender, unlike a desert sunset," she told him. "It makes it more feminine."

That drew a laugh, almost everything did. He buried his head in the menu, but she could see his reluctance.

"Have whatever you like, honey."

The server arrived with their drinks and took their dinner order. When she asked for his, Koda ordered the same meal Ashton and Peyton had chosen.

"The water looks like gold," he said, absorbed in the view.

"That's it. You're definitely a romantic."

Koda pressed his hands to the arms of his chair. He asked Ashton, whose head was buried in his phone, "Do you also live here?"

"No," Ashton replied, not lifting his head.

"But you live in California?"

"Yes."

"Were you born in California?"

"We always lived between Texas and California."

The server brought buttered toast and a plate of ceviche. With a turned down mouth, Koda eyed the seafood. "It's gray," he said, depressing his back to his chair.

Ashton scooped octopus onto a piece of toast. "Ceviche requires a refined palate."

Koda colored. "Is all of California this beautiful?"

"No."

Peyton said, "Ashton, stop being a pest."

Koda crunched a piece of toast. "Can I go to that beach down there?"

"Big River Beach," Peyton said. "We must. I go most days."

"I'm taking you there next, but we'll enter from the other end," Ashton said, choosing a golden piece of toast and topping it with a succulent scallop. He held it to Peyton's mouth, trying to feed her.

Starved for more than food, Peyton opened her mouth and locked eyes with him. She was losing her willpower.

The cioppino arrived in oversized bowls.

"What's this?" Koda looked as though he were peering into a clogged sink.

Peyton chuckled. "It's what you ordered… shrimp, fish, and shellfish in tomato-saffron broth. Delicious."

He tried the broth and furrowed his brow. "Not spicy."

Ashton rolled his eyes and excused himself.

Peyton signaled their server and ordered steak and fries for him. "Please put this bill on my card," she said, handing it to her. "My friend will want to pay for it, but tonight is on me." Koda looked embarrassed, so she said, "Your food should taste good. It's your first proper meal in California."

They lingered until the horizon, smudged pink and red, mutated into a backdrop of pelicans, loons, and grebes. Ashton checked his watch and gestured for the check.

Instead, the server brought Peyton's credit card back with the receipt for her to sign.

"It's been taken care of," she said. "We can go."

When he was angry, Ashton had a way of bringing his thumb and forefinger together. "Why did you do that?"

"Because Koda is my guest, not yours, and we're not dating."

"Whose fault is that? I wasn't the one who just disappeared one day and never returned!" He got to his feet, tossed his napkin on the table, and bailed.

"Did he leave us?" Koda asked.

Peyton flung a lazy hand his way. "For one thing, I have my own car just a few blocks away. But, no, he wouldn't. That's just Ashton. His feet move as fast as his feelings. Come on, he'll be in the car. He's a gentleman, after all."

Ashton was drumming his fingers on the steering wheel, looking straight ahead. He waited for Peyton and Koda to climb into the car, then turned up the music and raced to the beach.

"There's a bonfire on the beach. Awesome!" Koda hopped out and left them alone.

"It's your bonfire, Peyton. Your friends planned beer and a bong for you." He ran his fingers over the side of her neck. "Come back to me."

Four little words confiscated her breath, but Adler popped into her mind. He was a clean slate, single, transparent, and he made her feel safe. She'd bared her soul to him and all he'd seen was beauty. But he wasn't asking her to come to him, was he? In fact, he'd done the opposite. "We've been spotted," she said. "It's rude to just sit here. Come on, we'll talk later."

Koda was already on the edge of the sand, playing with it, when Peyton and Ashton joined him. "I'll introduce you. Everyone here is artistic or athletic. You'll like them," Peyton said. "Let's go eat s'mores."

Several of her friends met them as they walked down the beach and gave her condolences and hugs. Ashton took a beer, sat at the edge of the group, and watched Peyton as he always had, with the kind of attention that made it easy to forgive him almost anything. Scintillating liquid sapphire, the Pacific hooked Koda. He removed his sneakers, cuffed his pants, and let the ocean drown his ankles. Though she had many things to tell her friends, Peyton tuned to the boy facing the ocean alone.

She waited for him to step back on dry sand and joined him. "I always saw you as chipper, yet you're unhappy."

Caught off guard, Koda's classic Native face sharpened. "Why do you say that?"

She hugged him with the arms of a loving sister. "You're hurting."

His eyes welled. "I don't know what it is, but sometimes I feel like I could explode."

"You need new experiences, honey. Let's go sit by the fire."

Jane, short and round with thin blond hair and thick glasses, arrived with a bundt cake. Peyton gave her a hearty embrace. "Thank you for the gift card, you generous neighbor, you." Jane said. "You're here for such a short time, we were afraid we'd miss seeing you if we don't get together right away."

"I have amazing friends," Peyton said, inhaling the perfume of waves and flames.

Koda swayed to the sound of a Spanish guitar. "Sing something, Peyton, like you do on holidays."

"Give her the guitar," Ashton said to the man who was holding it. "Sing 'Leather and Lace.'"

It was a song about a man who enters a woman's house and never leaves. Peyton took the guitar and sat on a rock, her hair swaying in the breeze. She had already crossed the line, letting Ashton feed her. She didn't think she should serenade him, too. "I'll sing something we can all sing together." She didn't have to look at Ashton to know she aggravated him. "First off, 'Margaritaville.'"

Clapping and whistling ensued, lasting well into the next songs: "Free Fallin'" and "Sweet Home Alabama". Koda stayed close to Peyton, making sandcastles with a dreamy look on his face. He joined in on the choruses, but when she gave the guitar back, he got up, dusted off his pants, and returned to the waves. Some of the group went for a night swim, while others hung around the fire, toasting marshmallows.

Ashton plopped next to Peyton. "That was beautiful, my darling."

"Don't call me that."

"Okay, my love."

"Ashton, I don't understand at all." She looked at the most beautiful face she'd ever seen, illuminated by the campfire light, by their history. "There was a time when I would've done just about anything to keep you. But you didn't leave your wife, although you said you hated her so much you rarely saw her."

"You broke my heart," he mumbled, "leaving without a goodbye, and then blocking my number. I couldn't even call you."

She tucked her long hair behind her ears to keep the wind from whisking it over her face. "You knew all my reasons, knew where I lived. I don't understand why it was okay to ignore me for years, then suddenly act like you couldn't live without me."

"It wasn't sudden. I didn't seek you out because I was adamant you should come to me. You wounded me when I thought you couldn't possibly live without me. I counted on your attachment, and I admit I took you for granted." He wrapped an arm around her, warming her. "I can't tell you how sorry I am about that."

"I left when all I felt was pain and disappointment. I wanted normalcy, a family, to introduce you to my father, and invite you to spend holidays at the ranch. But none of that would've been okay because you were married. Walking away from you felt impossible. Your effect on me was too strong. It had to be done cold turkey. I didn't just love you, Ashton, I *lived* you."

He shook his head, as if hearing glass break. "I wanted to find you sooner, but my pride got in the way. I'm genuinely sorry about that, and I've grown up since then." He buried his fingers in her hair as he'd always loved to do.

She leaned into him and played with the sand. "Why were you thinking of me?"

"I didn't understand what I had. I told myself there'd be others like you, but no one came close. You're a rare combination of characteristics, but I was too young to appreciate that." He shifted closer, pressing against her.

"We're having the same conversation all over again," she said. "Why would we work now, when nothing has changed?"

"Not nothing. If what you want is a child, then we'll have one. I'm saying yes to that now."

"But do *you* want one?"

"It's enough you do."

"But I'll be raising them alone, while you're busy with your ambitions. I'll be the mistress with a child. I'm too good for that. Worse, should anything happen to you, your wife would have all the rights. Should you, God forbid, end up in some hospital, all the decisions would be hers."

"I'll have papers drawn, make sure you have legal protection."

"How will anything like that hold up when you have a wife?"

"I'll get a divorce, but it'll take time because there are businesses between us, not just personal property. It'll be ugly and drawn out. It'll pull in our fathers. One is a damned bear, the other a bull. But if you're by my side, I'll go through with it."

She felt torn and depleted. The waves crashing on the rocks, the merry chatter, and seagulls calling out exacerbated her longing. She wanted to forget about the will, Lexi's lawsuit, the letters, and whoever Recipient One was. It had been too long since she'd let a man hold her all night. Ashton read her right and kissed her the way he used to. She wanted it. Needed it. The longer he kissed her, the more she yearned for what he wasn't ready to give. She'd been craving intimacy, but was it wise to open the same door twice? An awful feeling from their past revisited her. "You know, when I'd go places with you and people would mistake me for your wife—"

"—I never corrected them."

"And you think that made me feel better? I felt like I was an imposter walking in someone else's shoes." She was lacerated, realizing she'd felt like a pseudo-artist, an imposter all her life. A copy. Harlow was the original. What had she done with that pain? She'd manifested a situation that made her feel the same inferiority. Not the wife. A copy of yet another woman. Maybe her psyche was permanently damaged, not just wounded. She hoped that wasn't true.

Something about her body language made him ask, "What happened just now?"

She shifted away, feeling lightheaded. "There's no way I'm choosing a situation that would make me the imposter ever again."

His reply was sharp. He pressed his thumb to his index finger, glowing in the bonfire light. "I see, being with me makes you feel like an imposter, but putting on a stupid hunt, as if you're some B&B doesn't?"

She hadn't told him she had nixed the idea. "You don't know what I have and don't have."

"Yes, I do, and I also know you're strapped."

Peyton snapped her neck, as if she'd been tasered. "I'm not strapped! What?"

"You need money. I have money. What's difficult to understand?"

She got to her feet, stumbling in her anger, but he caught her. "Yes, I need to save my estate. But do you think your money is a consideration? I loved you like a crazy woman once. I couldn't date anyone else for two whole years, and you think it had to do with your money? But what did you do? You took up with one woman after another as if I hadn't mattered at all. You did what my father did." Another realization punched her. Perhaps she wouldn't have been as angry about the floosies if Ashton hadn't dated so many women so soon after their breakup.

He grabbed her wrist. "Money matters, as you're finding out, and I may have dated many women, but that's because none of them were you. I had to keep substituting, and I'm sick of it. You don't want the life of an imposter, nor do I! This hunt, this ridiculous idea, won't save your precious estate, but I can." He slapped his chest. "Why are you lowering yourself this way when you have Ashton Grant behind you?"

"There's no shame in enterprise. It's what made your family's fortune."

He looked at her with frozen features. "I never thought the day would come that you'd refuse my help."

There was hurt in his voice. She took his hand. "I don't want you agonizing, but be honest, please. Are you offering to help me or are you offering to make me dependent on you?"

"What do you mean?"

"You want to give me millions of dollars at what price? What will my life look like after that?"

"You'll be with me, Peyton. What kind of question is that?"

She felt the sand swallow her ankles and took it as a sign. "The reason we worked those first two years was because I went with you everywhere, which cost me commissions and friendships. But with a child, I'll want stability, a partner who comes home in the evening, which means I'd become the invisible mistress who's always waiting for you. Then, when you show up, I'll have a child who needs my attention. Will you be happy with that? I won't, especially when I'm illegitimate and waiting." She squeezed his hand and resisted holding him. "I am not that person. If I allow you to reduce me to that, I'll grow to despise you, and I never want that."

The hurt in his eyes was fierce. "Have I once reduced you, though, have I?"

"No, but society will. You're still married. You'll never be able to introduce me or our child to your family. Can you explain how you'd be happy with a child you don't want and a girlfriend who feels excluded?"

He shook his head and ran his hands through his dark hair. "I'll be in the car when you're ready."

Koda approached her. "Are you alright?"

"Yes, why?"

"I don't know how to explain it. Around him, you go from being like Brocco to being like Lightning. On edge."

She put her arm around him. "It's what happens when love is stronger than commitment."

Ashton drove them home, at normal speed, and asked if Koda could let himself in, while she remained behind.

"You parked under the mock orange again."

Alone with her in his car, he seemed like his younger self. "Believe me, I'll get a divorce."

"If you don't leave your wife because it's what you need to do for yourself, then you'd be leaving her for the wrong reasons. I couldn't be your catalyst back then. Now... I don't want to be. Had you been serious, you'd be free today, but you're not."

"Maybe if you thought about it longer."

"Ashton, Ashton... there's a need that comes from love, and there's a love that comes from need. I want the former."

He took her hand and kissed it. "Peyton, to me, you're the only original."

Her heart nearly exploded, and a geyser of tears erupted. She ran to the house, locked the door behind her, and pressed her spine against it, shaking.

nineteen

With a long to-do list, Peyton sent Koda to the beach alone. She had a video conference scheduled with Geraint to decide which of her paintings to ship. But first, she needed to examine her work with fresh eyes. Mendocino shone a beam on her history and thrust a magnifying glass onto her present. She sorted through her paintings. Some were already hung. The rest she lined up against the walls. She sat on the floor, as if she were a campfire and her paintings, the watchers. Each told a story, but some parts were meant only for her. She assessed and analyzed every canvas until her inner messenger emerged.

The copies of her mother's works were of still and quiet subjects, but hers were full of motion, contortions, either in body movements or facial expressions. None of her figures were docile or resting. They were always toiling, adventuring, or engaged heart and soul with others. What had she been telling herself? She'd been urging herself to move on, hadn't she?

She had moved forward, but not moved on. Big difference.

She hugged herself and rocked, sobbing from wounds that lingered and from what healed crooked. She washed her face in the kitchen and was drinking a glass of water when she heard an obnoxious horn blare in her driveway.

She peeked through the screen door and saw Margot about to blare it again. "Don't do that! This is a quiet neighborhood."

Margot got out of the car wearing a tutu and did a little dance. "Hi, hi, hi… I'll bring up my bag."

Peyton watched her niece struggle to pull out a suitcase big enough to hide two bodies. "Wait for me. I'll have to help you with that."

Margot was already on the porch when she got there, frisky and giddy, springing in place. "Auntie Peyton!"

"Does your mother know you're here?"

"Nope."

Lexi always interpreted anything Peyton did for Margot as harm done to her. Her niece jostled and twisted her arms toward her. "Are we hugging, or are we dancing the Macarena?"

"Your house is vee Gucci, but is Mendocino near Canada or something? It took eight hours."

Peyton had asked Lexi to send Margot for visits in the past, but she never allowed it. It felt good that Margot was grownup enough to visit on her own. "I'm glad you're here, honey, but you'll have to return to L.A. the day after tomorrow."

"Why?" She ran through the first floor like a ten-year-old. "I'm nineteen. I can stay here by myself, can't I?"

"Absolutely not." Peyton surveyed the massive pile of luggage still lodged in Margot's trunk. "Bring up only what you need." Margot grabbed an armful at random and galloped upstairs. "Take the second room on the left."

By the time Peyton caught up with her gazelle niece, she'd already flung her stuff over Koda's bed. "This room is gorgeous."

"But not yours." Peyton gathered Margot's pile of clothes. "The other room faces the same view from at least one window."

"Oh, why?"

"This is Koda's room. He's a guest of mine. Stop harassing me and come get settled."

Margot did a cartwheel into the corridor. "Do you have Coke?"

"Honestly, Margot. I have valuable breakables in this house."

"Sorry. Coke and cookies?" she asked, entering the bedroom.

"Come here. Let me give you a proper hug." Peyton squeezed Margot's cheeks like she used to when she was little. "Happy you're here, honey, but slow down a tad and enjoy yourself."

"I'm ecstatic," she said. "Can we have some fun?"

Peyton blew her hair out of her eyes. "Let's go swimming, and I'll introduce you to Koda. He's already at the beach."

Margot started stripping and tossing her clothes wherever. "I think my bathing suit is still in the car."

"I'll go get it for you." Peyton hurried outside, riffled through her niece's bag, and found what looked like red elastic straps in the shape of a bikini. She stretched its many strips this way and that, snickering. "Is this a bikini or a squid? How do you wear this thing?"

Nude, springing up and down, Margot stood on the porch yelling, "That's it, that's the one."

"Get inside. What're you doing?" Peyton dashed to the porch and shoved her into the house. "Honey, this is not Rodeo Drive. You can't go naked in public."

Margot laughed hard enough to slip. "What about those cookies?"

"We'll have to buy you some, and put something over your bathing suit. We're walking there. Don't want you to get arrested."

Sandwiched between shops and the Pacific, they walked along the edge of headlands covered in purple sea thrift and yellow verbena, then trekked down the sandy path to the ochre beach.

"Hardly any seaweed," Margot remarked, whipped off her T-shirt, and ran into the water, while Peyton scanned the beachcombers for Koda. She spotted him making a sand igloo and dashed toward him. "Want to go for a swim?"

"Oh, hi!" He wiped his brow, covering his face with sand. "It's funny how the sand here smells different from the sand in the desert."

"How so?"

"It's pungent, like rising dough." He rubbed his hands over the sand sculpture, smoothing it.

"But the sand in the desert smells like bread?"

"Pretty much, yeah."

Peyton removed her beach dress, folded it, and piled it on top of the towels she'd brought. "I barely swam all summer. Can't tell you how odd this is. I'll need a swimming pool in Abiquiú. Coming?"

She sprinted to the waves, Koda running behind her. Into the Pacific she dove, swimming against powerful waves, warming her body with laborious strokes. By the time she looked back, Koda was standing with water up to his waist. She waved to him and searched for Margot, who was wading nearby. Peyton could tell Koda said something to her niece. She swam back until she could stand.

"It's not that cold," Koda said, with goosebumps all over.

"You've met?"

"I recognized Margot from the picture you showed me," he said.

"Let's get out of the water."

"That was sick, Auntie."

"My swim? Nah… sick are those open water swimmers over there in wetsuits, swimming miles a day. What do you think of our Koda?"

Margot looked him up and down. "He's straight fire."

Koda tucked his chin into his chest, hiding his face. "Did you have a pleasant drive?"

"It was dope! Different from SoCal."

Peyton spread three towels on the sand. Margot dove onto the one in the middle and tapped one for Koda.

"How long have you been growing your hair?" she asked him.

"Always."

"Me too," she said. "Want to go clubbing later?"

"This isn't that kind of place, Margot. There are bars, but you're not twenty-one."

"I have an ID that says I am." She shot to her feet and blazed away, kicking sand in Peyton's face.

"Where's she going?" Koda asked.

"Damned if I know." Peyton spit sand and flicked it from her eyelashes. "Go after her, please. I'll catch up."

She washed the sand from her eyes, put on her beach dress, and grabbed the towels. She could see Margot doing cartwheels on the bluff, in red dental floss, with Koda trailing her. Her niece had already exhausted her. She sauntered up the bluff, her mind drifting to her mother. When she reached her house, neither nineteen-year-old was back. She stood before *The Last Start*, hanging above the fireplace in her living room, and asked her mother why she hadn't finished her last painting.

She stood at the stove with a towel over her head, thawing frozen mushroom soup and preparing the table for three. Margot and Koda tore in. "Are you terribly sandy? I have an outdoor shower."

"We're good," Koda shouted.

They flew up the stairs and disappeared. Peyton let them be, ate soup, and checked her phone for messages and emails. If Ashton were to step back for good, would she regret it? Would Adler ever step forward? The hunt was off. How would she see him again? She remembered that he still had her clock. Hope remained.

Two emails needed attention. One was from Mark explaining that he'd submitted her affidavit and had managed to exclude *The Last Start* from the count. The second was from Kelcy Loving, confirming details of the archery competition.

Good news after a succession of setbacks. She could keep *The Last Start*. She closed her eyes and said a prayer of gratitude.

Margot came down wearing a tight black dress from Peyton's closet and caked on makeup, vaping as she slipped on stilettos. "Don't wait up."

"Don't vape indoors, and did you ask me if you could borrow that dress?"

"YOLO!" Margot replied, and left, cranked up her engine and disappeared.

Peyton Googled YOLO on her phone.

Koda came down in his best shirt, his aftershave too strong.

"Do you know what YOLO means?"

"You Only Live Once. Why?"

"I'm gauging just how old I'm getting."

He chuckled. "Where's Margot?"

"She left." Peyton read his face and bit her lip. "Were you supposed to go with her?" A memory spooled in her mind. She had seen her father running after her mother, who was driving off in her convertible with the edge of her dress caught in the door. He'd tripped on the gravel and sat on the ground in his dress pants, unable to get up.

Koda slipped his hands into his front pockets. "I thought so."

"Koda, there's something I need to confide in you." Misty eyes peered back at her. "Can I count on your discretion?"

He chose a chair and slumped in it.

"I suspect Margot is unwell on some level. Do you know what I mean?"

He shrugged one shoulder. "She's just energetic."

"No, Koda, it's more than that. I think you should realize she's likely to hurt you without meaning to. I don't think she can help herself right now. Whatever she promised you, she already forgot it."

"She only told me an hour ago we'd go out together."

"To her, an hour is long ago. If I were you, I'd treat her like a Siren and fear her like one."

He gave Peyton a vacant look. "Like the sound a cop car makes?"

"No, the Sirens from the *Odyssey*. Creatures whose singing mystifies sailors into crashing their ships and drowning. I'll lend you a copy. Anyway, Margot is breathtaking, but she'll rip you to shreds. Don't get involved with my niece."

"I guess I'll just go to bed, if that's okay."

"Won't you eat something first?"

"I'll pass. Thank you."

"All will be all right." She blew him a kiss and sank into her chair, thinking of how some wounds burn long after the flames have been extinguished.

Peyton was awakened by a strange noise. She sat up in bed, listening to the sound of a couple having sex, learning just how inadequate the sound insulation in her house was. She knew Koda was in a hurry to allow his loins to overtake his smarts, but she'd thought he'd let the sun rise first.

She waited until she was sure they'd fallen asleep, then skittered to her kitchen to clean out her fridge and freezer for the last time. She'd be leaving the house unoccupied for months, possibly readying it for sale. Peyton wrapped herself in a throw, made coffee and took it with her to the edge of the bluff where she could watch the sun rise over the trees. She thought of what she'd have to say to Margot, then pictured Adler fishing with the boys. It was too early to call him, but she did anyway.

"This is the best start to my day," he said. "Were you dreaming about me?"

"Not one bit, which is why I called you first thing."

He laughed and sounded as if he were scraping a razor over his chin.

She pictured him in underwear, leaning over a sink, and was ignited. Maybe she'd get to paint that. "How did fishing go?"

"They're good kids, but it would've been better if you'd come along."

"They make me look better equipped than I am." She pulled the throw tighter, her eyes watering from the cool sea breeze, listening to his warm chuckle. "Invite me again."

"It's a standing invitation, Peyton."

She bit her lower lip, smiled, and shrugged. "But this time, if there's trout in it, you're coming to dinner." She could hear water running and assumed he was rinsing his razor.

"Is that also a standing invitation?"

"Would you like it to be?"

"I wrote my number on a piece of paper, didn't I? What you don't know is only a handful of people have it, and none of them smell as good as you do."

"Thank you, sailor. I'll be using it again."

"I sure hope so."

Down the street, a French bakery churned, rousing the residents with the scent of warm bread. She could smell croissants and hear the chatter of early risers. She changed and headed there, admitting this could be the last time.

Later, after she finished sorting and cleaning, she sat in the living room and waited for Koda and Margot. They came downstairs holding hands. "Croissant, brioche?"

"I could eat a horse," Koda said, and sat at the kitchen table, spotlighted by the morning rays. He buttered a brioche and slathered jam onto a croissant. "Do I smell bacon?"

From a warm oven, Peyton plucked egg and bacon sandwiches, and set them on the table, watching Koda unwrap one and devour it. Margot vaped again, her eyes on the coffeemaker.

"I'll make you a cup," Peyton said. "But no vaping indoors."

Margot rubbed her smudged eyes until what remained of her mascara flaked over her cheeks. "Must you make this much noise chewing?"

"Sorry," Koda said and chewed less.

"If you're going to eat that other sandwich, do it somewhere else, 'kay? It's vee annoying."

Peyton said, "You have a hangover. Don't take it out on Koda. There's aspirin in my medicine cabinet upstairs." She placed the second sandwich in front of Koda and gestured for her niece to follow her. "Come upstairs, I'll help you."

"Awks, right?" Margot said.

"The only awkwardness here is of your own making." Peyton gave her niece the aspirin and damp cotton pads for her smudged eyes. "A few hours ago, you slept with Koda. Now you're treating him like vermin. Why?"

She waved her vaping pen. "He giggles like a girl. It's such a turnoff."

"Are you using protection, at least?"

Lexi's shouting reached them from downstairs. She was telling Koda to move out of her way and calling Margot. Peyton ran downstairs to find Koda doing his best to block Lexi.

"Leave Margot alone!" he said, with splayed arms.

Lexi looked past him to Peyton. "Why is this guy so concerned for my daughter? Is he using her and you're letting him?" She was wearing ripped black jeans and a cruiser motorcycle jacket.

"Have you lost it?" Peyton asked. "Here I am worried about Margot, when I should worry about you."

Lexi beckoned her daughter. "Come on, we're leaving."

Margot stood on the hardwood stairs behind Peyton, clasping the white railing with tense fingers. "I'm not a child anymore, Mom. You can't tell me what to do."

When Lexi's face hardened, it lost all its prettiness. "What ideas have you been putting in my daughter's head?"

Margot slipped past Peyton and dashed into the kitchen. She glowered at her mother with a stiff neck. "I'm not going with you. I have stuff to do here, and I'm not done."

Lexi smacked the kitchen table, chinking her jewelry on it. "Why are you letting your aunt come between us?"

Margot struck her thighs with her fists. "Auntie hasn't said one word about you. Not one. Why do you always blame her for everything?"

Lexi looked about to cry. Her jaw dimpled, but she gritted her teeth. "I'm your mother, not her!"

Peyton caught a familiar look in Margot's eyes. One she'd seen when her mother locked her out of the house in bitter cold weather for getting home ten minutes late. "Margot, please, go upstairs and catch your breath."

Lexi thumped her purse on the tiled floor. "Stay out of it, you fucking snake!"

Koda shouted louder than Peyton had ever heard him. "Don't speak like that to Peyton or Margot! Everything was fine until you showed up!"

"Koda, I think you and Margot should go upstairs," Peyton said, but no one moved.

"I'm taking you for every penny you've got!" Lexi shouted. "Oh, I heard about your bankrupt ranch. You're in the shit now, and you so fucking deserve it."

Margot screamed as if she'd been stabbed. "Why are you always wrecking my life? I came up here to get away from you. From *you*!"

Peyton said, "Lexi, you're pushing Margot too hard. She can't handle it."

"You always thought you were better than me. Even a better mother to my daughter. You're not. How can you be? No man wanted to have a child with you. Maybe the men can smell it on you."

Lexi's words were inaccurate, but they cut deeper than Peyton wanted to allow. She said what would best help her niece. "Margot is bipolar, like Mom was. Open your eyes and listen to me for once. She needs real help!"

"What?" asked Margot. "I'm bipolar?"

"Don't listen to her. You're fine." With hard eyes and features pulled to a point, Lexi looked about to hit her. "Stop inventing lies!"

Peyton knew she'd have to ask hard questions or lose the ability to help her niece. "Not lies. Think, Lexi. Did Mom hit you when she was in a mood? Did she kiss you and laugh with you the next day like nothing had happened? Don't you remember the time she had me with her in the car when she caught up with you on your way to school and basically stole you without telling anyone, not even your dad? The school was looking for you, thinking you'd been kidnapped."

Lexi rearranged her face. She recognized some truth in what Peyton said. She picked up her purse and lanced her with congealed eyes. "Margot is not Mom. And Mom wasn't crazy, though you might be."

"I didn't say Mom was crazy. I said she was an undiagnosed bipolar who ended up killing herself because no one got her help."

"Mom didn't kill herself. Stop it!" Lexi lunged at her daughter and grabbed her arm. "We're leaving this disgusting house full of lies."

As Margot yanked, trying to free her arm, her mother's bracelets sliced her, making her bleed. "I want to stay with Auntie and look what you did to my arm!"

Koda ripped paper towel sheets and wrapped the cut. "Let's go wash it in the sink."

"I'm sorry," Lexi said. "I didn't mean it."

Peyton was happy to see Koda and Margot separate from the situation. "I don't come between you and Margot or jeopardize her by making stuff up. She should be evaluated right away."

"You have fucking taken my daughter for the last time. I'll see you in court, and from what my lawyer is telling me, you'll have to liquidate everything before you can say bipolar one more time."

Peyton watched Lexi search for her keys, but she wasn't done. "Speaking of lawyers, mine told me you claim you don't have a single painting of Mom's. How can that be? You would have had at least some of the portraits she did of you."

Lexi's face morphed from anger to indignation. "That's a lie. Mom never sketched me or painted my portrait. If she did, I haven't seen any."

"You're sure?" Compassion flickered through Peyton. She believed her, but Harlow had painted her portrait and her father's multiple times. Why not Lexi's? "Have you ever thought that perhaps all this anger you direct toward me shouldn't all be mine? Is it possible some of it is toward Mom, but you project it on me instead? Because I just don't understand the extreme hatred in your heart for me. What have I done to you that deserves this much resentment?"

Tongue-tied, Lexi scowled, but something told Peyton she'd hit a nerve. "First you flew all the way to New Mexico to serve me papers, then you came a long way today. Could it be you need to see me for another reason?"

"Like what?" Lexi asked in a softer tone.

"I don't know. I'm asking you."

Lexi cuddled her purse against her torso like a security blanket.

"Sit down a minute. I'll get you a glass of water." When Peyton returned from the kitchen, she found Lexi in the living room, standing before *The Last Start*.

"Why do *you* hate me?" she asked in a small voice.

"What? I may not like you very much, but I don't hate you. What makes you think I do?" Peyton held out the glass of water, but Lexi didn't reach for it.

"I don't know," she said, with a trembling lower lip. She looked on the verge of tears, then in a flash, she hardened her face and stormed off.

Peyton shook from the adrenaline rush. She was breathing hard and pushing away more ugly memories.

Margot returned with a bandage on her arm. "I don't want to go home. Can I go with you to Abiquiú?"

Koda blurted, "That would be great!"

Peyton figured if anything else were to go wrong, she'd have to change her name and disappear. "Honey, I'm not returning home right away. I have a job to do. Before you suggest going on ahead of me, the answer is no. I need to be present."

Margot burst into tears, and shook her shoulder free of Koda's grip with an irritation that said she was still in an extreme place.

"But you can join me once I'm back, okay?"

"When?"

"I'll send you a ticket when I know."

Margot turned into one big grin, as if nothing had just happened. "I'm going out."

"Where?" Koda asked. "Without me?"

Peyton asked him to excuse them, and he ducked into the den off the kitchen. She whispered, "Don't just drop Koda. Don't make him feel used. He's sensitive and sheltered, not like you. Explain to him kindly that he's not to blame."

Margot touched Peyton's face as if she were high and disoriented. "I'll catch you later, 'kay? I'll go change."

Koda returned frowning and took the stairs two at a time.

Before long, Peyton heard Margot yelling. "You're acting like a virgin. Want me to marry you, honey, and save your honor?" She froze, pressing her temples.

"Will you just wait, please? Are you still going to a bar?"

A door slammed, then Margot came running down the stairs. "I'm sorry I slept with you. Cray! What's this? Fatal attraction?"

Peyton met her at the door. "Maybe you shouldn't go out just yet."

Margot ignored her, tripped on an accent chair, and stormed off the way her mother had.

Peyton climbed the stairs, tiptoeing like a cat-burglar. She eased the bedroom door open and peeked in. Koda was sitting on a bed piled with clothes. "Can I come in?"

He didn't move a muscle.

"I'm sorry, but Margot is not good for you."

He looked up at her with flared nostrils and red ears. "Can we go somewhere?"

"Want to go riding dune buggies on Blues Beach? I'll change. Meet me by the garage. We'll have to drive there."

By Monday morning, Peyton had packed the thirty-seven canvases Geraint wanted into padded boxes. She watched the delivery men load them up. There would be no going back now. Nightmare scenarios twisted her bowels. What if nobody showed up for her exhibit? She could sell nothing. She could be mocked. And on top of that, she could still lose the ranch. What would she have accomplished then?

To burn off nerves, she let loose on the house before closing it down, vacuuming and washing linens. Koda asked to help, so she gave him the job of unplugging appliances, shuttering and sealing the windows and doors.

Margot shoved her belongings into plastic bags and took them to her car. "Can I help?" she asked, now that it was time to leave.

"We're done." Peyton sensed that Margo was more like her usual self.

"I've been savage this whole time. I'm sorry, Auntie. Was Grandma really bipolar?"

"How much has your mother told you about Grandma?"

"Nothing. Don't you get it? She and I don't talk much at all."

Peyton sat down, urging Margot to join her. She tucked her niece's red hair behind her ears and stroked her hand. "Here are the symptoms: out of control behavior, angry outbursts, high sex drive or low sex drive, overspending, periods of oversleeping, periods of insomnia, lack of focus, risky behavior you wish you could stop, but can't. Not necessarily all the time. Just enough to disrupt your life. Does any of that sound familiar?"

Margot's eyes grew twice their size, and she covered her mouth with both hands. "All. Of. Them. I'm bipolar?"

"You need a proper diagnosis from a reputable psychiatrist. There's medication, therapy perhaps. Listen to the recommendations, do your own homework, and then decide. You can always call me, and we'll discuss it. That's what I believe you should do, honey."

"Will you tell Koda I'm sorry?"

"I think you should. It doesn't mean much coming from me."

Tears trickled down Margot's cheeks. "I can't. I'll text him."

"Oh dear, no. That's worse."

"I can't," she said, and rose to her feet. "Can I hug you before I go?"

"Of course, but please find your strength and don't leave Koda heartbroken."

"It was just one night. He can't be heartbroken." Margot stepped outside and let the front door slam behind her.

Peyton wiped her face and unfastened her ponytail. She found Koda, and said, "Margot just left."

"Without saying goodbye?" He swallowed, then exhaled hard. "Will you still invite her to Abiquiú?"

Peyton nodded, watching him get excited and promise himself more Margot mania. Was this her father once, fixated on someone exciting, yet unstable?

twenty

Salt Lake City was one of Peyton's favorite places. Built on moral precepts, sprawling on the banks of a giant lake, and sheltered by snowcapped mountains. Harlow's hometown is clean, modern, and aesthetic.

Peyton wasn't doing anything she hadn't done before or visiting somewhere she hadn't been, yet she felt isolated and fractured. She took walks before work, sat at cafés drinking copious amounts of coffee and arranging the details for an archery competition she hoped would turn her sparrow nest egg into an eagle's. She visited the Leonard Museum, where she'd found inspiration in the past. Not this time. Staring at one masterpiece after another rattled her confidence and made her regret the visit. As her commission was drawing to a close, she sat on the rooftop terrace of her hotel, gazing as the sun set over the sharp peaks of the Oquirrh mountains. When the sun dove, it left behind a fin of light, like a red whale nosediving into the sea, leaving its fluke protruding. She stared at Temple Square, massive enough to gobble up five square blocks, mesmerized by the Gothic Mormon Temple at its center, standing in contrast to the modern architecture surrounding it. With a margarita in hand, she called Layli.

"How're you?" Layli asked.

"Don't know, on the verge of tears often." Peyton heard Layli close a door and assumed she'd ducked into her sewing room.

"For you, it's been one race after another with little rest in between. I'm not surprised you feel frayed. Where's everything with Geraint?"

"He's already categorized my paintings. I titled them all, and he says the friendly reviews will come out soon, but that means nothing. The reviews that count won't come out until after the exhibit opens. It's the hearing with Lexi I'm dreading next, but I called about the boys." She watched the lights of the city come on, adding to the Christmas tree feeling. "There's an idea I want to run by you. I'd like to better bond with the kids, and I've had Ambrosia Yazzie on my mind. Monument Valley is seven hours away, and Abiquiú is another five. How do you feel about sending the boys to me for a road trip? We'll go slowly, visit a few national parks and monuments. We'll return before school starts, but they'll see places, like Arches and Canyonlands."

"Just the three of you?"

"I'm an idiot! Sorry, you too, of course. I'm not saying that because you asked. I just thought you could use the break."

Layli laughed. "Hell yes. I'm excited to have a week all to myself. Joe and I would love some grown up time alone."

"Adler's friend, Joe? Layli, you've been holding out on me. When? Spill."

"Just a fling, but thank you. You just made my day. When do you want them?"

"I'll book tickets to Salt Lake City and forward you the itinerary."

"Why are you going to see Ambrosia?"

"It's silly, but my gut says to talk to her, and I haven't been back to Monument Valley in forever." Peyton licked the salt ring on her margarita glass and took a sip. "Have you seen Adler at all?"

"Does this mean you haven't heard from him?"

Peyton bit her cheek and straightened her spine. "I called him a week ago, but he didn't return my call. Maybe that door got closed in my absence."

"You sound like you miss him."

Peyton turned her back to the view, sadder than she would've expected. "He compelled me to see myself as an artist first. It was inspiring and tender. I would've liked to have seen him again, but it looks like I won't."

"I like him a lot," Layli said. "He popped in to see Joe, brought the kids presents, ate with us, and asked a lot about you. He said he'd be back. You'll see him again."

Peyton supposed if a hunter didn't track her, it was a bad sign.

With coffee in the cup holder, Peyton was smelling a new dawn as she drove to the airport to pick up the boys. For the adventure ahead, she'd rented a roomy SUV and filled coolers with nutritious foods Ricky was likely to hate. She hoped that by the time their journey ended, they'd be close, and that occupying herself with them might distract her from the terrible scenarios playing in her head. She wore a short seafoam green dress and flat sandals that laced up her calves.

She grinned when she spied a blue mohawk, but had little chance to adjust her face before she faced their escort. Tall and tan, with one hand on his backpack strap and the other on Ricky's shoulder, Adler smiled at her. She'd been optimistic, but now she was thrilled. She was too young for hot flashes, but she felt them alright.

Mikey zipped toward her but stopped short of hugging distance. "Look at how blue my mohawk is now."

"It's vibrant. I love it!"

Ricky hugged her like a long-lost son, almost unbalancing her. He was taller, with erupting front teeth, though it had only been four weeks. "Hey there, champ. Don't you want blue hair too?"

"I brought the storybook you gave me. Can we read it?"

"Sure can." She ruffled his spiked hair, and at last gazed at Adler. "Hello, sailor."

"Is it okay I'm here?"

"And if I say it's not, would you just leave?"

"Ask and find out."

"You'll do what I say?"

"Ask."

She stared into his probing eyes, afraid she must be blushing every shade of pink. His smile lit up his face, and he ran a hand through his fresh haircut.

"The car is this way." The closer he came to her as they walked, the better she could smell his citrus and sandalwood cologne.

"Seafoam green is my second favorite color on you, though I can't imagine there's a color you can't wear."

She giggled, too excited not to bite her lower lip. "Mustard looks awful on me."

"Mustard should be outlawed. Looks awful on everyone."

Ricky clasped her arm. "Where're we going?"

She took him by the hand, "First to the Salt Lake Temple, then to outdoor adventures. I have such a wonderful trip planned for you. On your first day back at school, when the teacher asks what you've done this summer, you'll have lots to share." She looked at Adler. "We're spending the night in Moab."

"I know. Layli gave me the itinerary. I asked her not to tell you, then booked a room everywhere you did." He smiled and scrunched his nose. "Is that strange?"

"Bold, but impressive. I love a decisive, actionable man."

"I accept that tip."

At sunrise, Peyton and Adler sat beneath Mesa Arch, enchanted by the view. The golden hour turned the amber rocks to crimson. Suspended across the top of the mesa, the Arch is a window to a fantastical world of mountain chains layered like giant iguanas pressing against the snow-capped peaks of the La Sal Mountains. Hoodoos hailed them—watchmen of one of the largest canyons in the world. The boys climbed on rocks, balancing and daring each other.

"I've never been alone in this spot before and I've been here several times," Adler said. "It's always crawling with visitors."

Peyton asked for his pocketknife and peeled an orange she'd brought for her breakfast. "I love the smell of citrus." She finished peeling the fruit in one long, intact curl and held it up.

Adler shifted closer. "They say if you can peel an orange without breaking the skin, you'll go to heaven."

She wiped the blade on a napkin, gave it back to him, then handed him the bigger half of the orange. "This is heaven, right here."

He tore off a wedge. "What's your definition of heaven, sweet Pey?"

"Heaven is getting what you desire, when you need it, when there's nothing more you want."

"You don't want more?"

"I will once we leave."

He laughed and nudged her. "You're funny."

"Boys!" She shielded her eyes against the sunrise. "Don't stray far."

"I was at Layli's," he said. "Scarborough was there, too. Koda showed me Lightning. He's only made incremental progress with him. Phenomenal horse."

"Lightning can be tamed only so much." Peyton pressed her legs together and rubbed her arms. "He needs the right rider, someone capable of marshaling him."

"Isn't that the best horse?" He removed his jacket and laid it on her shoulders.

"It depends on whether you're riding him or betting on him." She studied his face. In the filtered morning light, his eyes glowed. "Your eyes aren't at all dark. They're positively golden."

"They change."

"Everything changes." She got to her feet and asked the boys if they were ready for their next stop. "Thank you for the jacket. You're thoughtful."

"Thank you for not asking me to leave."

She held his gilded gaze and wished she could cradle his face. "Have I once asked you to leave?"

Adler tucked his hands in his pockets. They had a thousand-mile view of green and purple striations and ochre buttes speckled blue agave and prickly pear cactus.

As if he had hoofs for feet, Mikey balanced on an escarpment. "There's a rim trail here at Canyonlands. Can we go there?"

"We must. It's my favorite. Now get down. You're making me nervous." Peyton gestured for them to walk back to the car. "Don't forget. When we reach the end of the rim trail, make a wish. You'll feel like you're suspended in mid-air, in the palm of the gods."

Ricky said, "What if they crush me?"

"The gods only crush the weak, dummy," Mikey replied in a spooky voice, and then dashed to the car, knowing his brother would race after him.

"Stop calling your brother names, Mikey!" she shouted as the boys hurled forward. To Adler, she said, "Mikey acts like he could care less about his brother's feelings, yet he watches over him all the time."

"What will you wish for, Peyton, in the palm of the gods?"

She gave him a sly smile. "If I tell you, the gods will reject my wishes."

"Only if what you wish for is not what God wishes for you."

"Been hanging out with Father Gabriel? Sounds like a discussion he and I had recently." She sized him up. "Do you allow yourself wishes?"

"It's interesting you should ask." He rubbed his chin. "I dream more than I wish."

"And there's a difference?"

"Dreaming points out possibilities a man might not have considered before. Wishing limits those possibilities."

"How so?"

"When we dream, the possibilities are endless, but when we wish, we limit the scope, and it can make us lazy." He brought his face closer until she could feel his warm breath. "Wishing too much makes us forget we earn our dreams with hard work, correct actions, and measured reactions."

Peyton wondered if he'd handed her the recipe to his heart. "Spoken like a true cowboy. You determine what you want, but don't insist on how you'll get it. You remain open to the how, because sometimes the answers arrive from mysterious places."

"Like how an art show trumps hunting for saving a working ranch."

"Bingo." She laughed, twined her hands behind her back, and smiled from an intimate place. "Complexity is beautiful because it's open to interpretation."

"Are you calling me beautiful?"

She snickered. "I'm calling you *not simple*."

He shoved her, playful in a way new to her. "I'm not opposed to being called beautiful, you know."

Peyton shoved him back. "Dream on, Captain."

They stopped for lunch at Comb Ridge Restaurant in Bluff. Peyton ordered a plate of cheese with apples and honey. "Everyone should have the pecan pie before we head over to Hovenweep," she said. "I swear the pie here is the best, like most everything on this menu."

Mikey, who had been drawing on a napkin, lifted his head and pinched his forehead into a unibrow. "Ho-ven-weep."

"That's right," Peyton said. "It's not as famous as some of the other parks, but it's one of my favorites."

"What's Hovenweep?" asked Ricky, eating the last of his grilled chicken.

Peyton rubbed her palms together. "Once, Hovenweep was home to thousands. The villages are ancient, from eight hundred years ago. But get this: many of those buildings are still standing. Can you imagine building something today that could last a thousand years?" She counted on her fingers. "Multistory towers perched on canyon rims, houses balanced on boulders, a canyon terraced with colorful rocks, and a mesa covered with wildflowers. It's a peaceful place."

"A high place to keep safe from invaders," Mikey said.

"That's right. How would you know that?"

The boy ran his fingers across his mohawk. "Don't know."

"I think we should also check out Natural Bridges," Adler said, wiping his face with his napkin.

"Anything you want," Peyton said.

"Anything?" He grinned. "We'll see."

At the bottom of the canyon, in the heart of one of the ancient villages of Hovenweep, they came across a green copper rattlesnake.

"If you don't bother it, guys, it won't bother you," Adler said, keeping a healthy distance.

Ricky said, "Grandma told us snakes are a bridge between our people and the Other World, but I'm scared of them."

Mikey looked at Peyton. "The snake says divine power is stronger on the way up."

"I hate climbing, and I'm tired," Ricky said, but Peyton sensed Mikey was referring to her spiritual climb.

Adler said, "I'll rest with Ricky for a couple of minutes. Go, we'll catch up."

Before he reached the top, Mikey gestured to a partially collapsed tower in the middle of a scarp. "That's where he stored grains for winter, lots of it."

"Who, honey?"

"Honovi," he replied. "And over there was his house. There were other families with him."

"Honovi?"

"Yes, who else?"

Peyton placed her hands on her knees, bringing her face closer to Mikey's. "Honey, how do you know this?"

"I see him." He pointed to a different side of the canyon. "He's showing me the crown dancers over there. They're cool."

Peyton followed his finger, but saw nothing. "Do you have visions, Mikey?"

"I've seen things, but not Honovi before."

"Do you know Honovi?"

"He says they had to leave when the rains didn't come for a long time. He was old and alone and missed his home. When he walked on, he returned here to be reunited with his family."

Adler appeared, jogging up the steep bank of the canyon with Ricky on his back. "Someone needed a taxi." He saw Peyton's face and put Ricky down. "What's wrong?"

"Nothing," she said, though his face revealed he knew otherwise.

"Does Ricky have visions like you?" she whispered.

"Yeah, of pizza and burgers." He laughed and ran along the path.

Ricky said, "Mikey has drawings of Hovenweep in his sketchbook."

"Like these buildings?" Adler asked.

"Yeah, like this whole place. The canyon, tower, and people with like masks and stuff."

"Drawings he made before?"

"Yeah, yeah…"

"Did Grandma ever say anything about this?"

He shrugged. "Grandma says Mikey has dreams with open eyes about people whose eyes are closed. Don't know what that means. Can I have a snack?"

Adler looked at Peyton. They studied Mikey, who was dancing around an invisible fire. "What're we dealing with here?" she asked.

"Nothing. It's Mikey who's dealing with things."

Peyton pulled a protein bar from her pocket and gave it to Ricky.

He fiddled with the bar but didn't open it. "Am I special like Mikey? Grandma says Mikey is very special."

Peyton contemplated what was best to say. Her eyes roamed over the sandstone-block structures, the boulder-dotted canyons, and the Sleeping Ute Mountain range looming in the east. "I haven't told you about the turtle and the fish."

"What's that?"

"Well, a turtle came upon a fish in a pond. The fish bragged about how big and clear his pond was. He told the turtle he commanded everything in the pond from top to bottom. 'Aren't you amazed?' he asked the turtle." Peyton bent on one knee until she was looking up at Ricky's round face. "What do you think the turtle did?"

"I don't know. What, what?"

Peyton gripped his hot cheek. "The turtle told the fish about the ocean, and it blew him right out of his pond."

Ricky laughed, his belly shaking. "I want to be a turtle then!"

"You *are* the turtle, Ricky. You're Awanata, and that means turtle. If you don't believe me, ask Father Gabriel."

"Wow, I'm the turtle? But I've never been to the ocean." Ricky unwrapped the protein bar, bit into it, and ran off to his brother.

Adler chuckled and clapped. "Well done, sweet Pey."

"I like when you call me that."

He held her gaze, ruminating, and she wished she knew about what. "Do they ever bother you?"

"If we lived in a tight space, they might, but the way our lives are structured, plus how cooperative they are, it's working out. Besides, I didn't see them for a while, so I missed them, and nothing grows patience like longing."

"Did you miss me?" he asked, then paused. His eyes told her a lot rode on her answer.

She leaned forward and lowered her voice. "Would you believe me if I told you I didn't?"

He grinned, creasing his cheeks, a hair. "If I remember correctly, you point-blank asked me to take you at your word. Be careful how you answer."

"I may have thought of you once or twice."

"An hour?" He laughed. It was masculine and hearty. He lowered his lips to her ear, giving her goosebumps everywhere. "You made all that up about the turtle and the fish, didn't you?"

She winked at him. "It was wonderful to have a storyteller for a father. Dad changed fables or made them up to fit whatever lesson he wanted to teach me. It rubbed off."

He moved closer, and she hoped he'd hold her hand, but he didn't.

On the drive back to the hotel, the boys fell asleep in the backseat. "We're not far now," Adler said, yawning with his hand over his mouth. "About tomorrow. Even though the hunt is off, I'd still like to visit BearClaw. If you remember, he's the one I was hoping would help me scout, and he lives close to Monument Valley."

"We'll do whatever you want."

He glanced at her as he turned into the hotel parking lot. "He lives in the middle of nowhere, and he can come on strong… If that's all right."

Peyton played with an emerald ring that once belonged to her mother. The only personal item she had of hers. "It's subtleness in people I find unsettling. Directness, I like. Just look at you."

Adler laughed. "Describing him as coming on strong might be an understatement."

Peyton watched the boys. "Slack in the back as they are, they look younger than their actual ages. You're superb with them."

He cut the engine. "Can I ask you something sensitive?"

"Sure."

"Might you have to sell the only painting you have left of your mother's?"

"*The Last Start* is incomplete. Can't be sold. But it's not the only painting I have of hers. You're only the second person I've told." She was thinking of the commissioned portrait she'd stolen as a child. "I asked myself whether I'd sacrifice *The Last Start* if it could save the ranch, and it felt as if I'd be sacrificing my mother to save my father. It's a strange feeling, but between them, the one I feel was a true parent to me was Dad. Some of it was circumstantial, some of it destiny. Anyhow, *The Last Start* is unfinished. No point dwelling on it."

"Do you think you'll forgive your father?"

"I have to, Adler, and I will. My father loved me as I loved him. As I love him always."

"Do you always forgive?"

"I try. You?"

"It depends on the offence. I may not be as quick to forgive as you are."

"I noticed." Peyton was thinking of his reaction during their first meeting by the lake. "But you *can* forgive?"

"Yes, just not every time. Intention matters."

She roused the kids. "Let's meet up at breakfast, no later than seven-thirty. I'm eager to get to Monument Valley."

"Anything you want," he said, stealing her line.

She cocked her head and stole his. "Anything? We'll see."

twenty-one

Adler parked the car on the shoulder of US-191 and got out to open a gate blocking a dirt road.

"There's a town here?" Mikey asked.

"If there's a town, only one man lives in it. There's a friend here. He lives behind this fence, way down there."

"Why would someone live here?" Ricky asked.

"To some people, nowhere is better than anywhere," Peyton replied.

Ricky grunted. "Are you sure we're not lost?"

"We're with Adler, so I'm sure," she replied, though she was glad the tires were new and the trunk well stocked.

They drove for over twenty minutes through a desolate landscape of red dirt, cliffroses, and brittlebushes before they arrived at a small house shaded by trees. The yard was bare dirt with a rusty pickup truck parked next to an old RV. Even the corral was empty. Adler called out BearClaw's name as they disgorged from the car. Mikey brought out his sketchbook, his constant companion, and Ricky his storybook.

Now the engine was silent, she felt the space.

Ricky whispered, "The quiet here is the quietest ever."

The front door of a prefabricated house swung open, spewing out a man with a scruffy beard and three parallel scars on his cheek. "Did you kidnap those boys?" BearClaw asked.

Adler cracked his biggest smile and embraced his friend. "You're still alive? Howdy, Papa Bear!"

Though swift in his movements, BearClaw hobbled. "Who're these people? Let me get a good look."

"These are my friends." Adler introduced everybody, while BearClaw studied them. The man had no compunction about staring too long or standing too close. He shook Peyton's hand and wouldn't let go. "What's a girl like you doing with this mustang?"

"As in a horse?"

BearClaw winked at Adler with pride. "As in one of the few enlisted in the Navy who become officers."

"I think my friend would like her hand back, Willie," Adler said.

"He may be two stories tall, but Mustang is sweet on you, and you like him too, don't you?"

Peyton looked at Adler, not hiding her feelings, and was happy he didn't hide his. It felt satisfying on the low end and thrilling on the high one.

BearClaw took a pack of cigarettes from his shirt pocket and tapped one out. He offered some to his guests, including the boys. "Where're your parents, rug rats?"

Mikey played with his mohawk. "Don't know."

"Hell, I don't know where mine are either." BearClaw wheezed more than laughed.

Peyton gathered the boys to her.

Mikey said, "I think you scare my brother."

"I scare myself half the time."

The boys laughed and relaxed somewhat.

"What's so terrible you find yourselves out here?"

"We were in your neck of the woods," Adler replied. "Stopped to say hello."

He flung the cigarette in a rusty trough full of butts, lit another, and gawked at Mikey. "A golden eagle sat in my tree for some time yesterday. They don't come down this far, usually. I knew it was a totem, just not mine."

Peyton wondered what transfixed the man. He tilted his head, studying the boy as if he were a specimen.

"Why did Adler call you Papa Bear?" Ricky asked.

"Well, I have two sons. One is a toddler, the other a grizzly."

"Nah…" Ricky said, giggling.

"Ask your brother," BearClaw said, smoke swirling between his teeth. "He knows, but he better quit probing my ancestors or I'll have to bring out my rattle and probe his."

Mikey looked away, smirking.

BearClaw fished out his phone and found a picture. "On the left is my toddler, River. On the right is my big son, Smokey. As you can see, he's near eight feet tall." He chuckled and played with his lighter. "Sent this out for a Christmas portrait last year. Nothing good came of it."

"Why?" Ricky asked, already turning red from the heat.

"Well, my wife took off with River. Said I wasn't responsible enough, offering him up as a snack like that. I was only getting him together with his older brother. Family time, ya know? Was she right?"

Peyton asked, "How do you manage to live so far out by yourself?"

He gave her a knowing grin. "Oh, you agree with the wife, I see. All right."

"But how do you?" asked Ricky.

"I have solar panels and a generator, a satellite dish, a water well, lots of guns, and sometimes, a grizzly patrols the property. That's how."

"Willie, we have cold drinks in the car and chips and whatnot," Adler said. "Want some?"

Again, BearClaw focused his attention on Mikey. "I want to spend an hour in my sweat lodge with this boy."

Peyton stepped in front of Mikey with outstretched arms. "No way."

Adler asked to have a word and came close enough for her to smell his aftershave. "I've done sweat ceremonies before. I know what we're up against. We won't heat the stones too much, nor linger for too long. Mikey is a beginner and a child. I'll be there, and I'll watch him like a hawk. If he isn't able to handle it, I'll get him out of there."

"Why're you indulging this guy? The kids are off limits."

"Willie is no ordinary man, however coarse he seems. He saved my life, and it wasn't by mere luck. Believe me, he gets Mikey better than either of us ever will. That's partly why I brought us here. I saw what Mikey can do. Trust me on this."

"I trust you."

His eyes said being trusted was something he needed.

"And if Mikey can gain a mentor for his gift, then I'm all for it."

Mikey came up to them with a stiff spine and paused, blinking too much. "You should do it too, Peyton."

"What?"

He opened his sketchbook to a drawing he had done in charcoal. It was a woman sitting in a vast desert, under a starry sky, with hair flailing about her in the image of galloping horses. "This is you."

"You have real talent." Peyton took the sketchbook from him and brought the drawing closer to her face. "Who's this standing on top of the hill watching me?"

"The stuck woman," he replied. "You must hurry now."

Peyton knew Mikey was telling her something significant, but she didn't understand. "Can you tell me more?"

"I did," he said, took back his sketchbook, and fanned himself with it.

"You're a remarkable person, never mind a nine-year-old at that." Peyton was standing in the middle of nowhere, surrounded by raw desert on a sweltering day, but she was blissful.

"I'm ten tomorrow."

"Oh my! Why didn't you say something? We have to get you a cake and a present."

"Can I do the sweat lodge thing?" he asked.

"It'll be uncomfortable. It can even be painful. Why do you want to do it, Mikey?"

"It's the womb of Mother Earth, where my people can heal."

Peyton felt honored to have these kids, especially Mikey. She'd hoped for soulful healing on this journey. What she found was even more humbling. "Where does your mature language come from, honey?"

"Don't know."

Peyton bent lower and studied his spirited dark eyes. "Are you absolutely sure you want to do it?"

He nodded and caged his sketchbook to his chest.

"Adler, don't the stones take a while to heat?"

Ricky fanned himself and wiped his beaded forehead and upper lip.

Adler said, "Yes, not fair to Ricky, but we're close to Monument Valley. If we start now, we can still check in at The View Hotel, though somewhat late." He gave her an assured look. "We'll look for Ambrosia first thing tomorrow."

BearClaw was piling up the grandfather basalt stones he'd need to fuel the sweat lodge and telling the boys about them. "Mikey has new folks now, doesn't he?"

"The boys are with me," Peyton said.

BearClaw pinched a lit cigarette between his lips, not bothered by the ash dropping on his faded blue T-shirt. "I'd like to see them again soon."

Peyton watched the men and listened to them, but kept quiet, giving old friends their space.

Adler fetched more wood and carried the logs to BearClaw. "Peyton lives on a ranch, down in Abiquiú. There's an archery competition on her property soon. Come down. We'll go together, and you'll see the boys again."

"Mikey's spirit is an eagle. It doesn't get more sacred than that." BearClaw leaned on one hip and inhaled the last of his cigarette. "I don't venture out much these days and my truck is temperamental, like the missing wife."

"Is that a no?" Adler asked.

BearClaw looked into Mikey's eyes and took a deep breath. "We pass it forward. I owe the boys, especially that Mikey. Someone gotta teach him how to process that amazing power of his. He's got more medicine in him than all of Bear's Ears, and that place is sacrosanct. So that's an affirmative, Captain."

Adler nodded. "Good call, Lieutenant. It would be great to see you. Hope you stay a long while."

Peyton carried out a cooler and placed it on a torn and rusty metal beach chair, while BearClaw staggered under the weight of the stones and built a pyramid of logs around them. The kindle took, and a bonfire licked the air, baking the stones.

"Let's do this right. Help me, Adler."

They went into the house and brought out a large four-handled drum covered in brindled steer hide. They placed it under an ironwood tree, from which a heavily scored target board hung. "Come here, Ricky, you're going to help us drum and chant." BearClaw handed each boy a stick wrapped with hand-sewn deerskin heads filled with raw sheep's wool. "Grab chairs and let's go. Just follow my lead." He started the drumming and chanting. With patience reserved for fragile souls, he encouraged the boys to imitate everything he did. To Peyton's surprise, Ricky took to the chanting like a warbler.

"I'll bet Ricky can carry a tune," Peyton told Adler. "He might have a musical ear, and he isn't shy with his vocals. Just listen to his range."

"Why are the boys here, Peyton?" Adler asked. "They're the reason I get to be with you. I'm glad, but why did you want them on this trip?"

"We three need the same things."

"What's that?"

Peyton looked into his golden eyes. "Family. Recovery. Release."

He took her hand and entwined his long fingers with hers, which she thought was overdue. "My parents are dead, and my only brother drowned at sixteen. I understand what you mean."

She squeezed his hand. "Maybe you need that, too."

BearClaw changed to a lower pitch and slower rhythm.

"What will you do while we broil ourselves in the sweat lodge?" Adler asked.

"Read to Ricky and think about Mikey's drawing. He's been trying to tell me something important ever since I met him, but I'm too dumb or blind to get it."

Adler turned over her palm and ran a finger along her lifeline. "They're praying their way. Want to pray with me our way?"

She shook her head and craned her neck. With closed eyes, holding hands, they said The Lord's Prayer to piercing Native chants—a living shrine of the Three Cultures Monument of the Spaniard, Cowboy, and Chief.

When the fire burned down, the grandfather stones glowed like embers. BearClaw and Adler wrapped them with leather straps and carried them to the sweat lodge. Stripped to breechclouts, they went inside and huddled around the stones, watching BearClaw slather medicine and pour water on them. Steam scented with sage and pine filled the lodge, and filled Peyton with apprehension and excitement. And it wasn't only because she got to see Adler almost naked.

She closed the flap to the sweat lodge and sat with Ricky at her side. "We'll just stay here and keep a close eye on them."

"Good thing we have drinks," Ricky said. "I'm thirsty."

"What do you say we read a great story?" Peyton pulled two bottles of cold water from the cooler. "Do you know why the Diné are such master weavers?"

"Who?" he asked.

"The Diné is what the Navajo were originally called."

He laughed before he answered. "Their fingers are fast?"

"Well, let's read about Spider Woman and the Holy Ones, and you'll learn why."

Peyton began reading and adding tunes to get Ricky to sing along. By the time he learned about old mysteries and new magic, she was sure he had a trainable voice. "Do you think maybe you'd like to learn how to sing?"

"Do turtles sing?"

"You know, this might be hard to understand, but I'll say it, anyway. If you learn to sing well, music will become the ocean you use to tell off bragging fish. We all need something to bolster our confidence in this life. Yours can be music."

Ricky's face wore an expression of deep thought.

Peyton wanted him to make the connection himself, as her father would do with her. "Do you remember the paintings of music we saw at the Georgia O'Keeffe museum?"

He gushed enthusiasm. "Is that why she painted music like the sea, in waves of blue and green?"

"That's right!" Peyton kissed his pomegranate cheeks. "Take it from me, Awanata, you're special, too. That was a brilliant observation, and I thought you didn't enjoy the museum much." She checked the time again. "Looks like they should be done."

Mikey was out first, flushed, drenched, with a big smile on his face. And another expression Peyton couldn't read. "The air out here is refreshing," he said, despite the ninety-eight degrees.

"Do you feel all right, Mikey?" Peyton grabbed a bottle of water and offered it to him. To her astonishment, he hugged her and let loose, sobbing for the first time since his grandmother's passing. When he wouldn't let go, she lifted him in her arms and rocked him, letting him rest his head on her shoulder. He'd have to let go first.

Ricky looked at his brother with an open mouth and wide eyes.

"He'll be all right," Peyton said. "We're all going to be all right."

When he stopped wailing, Mikey wiped his face on his forearms. "I'm sorry."

Peyton put him down. "Oh no, Mikey, don't be. We honor this life best when we cry all our tears, so we get to laugh all our laughter."

They left BearClaw, who was wearing nothing but his breechclout and smoking yet another cigarette. The light over Monument Valley was changing into an orange glow. They trundled down Route 163, encountering no other cars. Peyton asked to take pictures of the iconic Monument Valley buttes in the distance. Adler pulled over, she handed him her phone and chose just the right spot with the famed Mitten butte and a gleaming sky behind them.

"Take many, please," she said, standing between the boys, cradling them tight.

Adler aimed her phone at them, and said, "Who's going to take my pic with Peyton next?"

Ricky bounced. "Me, me!"

Adler was merry, laughing as the kids struck exaggerated poses and made hand gestures. Several snaps later, he thrust Peyton's phone in her direction, all merriment absent now.

Ricky said, "My turn, my turn. Where do I press to take the pics?"

"It's getting dark. Let's go." Adler touched Ricky on the shoulder. "Another day, buddy."

She waited until getting back on the road and the boys grew preoccupied in the backseat. "What happened? You seemed just fine a moment ago." When he didn't reply, just stared ahead, Peyton leaned closer. "Adler, you're obviously miffed. What's going on?"

"Your text messages got in the way."

Peyton checked her phone and found two messages from Ashton. The first text read: *I hope you've been thinking of my proposal, my love. It's not too late.* And the second: *BTW, I have been reflecting hard on our conversation on the beach. And it's always special when you sing to me.*

twenty-two

Anger and dismay competed within her. Not only were Ashton's texts inappropriate and dreadfully timed, but his tenacity was both annoying and flattering. He was doing everything she'd wanted him to do after their breakup. Seek her. Explain and listen. Fight for her. She kept her eyes on the road, unsure how to address the situation. They drove through Monument Valley, one of the most ethereal places on earth, with iconic buttes and Martian character, yet Peyton was too absorbed in her thoughts to notice.

At the hotel, she unloaded the luggage, ordered dinner for the kids and left them to shower, then went down to the lobby in search of proper coffee. Near the elevators, she bumped into Adler and noticed he was carrying a packet of ibuprofen. "Do you have a headache?"

"Are you seeing your ex again?"

"No, regardless of what the texts say."

Distrust shone through his eyes, darker now, more intense. "The texts didn't seem open to interpretation."

She trained a critical stare at him. "Are you asking me or are you accusing me? Because it seems to me you've already made up your mind."

"You said there was nothing between you and that guy. It didn't occur to me you'd run off to some beach somewhere together. I feel stupid flying to Salt Lake City when you're involved with someone else."

"You were right to come with the boys. No mistake there. But you have a horrible way of presuming what isn't true. You didn't ask me, just assumed. And I wasn't the one who asked to put everything on hold."

He tried to touch her, but she moved away. "I'm out of your league, remember?" She saw the hurt in his eyes and softened. "Look, I'm sorry. It was a resentful thing to say. I don't believe that's the case at all."

He balled the packet of ibuprofen in his palm. "I don't know how to take this."

Peyton feared she was on the verge of ruining their progress. She wanted him, but he had to want her just as much. "I'm going to my room. If you have questions, you'd like me to answer, come knocking. You can ask me anything you like, and I'll answer honestly. That's how I am. But you have to be willing to believe me, otherwise, there's no point."

He wished her goodnight and used a different elevator.

What if he didn't come? What if Ashton's texts had sent them back to square one, if not negative two? She felt sick to her stomach. Coffee lost its appeal. Everything did.

She was in bed reading little and wondering a lot, while the boys slept in the room adjoining hers. She heard a gentle rap at her door, got up, and peered through the peephole at Adler.

"Can I talk to you?"

"I'd like that."

He was clean-shaven with wet hair, smelling of shampoo. "I came to apologize. I have no excuse. Some things can needle me, then I shut down, but I can work on that."

"I don't lead people on, Adler. I think I've been obvious. Few men attract me, but you do. I see the depth of you and want to discover all of it."

"In Moab, you said things always change." He shuffled closer, and it felt natural. "Let me start over, asking rather than accusing."

He waited until she fractured a smile.

"Who is he?"

She sat cross-legged on the bed in leggings and a cropped T-shirt. "Pull up a chair," she said. "Ashton Grant was the one deep and long relationship of my life. He wants us to start over, but the things that tore us apart in the first place remain. Ashton is gifted—hardly anything he can't do, but he can be grandiose and domineering, as he was in the texts you read. He can also be tenacious, gets what he sets his mind to, but it won't work this time."

"He was with you in Mendocino?"

She stretched to the nightstand and turned on the lamp. "You can't understand Ashton till you see him in action. He knows how to be strategic and charming."

Adler's face showed he'd seen none of that charm.

"He's successful, has a brilliant head for business. It's not all legacy money. A lot of it is his personal shrewdness. He applies the same tactics elsewhere, and though I used to fall for them, I don't anymore."

"Sounds like quite the catch," Adler said, rubbing the back of his neck.

"He is. My standards are high. You should look in the mirror." It felt good to see him smile and lean forward. "Ashton is many wonderful things, but he's not for me at this juncture." She could see he wasn't reassured. "He showed up in Mendocino uninvited, but I made up my mind long ago, before I met you. No matter what Ashton wants or doesn't want, I can't go back. It was all about him once. This time it's about me. If he hasn't believed me yet, he will."

"Are you happy I'm here?"

"Blake, your mere presence is enough. I thought I'd made that clear."

He sat on the bed beside her, emotions scoring his strong features. "I hunt, deep-sea fish, and take on dangerous situations in my security business.

You can say I'm hardly short on adrenaline, but nothing pumps life into me like being with you." He kissed her, then pressed his weight against her, pushing her back until their bodies met, and gave her another long kiss. Peyton summoned her head to overrule her heart. She pressed a hand to his chest and pushed him away. "What changed since Royce's party?"

"I missed you, and I miss hardly anyone. Besides, you no longer needed me, but I still counted with you."

"You missed me?" She could hear the coquetry in her voice, loved how he brought out her lightest side.

"Thought of you often, and before you ask, I didn't call because I thought showing up in person was more meaningful."

"It is. You sure go for audacious moves. Now tell me, why aren't you with someone?"

"If you haven't noticed, I'm picky."

"And extra cautious."

"Perhaps."

Trust issues. A high hurdle. "What's your story? Were you ever seriously involved?"

"There was someone in my early military years. We lived together, but I was on duty, got sent to many places. She didn't take it well. Had an affair. I didn't stray, didn't even consider it, but after that I met no one I wanted to invest in… till now."

Adler was conservative, a risk assessor who took few chances and protected his heart more than she'd expected. If she were to win him over, she couldn't make too many mistakes. "I have to divulge one more thing. It could be a deal breaker for you. When I met Ashton, he lived alone, and when he wasn't working, his time was all mine. A month into the relationship, I found out he was married. I could've left, but I was too attached to him by then. It's not something I'm proud of, but if this changes the way you see me, I want to know early, before one of us gets hurt."

His expression was difficult to read. He removed the hand that had been on her knee. "I appreciate everything you said," he told her. "Thank you for sharing something most women would withhold."

"You don't like surprises." Peyton held out her hand, testing his reaction. When he didn't hesitate to take it, she felt better. "Are you unsure of me now?"

"I wouldn't say that." His look was probing. "We all have a past. I can only evaluate you in the present."

"And what have your evaluations divulged?"

"They told me to hop on a plane and come to you. Not seeing you for weeks felt like punishment."

She considered his history and hers. "Tell you what, Captain, when you can put down your shield and trust me to the degree I trust you, I'll come to you."

He stretched to his full height and clasped her hands. "Why do you trust me?"

"Because the only way to find out if you can trust someone is to trust them. Besides, your eyes tell me I can, and your behavior confirms it."

"Maybe I trust you already," he said, lowering his face to hers for another kiss.

"No, not fully. Fair enough, though. I laid a lot on you tonight. You want to trust me, I can see that. But you're not there yet. Tell you what, when you do—"

"—when I do, yes?"

"When you do, Blake, I'll show you the view from my room."

He chuckled, lifted her hand to his mouth, and kept it there for a minute. "I love when you call me by my Christian name, the name my mother used."

"I know. You discourage people from using it. It clued me in, and I'm touched you allow me to use it."

"You're not people."

"Who am I, then?"

"Since I arrived, we started with Arches National Park and didn't stop until Mesa Verde. Let's say you require a lot of hikes."

She tittered. "Glad you're athletic."

The local post office was Peyton's best chance of finding out where Ambrosia lived. She still hoped the old cook could shed light on her mother's sudden death. She asked the only employee. He mumbled something about privacy laws and looked past her to the next customer.

A man dressed in chaps and a baseball cap, who was filling out a label, said, "Young lady, if you want old Ambrosia, then you'll have to be asking for Pat Yazzie, her grandson. He lives past the wall of petroglyphs. You'll know it's his house when you spot longhorn cows and a mean yellow dog."

"Thank you, sir."

"I may not be doing you any favors sending you down there. The dog is rabid, Pat more so. Good luck if you decide to go. There are two hogans there. Only enter the domed one, not the forked one, you hear? Women aren't allowed in the forked one."

Back in the car, she gave Adler the instructions.

"Very specific address. It's like being back in Afghanistan," he said, and cranked up the engine.

"That guy sort of soured me. He made it sound rather bleak."

"What does bleak mean?" Ricky asked.

Mikey slammed his sketchbook shut. "If you ask Peyton to explain all of her big words, it'll never end."

"There are no big words and small words," Adler said. "There's only precision or vagueness. Peyton is precise with her words the way you're careful with your drawings."

Peyton stuck her tongue out at Mikey. "Funny…" she told Adler, "you're so open, yet so disciplined."

He smirked. "What can I say? I'm persnickety."

"What's persnickety?" Ricky asked.

"Oh my God!" Mikey shouted and covered his ears with his hands.

They drove down a dirt road, passing buttes and houses without addresses. They seemed to be driving aimlessly, and the road was looping back. What if Ambrosia was the key to uncovering her family's secrets? She had to find her. Adler flagged down a pickup truck with a cracked windshield.

A man with a wrinkled, kind face rolled down his window. "Lost, son?" he asked, and spit chewing tobacco.

"Looking for the Yazzie family… err… longhorn cows, yellow dog?"

The man reached for his can of chewing tobacco and prepared a fresh lump. "If you mean Pat, then ask permission of that house over there to enter their yard, and then walk straight back. You'll get your wish. If you see Pat, don't speak to him. Speak only to the women. Pat is a boozing, mean bastard."

Peyton asked, "Is there an Ambrosia who lives there, sir?"

"If you mean a lunatic weighing a peanut, then yes, ma'am, there is."

They thanked the man, followed his advice, and were granted permission to enter the yard. They'd brought a box of provisions—tobacco and dried goods—and Adler carried it as they made their way through a flock of chickens and a herd of mules. The old residence consisted of several structures, part modern, part traditional, part rundown, a quilt of mismatched materials. The roof was part tin, part mud, the windows were a chaos of sizes, and the doorsill was crooked. Not a lick of paint anywhere, although specks of faded turquoise still clung to the front door. Even the door handle was loose. Patterned sheets hung in the windows in place of curtains. Two hogans flanked the structure, and a yellow dog lay on his back, spread eagle, not at all interested in them.

"This could be the place," Peyton said. "The man at the post office said to only enter the domed hogan. I'll go check." She left Adler holding the box with the boys at his side. The traditional Diné hut had been constructed of piñon and ponderosa pine bark covered with clay and mud, exactly as it would've been built a thousand years ago. Two women were praying inside. Peyton didn't approach for fear of offending them. After a few minutes, a middle-aged woman looked up and noticed her. "All are welcome here," she said. "Don't be shy."

"Thank you. May I invite my friends?"

"Yes, of course."

The boys entered first and tried to sit on a long rustic bench. "No, boys, you can't sit while the elders are still standing," Peyton said.

"That's right," an older woman said. Peyton assumed she must be the other woman's mother. She was wearing a long floral skirt and a fuchsia blouse, cinched with the beaded belt Diné women favored.

"We're sorry for showing up unannounced, but we're here to visit Ambrosia. We brought her a small gift and would love to talk with her."

Adler said hello and raised the box in his arms. "I can put this down anywhere."

The mother said, "Oh, how thoughtful and generous of you. Thank you."

"How do you know Great Granny?" the younger woman asked.

"She used to be the cook at Pioneer Ranch down in New Mexico, didn't she? I'm Peyton Chase. My father had fond memories of your great grandmother."

"Blessed be," said the mother. "You've answered our prayers!"

"I have?"

She clasped her daughter's hand, and glued a palm to her chest, then rushed at Peyton. "We've been meaning to tell your father to stop sending checks to the post office. My brother Pat steals them and drinks up the money. Poor Granny sees none of it, and she needs her medications."

"I'm sure my lawyer can send it anywhere you like." Peyton looked around and decided they could use a significant raise.

The woman hugged her as if she were a fruit tree in the desert. "If you can do that, you'll be making a big difference for us."

"Shouldn't be a problem. I'll make it happen."

"Come with me if you want to see Granny. She's in the house, but I must warn you. She only remembers the distant past."

The women insisted Peyton enter first, followed by Adler and the boys. The rustic space was cool and neat, though dark at first. A straw rug covered a cracked cement floor, and a tiny figure sat on a low platform bed.

"Granny," whispered the mother, squatting next to her, "there's someone here to see you." She gestured for Peyton to come closer. "Let her take a good look at you."

Peyton's heart ached when she saw Ambrosia. Her knuckles were gnarly, her back hunched, and her eyes clouded with cataracts. She should've expected her to be in a bad state. Ambrosia tapped a spot beside her. When Peyton took it, the mattress sank like a seesaw.

"Granny, this is Peyton Chase, daughter of Mr. Chase."

The cook studied Peyton's face and splintered a smile. She asked for her dentures, kept in a glass of water on a rickety table. "Oh, Mrs. Chase, I'm thrilled you made it."

"Oh no, I'm Harlow's daughter, Peyton. I was small when you last saw me."

"Mrs. Chase, when did you return from the hospital? No one told me!" Ambrosia tried to stand. "I would've made your favorite dinner. I can still make it."

"Please, don't get up." Peyton turned to the women. "I look like my mother. I must be confusing her."

"When I saw all that blood, I called out for Mr. Chase right away."

"Blood?" Peyton piled her hands over her mouth. She'd long suspected that her mother had committed suicide, but she wasn't sure how, and hadn't pictured violence.

"Forgive me for leaving you lying on the bathroom floor in a pool of blood, but you needed help, and I didn't know what to do. Forgive me, please. Mr. Chase knew what to do. He took the gun away, took care of you, and now you're back."

So her mother shot herself. Afterward, her father bought an ammunition safe box and kept it in the carriage house under Scarborough's watchful eye. He'd also remodeled their ensuite bathroom. Peyton's throat went dry, but she forced herself to say, "Of course I forgive you, Ambrosia. I'm fine now, see? All better. No blood and no hospitals."

"It's because I prayed for you and left your picture at the Sanctuario de Chimayo. God doesn't forget."

Peyton finally had some answers. She'd known her mother had had a terrible end, but picturing her covered in blood was worse. Her father had been traumatized and had to live with the secret of the suicide. The annuity he provided Ambrosia must have been part generosity and part hush money. "Thank you, Ambrosia. I'm very grateful," Peyton said. She felt claustrophobic, as if her lungs were caving in on her.

The women gave her sympathetic smiles. "She doesn't know us most of the time. Sorry, we thought maybe she'd recognize you."

Adler put his hand on her shoulder and rubbed. "Let's get you some air," he said, and guided her outside as the boys followed.

She took a deep breath of fresh air and burst into tears. That day, her father had asked Royce to keep her overnight. Now she understood that he'd needed time to clean up and cover up.

Adler held her, and she buried her head in his chest, sobbing.

"I'm so sorry, Peyton."

The younger woman brought her a glass of water and brown paper towels. "Is your mother all right now? Sounds like she survived an accident."

"Rest her soul," Adler said. "Mrs. Chase passed away a long time ago. Thank you for letting us speak to your great grandmother."

"Sorry, you didn't find enough here, and thank you for bringing such generous gifts."

Peyton could only nod.

Mikey inserted his hand in Peyton's. "She's been waiting for you."

"Who, honey?"

"Your mother."

Peyton squeezed his hand. "My mother is dead, honey."

The older woman came out of the hogan carrying a bowl of dough. "My daughter is making fry bread. You must stay and have some."

Peyton knew that in Dinè culture, hospitality must be accepted, and nodded.

"Can I help?" Ricky asked.

"You're our guests. You just eat, and that's it."

Peyton went back inside and squatted beside Ambrosia. "What was I doing the day you found me bleeding?"

"You were in your room all day, Mrs. Chase."

Peyton knew the rest. She'd never forgotten the image of her mother piling shoes into a suitcase, upset and talking to herself.

"Didn't eat breakfast or lunch. I baked a chocolate cake to cheer you up."

Peyton snapped to her feet and called to Adler and the boys. "I almost forgot. Today is Mikey's birthday."

"We'll have to stop in Farmington for cake," Adler said.

The women returned, too. The older one pointed to Mikey. "You're the birthday boy, aren't you?"

Mikey raised his hand. "I am Honovi, son of the Utes."

The women exchanged looks. "Well, Honovi, a gift has been waiting for you for quite some time." The mother opened a chest and took out a bracelet hidden in a ball of socks. "Give me your arm," she said, and wrapped his biceps with a silver bracelet engraved with feathers and inlaid with turquoise and mother-of-pearl. "We kept this safe for you. You'll grow into it in no time."

"It was your father's," Mikey said, playing with it. "He was Medicine Man."

The Diné women didn't ask how he knew. "He said you'd come one day."

They were quiet as they drove to Farmington. Ricky played a game on his tablet, and Mikey examined his ornate bracelet. Adler drove silently, giving Peyton her space.

"What is it?" she asked. "You keep looking at me."

"You just learned something dreadful about your mother, didn't you? Something you were never supposed to know." He held out his hand, and she took it.

"You understood how hard it was for me to speak," she said, "and you stepped in. You had my back." She didn't bother to wipe away the tears streaming down her face. "I always suspected she committed suicide. But with a gun? Makes it extra gruesome."

"How did your father say she died?"

"Not from a hemorrhage, that's for sure."

Ricky took out his earbuds. "Are we going home now, Peyton?"

"Yes, and we're close. I texted Layli, told her what time to expect us, and now she's planning a birthday party."

Adler gave her a poignant look.

"Is it bittersweet, Ricky? You're happy to be going home, but you also wish this trip wasn't over. Right?"

He held up his storybook. "Will you still read to me at the ranch? It's so cozy."

"I'll read to you every day, if I can. How about you, Mikey? Happy to be going home this afternoon?"

"Will you take me to the Georgia O'Keeffe museum again?"

She loved that he was able to ask for things. "I'd like to take you to many museums and galleries. There are lots of artists worth studying, and I still haven't shown you the bookcase filled with books about art. We'll go to concerts, too, Ricky."

Adler asked quietly, "How can I help you?"

"I have to help myself." A faded smile fractured her lips. "Whatever it is I need from you, you've been doing it. I can't ask for more."

"Yes, you can, sweet Pey."

She wondered why she was taking the news of her mother's death so hard. She'd suspected it for a long time. On the day she shot herself, her mother had hit her hard, and Peyton might have found her body before anyone else. Just how distraught was her mother? And why had her father never told her the truth? She didn't always remain a child.

Adler dropped the kids off at Layli's cabin. Then drove to the Big House and helped her unload her luggage. "I'll leave the rental, pick up Nuke, and take my Jeep home."

"Thank you for everything."

They stood in the mudroom's quiet, he not asking to stay, she not asking him to leave.

He said, "The past few days have been remarkable, but be patient with me."

"We might need to be patient with each other."

"I've been saving this for last," he said. "I had to order a couple of parts for the banjo. They're hard to find, which is why it's taken so long."

"Thank you, but you should let me pay for them. It's Dad's clock, and—"

"—never say something like that to me again."

She pulled at his sleeve. "It's quite generous of you."

"I'm only bringing it up to let you know I haven't forgotten about it. The parts should be waiting for me. I can bring the clock back on the day of the archery competition."

"We'll do dinner alone afterward?"

He pulled her to him, raising her temperature. "What'll you do in my absence?"

She huffed. "I have a court hearing. My sister wants half of Mom's paintings. Only I don't have them."

Adler's expression morphed from flirtation to fight. "Will that be exorbitant for you?"

"Why do you think I'm honoring the competition? My house in Mendocino won't fetch the full amount the courts are likely to award her. I'm hoping the competition might raise some additional funds."

"Will you let me know the outcome?"

"You'll be the first to know." She stretched her neck, hoping for a kiss, and he didn't disappoint. There was fire in that kiss, and it spread to her loins.

twenty-three

The boys' first day of school coincided with Peyton's court date. For the first time, they had new backpacks, clothes, and fresh haircuts. She'd bought Mikey a blue topaz earring to go with his blue mohawk, and for Ricky, a sterling silver necklace with a turtle pendant.

Peyton drove them down the three-mile access road to the school bus stop. When they saw it barreling down the road, she gave Ricky a hug and a cheek squeeze. Mikey's preferred form of affection was a fist bump, but when she turned to him, he surprised her with a hug.

"Sometimes we lose a lot, including family, but it frees us up to start something new," she said. "Happy first day of school, my boys."

Mikey gave her soulful, dark eyes. "But we're not tied by blood."

"But we are—by artist's blood."

As she drove down to the capital, she mulled over her exchange with Mikey. She was wearing the same tailored black suit she'd worn to her father's funeral, and entered the courtroom with an ominous feeling. The room was dismal—beige walls and brown furniture. She spotted her sister with her face in her phone and wondered what their mother would have thought of this lawsuit.

The atmosphere wasn't what she'd expected. Seats were arranged in a horseshoe, better suited to an AA meeting than a court case. The judge, ironically a woman Harlow's age and also a redhead, wore her robe open, exposing jeans and a silk blouse. She wasn't barricaded behind a desk on a dais, but standing with the lawyers, like a coterie enjoying a cocktail party. When he saw Peyton, Mark excused himself and greeted her with a hug, but it didn't help.

"Glad the atmosphere is relaxed," she said.

"It's family court with a straightforward question, not a murder trial," he said and escorted her to the defendant's side of the room.

Peyton glanced at Lexi and was surprised at her sedate demeanor, when up to that point, she'd been sadistic. The informal atmosphere eased her anxiety, but she knew she'd lose, and more than her house. After this, there would be no reconciling with Lexi. Did she care when Lexi was unjust, unreasonable, and downright cruel? Lexi was also a child who got caught in Harlow's crosshairs. The only other witness.

An affidavit from a handwriting expert, and another from a laboratory on the date and type of ink and paper used authenticated Harlow's letter. Peyton didn't dispute it. Who was she to stand in the way of her mother's intentions? But she wished she still had the paintings she was expected to hand over, not be forced to sacrifice what she had worked so hard to build in California. She struggled to accept that she was expected to settle her parents' debts. Then it hit her: *The sins of the father and the mother are their own inheritance.*

The case was straightforward. The judge declared she'd deliver a verdict to the lawyers that neither Lexi nor Peyton would need to return to the courthouse, and dismissed the court.

Mark's silver hair was growing thinner, exposing a pink scalp splotched with liver spots. "As I initially explained," he said, "the odds are, Lexi will get half. If coming up with the money for your sister still rests on selling your house, then list it. Sorry, honey, inheritance law is clear."

Lexi was wearing a cream pantsuit and more smugness on her face than makeup. "You thought you'd always win, didn't you?"

Peyton stood and grabbed her purse. "You've been in a one-woman race all your life, Lexi. I only compete with myself." Peyton was too deflated to argue with anyone, let alone Lexi, but she realized she'd been running her own one-woman race with her mother, and she had to stop. Seeing herself from all directions wasn't easy. Reality scissored her present into pieces. "You'll get your money soon."

"Why didn't you protest anything?" Lexi asked without her usual edge.

Peyton braced herself on the back of a chair. "Because you're entitled just as much, though you didn't have to sue me. You could've tried to solve it between us first."

A faint guilty look diluted Lexi's smugness. She opened her mouth, then closed it.

Peyton surmised winning must not taste as sweet as Lexi had expected. How could it when they were each other's only sibling?

Mark stowed his files in his briefcase and led Peyton out. "Let me treat you to lunch after all this stress."

"Thank you, Uncle Mark, but I have zero appetite. I need to sell my house and arrange for my furniture to be shipped, but I don't know where to send it. What if I end up losing the ranch, too? Should I ship it to New Mexico or store it in California?" Fear was swallowing her whole, and she didn't know how to escape it.

She drove back to the ranch like a homing pigeon, the windows down, her thoughts wheeling faster than her car. If her furniture in Mendocino had no destination, what would she do with centuries of furniture and artifacts at the Big House? Was she about to lose everything? In her panic, she thought maybe she should take Ashton up on his offer. She'd once loved him more than life itself. He would give her a child and save her ranch. Her house, too. All she had to do was ask. Then Adler's face emerged in her heart and mind. His beautiful smile, depth of soul, honesty, and the way he made her feel safe and understood. He could give her a proper family, and he'd already accepted the boys, even liked them. Ashton hadn't responded kindly to Koda. He'd never embrace the boys. He'd despise them and expect her to go back on her promises. And she'd promised herself to be brave, never to play the imposter again. She'd have to face the firing squad. She still had a chance. A small one, but it was there. As she drove on stunning country roads cut through vibrant rocks, she knew the only way out was through.

The key players showed up at the archery competition early to discuss logistics and rules. Royce joined them at Peyton's behest to advise on the preparations. She knew most of those present and sparked any gathering like kerosene.

Kelcy showed up in jeans and a hat the size of Dallas. He would be competing against an opponent he liked and was determined to keep it friendly.

"Seen William?"

"He's with Mikey and Ricky," Peyton replied. "Let's go find them."

"Ever since I brought that boy to your ranch for riding lessons, he's wanted to stay here all the time. We're going back down to Texas soon. He'll sure miss the boys."

"Come back for the holidays," Peyton said, then remembered she might no longer own the ranch then, and swallowed.

"Layli gave me a tour of your casita last week. I can rent it, maybe? Stay a stretch?"

Peyton had never had a paying guest. It felt strange, not what her family did. So long as she remained on the estate, she'd maintain the family standards. "Come and stay for a weekend as my guest. Then we'll take it from there."

Kelcy flashed his puckish smile. "Little lady, that's kind of you. I'm as bashful as a bison. Will take you up on your offer."

"It's my pleasure."

As they walked to the back door, she gave him a brief history of the ranch. They found William squatting on the ground by the kitchen garden, while Layli tied one of his laces.

"Okay, now you tie the other one like I showed you," she instructed.

William tucked his tongue into the corner of his mouth, focusing hard, and when he managed it, he screamed with joy and jumped to his feet. "I'm a good tie-er now!"

Kelcy's belly laugh resounded. He bent down and squeezed his grandson's cheeks. "Just like good-er is not a word, tie-er isn't one, either." He looked at Layli with soft, blue eyes. "You taught him what no one else could. How'd you do that?"

She winked. "Maybe I can teach his grandpa archery."

He slanted eyes at her and stabbed a thumb to the ground. "You're going down, Layli Hoarnhorse, and you're going down hard."

She gave an evil laugh. "William asked to sleep over. Would be nice if you let him."

"Ditching me already, William?"

"I'll be sleeping in a tepee with Ricky."

"A tepee?" He elbowed Layli. "Want to build me a tepee in my room?"

She wagged a finger. "Kelcy, you're so bad."

"I wish you'd find out just how much."

She shook her head, checked the time, and excused herself.

Mikey, who had been sketching, closed his sketchpad. "Stay here, Layli. He's coming."

"Who's coming?"

"Papa Bear."

Kelcy laughed. "Dreaming of Goldilocks, son?"

In a voice much too solemn for his age, Mikey said, "Goldilocks is fictional. Papa Bear is real."

"For a boy, you're darn serious."

Mikey played with his blue mohawk. "I'm serious about Papa Bear."

"Come, Tiger, let's go."

"Can I sleep over?" William asked, stretching his vowels.

"Yes, why not? Layli should win something. She sure won't win the match. Now, don't forget the judge comes in an hour." Kelcy doffed his hat, took his grandson by the hand, and headed to the targets.

As Mikey predicted, Willie BearClaw arrived in a pickup as old as an icebox, smoking a cigarette, his long hair in two braids and a red bandana tied around his neck.

He slid off the driver's seat, patched up in duct tape. "Parked her back here on account of she's ugly," he said. "Don't want to scare your guests or nothin'."

"Papa Bear!" Mikey exclaimed.

Peyton said, "Mikey knew you were coming. He just told us."

"I bet that boy knows the day I'll die." He laughed, extinguished his butt on the door of his truck, and flung it inside the cab. "Whatever he tells you, believe him." He scratched at the three parallel scars on his cheek, then extended his hand to Peyton. When she shook it, he closed his eyes and chanted something hair-raisingly beautiful. "Good energy," he said. "You're not afraid of me."

"Should I be?"

"The good ones never are." He smiled and eyed her house. "You're on your way to losing some. You prepared for that?"

She pictured strangers moving into her house in Mendocino, and her heart broke. She hoped BearClaw didn't sense she'd lose the ranch, too.

Layli speared out of the house carrying two mugs of coffee. She eyed BearClaw's truck with disgust, took his measure and said, "You're the one Mikey calls the Sky Partitioner."

BearClaw smirked, looked at Mikey with the pride of a Papa Bear, took his cigarettes from his shirt pocket and tapped one out, then offered them to everyone present, including Mikey. "Willie BearClaw is the name."

He reached for a mug, though Layli hadn't offered it, and slurped. "Just how I like it, rich and sweet."

It struck Peyton as odd that he didn't shake hands with Layli. He was happy to take hers and hang on to it. "This is Layli Hoarnhorse. She is—"

"—a guardian angel. Oh, I know."

"Which nation?"

He puffed smoke in little rings. "Lakota and Cherokee, but Scandinavian on my mother's side, like the boys are on theirs."

Layli arranged her hair and hooked her thumbs into her silver and turquoise belt. "How do you know that?"

"I know that the way I know, whoever gave you that belt broke your heart into a million pieces. Yet, you wear it all the time, don't you?"

Never had Peyton seen Layli so startled. Her face fell and her eyes darkened. To soften the moment, she said, "We're serving lunch in a while. You must be hungry."

"Stay with us, BearClaw," Mikey said. "We're having ice cream after."

"Okay, but only because Layli wants me to." He reached into his truck for his rifles; left the windows down and the doors unlocked. "This time, I'll follow you," he told her.

"This time?" Peyton asked. "Didn't you just meet?"

"First time in *this* lifetime," he said without bothering to remove the cigarette from his mouth. "Layli knows."

"Actually, I have no idea," she replied, "but I'm glad to give you room and board."

Peyton had expected him to arrive with Adler. "Is Adler still coming?"

He gave her a knowing smile. "Mustang promises nothing he can't deliver on. We were to meet up in Chama. But the Great Spirit sent me on ahead."

Royce spilled out of the backdoor calling "yoohoo!" Her outfit was worthy of the Great Gatsby, all sequins and fringe. When she saw BearClaw, she made an interesting face. "You look like a cross between Tarzan and Inigo Montoya in *The Princess Bride*. Hello."

He snapped his fingers, helping himself recall. "And you look like what's her name, from *Harry Potter*."

"Madame Olympe Maxime," Mikey reminded him. "The giantess headmistress."

Royce squinted and flared her nostrils. "Really, why not Hagrid?"

BearClaw laughed. "Didn't mean it like that, ma'am. I meant you're elegant like her."

"Uh-huh. It's every woman's dream to be called an elegant giantess." She looked him up and down, then looked at Peyton. "Mark will be here soon. He said the betting closes in an hour."

Peyton thought of the fifty grand she'd already wagered and hoped to God she didn't end up losing that, too. "Thank you for coming. I need your input on everything we've done so far."

"It's what I do. Now, if you'll excuse me, I'll go back to my academy of witches."

Layli snickered. "Mikey, will you take BearClaw to meet Scarborough and ask him to lock his rifles in the safe at the carriage house? BearClaw, we'll catch up with you. We have to meet the judge and go over the details. If you see a Texas cowboy with a chevron mustache, don't shoot him."

He chuckled, mainlining another cigarette. "I like a woman who gets me."

When they were alone, Peyton asked Layli, "Was BearClaw right about your belt?"

Layli caressed the belt she wore almost every day. "His name was Corbin. He was strong and confident. On my birthday, he bought me a twelve-thousand-dollar belt. Then, just like that, he sent me packing."

"An extravagant gift. You must have known each other well."

"Someone I loved more than my liver chased me out at the price of twelve thousand dollars. That was my worth to him—the price of a funeral, ironically. I felt he buried me with it."

"Then why wear it so much?"

"To remind myself never to be with anyone who fears me or puts a price tag on me. He thought an expensive gift would make me believe he cared. Instead, it made me feel cheap and disposable."

"Loved anyone else after him?"

"No one ever bought me a twelve-thousand-dollar gift. Corbin was why I left home. I was so young… Let everything ride on him. The experience left me shattered. After that, I was happy relying on myself. Don't get me wrong. Men are great. But life without them can be great, too."

"That's true," Peyton said. "I got you something, and this is the ideal time to give it to you."

She led Layli to her bedroom. She'd left a big black box on the bench at the bottom of the bed. "Open it."

Layli lifted the top from the box and peeked inside. "You're kidding me!" She unfurled a tailored white suede bodice, and a matching tapered jacket with fringe and intricate beading. "Leather pants, too? Oh my God! This cost a fortune, I know it!"

"This outfit says warrior princess—what you are, Layli." She clapped. "It's something Ashton bought me toward the end, but I've never worn it, reminded me too much of him, so I tucked it away. I brought it with me from Mendocino. You'll rock in it."

"It might be small for me."

"It's stretchy."

"Oh, I'm wearing it, if I have to grease my thighs." Layli laughed and held up the bodice. "This is so sexy. I don't want to let you down. You have so much money riding on me. What if I lose?"

"Here's how I see it. We're both doing all we can. You with a bow and arrow and me with a brush and canvas. We're in it together, Layli. All we can do is give it our all."

Layli ran a gentle hand over the soft deerskin. "Do you think BearClaw will dig this outfit?"

"Willie BearClaw? Don't tell me you like him."

"What's not to like?" She returned the clothes to the box. "He's sexy, isn't he?"

Peyton laced her fingers together. "He's small, wobbles, and reeks of nicotine. Sexy, you say?"

"Ugly sexy, but sexy. Intense as hell. I find him irresistible."

"Whatever happened to handsome sexy?"

"They can't all be calendar worthy, like some people, okay?"

Peyton raised her hands. "Well, I feel sorry for Joe. Between Kelcy and BearClaw, he hasn't got a chance."

Layli did a suave trot. "I'm enough woman for all three."

Peyton cackled and attempted a whistle she couldn't muster. "Just remember, everyone involved has a gun."

"So do I, Flower Child."

"You're serious about BearClaw?"

"Are you serious about Adler?"

"Were the Spanish monks serious about their missions?" Peyton foresaw the tempest to come. If she lost her estate, would Adler go with her to California? Could she give up the Pacific for New Mexico without Pioneer Ranch?

Peyton changed clothes and prepared to meet the guests. Word of the competition had spread, and strange faces arrived along with familiar ones. Cameras streamed, and the betting window was about to close.

On that perfect September day, the aspens' gold foliage twinkled against white bark, and the sage flowered purple. In the distance, a herd of horned Guzerat cows ambled from one pasture to another. Targets dotted the greensward amidst scattered orange and red leaves.

Layli wasn't the only warrior princess. Peyton was fighting her own battle and dressed the part in cowgirl boots and an emerald-green dress that billowed behind her, exposing her thighs. She hoped that when Alder got there, he'd calm her down. They'd spoken on the phone, but she hadn't seen him since they returned from Utah.

Punctual as the clocks her father loved, he arrived on time. When she saw him getting out of his Jeep with Nuke, she hurried toward him. She knew eyes were on them and that Adler loathed public displays. They were too familiar for handshakes, but not involved enough to kiss in public. She stopped a step away and let him make the first move.

"You're breathtaking," he said, pulled her into an embrace and kept her there. "The list of my favorite colors on you is getting longer and longer."

"You look handsome yourself. I like it when you hug me like this."

He studied their surroundings. "I want so much to kiss you, but too many folks around." He squeezed her hand. "Brought you something, but it'll have to wait until after the competition."

"You didn't have to bring me anything. It's enough you're here."

"This you want," he said. "Sorry the lawsuit didn't go better."

"Can't win them all." She smiled, though she felt like weeping. "I'm able to handle today better, now you're here."

"I like when you tell me how you feel and what you think."

"You make it easy." She touched his cheek, then ran a finger down his neck to his breastbone.

He grinned and pressed her hand over his heart. "Are you seducing me, Ms. Chase?"

"Not sure I ever stopped." She saw Koda round the corner and did a mute clap. "My niece is here!" Margot got out of the car dressed in ripped jeans and a pink halter top. Peyton dashed to her, splaying her arms. "Welcome to New Mexico."

"Margot, this is Adler. Adler, my niece Margot."

He smiled, doffed his hat, shook her hand, and pasted eyes on Koda, who was struggling with Margot's enormous suitcases.

"Is he your boyfriend or something?"

"Adler is my date." She caught his eye and was glad to see him smiling.

"I'll help Koda take up the suitcases," he said.

"Koda, put them in the lavender and yellow room, please. And thank you so much." She kissed her niece's cheek. "Does your mom know I invited you?"

"Dad knows. He'll tell her eventually like a little bitch." She bit a cuticle. "He's down in the dumps."

Peyton crossed her arms over her chest as she looked at a younger version of herself with more scarlet in her hair and attitude. "While you're here, please mind how you treat people, especially Koda."

"He's always in my DMs. Not the other way around!"

"More the reason. Don't lead him on, Margot."

"'kay." She fluffed her thick hair. "What smells so good?"

Peyton placed a hand on Margot's ever disappearing waist and guided her toward the food tent, where taquitos, flautas, and chimichangas were being served. "We grill on woodchips. It'll smell even better when we toss some steaks on those flames. Eat lots, honey."

"Ooh, a full bar," Margot said, promising the day wouldn't remain peaceful.

Peyton could hear Lexi accusing her of turning Margot into a drunk. "Just have one drink, okay?"

Margot nodded like a rascal, promising not to loot the cookie jar.

Scarborough pealed the bells, and Layli strode to the center of the crowd, resplendent in her new outfit, with a red bar painted over her eyes, gold lips, and three parallel stripes on one cheek. She wore feathers and beads in her hair and thick gold bands on her wrists.

Kelcy came closer. "Christ! War paint? Bodice? Are you trying to give me a heart attack? I'm not that young anymore."

"Just want to say win or lose, you're an upstanding guy and a remarkable archer."

Kelcy put down his whisky glass. "Win or lose, let me take you out."

"Just why do I interest you, Kelcy?"

"Because you don't back down. It turns me on, damn it."

"You're not my type, and you've got too many miles on you."

He gave a belly laugh. "Darlin', that's why I know how to treat a lady. Don't hate me when I beat you later and don't go changing your mind."

"I agree to nothing." Layli eyed BearClaw. "I have my eye on someone, and he ain't you, so prepare for a beating."

"It depends on the beating you have in mind."

"You're so bad, Kelcy."

The crowd went quiet as the competition began. Kelcy had gone to some expense, ordering pre-printed targets with black dots in various shapes. An impartial judge had been hired to evaluate the results and declare a winner. An archery champ himself, he was a man in his forties with disproportionately muscular arms. Contestants had to pierce each dot with an arrow. The most accurate archer would win.

With pomp in the air like confetti, the guests raised their phones to shoot videos. A live feed had been set up to enable remote betting.

Royce and Peyton stood with Mikey, Ricky and William, making sure they were quiet and safe.

Adler discretely took her hand. "Layli is going to lose," he said.

"Why do you say that?"

"Kelcy's wrist isn't bothering him anymore, and he stands like a hunter. She stands like she's at target practice. It means he knows how to take a shot under duress. Can she? She's not used to an audience, might suffer target panic."

"She won the first time," Peyton said.

"Yeah, but this is no rodeo. It's big money."

Royce said, "Let's hope Layli's cleavage distracts Kelcy. Otherwise, she's going down."

"Layli is a warrior," Peyton said.

Royce played with her massive ruby earrings. "When warriors fall, it's usually in battle, honey."

The judge stepped to the center and stated the rules. He discussed safety, reminding all present to stay back. "A winner is declared when four out of seven matches are won," he explained. "Be as quiet as you would at a golf tournament to allow the contestants to concentrate."

He tossed a coin. Kelcy called heads, and heads it was.

He cemented his position and pulled his bow. "Remember, don't hate me." His first shots were accurate, and Peyton braced herself.

Layli's bow wasn't as sophisticated as Kelcy's, but she was sure of her skill. Snorting horses and barking dogs were the only sounds as she drew back her bow, took aim, and fired. Her accuracy was astonishing.

"They look about even," Peyton said.

The judge went to the targets and measured, then declared Layli the winner by the slimmest of margins.

"The rounds get more complex," Kelcy teased.

Layli sneered, but he blew her kisses that made her laugh. "You think that gives you an advantage?"

"Hell, yes! My bow doesn't need as much stringing as yours."

Kelcy won the next round. The third round went to Layli, the fourth to Kelcy, making them three to three going into the seventh and final round. Layli's fingers were getting red and Peyton started praying.

Adler pressed against her. When she looked up at him, he lowered his face to hers. "Don't worry, sweets. I'm with you."

Mikey was riveted, but Ricky turned away.

"Layli Hoarnhorse, I told you that when my wrist healed, you couldn't beat me."

Layli stretched her fingers and took her position for the last time. A gust of wind whipped up, making her eyes water, and she fired an arrow slightly off. The crowd was stunned, but didn't know who had won. The judge started measuring, then called Mark over as a witness.

The judge faced the spectators and said, "By a margin of two-tenth of an inch, Kelcy is the winner!"

The crowd applauded and whistled. William ran wildly to his grandfather. Without an experienced trainer and an elite bow, Layli had lost the competition by a hair.

Kelcy didn't gloat, didn't even seem happy. He looked at Layli and said, "You're remarkable, and you don't owe me anything, you know."

"You're impressive. Congratulations." Layli put down her bow and slipped on her jacket.

"I hope you knew she'd lose," Royce said. "Sometimes your optimism works against you."

Peyton's heartbeat was drumming in her head. She'd lost her Victorian house and two-thirds of her nest egg, and it tumbled down on her like a rockslide. She stood punished, but that's what atonement is—a quart of blood and two tons of gold. As she studied Layli, she understood how crushed she felt, despite her efforts to hide it. She would have liked to hug her, but like her brother, Layli was averse to sympathy. "Don't blame yourself. You did your best."

Glass-eyed, Layli said nothing.

"You're a phenomenal archer, Layli."

Most guests applauded, a few booed, but they were silenced when BearClaw threw a knife that knocked one of Kelcy's arrows right out of its target.

"What the hell was that?" Kelcy asked.

He stepped forward and looked Kelcy dead in the eyes. "Quadruple or nothing on the chance, I knock out all arrows. Quadruple or nothing on the bet, I can repeat this accuracy eleven more times."

If BearClaw were to win, Peyton's fifty-thousand-dollar bet would turn to a one hundred thousand dollar win, but if he failed, she'd have to fork up one hundred thousand. She'd have to give up the rest of her nest egg and sell her car. She wasn't a high risk-taker unless challenged, and when had life challenged her more?

twenty-four

Kelcy nicked the end from a Cuban cigar and light it. "You got such money?"

"I'm not betting," BearClaw replied. "You and the fat-cats are."

Mark, the self-appointed bookie, announced with full lungs. "This works only if most of you are still in. Quadruple or nothing. Who's in?"

Kelcy asked to examine BearClaw's knife. It was a stainless-steel thrower knife. Basic. "You're sure? Your friends can lose extra. Eleven more times, hitting it exactly right is an awful lot."

Mark said, "It's better odds than a perfect game in bowling, and that has happened."

Peyton's gut said to hazard more, but she was petrified, and consulted Adler. "Sorry to ask, but should I do it?"

"If you don't bet, you've lost fifty thousand for sure. On his lonesome, Willie practices every day, and he has the eye of the tiger. I know this look. He's in the zone right now. I'm betting. If he can make it happen, I'll split the winnings with him."

Soon Mark announced the betting closed.

Mikey shifted from foot to foot, humming a chant BearClaw taught him. Ricky buried his face in Peyton's dress.

Adler squatted beside him. "Look at me, Ricky. We might not be born with courage, but we mustn't die without it. BearClaw would want you to witness what he's doing and learn from it. You owe him your attention."

"What if he loses?"

"We don't fear loss. We fear never trying. At times, we all lose but win on another day."

Peyton held her breath as BearClaw knocked off Kelcy's arrows one-by-one, throwing the same knife over and over with confidence and ease.

Kelcy, who now owed ridiculous money, applauded. "Might be the best money I ever lost," he said. "I can't remember when I had this much fun." He took a draw on his cigar. "Ever kill anyone with that knife?"

BearClaw held his knife up, blessed, and sheathed it. "Why, got a target?"

Peyton gripped her belly, laughing. She still hated that her house was on the market, but she was relieved. With the added one hundred thousand, she could pay Lexi the money the judge was likely to award her and share some with Layli.

"Sir, you're unbelievably gracious," Adler said, shaking hands with Kelcy. "I have no words."

Peyton promised him a special dinner should he visit them overnight. "You really went for it, Kelcy. I'm sorry you lost, but you made a significant difference."

"I don't settle," he said, and relit his cigar. "I go for the stars. Those who settle are in a hurry. Too dumb to know good enough is also bad enough. Did that once. Ended up in a divorce that gave me not two burro ears, but four."

Royce said, "You probably had six before."

He pointed to Adler, laughing. "Son, are you taking me and my Charles hunting or what? He has bad luck. Can use guidance. We'll pay."

"I've never charged anyone for joining me in the wild. And after what you did today, it'll be an honor. January is the best month. We'll plan something."

"Come back with William soon," Peyton said. "Ricky would love it, and so would we." She glanced around and saw an exchange between BearClaw and Layli. He was running a hand over the three painted lines on her cheek. Whatever he said made her tear up.

Royce asked about BearClaw.

"He's no ordinary man," Peyton said. "Lives alone in the middle of the wilderness."

"Didn't I say it? He's Tarzan. Dunk him in Listerine and bring him to my hut."

Peyton cracked up. "You, too? Layli thinks he's hot stuff."

Royce eyed BearClaw. "He's twisted, strange, scruffy. Hot stuff is about right."

Peyton shrugged. "Well, shows how much I know."

Mark was settling the bets, and Scarborough's crew began dismantling the targets and tent. Guests headed to their vehicles, and Layli to her cabin where Peyton knew she would snip and tailor her feelings until stitched mute.

Adler said, "I have to fetch something from my car. I'll meet you in the study."

For the second time, they stood in her father's personal space. Adler was carrying a small gift bag and the banjo clock.

"Thank you so much for fixing that," Peyton said. "Dad's study wasn't the same without it."

He returned the clock to its original spot on the wall, then snatched her in his brawny arms. "You're all mine now." He kissed her hard and long. "First, look inside that bag."

Peyton found a pair of riding gloves. "Toggi Salisburys! Aww, these are adorable. What a thoughtful gift."

"They eliminate the problem of tan lines to the hands and wrists during the summer months. I always hated that problem."

Her memories wheeled back in time to when she dropped her gloves, and he ran after her, all those years ago. "Are you going to specialize in handing me gloves?"

"I might be destined to do that."

Peyton came closer, rose on her toes, and kissed him like an open invitation. "I've been thinking about this for days."

He tightened his grip on the back of her neck and kissed her again. "I was hoping to stay. But you might not want that once I show you what else I brought." He lifted the glass door to the banjo and depressed a piece of wood. A lever popped. Adler pulled on it until it shifted, exposing a slot full of letters.

"To fix the clock and clean all its parts, I had to take it completely apart. The hidden compartment is ingenious. Never seen such seamlessness."

"You found Dad's letters?" She reached for them and noticed the one on top was dated only a week before his passing. "Wow, Adler, I can't tell you how struck I am. I looked for these letters everywhere."

"Your father mustn't have wanted them found. They're sealed, no idea what's in them, and I wouldn't have read them, anyway. They're dated though, going back twenty-one years."

Peyton brought a hand to her mouth. "The year my mother died."

He kissed her forehead and rubbed his hands up and down her back. "If you want to dive into them, we'll postpone everything."

Peyton dreaded those letters, but knew they were likely to reveal the emotions her father had kept bottled up. "Okay, but can it be soon? I feel bad asking you to drive down again. If it's too much, I'll drive up to you."

"First read them, then tell me what you need, and I'll give it to you."

Peyton kept the bundle of letters glued to her chest as she saw him off. What they revealed might complicate her life even further. She thought of Recipient One, who could be a secret half-sibling and couldn't face those letters alone. She dialed Royce and headed over to see her.

Royce met her on the loggia. "You look blue. Did you forget to breathe on the way?" She checked her hair in the foyer mirror. "I'm balding. Soon, I'll look like Mr. Clean."

They sat together on the divan in the tearoom. Peyton stacked the letters on the table. "They're in chronological order. I just couldn't read them without the company of someone I trust. Thank you for letting me come here."

"Lordy, I'm dying to know what's in them."

Peyton opened the first letter and read it with fast moving eyes. "This is Dad expressing his grief. He's astonished he wasn't the first to go." She picked up the second letter, slowly bringing a hand to her mouth and tearing up.

"What, what?"

"He writes of how devastated he was to find Mom covered in blood. He says he'll never have a gun in the house again."

"She shot herself?" Royce poured herself a whiskey. "If there was ever an excuse to start early." She offered Peyton the bottle.

"Can't handle a drink right now."

"And the third letter?"

"This one is dated a month after Mom's funeral." Peyton shook her head. "Listen to this, I'll read it to you. 'I'm furious you tried to kill yourself, Harlow. I'm wrathful that you can't understand a word I say when I visit you. Livid that you left Peyton without her mother and frustrated you didn't die. If only you'd died. I wouldn't have to see you mangled and unconscious. Wouldn't have to lie to the world. That would be too easy for me. You have to punish me, even now.'"

"What does that mean?" Royce poured herself another inch of whiskey.

"He said she was dead when she wasn't, but why lie about that?" She'd never known her father to be a liar, yet here was a whale of a lie she couldn't comprehend. How much of her history did she understand?

"Open the fourth letter, hurry."

Peyton raked eyes like quicksand over a single page. "He swears he'll never forgive her, wishes he could stop visiting her, but loves her still." She remembered her father's survival strategy. How he'd enter carpentry mode, carving his feelings and wedging them where they couldn't obstruct his routine.

"When did she die?"

Peyton opened letter number five, read it slowly, and smiled through tears. "He's telling her about my birthday party, and how I seemed much older at thirteen than twelve, as if I'd matured years, not months."

Royce drained her glass. "You'll have to keep reading. We need to know the real date Harlow passed."

The other letters spoke of his loneliness, his unremitting anger, his loss of faith, and how much he hated his inability to let Harlow go.

"He never writes that she died!" Peyton said. "Can she still be alive?"

"It would explain why he sold the paintings. It sounds to me like Harlow put herself in a coma. The price of her care would've been exorbitant."

Mikey's words returned to her: *You're stuck because she is. She's waiting for you.* Could her mother have hung on for two decades, waiting to see her? Was Harlow Recipient One? She struggled to breathe, which made Royce rap her back and force her to take a glass of whiskey.

"Drink it, for God's sake!"

Peyton did, and though she hated whiskey, the burning in her chest reduced the burning in her spirit. "I'm calling Uncle Mark."

He answered right away. "It's good you called. I need to see you."

Peyton figured he must have heard from the judge. But the crisis at hand was ever more critical. She explained the situation.

"What an unexpected turn of events! I'm so sorry, honey."

"Can you go to Mr. Jennings and extract the truth?"

"At this hour, he'll be in his loungewear, not fenced behind his desk. Might fess up. Where're you?"

"At Royce's."

"Let me see what I can do."

Peyton shot up and paced, fiddling with her nails. "What if Mr. Jennings refuses to tell us?"

"I'll have to break his glasses and all his pencils, won't I? Darling girl, lawyers know how to speak to one another, and Mark was attorney general of this state. He knows how to cross-examine, believe me."

"I'm trying to accept Mom might be alive, but it feels like a lie."

"You want to see her, don't you?"

Peyton wasn't sure she could. "Dare I?" She sat on the divan, took off her boots, and tucked a throw pillow in her lap. "I got from Dad's letters that she's alive but catatonic or something. What did you get?"

"Something like that."

"That would make her the living dead," Peyton said. "No one deserves that."

"I have to eat something. Shock makes me hungry. Well, lack of shock makes me hungry, too."

"Not at all hungry, but I'll take a bucket of coffee, please."

"You look like you lost ten pounds since Sorensen's funeral, and you never needed to lose a single one." Royce called the housekeeper. "How Sorensen suffered in silence."

"I knew Dad protected me, but I didn't know how much." Peyton couldn't stop sobbing. Perhaps it wasn't her father who needed forgiveness, she did.

Ninety minutes later, the housekeeper knocked on the door and entered. "Two gentlemen are here for you, Mrs. Kent. Would you like them to join you here?"

"If they look like Laurel and Hardy, yes, please."

Mark entered first, joking that the cops would soon rescue Mr. Jennings from his kidnappers. "I'll have you know this will cost you at least cocktails."

"I can't believe you showed up in person," Peyton said, slipping her boots back on. She hugged Mark and shook hands with Mr. Jennings. "I'm being a complete pest. Please forgive me, but I must know some things."

"I confided in Mark as my attorney," Mr. Jennings said. "If he wishes to risk getting disbarred by revealing information to you, that's on him… Of course, I'll have to report him first and prove it."

"There's a trust of consequence funded by the Pioneer Ranch Estate, for which you are sole beneficiary," Mark said. "It provides medical care in a private facility to a quadriplegic with no cognizance—a big trust fund." He looked at Mr. Jennings for confirmation. "Upon her passing, all remaining funds revert to you, Peyton, not Lexi, since the principle came from the paternal line alone."

"Is Harlow in a hospital in Santa Fe?" Royce asked.

Mark looked to Mr. Jennings for answers.

He shook his head, flaring his nostrils, then took a notepad from his pocket and scribbled the name of a doctor, an address, and a phone number. "I recommend Mark do the contacting on your behalf, as your lawyer. You won't encounter any resistance. Dr. Clay is looking to retire." He handed the paper to Mark. "I'll leave now and wait in your car. I was never here."

Peyton crossed her hands over her heart. "I don't know how to thank you, Mr. Jennings."

He gave her a mischievous smile. "I wouldn't mind a steak and some bourbon."

"Say when." Peyton sighed and winced at her next thought. "Is Mom in horrible shape?"

Mark patted her back. "Manny has been checking on her now Sorensen is no longer with us. He said she's unrecognizable. Her muscles have atrophied. You can only imagine, Peyton dear."

"I'll go with you, darling," Royce said. She gave her big hands to Mark. "You are the hero of the hour."

"One more thing, Peyton. It comes as no surprise that the judge found for Lexi. I know you think it's fair, but nine hundred, twenty thousand dollars is a lot of money to give away. I'm sorry."

Royce frowned. "That's highway robbery!"

Peyton said, "That's about right for half their value. Might be a little low, even." She didn't wait for Mark to ask about her next move. "The real estate agent was confident my house would sell quickly, given its location, size, and condition. Looks like I'll be able to cover the funds."

Royce gave her sad eyes. "You were so selective restoring that house and thought you'd be in it indefinitely. Oh, darling girl…"

"Like Scarborough always says… We're only borrowers."

"I'll skedaddle." Mark closed the door behind him.

"This is a humongous mess," Royce whispered. She handed Peyton her phone. "Call Ashton. If Harlow has lasted twenty-one years, your trust fund might not revert to you for quite a while. You can't afford to lose everything. Call him."

Peyton stared at the coffee ring at the bottom of her cup. The longer she gawked at it, the more trepidation noosed her.

"Fine. You can call him later, but by God, do it." Royce sat beside her and squeezed her wrist. "Listen to me on this one. He's precious and dying to get you back. I know you like this Adler guy, but he can't fix things for you. You can have everything with Ashton. Just say the word."

Peyton kept the letters on her lap on her drive home. Harlow had two daughters. Lexi should know, but she and Peyton had been on terrible terms. She thought it would be best to visit Harlow alone, before letting her sister know their mother was still alive. Mikey's messages resurfaced, signaling life. She dissected everything he'd said, one cryptic line at a time. What else did he know about her mother?

twenty-five

Mikey was in his favorite spot, the billiard room, playing a video game. As soon as Peyton sat beside him, he put down the controller.

Her heart thundered, and her eyes ached from too much crying. "Honey, I'm going to ask you something, if you can't answer me, that's okay, all right?"

"Your mom is not dead. I told you."

"Yes, that's right, and thank you. I didn't understand before."

He stared without blinking. "She shouldn't still be alive, but she has something to say to you. If I go with you, she can say it."

"Go with me?" Peyton pictured her mother as Mr. Jennings had described her and couldn't expose Mikey to that. "It's too much to ask of you."

"She has no face. I know. She showed me."

Peyton remembered the drawing Mikey had shared with her in Utah. "Was the figure on the hill watching me, my mom?"

He nodded. "I drew her far because she has no face and feels isolated, but her spirit is close." His tranquil air and straight answers were hair-raising. "Can we paint together soon?"

"I hope to always paint alongside you." Peyton had been feeling a new composition coming on, the way she birthed all her paintings. She'd hold the brush and let the canvas create itself. This time was no different, except she'd been mired in one crisis after another. Her studio was in Mendocino, but she had her restoration kit, and there were still plenty of canvases at the ranch. "Thank you, Mikey. What you said to me is better than anything."

He tapped her hand as if he were her senior. "Don't be afraid, Peyton. I'll go with you."

She twisted her body toward him. "Are you ever afraid of your visions?"

He shook his head. "The old ones don't scare me. People do."

Peyton set up in a den they rarely used and sat on a stool, painting the edges of a canvas. She knew a face would emerge. Whose? She furiously painted in colors inspired by the last vestiges of summer when the blooms and fruits evanesce, shades of green, gray-blue, pale pink, and buttercream. The longer she painted, the more eager she became to see her mother.

Against Royce's advice, Peyton brought Mikey to see her mother. She was afraid that if he saw Harlow's deformity, he'd have nightmares, and made him promise to stay at the door.

Harlow was a patient at a luxury clinic, a Spanish adobe behind a secured gate at the end of a long driveway. When they arrived, they were vetted by a chic, heavily Botoxed receptionist, then ushered into Dr. Clay's office.

He was a heavyset man with droopy cheeks, keen blue eyes, and thinning white hair combed forward. "I never thought I'd see you in person, Ms. Chase. Your pictures are all over your mother's room. Through them, I've watched you grow up. It's a little strange seeing you in the flesh now."

Peyton took a deep breath. "Is Mom completely unable to recognize anyone?"

"That's correct. She's kept alive artificially through a feeding tube, and has been unresponsive since she arrived."

"Can life support last forever?"

"No, and it shouldn't. Your mother has been overmedicated, at minimum. Some years ago, we administered a trial drug that killed most of the patients, but not Harlow. She hung on."

"Might we see her now?" Royce asked.

The doctor looked at Mikey. "How old is he?"

"He can hear this, that's okay," Peyton replied. "It's facts of life."

"I must warn you. The bullet shattered the bones in her face, destroying her brain. Are you sure, Ms. Chase, you want to see your mother in this condition? Your father wanted to spare you that."

"He was sparing his little girl, but I'm a woman now. If he could handle it, so can I." She angled her body toward the door. "Thank you for the warning. I appreciate it."

Dr. Clay nodded and led the way to a large room. The bed faced away from the door toward a long view below of Sante Fe's terracotta roofs, salt cedar, and Russian olive trees. She spotted her mother's hand resting on the edge of the bed before seeing the rest of her. It wasn't manicured, rather veiny and jaundiced, and her hair was gray and short, though brushed.

"She gets visits from a stylist and a masseuse, even a cat," Dr. Clay said. "We play audiotapes and music. Two full-time nurses rotate. Your mother is never alone. Basically, this house and its staff are dedicated to your mother's care. Your father wanted her to be well kept in case she awakened. His grief was strong."

Her father had been so angry at his grief. She took her mother's hand. It was heavy, though bony, lifeless. "Will Mom ever wake up?"

"No, which is why I appreciate your coming. Sorensen's Catholic faith interfered. He wouldn't terminate your mother's care, but I'm hoping you're of a different mind."

Royce asked, "Terminate?"

"End life support. Given the quality of life, I think it's time. I hope you're not tempted to object. We are still being paid to care for you mother, but she hasn't made progress in twenty-one years. There's no justification for keeping her alive."

"Can we have a moment alone with her, please, Dr. Clay?"

"Yes, of course. The nurse will wait outside."

"Are you okay, darling?" Royce asked.

Harlow had no distinguishable features. If Peyton had been shown a picture of her mother's face today, she wouldn't have realized it was anything human. It was a caved in groove of scars and crushed bone. "How had Dad handled all this alone?" She squeezed her mother's hand and sobbed.

Royce said, "She wouldn't want this prison of the flesh for herself. Was this Sorensen's way of helping her?"

"My guess is he thought she punished herself. She had made her bed, and he wanted her to lie in it." She realized the conflicted relationship she had with her mother might not have been unique to her. He must have felt the same way. Had Lexi?

Royce scoured the drawers and found needles, gauze, and ointments. "The Harlow I knew would have had perfumes, creams, and lace underwear. Not this. No, not this."

Though Mikey had obediently stayed behind where he couldn't see Harlow, Peyton worried. "Honey, are you doing okay?" Harlow's heart monitor twitched, making Peyton wonder if her mother felt her presence. An image of the portrait she'd stolen on the day her parents stopped forgiving each other flashed in her mind. "Mom, if you can hear me, I'm so sorry."

Mikey took a step forward. "She wants to speak to you."

"Royce, may I have a minute with Mom alone, but I need Mikey to stay."

Royce was reluctant to leave but hustled out.

Father Gabriel had given her absolution, but Peyton felt the need to atone. "I may have pushed you over the edge, Mom, and I shouldn't have done what I did. Forgive me."

Mikey spoke in an even tone, as if delivering a generic message. "She knew it was you who took the painting, but she wants you to know it wasn't your fault."

Peyton stifled her cries in fear of alarming Mikey.

"She put paint on your face because, like her, you have it in your blood. She says it's not you who should be sorry. It's her."

Peyton clung to her mother's hand. "Does she forgive me?"

"She says you did nothing wrong, don't need forgiveness, but asks that you forgive her."

Peyton was filled with love and forgiveness. "I do, Mom, and I'm really sorry."

Harlow's monitor twitched again, sending the nurse into the room. "I've never seen her respond before." She fiddled with the equipment. "Remarkable."

"Is it okay to keep visiting?" Peyton asked.

"Yes, but I'll have to inform Dr. Clay," she said and left.

Peyton asked, "Is there a message for Lexi?"

"She'd like to see her, too. Wants her to know she wasn't a disappointment."

"Anything else?"

Mikey closed his eyes and scrunched his face as though he were in pain. "She isn't speaking to me anymore."

Peyton walked over to him and kissed his forehead. "You might think I'm saving you, honey, but it's you who are saving me."

He wrapped his slender arms around her waist and let her hold him.

"I love you, my boy." She truly felt he was her son, no matter the obstacles. He had brought her mother back to her, and in turn, she'd be the best mother she could to him and his brother. "There's hardly anything I won't do to keep you and Ricky safe and loved."

Peyton tucked the boys in at Layli's cabin, then returned to the unfinished canvas. She felt a sense of urgency so great, she could barely stay seated on the stool, had to paint standing. She raised the easel and began sketching features with charcoal. Soon she realized she was drawing Lexi's face. Harlow had never done a portrait of Lexi. By paying her mother's debt, Peyton atoned, trading the portrait she'd stolen for one she created on her mother's behalf. Lexi deserved to be loved with paint, not the adult Lexi who took pleasure in tormenting her, but the child Lexi, who felt replaced and neglected.

As she fleshed out her sister's portrait, she heard the banjo clock strike midnight and took it as approval from her father, who had taught her generosity of the soul. She didn't know if Lexi would appreciate the portrait or even agree to see it, but that was beyond her control. As she often did after capturing the essence of her composition, she stepped back and evaluated her work, approving. She picked a needle from her conservation kit, pricked her left pinky, and squeezed until a sizeable drop of blood formed. She dipped her brush into it and added it to the pink lips she had given Lexi, turning them a rosier shade. Then she squeezed another drop of blood onto her palette and mixed it with dark pigment, dipped her brush, and signed the painting. A blood sacrifice for a family that had been sacrificed by circumstance, history, and human frailty. She titled the work *Blood and Paint*. It wouldn't be finished to her standards for a while, but it was already clear and moving.

She was exhausted but more serene than she'd been in a long time and aching to speak to Adler. She needed him to hold her. More than that. Needed him to lie with her and spoon her in a healing and sheltering embrace. She didn't know how much she could ask of him. Hadn't her parents, each in their own way, pushed her to be less needy? She paused. In the stillness, she heard the banjo clock ticking the seconds, acknowledging a new truth. Life had pivoted. She could no longer source her feelings from the past. She'd have to plumb them from her present.

It was the middle of the night, too late to call Adler, but she could text him. *If you're awake, can I call you?*

She waited a few minutes, but no reply came. She wished she hadn't sent the text. After the spiritual cleansing, she needed a good scrubbing, and took a soothing shower, a baptism for her rebirth. She pulled on a pair of shorts and a tank top, brushed her hair and teeth, then checked her phone and discovered that Adler had texted back saying to call him.

"I'm so happy you can talk, but is it really okay?" she asked. "I feel I'm imposing."

"I don't want to talk on the phone," he said. "I'd rather do it in person, if that's all right."

She snapped awake. "Are you close by?"

"At the end of your driveway. I left when I saw your text."

Peyton danced around. "I'll meet you at the backdoor."

She stood in the doorway, her hair wet, waving as he walked toward her, grinning.

"What're you doing calling up men in the middle of the night?" He hugged her, lifting her off the floor. "You smell of soap. It's my favorite scent, funny enough."

"I needed you and here you are."

"I was down here having a beer with the guys and playing cards. Your timing was impeccable. You needed me?" His voice and demeanor showed her he loved that she'd said that.

She took his hand and led him into the kitchen. "Want something to eat?"

"Did you call me because you thought I'd be hungry?"

She laughed. "Will you hold me?"

"For as long as you need."

"Did you want to tell me something specific, sweet Pey, maybe about those letters?"

"I'll tell you everything. So much happened yesterday and today, but I don't want to spend another minute crying."

He lifted her and kissed her. "Are you ever going to show me the view from your room?"

"It's dark now," she replied, giggling.

"Good. I intend to draw the blinds." He hoisted her over his shoulder and ran up the steps to the second floor as she laughed and shrieked.

It had been years since Peyton awakened in the arms of someone who felt a part of her. Twined in his arms and legs, facing him, she told him about seeing her mother, explained her father's journey, and her own emotional state.

"I've been aching to wake up with you by my side," he said.

"Does this mean you trust me now?" She held him against her skin. "When I asked to talk, I didn't think you'd come over."

"You've been consistent and transparent in ways I'm not used to. Despite your grief and stress, you're clear about me in your heart and mind." Soft morning rays fell on his tranquil face. "Besides, a man can wait only so long to hold a woman he thinks about constantly. Sweet Pey, what'll you do if you can't raise enough money to keep the ranch?"

She'd debated this hundreds of times, but hadn't found an acceptable answer. "If I lose it, I'll be the one who fell far from my father's tree, not just my mother's. I can't lose it. I'll try just about anything not to."

"I don't want you returning to California full time. If you lose this ranch, might you?"

Adler lived in New Mexico. So did the kids and other people she loved. Yet New Mexico had always been Pioneer Ranch. "I don't have everything figured out."

"Maybe I haven't made myself clear enough. We both want children, and I'm getting long in the tooth to keep on waiting. We're Catholics from northern New Mexico. What runs in your veins also runs in mine, and though we haven't known each other for long, we're mature and self-aware. I want us to move in that direction."

"You slay me, know that? You massacre me."

He kissed her intensely. "Then stay and start a family with me."

She felt a torrent of emotion. "Do you have any idea how sexy those words are?" She fondled his chest. "There's something I want to know."

He raised his head, alert, reminding her of the hunter he was.

"Why did you back away from me? We sort of talked about it, but I want to know more. It couldn't have been intimidation. What was it?"

He lay on his back and guided her to lie on top of him. "I had to be sure," he said, resting his hands on her buttocks.

"Sure of what?"

"I needed you to choose me for who I am, not so you could change me. We've led different lives. I questioned whether I'd be enough, or whether you'd be too much."

"Why would you doubt that?"

"Because most people either don't see the one they choose, or if they see them, they set out to change them. How could I be sure you'd be different?"

Peyton thought of Ashton. She'd once thought he'd change his life, even change his views for her. "Oh, I learned that lesson, believe me."

"I didn't want a shallow attachment based on good sex and fun times. I wanted something soulful, real, founded on shared values. Because of the circumstances, our mature ages, and the question of your permanent address, I knew we'd get just one shot. Had to get it right."

She gave him a naughty look. "You knew the sex would be good?"

"Are you telling me it's just good, not great?" He tickled her, then cemented her hands to his chest. "Whatever you want from me, ask it. I may not always perceive you well, but I'm learning. I want to hear what you need."

"Same here." *Blood and Paint* was no longer the title of a painting. It had become the title of her life. "Am I too much for you, like you initially feared I could be?"

"You're where I belong." He touched her face with his fingers. "I'm not too little for you?"

She eased out of bed to stand naked before him. It was no seduction. "I am as you see," she said. "Just as I can't show you more skin, I can't show you more soul. You know my deepest secrets. I've shown you my sins, lumps and wounds, and you've never pushed on them. You deserve only light and love."

For a second he stared at her, then he flung off the sheets, sprang out of bed, and lifted her. "If anyone had ever told me our paths would cross again, then overlap, I wouldn't have believed it. And if they had said a woman can fill me to the brim, I'd have called them a liar. That's what you mean to me, sweet Pey."

She wrapped her legs around his back and pecked kisses on his lips, cheeks, and eyes. "While we're on the same path, feel free to hoist me over your shoulder again. That was thrilling."

After Adler went home to change and pack a bag, Peyton stood before her sister's portrait, fresh as her many new awakenings. She had to attempt the conversation she dreaded. She called her sister, and to her surprise, she answered.

"What?" Lexi asked. "Did you call to tell me my daughter is driving you crazy? Or maybe you're calling to tell me you got my money?"

"There's something serious I need to tell you about Mom. Can you cut the antagonism for five minutes? And you should sit down for this." When she didn't reply but didn't hang up either, Peyton said, "Mom is still alive, but comatose. If you—"

"—what? Why haven't you ever told me? What's wrong with you?"

"Will you let me explain? I only just found out the hard way and doing the decent thing by telling you. I didn't have to tell you, did I?"

Lexi sobbed into the phone. "So, your precious father lied? Not so perfect now, was he?" She blew her nose. "I want to see Mom right away."

"She wants to see you, too."

"How do you know that?" Lexi asked, back to her sharp tone.

Peyton would never explain Mikey to someone cynical. "It's only natural."

"But she's corpse-like, grotesque, right?"

Most everything Lexi said made Peyton cringe. How different they were. "I'll send you the address and tell the doctor overseeing her care you're coming," she said, staring at Lexi's portrait.

"You're not gonna be there?"

The fear in her sister's voice at being alone with their mother astonished her. "Don't you prefer it that way?"

Lexi didn't answer.

"You deserve Mom all to yourself."

"Deserve? Never thought you'd think I deserved anything good."

"You're so off base, it's not even funny. If I wanted to hurt you, I wouldn't feel love for your daughter. Wouldn't have gotten to know her. Didn't that ever occur to you?"

"Maybe you only did it to fuck with me."

"I'm not devious. And there are easier ways to hurt you. I may not be thrilled at the sight of you, but I've always wished you well. Why you can't believe that is beyond me."

"Yeah? Then, send me my goddamn money!" She hung up, leaving Peyton to grieve over all the wrong that was never righted.

Margot came in wearing one of Peyton's dresses. "You paint like Grandma! Mom looks different."

"Different how?"

"Sweet or something, but she's not. She's always angry or distracted."

Peyton had had enough of daughters blaming mothers. "Your mom made mistakes. Some of them were because she didn't have her mother. When she did, she didn't have the best example. Grandma gave us fun memories, but also difficult ones. She left your mom for her dad to raise alone, then one day, she died. But your mom never left you, never gave up on you, and loves you." Peyton reached for Margot and hugged her. "My earliest memories of your mom are nice. I don't know what happened along the way. I painted the woman your mom could be."

Margot bit a cuticle, staring at the floor. "I'm scared."

Peyton placed her hands on her shoulders. "You're not Grandma. Today her condition is understood well. There's expert help if you want it."

"I'll go find someone in my insurance network."

"Great idea. And, sweetheart, ask before going in my closet and taking anything. Although this dress looks better on you. Keep it."

"Really? I love designer stuff." Margot buried her face in her phone and left.

Layli passed her in the hall. She said, "That girl, who is practically a child, has turned my brother into a doting puppy, and I can't even get BearClaw to kiss me."

"You don't have to tell me, but what did he say after the competition when he pointed at the three lines you painted on your cheek?"

Layli closed her eyes. "He said he didn't want to give me his scars. I should go wash mine off."

"How do you feel about that?"

"BearClaw is afraid that getting involved with me will interfere with him mentoring the boys. He said he wrecks women, so I should back off. All I do is lose. I wouldn't care this much about being rejected if I hadn't also lost the match. I thought I was old enough to fail better. Just disappointed in myself."

Peyton understood her fragility. "And Joe?"

"Just a fling. Anyway, I'm cursed in love." She gave Peyton playful eyes. "But you're not. I saw Adler strut to his truck like a man who got him some."

Peyton giggled. "He got some last night and more this morning."

"Well, it's about time. What the hell have you two been waiting for? Just how hot was it?"

"Let's just say I can't wait for him to come back."

"Are you ready for your show in L.A.?"

"Don't remind me. And that's not all. I have to pack up the house in Mendocino now that it's sold." The thought of her exhibition coiled her intestines into wild vines. She sat down in slow motion and rubbed her palms on her knees. "I hope I don't blow up my reputation and lose the ranch, too." She bit her lower lip. "Don't know how I'd survive that." The exhibition could launch her career as an artist or end it before it started. Expectations of Harlow's daughter would be high.

"What'll you do?"

"All I can do is the next right thing."

When Lexi said she'd fly in to see Harlow, Peyton didn't expect it would be the next day. Lexi didn't inform her, but Dr. Clay did. She was in the garden, working, when she took his call.

"Can you come down right away?" he asked. "I'm so sorry, Ms. Chase, but your mom passed away a few minutes ago. Your sister was with her, and had a terrible reaction, threw a fit, accused us of neglect and abuse, and the situation escalated from there. I had to call for help and sedate her for her own safety."

Celebration packed Peyton's heart. Her mother was free. And if her waiting had been penance, she hoped she'd found salvation. "I'm so sorry. I know you've done your best for Mom all these years. I'll leave right away."

Peyton couldn't remember the last time she'd seen Lexi less than wound up, tense, and aggressive. She found her on a recliner in a room with green walls, a blue sofa, and a single large window overlooking the driveway. Between the shock, grief, and sedation, she was lethargic, acting as though she were high, giggling one minute, crying the next.

The doctor said, "The effects will wear off gradually. She'll be back to herself by late afternoon."

"What's next with Mom?"

"Your father planned everything, down to the coffin and dress. She's to be interred in the sarcophagus next to his. Her name is already carved on it, as you know."

Peyton shed bigger tears for her father than her mother. How he'd protected her! And she'd blamed him out of ignorance and anger.

Lexi used the electric button on the side of the recliner to bring herself to a seated position. "Am I in hell?"

Peyton said, "No, you're in recovery."

"That sounds like something the devil would say."

The doctor chuckled. "Sedated patients say the funniest things."

"I'm Peyton, not the devil," she replied, though she knew Lexi would claim they were one and the same.

"Peyton, you look lovely. Did you change your hair?"

"My hair has always been chestnut and long."

"But you're a redhead."

"Nope, you and Margot are like Mom. I took Dad's coloring. Doctor, did my sister arrive by car or taxi?"

"An Uber, and we can take care of everything for Harlow. You only have to choose a date."

"Can we see Mom once more before we leave? Lexi won't cause another scene now, right?"

"Correct. The recliner is on wheels if you want to move your sister."

"Want to see Mom one last time, Lexi?"

"Yeah… why not?"

Peyton parked her sister's chair beside Harlow's bed. She needed to say a proper goodbye. She removed the white sheet from her mother's face and petted the crown of her head. "I now know what you did wasn't all your fault, Mom. You needed help, and had you gotten it, things would've been better, but they weren't all bad. We played and laughed. I remember hugs and kisses, and because of you, the smell of paint might be my favorite. From you, I got my ability to hold a brush in my hand and soul. Thank you for that."

Lexi asked, "What did Mom give me?"

"She gave you wit, spunk, and that fuck-you attitude you swing about like a sickle at harvest time."

Laughter gripped Lexi. She attempted to stand, but was too uncoordinated. "I am a firecracker, aren't I?"

Peyton spoke her pure truth. "Mom didn't give us certain things. Couldn't. But maybe, just maybe… she left us each other. You and Margot are my only blood. Can we forgive each other?"

Lexi focused her blue eyes. "Maybe if you give me lunch."

Peyton wondered if her sister would remember this kind exchange.

Lexi slept in the car as they drove to the ranch, her head against the window, her expression docile. Peyton felt like the older sister, watching over the younger one. Without hiking up her features into her hairline in anger, Lexi resembled her portrait, pretty and at peace. When they pulled up at the house, she shook her awake. "Lexi, can you walk?"

She rubbed her eyes and yawned. Her pupils were less dilated, but she seemed bleary. "Am I at your house?"

"Yes. I'll take you to see Margot and get you some food. I let her know we were on our way." Peyton walked to the passenger side and opened the door.

Lexi got out, bracing herself against the car. "I can walk, but I can use a hand."

Peyton helped her into the kitchen and sat her at the long table. "I feel nauseated."

"You need to eat." Peyton had leftover pumpkin soup. She texted Margot, washed her hands, and popped a bowl in the microwave. "Do you still like chicken with Dijon on rye?"

"Are you tricking me?" Lexi asked, becoming alert. "Why are you so nice?"

"You may not believe it, but I *am* nice, and you're my sister." Peyton placed napkins, a spoon, and the soup on the table. "Eat."

Lexi looked at her and burst into tears. "I don't want Margot to end up like Mom."

"Right," Peyton said. "She won't, and she's more open to an evaluation now."

"So, Mom was bipolar?" Lexi mopped her face, though she continued to cry. "I was five years old when she divorced Dad. She told me she'd always stay close, that I wasn't losing her, and then she met your dad and moved to New Mexico. I went from seeing her every week to only a handful of times a year."

Peyton was crying, too. "Then she had me and you felt replaced."

"Yes, she lied so much."

"Mom didn't keep some promises because she was impetuous and, at times, out of control. I don't think she meant to lie." Peyton pinched her temples, remembering the few things her father had divulged. "I asked Dad how he met Mom and why he asked her to marry him. He said she brought a suitcase and a trunk of art supplies one day and never left. It appears she came for a sojourn, and it turned into a marriage. Mom didn't plan much. I don't believe her impulses allowed for strategic anything. I'm so sorry, Lexi, but we both got stars and scars from our mother." Peyton saw it was time to deliver Mikey's message. "Mom didn't think you were a disappointment. You should know."

Lexi looked surprised but distressed. "Why do you say that?"

She wasn't ready to bring up Mikey's clairvoyance. "Stuff Dad said to me. I suspected you felt you disappointed Mom, but you didn't."

Margot came into the kitchen wearing Daisy Duke shorts and a halter top, carrying Peyton's portrait. "Look, Mom. Auntie painted you."

"Me?" Lexi brought her manicured hands to her mouth, her eyes wide and awake. "Oh my God, you painted me?"

"Why are you crying?" Margot asked. "You should be happy."

"You made me pretty," Lexi said. "I didn't get Mom's beauty like you and Margot. It skipped me. I thought that's why Mom never painted my portrait. I thought I disappointed her in every way."

"You're very pretty, Lexi." Peyton carefully took the painting from

Margot and put it down. "I titled it *Blood and Paint*, because that's what we are in this family."

Lexi pressed her hand over her chest to steady her breathing. "Am I really pretty? I felt mousy compared to the three of you."

"You never told me I was pretty," Margot said, "only Auntie has."

"My darling, you're gorgeous." Lexi opened her arms for her daughter. "I'm so sorry I withhold compliments. Grandma screwed up with me, and I screwed up with you."

Margot knelt beside her mother and buried her face in her lap. Peyton watched them embrace and sob and thought of tender moments she'd shared with Harlow. The longer she studied them, the surer she was that her next painting would be of Harlow and all her daughters.

"You're giving me this painting?" Lexi asked. "But I made you sell your house."

"I know what you did, and I'm not over it yet, but since Mom didn't paint you, as far as we know, I did." Peyton remembered that Harlow had planned on selling the portrait she'd stolen, *Peyton at Nine*. "Or if she did paint your portrait, someone somewhere owns it. I'll make sure Harlow's daughters and granddaughter are enshrined in paint."

"Blood and paint," said Margot, standing up and wiping her tears.

"That's right, honey." Peyton hugged her niece.

Lexi extended her hand, and Peyton accepted it. "I'm sorry I've been so enraged for so long."

Margot asked, "So you're not anymore?"

"I didn't say that," Lexi replied, making them burst into laughter.

"One day at a time," Peyton said. "You always should've had half the paintings, which I, unfortunately, no longer own. I just wish we'd gone about it differently."

"Sisters?" Lexi asked, as if testing a new path.

"Sisters," Peyton replied, hoping they were making inroads in their contentious relationship.

<h1 style="text-align:center">twenty-six</h1>

Peyton shipped her furniture from Mendocino to Abiquiú. She said goodbye to the Northern California coast by hiking Russian Gulch Waterfall, strolling the Pudding Creek Trestle, driving the Redwood highway, and visiting the Gualala Art Center. Then she said goodbye to her friends. She doubted she'd return soon.

Her trials weren't over. She was about to take the boldest move of her life. She'd have to race bareback again, and this time, if she were to fall, she'd break more than bones, tear more than flesh.

But there comes a time in a woman's life when she stands on the edge of a cliff by herself and decides whether she'll surrender to the entrapping jungle behind her or leap and grow wings on the way down.

Peyton determined she could fly.

On the day of the exhibition, Peyton was in the gallery, seeing to the finishing touches. Geraint had been promoting the show for weeks and closed the gallery on the day of the opening.

"I bet your cattle drive painting will sell fast," he said, standing beside her in skintight jeans. "The other is you-know-whose portrait."

Peyton had resisted offering any of the portraits she'd done of Ashton, but Geraint insisted on at least one. It felt as if she tore a page from her diary and was offering it for sale. If she hadn't been desperate to save the ranch, she wouldn't have agreed to it. "You invited him, didn't you?"

"Would *I* do that? Not like he's more loaded than the House of Windsor, or anything."

Could she see Ashton this soon? She wondered if he'd show up. He was one extreme or another. He'd either descend on her with full force, or disappear like a politician's promise.

Surrounded by paintings she'd created in solitude and secrecy, Peyton was equally elated and frightened. "You're sure the pricing is right, Geraint? The cheapest painting here is thirty-six thousand."

"If you'd been obscure, I'd have halved the prices. The smallest painting here is thirty-two by forty-eight inches. That's large, as you know, and you're Harlow's daughter, to boot, well known in your own right. The pricing is appropriate. Hopefully, not too low." He made his eyebrows dance. "Besides, yours truly invited only deep pockets, some with a particular interest in Southwestern and Coastal art." He gave her a light shove. "Trust me, will you?"

Peyton pondered, tapping her fingers on her hip. She looked around the gallery. The bar had been set up. They'd tested the live streaming and adjusted the lighting. "All done?"

"Yes. Now get out of your Old Macdonald outfit and get dressed to kill. I want you to make a splash in something avant-garde that says you have panache and temperamental talent, because Geraint spent a fortune orchestrating this show for you and needs to reap a blazing profit. Shoo. See you at seven thirty."

Peyton knew everybody from Abiquiú who mattered would attend. Adler had a critical case in his IT security business he couldn't cancel, and Ashton was a wildcard. At least Geraint had prepared her for the possibility of seeing him. Inspired by the decade that launched an artistic revolution, she dressed in a 1960s style red micro-miniskirt with a slender top and white knee-high go-go boots. She teased her hair and wore thick black eyeliner, false lashes, and frosty pale lipstick of the era.

She arrived early, as planned. "You take directions exceedingly well," Geraint said. "I'm gobsmacked."

Peyton did a full twirl. "I don't look like I'm at a costume party?"

"Not one bit. You dived into the sixties and came out a modern-day Brigitte Bardot." He made a mute clap, then displayed a bittersweet pout. "I see Harlow in you even more. If you only had red hair and a wide headband."

She hoped Harlow's shadow would shelter her from the heat, rather than block the light. Her skin prickled with apprehension. The reviews would begin to be published the next day. She'd lowered her expectations and steeled herself, but she wasn't ready.

Royce and Mark showed up first, she, in a dizzying sequined dress, he, as usual, wearing an outfit that could pass for pajamas.

Royce hugged and complimented her. "Mark said I look like a disco babe."

"What I said was disco *ball*," he corrected, earning a jab in the ribs.

"Better a disco ball than club bed," Royce retorted, then ran fast eyes on the paintings in the main room. "I can't believe you hid this kind of talent. Honey, you can paint."

Mark said, "You say it as if she's a painter from Sherwin Williams. Our girl is an *artiste*."

Peyton laughed and danced around to burn off nerves. "I'm humbled and grateful you're here. You may be the only ones who show up."

Scarborough, who almost never left his stronghold, joined them. "Ma'am, it thrills my heart to see such active and brave cowboys all over these walls. L.A. needs hardcore men on treacherous, dusty terrain."

Royce patted her stiff coiffure. "She does. It's called traffic."

Layli moved from painting to painting, until Koda came in, looking like the lead singer of an indie band with a quiff pompadour, faded denim jacket, a black tee, and Doc Martens boots. Peyton saw he sheared his hair and looked immediately to Layli for her reaction.

"Is Margot here yet?" He ran eyes everywhere, wide-eyed, grinning.

"Not yet. Margot isn't known for her punctuality, but you look fab," Peyton said. "And your hair!"

Layli zipped in their direction, glowering at her brother. "You did that to your hair over a girl?"

"*For* a girl," Royce said. "I like it."

"Leave the city slicker alone," Scarborough said, chuckling.

Mikey pressed beside Peyton. "Koda is leaving."

"He's standing right here, kid," Royce said.

Peyton knew that Koda was rocking more than a new look.

"Is Mikey right?" Layli asked. "Leaving for where?"

"I was going to tell you," Koda said. "I got accepted at the University of California San Diego in La Jolla. They gave me a scholarship. I'll borrow the rest and get a job. There's also the money from winning with Lightning. I'm interested in their veterinary program. I'll be all right."

Peyton hoped if the paintings sold, she'd be able to save the ranch and support his studies, but she kept that to herself. She touched Layli's arm, her way of reminding her to take it easy.

"That's great news," Layli said, though she seemed galled. "But you're coming home during breaks, okay?"

Koda fixed the collar of his jacket, then gave Mikey narrow eyes. "Thank you for outing me like that, bro."

Mikey shrugged, as if that wasn't his problem, and played with his blue mohawk. "Peyton, I like how you use orange and blue together without making weird colors in between."

"You so have my blood." She tugged him closer, as proud as any mother. "It took four years of advanced classes to learn how to do that, but I'll show you." She laughed. "Then you can explain it to me."

Margot arrived in what could pass for a bathing suit with a train, swinging her small purse like a bullroarer. She gave Peyton a hug and threw eyes on the paintings. "You're like a real painter."

"Versus?" Peyton asked, frowning.

"When will you paint me?" She turned her attention to Koda. "Slay! Welcome to California." She grabbed his hand. "We're gonna go do our thing, 'kay? Like for two or three days."

"Days? Where're you going?" Peyton asked.

"Chill, Auntie. Santa Catalina, not Argentina."

Koda rushed out the door with her. "YOLO!"

Layli crossed her arms over her chest and leaned on a hip. "Your niece may ruin my brother."

"Or expand his horizons," Royce said. "Peyton honey, which ones should I buy? I love them all but would prefer to buy what you'd rather keep close."

"You're serious? I only wanted you here for moral support."

"Lordy, this is my moral support—three hundred thousand dollars' worth. I told you I can come up with that much. It's a win-win. One day they'll be worth more. Besides, I'm getting old and plan on eating much more Sophia cake with you."

Peyton knew Royce would be instrumental in getting her through the evening, but she hadn't counted on her generosity. "I don't know what to say. Wow."

"Say, you love cake. And Mark will buy some too, or I'll burn all his pajamas."

Peyton hugged Royce and pointed out her favorite pieces, then slipped behind a partition to hide while she studied the looks on the guests' faces. Were they impressed, moved, or turned off? From what she could read, their expressions were favorable.

Geraint startled her. "Come out, come out, wherever you are," he said. "Tonight, you're the cowboys, not the drowning calves. Be the center of attention. Clients are asking to see you. Let's go."

He introduced her to a couple who looked more like siblings than husband and wife, with identical short haircuts, pants and shirts, as if they were sharing one wardrobe to save money. He'd only invited big spenders, and Peyton tried to trust that, although these two looked like they shopped consignment and arrived by RV. Then they asked her what her mother was like.

"Mom was a desert rose, bloomed wherever she went," Peyton said, crushed. They saw her as Harlow's daughter, not Peyton Chase. This was just the beginning of the beginning. She had a long way to go before her own prominence overshadowed her mother's notoriety.

A famous critic with a Van Dyke goatee and horn-rimmed glasses gave her works cursory looks. She could see he was using a digital recorder, and her intestines growled. But she could only control what hung on the walls.

Geraint caught her attention and mouthed that the guy approaching her was also a critic. He introduced himself as Tom, without declaring his purpose or profession. Peyton thought he was odd, with a wide nose, small eyes, and a tie but no jacket. "Which are your more recent paintings?"

"The bigger they get, the more recent they are."

The man pinched his chin, resting an elbow on an arm folded across his chest. "You grew more daring over time, Ms. Chase. I adore your mother's work, but you are her reverse. She started off with risk and abandon but finished with control and precision."

"Call me Peyton, please." She thought his comment was astute. Perhaps Harlow had courage she herself lacked. Then as her mental illness progressed, she'd imposed order and precision on her inner bedlam. "Mom had a phenomenal instinct for colors and textures, and ridiculous patience. Some things can't be taught."

"Others can be over taught," he replied.

Peyton wondered if he was implying that her work was overdone. "Tom, how do my paintings make you feel?"

"Hmm... feel?" He turned to survey the paintings. "You and your mother together make the genius the world sees in Marco Grassi, the young one, not the guy from the sixties."

Peyton knew Grassi's work well. "What do you mean, together?"

"Harlow Peyton created hyperrealism, capturing solitude or loneliness. She'd show her subjects at work but pulled into themselves. I'm not saying your figures don't have depth, but they're more extraverted. You create emotive, active figures who collaborate or share, with a slightly unfocused feeling I love."

Peyton stood taller. "The *sfumato* effect, you mean?"

"Correct, but Marco Grassi does all that combined, as I'm sure you know."

She sensed blood and paint. What Adler had told her was true. She and her mother shared the same journey. Perhaps the same brush, too.

"May I ask you a question about your mother?"

Peyton nodded, thinking she'd be asked about her mother for the rest of her life.

"I once read that she painted standing, preferred to be barefoot, and often paced back and forth while working. Is that true?"

"Why do you think it matters?"

"Because she focused on stillness so much, I find it a contradiction."

"She'd kick off her shoes, especially when she had a burst of energy. My guess is it helped her to steady the brush. And she had to move in order to cover wide psychological terrains in her figures."

The irony was that Peyton had to do the opposite, cover wide psychological terrains to save the physical, the ranch. On the day Harlow died, she'd packed away her shoes, consciously preparing for her walk. In some ways, Peyton stood in contrast to her mother, but in others, they complemented each other. Maybe being Harlow's daughter wasn't a curse, after all. She said, "You have a generosity of soul, Tom. Thank you. I've been nervous leading up to today, but you helped me be less so. It's kind."

He bobbed his head from side to side, as if she were telling half-truths. "Reality is kind. I only voice it."

Geraint grabbed her by the arm and whispered, "That was Tom Clark. He counts big time. Just might give us a good review, the way he was grinning."

"Fingers crossed," she whispered back, "and I enjoyed the conversation with a critic. Shocker. Though Mr. Van Dyke goatee, over there, looks like he hates everything he sees."

"Fuck him. There's a reason everyone calls him Van Dick." Geraint touched up the tips of his white hair and adjusted his belt. "Don't look now, but guess who's here?"

Ashton looked L.A. hip in designer jeans and an Amiri black and white shirt. Someone carrying a museum worthy bouquet trailed behind him.

"Be nice, lassie. We need every sale." Geraint said.

Ashton pulled her to a corner and presented the bouquet. "You look dazzling."

"So do you," she replied. A certain sailor resided in her heart and soul, but she reserved something for Ashton.

Royce approached them and greeted Ashton with kisses. "Go, have a private word in the back." She gave Peyton encouraging eyes. "Go."

Ashton pointed to his portrait as he led her by the elbow to the back of the gallery. "You're auctioning me off?"

"Your image, not you."

"Are you selling all three?"

"No, just this one, and I'm so sorry. I wouldn't have if I didn't need to."

"I'm sorry you're struggling."

"Let's talk of cheerful things," she said.

Ashton cracked his half-angel, half-shark smile. "You couldn't part with the other two, eh? Does this mean you'll hang them in your bedroom?"

"Thank you for coming down to support me, and I'm sorry our last exchange was tense."

His cinnamon eyes were filled with feeling. "You sold your house. You're leaving California. Why? Did you decide to wither away on some ranch in the middle of nowhere?"

Ashton didn't understand her attachment to Pioneer Ranch, but Adler did. "It's not some ranch. It's centuries of history, trials, and sacrifice."

"You've changed."

"We all do."

"Do you hate me now?"

She loved when he exposed his soft spots. "No, of course not. Do you not know me at all?"

He clenched his jaw. "You were obstinate the last time. I'd never heard you speak to me with such finality."

"You don't hear me very well. And you're still parking under the mock orange. You know this about yourself, right?"

"The tree you no longer own? I could've saved it for you, Peyton." He didn't smile, didn't frown; stood there, looking at her. "I'm getting divorced. I wish you'd slow it down with this guy."

"Did you file officially in court?" she asked, knowing he hadn't. He would've shouted it from the rooftops if he had. "His name is Adler. He's single, wants a family, and it's serious with him."

"Am I so easily effaced?"

"I loved you first, loved you fast, loved you hard."

"But not anymore?"

"A love like ours doesn't dissolve. It goes into a separate folder. Timing is everything. It wasn't our time then, and it's not our time now."

"But why?"

She recalled a conversation with the friar about destiny. "Some people melt us down, others re-forge us. You're excellent at melting me down, Ashton, but not at re-forging me. The thing is, re-forging is what I need."

He pressed against her, and she didn't push him away. "Come back to California, live with me in Malibu again, and I swear I'll show up at your porch this time. Camp on it if necessary."

"That's because it'll be *your* porch. When it was mine, you were nowhere in sight. You want me to join your life, not build a new one for us."

"I miss you something painful." He glued gentle lips to hers longer than she should've allowed. "A part of you loves me still, Peyton, don't deny it."

"A part of me may always love you, but I question long-term happiness with you."

He clasped her hand. "You can have anything, my love."

He was asking her to be the imposter again. "Oh, Ashton, with you, I can have anything if I sacrifice *everything*. This time, I'm not betting the pot. I can't afford you."

"You're absolutely sure?"

The tenderness in his question cut. She stared at his beautiful face, smelled his signature cologne, and was beset by the best version of him. "I can't just keep moving forward. I have to move on."

He hung his head. "If you decide to sell the other portraits, offer them to me. Don't sell them to anyone else."

"I'm keeping them."

He fractured a desolate smile and scuttled down the corridor, out of view. As she watched him leave, a pang funneled in her chest. A part of her wanted to stop him, but another part knew she shouldn't.

Royce, who had never been out of earshot, returned with stealth steps. "I don't envy you your dilemma."

As they returned to the exhibition rooms, Peyton said, "I don't have a dilemma. I know what I want. It took me forever to figure it out. What I don't understand is why I can't marry two guys."

Royce keeled over, laughing. "One leg in California and the other in New Mexico. Who would refuse such a spread?" She adjusted the straps of her sequined dress and glanced at the big plate-glass window to the valet parking outside the gallery. "Keep your powder dry, honey. I'm looking at your men exchange words."

Peyton turned to see what Royce was looking at. "What? I thought Adler couldn't make it." But there he was at the valet stand, holding a bouquet. The two men who mattered most to her were more alike than they realized, both of them strong, determined, enterprising, and sharp. And they had the same taste in women.

"Excessive machismo," Royce said. "Prepare to sprinkle some estrogen on it, darling. Smile big, now. Your sailor is coming."

Peyton's heart leapt as Adler took big steps toward her. "I can't believe you made it!"

"I was always going to come. I wanted to surprise you." He handed her a bouquet of orchids, Asiatic lilies, pincushions, and ginger flowers, and hugged her. "Hello, Royce."

She glanced at the flowers he brought, and though worthy of such an evening, Royce's face said: *a smaller bouquet.* "Don't monopolize the star for long," she said, and left.

"She hates me."

"No, Royce thinks you resent her lifestyle and judge it, but I want you two to give each other a real chance." Peyton was dying to wrap her body around him, but she knew he detested public displays of affection, so she pulled him to the back of the gallery, put down the bouquet, and kissed him. "I haven't seen you for a week. It feels like a month."

He caged her to his body, but tensed his neck.

"What is it, baby?"

"This is about my baggage, not yours. You're a magnificent and trustworthy woman, but I must ask. You're happy with our exclusivity, right?"

"Yes, one hundred percent." She kissed him, not just to reassure him. "Is this because of something Ashton said?"

"It doesn't matter what he said." His taut posture said otherwise.

"Tell me anyway."

"He said I don't deserve you." His face revealed that he thought it was true.

"He can't know that when he doesn't know you. Let it go."

"If he were divorced, would you still have chosen me?"

"If Ashton had been divorced, you'd never have bleeped on my radar. But you did." She looked at him with the nakedness she'd shown him all along. "I see you as a life I want to share. I've suffered from so many secrets, and want none between us."

"Though the truth can be hurtful? Because I sure fire away."

"You do, Captain." Geraint had told her what she knew in her blood to be true. "Truth hurts, but secrets damage."

He said, "You deserve the best."

She kissed him, pulling on his shirt. "I have the best."

"How're you holding up?"

"I don't know what, if anything sold. And the reviews to come petrify me, but I'm still standing. Thank you for letting me lean on you. Whenever you're around, I feel everything will be all right."

"I'll carry you if I have to." He hugged her tightly and sliced a naughty grin. "Hoist you over my shoulder, at least."

Geraint called her name.

"Here," she called back.

"Oh, sorry, but who's this tower of testosterone?" Geraint smiled big, looking Adler up and down.

"This is my guy." She introduced them to each other.

"Oh, you're *the* Blake Adler, who reserved Peyton's *Cowboys Brewing Coffee*. Have no fear, it's tagged and awaiting your signature."

"Oh my God, no, baby! It's so expensive. You can't buy something I created. I'll just give it to you."

Geraint made bug-eyes at her. "What? That's an in-house decision and we offer no refunds."

"None of us are buying from you," Adler said, laughing. "We're investing in you."

"That's right. I like him." Geraint gave Peyton a chastising look. "Remind me never to leave you in charge of sales. Good grief." He checked out Adler again. "You're the perfect look, deary. I'll be seeing you in many of Peyton's future paintings."

Adler chuckled. "I've never posed for anyone, but Peyton is *the* someone, so…"

Geraint asked him, squinting his eyes. "May I steal her from you for just a minute? Don't mean to be rude."

Adler left and Geraint bounced in place. "I think we've sold everything were' going to sell this evening, and it's a triumph!"

Peyton needed to brace herself against something. "Triumph? What does that mean? How much did we raise?"

"If I sell even one painting from an artist's first show, it's a win. We sold half yours, and that's a record for me." He kissed her on both cheeks. "Congratulations, lassie! Your friends bought several, three of your paintings went to top clients, some Texan named Kelcy phoned in and said to send him one hundred thousand dollars' worth, as if we sold ground beef, and Ashton Grant bought his portrait, like I knew he would." He brought his hands to his cheeks and bounced again. "That's almost a million dollars' worth, Peyton. A million fucking dollars! You're my good luck charm."

"But that's not enough." After consigning Geraint's commission, Peyton dreaded that for her trust and income to cover the estate's deficits, she'd have to lower the mortgage some more, but how?

"What's the matter with you, Peyton? This is a massive success."

Hard as she tried, she couldn't stop her tears. "No, not really. Only three paintings sold to strangers. And I still haven't raised all the funds."

"Silly goose! Who cares? All the market knows is you outsold any artist's first show. This means I can charge more for the rest. They'll sell at a slower pace, granted, but for higher prices."

"I don't mean to sound ungrateful, but I need the money now, or I'll lose the ranch."

"I'd hug you, but your face is a mess, and this is an expensive shirt."

She snickered through tears. "It's going to be a long time before I have a proper income from sales of originals and limited edition *giclées*."

"That's true," he said, and grabbed her arm. "How much more do you need?"

"At least a cool million or close to it."

"That much? Should I say it or will you?"

What does a Chase do? Only one door remained open. An excruciating one. She sobbed into her hands.

"Okay, I'll say it. You have to sell *The Last Start*. It'll have to be auctioned to fetch such an enormous sum. And it might not. If it were to sell that high, it would set a record for Harlow. But you'll have to finish it first."

"Me? What if I ruin it? You said when I copy Mom's work, it comes across as rigid."

"Hello! Anyone home? Peyton Chase, you're a restorer and the best in my book. You're only finishing it, not recreating it, and this time it's the painter in you doing it, not just the restorer, and that's bigger." He formed his hands into a Buddhist mudra. "Meditate. Channel your mother's aura. Believe in yourself over a million bucks worth, then get some goddamned therapy for all that rubbish you're lugging around."

"The commission is thirty percent. It'll have to sell for at least one million four hundred thousand!"

"*The Last Start* is Harlow's last work before her untimely death. It's never been seen. We'll generate lots of hype. The subject is death and the afterlife—butterflies again—and now that you showed such strong sales tonight, the daughter will boost the mother's work."

Peyton lifted her head. "What? I can boost the value of Mom's painting?" All her life, it had been the reverse. Peyton had an advantage both as an art restorer and as an artist because Harlow was her mother. She could return the favor in a small way. But to sell a painting she'd lived with all her life, a painting she took everywhere, felt like excising her soul.

"A painting started by Harlow, then finished by her talented painter daughter a couple of decades later, has sentimental value, and it would be the only painting in existence accredited to both of you. It'll be unique and should outsell all previous works by Harlow or you."

"I'll need four weeks, at least, to do it justice."

"I'll need that much time to lock a date with the auction house, advertise, and personally call every one of my high rollers. What're you thinking, racoon-face? Are we auctioning *The Last Start*?"

Peyton's mother had recently embarked on her last start. Maybe that was reason enough. She thought of her mother's early settler roots. Of her ancestors who traveled west, risking everything to defend their way of life. How much had they lost?

twenty-seven

Peyton had been standing before *The Last Start* for an hour, unable to touch it, though everything she needed was laid out. She paced back and forth, retracing her mother's steps.

"Did you start already, or can I interrupt you?" Adler asked, peeking his head in the door.

"No, I'm stumped. Come in."

He was barefoot, in jeans and a black sweater, holding an adorable pup with the biggest ears she'd ever seen. "She's a fennec fox, got her young so she'll bond with you."

"My goodness, are you kidding?" The pup looked at Peyton with large brown eyes. Her fur was white as sand and her paws too big for her body. "I've never seen a fennec in person before."

"Gorgeous, isn't she? I had to put us on a waiting list to get her." The pup shivered and yawned. "It's like she just arrived from the maternity ward."

Peyton took the tiny fox, kissed her head, and petted her. "She looks more like you than me."

"Are you saying I have big ears?" Adler laughed and lifted her off her feet.

"I needed this. Thank you, baby."

He let her shelter against his majestic frame. "Talk to me."

"I'm afraid of touching *The Last Start*."

"You get your gift from your mother. How can you possibly ruin it?"

"Remember that you told me I may be meant to carry on her legacy?"

"Yes, it's what I believe. And now you are."

The pup began to fuss, and Peyton put her down. "All my life, I've competed with Mom and fell short."

"And now?"

A peaceful smile spread from her heart to her face. "Now she's my partner, my complement. I fear letting her down worse than ever." She buried her face in his chest. "Can you stay with me until I start it? But first I want to play with this cutie patootie."

"Wherever and whenever you need me, there I'll be." He sat in a chair facing the easel and the magnificent view of the mountains, the Chama River, fields of pumpkins and sweet peppers, and Brahman cows grazing in green pastures.

Peyton crouched on the parquet floor with the pup, who nuzzled against her, docile and consoling. "I'm naming her Solace."

"You said *I'm* your solace."

"The Appaloosa is Blake—my secret name for him—and the fox is Solace. I name all our children after you." She took a deep breath. "Okay, my angst has dropped a smidgeon. Maybe now I can." She began her ritual, reciting the Leonardo da Vinci quote that marked the beginning of every restoration project. This time, she was restoring her relationship with her mother. "While I thought that I was learning how to live, I have been learning how to die."

She sat on the stool with Solace leaning against her ankle, nipping the rubber toy Adler brought.

"I'll leave you to do your magic." He kissed her and left her with Solace and Harlow.

Peyton worked with precision, using a magnifying glass, tiny Fude Japanese goat-hair brushes, and paints she mixed herself. After a month, her work was nearly completed, but one critical ingredient was lacking. Harlow had left soul in the painting and Peyton had left spirit, but what they shared was missing. She pricked her pinky finger, squeezed out a drop of blood, and mixed it into the paint she used to sign it. "Blood and paint," she murmured—a promise to her mother and to herself.

Peyton arrived at the auction early. She wanted to spend time alone with her mother's last painting. Bidders would soon arrive, and the phones would open for remote bids. She stood before *The Last Start* to say her goodbyes. The painting was on a dais, spot lit and waiting. Lexi called her name, and she turned to see her sister cradling a jewelry box. They hadn't seen each other since they buried their mother, and though they hadn't turned into the closest of relations, Peyton was glad she'd come. "What's this?" she asked.

"I'm not here to cause trouble. Came to show solidarity. I know by completing *The Last Start*, you made it your own, and I'm okay with that." Lexi deposited the box on the edge of the dais.

Peyton recognized the jewelry box Lexi had stolen the day of their mother's first funeral.

"Every piece of Mom's jewelry is in this box. I think this time we should take turns choosing until we split them fairly."

Peyton's tears were effortless.

"I'm sorry I stole them. I felt you had everything and me nothing. But I was wrong and now I feel guilty about it."

Peyton hugged her, and to her surprise, Lexi clung to her.

"They don't make up for *The Last Start*," Lexi said. "But they're something of Mom's, too."

"Thank you. I needed this. I really did."

They took turns picking by category. First the necklaces. Then the bracelets, rings, and watches. They laughed as they put on jewelry until they looked like Liberace on crack.

"Thank you, Lexi. This makes me feel as though Mom is here with us."

"Margot has seen a psychiatrist who diagnosed her with bipolar disorder and attention deficit disorder. She's getting the help she needs, thanks to you."

"Thanks to you, too. It takes all of us. I'm sorry, but we can't control our genes."

She covered Peyton's hand with hers. "I had the portrait you made of me appraised. Not bad, sis."

"How much? Tell me."

"At least seventy, the guy said, based on the price of your other work. Also said it was poignant and stirring. One day, it could be worth significantly more. So, I won't mind more portraits from you."

Peyton shook her head, smiling. "Telling me this is also a gift."

"Hope you brought a big purse." Lexi handed her the jewelry pouches. "I read some of your reviews."

Peyton looked at the ceiling. Some reviews had been less than stellar. One critic called her work thematic and puerile. After that, she took Geraint's advice and hadn't read them. "Don't tell me, be it good or bad."

"The one I read said Mom would've been proud of you."

"Mom would be proud of you, too."

"Is your man with you? I'd like to meet him. Margot said he's a stallion."

A stallion with a name. He had taken her places, but he always brought her back. "Adler is here. He wanted to give me time alone with Mom's painting."

Ushers opened the doors as Peyton and Lexi tucked the jewelry away and took their seats. When Adler joined them, Peyton made the introductions.

The bell rang, signaling the start of the auction. Peyton prayed hard for a favorable outcome. Most of the bids were placed by phone or live streaming. The reserve price was three hundred thousand dollars and bids were accepted in increments of twenty-five thousand. When the price reached six hundred thousand, increments of ten thousand dollars were accepted.

At one point, an operator taking phone bids, shouted, "One million dollars!"

Peyton couldn't believe it, but it still wasn't enough to save the ranch. Chatter in the room rose with speculation on the identity of the high bidder. The auctioneer called for a higher bid.

A museum curator raised her number. "One million, one hundred thousand."

A gasp resounded as the phone bidder doubled the price, and the bidding ceased. The auctioneer called, "Going once, going twice, SOLD for two million, two hundred thousand dollars!"

Peyton couldn't move. "Did I hear that right?"

Adler chuckled and cuddled her. "You're not hard of hearing."

Press photographers hurried over, but she was too dazed to react until one reporter asked her to pose with *The Last Start*.

"Harlow had two daughters," Peyton said and introduced Lexi. "It's befitting we should flank *The Last Start* as though we were standing with Mom."

Lexi nodded, tearing up.

The value of both Harlow's paintings and Peyton's had been significantly elevated. She could plop a sizeable chunk down on the mortgage and refinance enough that her trust fund and personal income could easily cover. But she was sad. She excused herself and sought Geraint, hoping to discover the identity of the secret outbidder. "Do you know who it is?"

"No clue, but I'll dig. Might take some finessing." He kissed her cheek. "You did it, lassie. So proud of you! Turns out you've got *dewrder*, as we say in Welsh—pluck!"

⌘

For the first time since her father's passing, Peyton awakened to the knowledge the estate was hers. She could keep what mattered of his legacy in her heart, enshrined in the stone and grasses of Pioneer Ranch, and preserve what mattered to her mother in blood and paint. She felt good. And she felt bad. She'd sacrificed deeds and certificates but gained spirit and an authentic self. What she'd lost had a price, but what she'd gained was priceless. That's what a Chase does.

On that nippy October morning, the air smelled of dead leaves, wet soil, and wood-burning fire. She needed to gift those who had stood by her, supported and encouraged her, beginning with Adler. But the identity of *The Last Start's* new owner still dogged her.

Adler was crossing the bridge over the creek when she brought the saddled horses out. He had Nuke with him, and she had Cooper.

"Baroness is for me, but Lightning is for you," she told him. "He's the most challenging horse I've ever handled, and he's all yours."

"What?"

She had ordered a saddle for the horse, embroidered with Blake's name. "He's fast, built for endurance, powerful, and adamant. He fits you to a tee."

"You're giving me a prize-winning horse? But Peyton—"

"—but nothing. You should have your own horse now. You practically live here. No one will ride Lightning but you. He's still a colt. He'll get bigger."

Adler ran his hands over the Appaloosa. "This is a hunter's saddle. I can bring shot guns, long and short, even holster an additional handgun."

"Well, yes, Mr. Hunter. Did you think I wouldn't factor in your needs?"

"No one knows me like you do." He pressed his forehead to hers and kissed her, then traced the embroidery with his fingers. "Is he Blake, or am I?"

"Easy. You're both stallions. But only one of you is a mustang, Captain."

He chuckled. "Tell me why you named him Lightning."

"Because Mark Twain put it best. 'Thunder is good, thunder is impressive; but it is lightning that does the work.' From our earliest acquaintance, you struck me. Might have been your rudeness. But I suspect you'll always leave your mark."

"Just remember who struck whom first, Rodeo Queen."

"Emphasis on queen, thank you. But let's hurry before our friends arrive."

Peyton had invited her supporters to lunch in celebration of her permanent move to the ranch. She was in the kitchen, poaching salmon and baking bread pudding for a dozen people, when Geraint called.

"I *lurv* him, you know. What a special man."

"Who was it?"

"Ashton Grant! Your prince made us a pile of money."

Geraint confirmed her suspicions. She wasn't sure whether she felt better or worse. "Thank you for telling me, but he's not *my* prince."

"You want to lie to yourself, go ahead, but don't lie to me. And I'm including four of your paintings in my Christmas art festival. I already have interest. But I hope this doesn't mean you'll stop restoring stuff for me. Please, say you won't."

"Why would I? I owe you one, but I also don't see why I can't do both. I have a big studio now. You'll have to ship more to me, though. I don't want to fly to so many locations. We'll split the difference. I'll come to you at times, but you ship to me at others. Fair?"

"No, not fair, and you should always return to Los Angeles. But whatever Peyton wants…"

"California is in my blood, don't worry."

Like a burglar, Peyton peeked around the corner to be sure she was alone, then scuttled to her father's study, closed the door, and called Ashton. He picked up right away.

"I'm beyond moved and grateful, but why?"

"Isn't it obvious?"

She had accused him of offering to make her dependent on him. By betting incognito and very high, he'd helped her, yet left her independent of him. His gesture rattled her core.

"I can't let you forget me, can I?"

The sound of surf and gulls told her he had stepped onto the balcony of his Malibu house. She missed awakening to that. Missed him more. But she didn't miss feeling like the substitute wife. "Oh, Ashton, I may have tucked you away like a photograph in a locket. But what are lockets for? Forget you? Not when I'm old and senile." A sob rose to her throat, but she stifled it.

"Anyhow, I didn't want you to lose what I knew you loved dearly."

She wondered if he still talked about the painting. "At least I know it's in excellent hands. Thank you."

"You have my address, Peyton. When you miss it enough, you'll know where to find it. And I haven't changed the passcode to the gate and front door. All those years, you could've come. Wish you had. I've given no one else access, not before or since."

Peyton wiped her tears. "You made a crucial difference in my life."

"But not enough," he replied in a pained, low voice.

"Yes, it is. You redeemed Mom's premature death and helped me remain the Chase my dad raised me to be. My future sales will be significantly higher, thanks to you. I'll be able to pay off the mortgage that much sooner."

"And buy a house in California again?"

Peyton thought she would, but didn't want to raise his hopes. "I don't know."

"Yes, you will. This time make it SoCal." He fell quiet, and she gave him space. "I should've stepped in sooner, regardless of your protests. Should've saved your Mendocino house."

"You've done more than enough, Ashton. You also helped me see."

"See what?"

Peyton bit her lip, frozen in a moment the size of Jupiter. It was time to say goodbye. "I have to go, but I'm eternally grateful."

"I'll be seeing you, Peyton."

"Ashton…"

"Of course, I will."

She ran to her closet and parted the clothes. She'd restored the painting she'd stolen as a child and kept it in a hidden compartment. No one alive today had ever seen it. She took it out of the acid-free case and stared at it.

Peyton at nine years old, with paint on her face, stared back at Peyton at thirty-three with paint in her arteries.

She carried the portrait to the great room, dragged a chair, stood on it, and hooked the portrait above the Kiva fireplace, where *The Last Start* once hung.

The portrait that had humiliated her as a child, that had told her she lacked talent and fell short of Harlow's expectations, now represented something entirely different. It said blood and paint. Like talented mother, like talented daughter.

Adler found her standing before the portrait in tears. "What is it, sweet Pey? You're supposed to be joyful."

"I am. Mom brought me face-to-face with my authentic portrait." Her father, Lexi, and Margot had done that, too. Her father in the pages of the books he left behind, in the lessons he imparted, and in his relentless love of American artifacts. She wasn't the Chase who lost Pioneer Ranch. She was the Chase who hunted the past to rescue the future. "This was the first painting I restored," she said, "a portrait of me I thought was ugly and humiliating. How amazing that it's the one that restored me." She smiled and wiped her tears. "I understand at last."

"Understand what?" He cuddled her and stared at the painting. "Harlow was incredible," he said. "She put so much life in those hazel eyes. Your portrait looks like a photograph. I can see each individual strand of hair. Too bad she died young."

"Mom died, then showed me…" Peyton both laughed and cried, finally at peace. "She died, then showed me I'm worthy. An original. Not a copy."

Dear reader,

Thank you for joining me on this literary journey. I hope you enjoyed the adventure and found the story captivating. Your feedback is essential to me as an author, and I'd be incredibly grateful if you could take a moment to leave an honest review on Amazon or your favorite venue. Your review will not only help other readers discover this book, but it'll also inspire me to continue crafting more captivating stories for you. Thank you for your support!

Acknowledgments

No one accomplishes a feat like publishing a book alone. I have been incredibly fortunate to have had the support of a remarkable team of professionals whose expertise and insights have made all the difference.

In alphabetical order, I would like to extend my sincerest thanks to Danielle Acee for her exceptional work in proofreading, formatting, and marketing. Tim Barber, your book design skills have given my words a visually captivating presence. Joie Davidow, your editing prowess has been nothing short of superb. And to Hayley Webster, your gifted editing and deep understanding has brought my manuscript to new heights.

Though we may be spread across the globe, your collective efforts have propelled me to a place of extraordinary accomplishment. I am immensely grateful for your invaluable contributions to this project. Your dedication, talents, and astute feedback have transformed my manuscript into a true work of art.

Thank you for sharing your expertise and for being an integral part of this incredible journey. I am truly honored to have collaborated with such an exceptional team of professionals.